DEAD CAN LEARN

Tom Griffin

ARTHUR H. STOCKWELL LTD
Torrs Park, Ilfracombe, Devon, EX34 8BA
Established 1898
www.ahstockwell.co.uk

British Library Cataloguing-in-Publication Data.
A catalogue record for this book is available
from the British Library.

I dedicate this book to Richard Wood Duncan (Dick),
my late stepfather, who inspired me to write this book.
Dick received the Imperial Service Medal from
Her Majesty Queen Elizabeth II for forty-five years of
supporting, playing and tutoring Highland bagpipes, and
competing in numerous pipe-band competitions.
Thank you to Ross Coventry and Ross Noble, both fine pipers,
who provided me with the piping tunes referenced in this novel.

ISBN 978-0-7223-4737-9
Printed in Great Britain by
Arthur H. Stockwell Ltd
Torrs Park   Ilfracombe
Devon EX34 8BA

PROLOGUE

You could call my story *The Light Switch*. In February 2001, I was returning to Fort McMurray, Northern Alberta, Canada, from meetings in Houston, Texas, USA. The flight had an hour or so layover in Calgary, Alberta; just enough time for a light lunch in the airport terminal. Sitting down to soup was the last thing I remember. Without warning, without any sensation of pain or discomfort, I fell unconscious to the floor. It was just like a light switch. One minute I was getting ready to eat; the next, the lights went out.

The rest of the story has been reconstructed from eyewitness reports. A doctor and nurse who were sitting at a table behind me sprang into action, determining that I had suffered sudden cardiac arrest. As one removed my shirt, the other called 911. Emergency Medical Services at the airport responded in a few minutes, bringing with them an AED, or Automated External Defibrillator.

Only four weeks prior to my sudden cardiac arrest, the Calgary Municipal Airport Authority had purchased AEDs and incorporated them into their emergency response plan. Well equipped, well trained, and well prepared, the EMS team was able to save me. I was stabilized, suffered no brain damage, and was transferred to hospital for further care.

After a week's stay in hospital, I was told there was nothing wrong with my heart. I rejected that analysis and was sent to another hospital in Calgary, where I came under the care of two specialists in arrhythmia. After multiple tests, they determined that I suffered from Brugada syndrome, a genetic defect which had only come to light when it presented in some highly active athletes.

Still hospitalized, I avidly began researching the syndrome and connected with eight specialists in Canada who had done work in this area. Eventually I was selected for a case study in the Mayo Clinic's Brugada Syndrome Research Project, contributing valuable data and DNA samples which may someday lead to a cure.

With diagnosis in hand, my cardiologist elected to place a small ICD, or implantable cardioverter defibrillator, above my heart. Situated just below my left shoulder, the device automatically detects the onset of abnormal heart rhythms; and within seconds of detecting fibrillation, the ICD delivers a biphasic shock to the heart to restore its normal rhythm.

I returned to my job and continue to live a normal life – golfing, Scottish country dancing, cycling, travelling around the world – and am a promoter of community PAD programs. I have also spent a considerable amount of my time researching family history. I travelled to Scotland and England and obtained information on the family history from my aunts, uncles and cousins. I also visited family members in Australia and New Zealand and obtained their history since emigrating down under all those years ago. It soon became very apparent to me that many of the male members of my family had experienced sudden deaths due to heart attacks. For example, my grandfather in Port Glasgow, aged fifty-eight, died very suddenly when visiting one of his five sons. Doctors did not know the cause of death. I also learned that several younger male members of the family experienced sudden deaths, but no one knew why these deaths occurred. It became all too apparent to me that I did not know much about my family's Scottish history including why they changed their name from MacGregor to Griffin. This led me to conduct further research and resulted in my first manuscript, a historical drama.

Chapter 1

ROYAL IS MY RACE
(S Rioghal Mo Dhream)

On a cool and damp evening in early May 1794, which was typical of the weather for the west coast of Scotland at this time of year, Andrew Griffin is interrupted by loud knocking on his front door. Placing his chanter on the table, Andrew makes his way down the long hallway wondering who could be visiting on a foul evening. As he opens the front door in rushes Gregor MacGregor, Andrew's cousin, wearing a balmoral bonnet containing the clansman's crest badge. The clan crest is a lion's head with a crown inside a plain circle, and underneath is the clan motto, 'S Rioghal Mo Dhream'. Three eagle feathers mounted above the clan crest indicates Gregor is chief of the Clan MacGregor.

"Oh, what a nasty night, Andrew!" exclaims Gregor as he removes his bonnet and Inverness cape and places his clothes on a hall table located near the front door.

"Gregor, come in, come in, man. It's great to see you," says Andrew with a startled look on his face.

The two men make their way to the sitting room and Andrew invites Gregor to take a seat by the fire. Soon the cousins are sampling a peaty-flavoured Scotch whisky from the Dumbeck Distillers, located close to Port Glasgow.

"And what brings you here on such a foul night, Gregor?" enquires Andrew as he settles into the chair opposite Gregor.

"I received the news," states Gregor as he finishes his glass of Scotch.

"News, Gregor? What news would that be?" asks Andrew, pulling his chair closer to his cousin.

"Last night I was visited by a messenger with an urgent letter from the new Duke of Argyll, no less," states Gregor excitedly.

"Thomas Campbell Gregor?"

Andrew refills his cousin's whisky glass.

"The very same, Andrew, yes."

"So what did the letter say?" asks Andrew with great curiosity in his voice.

Gregor opens his kilt sporran and produces a folded document.

Andrew reads the two-page document carefully and pays special attention to the young duke's signature and seal at the end of the letter.

"The letter appears genuine, Gregor. The paper is of a rich texture, the handwriting is bold and confident and the seal appears to be that of the Duke of Argyll. But what is this reference in the letter to a secret meeting with you and the other clan chiefs o' Scotland in your old abandoned home in Aberfoyle in two weeks' time?"

"I have no idea, Andrew. At first I thought it may be another Campbell trap, but as you see in the letter young Campbell is only bringing a small bodyguard of eight men with him," explains Gregor.

"Do you trust Thomas Campbell, Gregor?" Andrew asks, looking his cousin straight in the eyes.

"I'm no sure, Andrew. I only met the lad when his father attended a meeting with the clan chiefs ten years ago. At that time Thomas Campbell was about ten years old," recounts Gregor staring into the fire.

"So what's the plan, Gregor?"

"Well, I have sent out runners to the other clan chiefs with a message asking them to join me at the meeting with Thomas Campbell, so I should have replies when I return to Aberfoyle, you ken," replies Gregor, slouching back into his chair exhausted by the long ride and cool, damp weather.

Gregor is fifteen years older than Andrew and has been clan chief of the Clan MacGregor for the past ten years. Gregor's sandy-coloured hair is peppered with streaks of grey. He is slightly shorter than his cousin Andrew, who is a tad over six feet tall, but Gregor has inherited his grandfather Rob Roy MacGregor's powerful long arms and stouter build.

"Gregor, you must be hungry. I will get some food."

Andrew leaves the room and walks down the hallway to the back of the house, where the kitchen is located. Preparing meals is certainly not one of Andrew's many skills. The cook, Mrs Purdie, prepares all of the meals, but due to the late hour she's gone home. Sifting through the larder Andrew comes across one half of a cooked chicken, some bread and cheese.

"Here we are, Gregor, this should do the trick," says Andrew as he places the tray of food on the table adjacent to his cousin.

"Thanks, Andrew. What about you – are you not hungry?" asks Gregor as he starts to eat a welcome meal.

"You get stuck in, Gregor. I had a big meal a few hours ago."

"So when did ye move into this house?" enquires Gregor as his eyes scan the large well-furnished sitting room.

"Two months ago. I won the house from a retired sea captain, Sandy Gunn. He was unable to settle his gambling debts during a marathon game o' cards at The Tickled Trout Inn, a tavern located just down the road."

"Do you have any servants, Andrew, for such a big house?"

"Aye, a Mrs Purdie does the cooking and her sister-in-law Jessie Murray sees to the cleaning, Gregor. They both live a few minutes' walk from here."

"Do you no find it a wee bit lonely living on your own, Andrew, in such a big house as this?" asks Gregor curiously.

"Well, I don't spend that much time here. My job at the shipyards here in Port Glasgow keeps me out all day and travelling to students' homes to teach piping in the evenings, and playing cards at The Tickled Trout Inn consumes much o' the remainder of my time, Gregor."

"What about the men that work for you at the shipyards? Are they a good bunch o' lads, Andrew?" asks Gregor as he starts smoking his pipe filled with thick black tobacco.

"Well, they're fairly good workers, but they hate the Highlanders," explains Andrew.

"Do they know that you are from the Highlands o' Scotland and that you were born a MacGregor?"

"No, no, I have not got round to telling them about my real name or that I am a Highlander," replies Andrew sheepishly.

"I think", says Gregor carefully, "that you might consider changing your name back to MacGregor. It's no just me as clan chief who is asking the question, it's all of your family and friends up north, ye ken," states Gregor thoughtfully.

Andrew knows that Gregor is absolutely right. Some of the men that he supervises at the Telfer Bros. Shipyards in Port Glasgow are a band of rough, tough, brawling Lowlanders, who mock and bully the men from the Highlands of Scotland at every opportunity. Andrew has thought many times about taking back his clan name, but he always finds a reason why he should defer the decision. He also realizes that members of the Clan MacGregor have royal blood in their veins. Like Clan Fletcher, the MacGregors were Siol Alpin, descended from Kenneth MacAlpin, the king who united Scots and Picts in the ninth century, but still he does not seem to be able to muster enough courage or motivation to apply to change his name back to MacGregor.

"Aye, I have thought about it many times, Gregor, and I know I will get to it sooner or later," promises Andrew with little conviction in his voice to convince his cousin that this is imminent.

Gregor leans back in his chair looking curiously at his host, recognizing the thinly veiled promise. Gregor senses Andrew is uncomfortable with this discussion, so he switches the conversation back to Thomas Campbell's request for a secret meeting.

"Andrew, I would like you to accompany me to this secret meeting in Aberfoyle in two weeks' time and act as ma advisor. Do you think you can arrange a few days off work?"

Andrew is startled at first by his cousin's request. To be asked by his clan chief to act as an advisor at a meeting with the Duke of Argyll is indeed a great compliment.

"I would be honoured to accompany you, Gregor," replies Andrew, shaking his cousin's hand.

Chapter 2

A SECRET MEETING

Blood and flesh and dirty rags had long sunk into the bog. Only the occasional sight of shattered bones and blackened sword fragments recalled the battle's violence. The screams of clansmen, now lost, have long been replaced with the cries of ravens.

The ten riders glance neither left nor right, concentrating on the road as they move swiftly yet warily past stream and bog. Bordered by broom and heather, the fields are punctured everywhere with scree. The ceaseless murmuring of water, seeping in around and down between the sparse grasses and sheep droppings, is not heard by the riders as much as it penetrates their very souls. These horsemen, all Campbells – gentlemen the lot of them, for only the gentry can afford horses – move quickly in the deepening gloom, shining swords sheathed in richly tooled leather scabbards concealed beneath finely woven woollen capes. Their tartan, muted as the May evening, keeps the trenchant chill from their warm damp bodies. It is 1794; the smell of war fills the land.

In the lead, astride Peggy, a white mare over sixteen hands high, a lad, barely twenty years old, stares straight ahead, eyes penetrating the soft landscape. He sits loosely in the saddle, a contrast to the red-haired, fiercely moustached older man stiffly straddling a handsome bay. The young man wears the rich garb of nobility. Dark locks curl from under a finely tailored plain balmoral bonnet in bottle green. On his black leather shoulder strap, a silver brooch shaped like a boar's head and surrounded by emeralds symbolizes the rank and power of the Campbells. Eight soldiers, each armed with sword, pistol and musket, shield the young noble and his standard-bearer.

As the horsemen stealthily approach the village of Rowardennan, ten miles west of Aberfoyle, word of their encroachment mysteriously precedes them. Flocksmen, ghillies and cottars returning from daily chores stand silently at the side of the road as the riders pass, watching, not as children would a parade, but as sheep guardedly scrutinizing a distant pack of wolves. The sight of the Campbell sashes and flag stirs ripples of sounds in the wake of the passing riders – first a muttering of obscenities, then scattered shouts, and eventually mournful wails from the women.

"Get oot o' here, you dirty Campbells," shouts a young man whose father was killed years before by men wearing the very same tartan sashes.

One of the flocksmen, who is guarding his sheep, ushers them on to the road. The Campbells are now hemmed in by the sheep and by the walls at the edge of the village. The soldiers draw their swords. The young lord slowly raises his hand and stops the forward progress of the horsemen.

"Let me deal with them, My Lord. I'll teach these scum a lesson or two," shouts the standard-bearer, Sandy Ross.

But Thomas Campbell bids him stay his hand. He has on this journey a very different objective.

"No, Ross, leave them be," orders Campbell. "Leave them be."

After a few moments, the sheep disperse, and the riders move on past the jeers of the locals. They have made their point, and so too, in his way, has Thomas Campbell.

As the horsemen enter the village of Rowardennan a tavern comes into view. The sign, hanging from the roof, flaps in the evening breeze and reads, 'The Mill Inn'.

"We'll stay here the night, Ross. Make the arrangements," orders the young lord.

The landlord of the tavern, a large, jolly, bald-headed man, appears with staff as the horsemen dismount.

"Rooms for the night," shouts Ross to the burly landlord.

"At your service, sir," replies the innkeeper.

Unlike the village folk, the innkeeper has no qualms about these gentlemen. If they can pay in cash or gold they are welcome, even if they are the dreaded Campbells from Argyll.

The riders are taken to a large dining room, where they are greeted by a brightly burning fire.

"Best wine, landlord," orders Ross.

As Campbell takes a seat by the welcoming fire Ross deploys the soldiers. Two guard the entrance to the front door while another is sent to the rear of the building.

The staff in the tavern provides a bill of fare for their guests. Within the hour the Campbells of Argyll are served with hot food and plenty of wine. After eating, Campbell and Ross retire to an upstairs room. Thomas Campbell orders a guard to be posted at the entrance to ensure no one enters the room while the Duke and Sandy Ross converse about the secret meeting with the clan chiefs of Scotland.

The room is ordinary and lit by candles, which barely give off enough light to enable the occupants to move around their accommodation. The furnishings are poor, certainly not equal to even the standards of Campbell's servants' hall at his great castle in southern Argyll, near the town of Killean.

"I will come straight to the point, Ross," says the young lord sternly. "Ma father, before he died, charged me wi' a secret mission involving the Clan MacGregor and other local clans. It's a delicate business and we will all need to show great patience. Do you understand, man?"

"Aye," Ross replies grudgingly.

"Ma father's last request was that we settle our differences with the MacGregors and the other clans. The fighting must end. Also, the King wants a new army division consisting o' three Highland regiments formed," explains Campbell.

Ross's face holds the look of man who has just heard some startling news. The Clan Ross had sided with the Duke of Cumberland against Bonnie Prince Charlie at the Battle of Culloden.

"Highland division, my lord? Secret mission? What can this mean?"

"It means, Ross, that the remaining clans will stop fighting amongst themselves. It means that the Campbells and the MacGregors will stop killing one another; it means that all o' the clans will unite under one banner and form Highland regiments and fight the French," explains Campbell with great conviction.

Sandy Ross's father is a retired army officer with the rank of major and Ross continues the family tradition by joining the British Army as a young lieutenant before becoming kinsman to the late Duke of Argyll, John Campbell. As lieutenant, Ross fought in many deadly encounters against Highlanders and has great difficulty in comprehending what his master is proposing.

"For God's sake, ma Lord, the clans will no go for it – there's too much bad blood, too much," cries Ross, whose face is red with rage.

"Aye, there is bad blood, but the King has given us his blessing and if all goes well I'll raise the King's standard at Stirling on the first day o' July 1794."

Ross is speechless and realizes that Thomas Campbell is totally committed to his father's deathbed wish.

It is mid-morning before the Campbells stir. Three days of hard riding has taken its toll on the horses and the men. The young duke orders the men to rest. The outcome of the day's meeting with the clan chiefs of Scotland is uncertain and could be very dangerous.

After a hearty lunch and with the horses well rested, the cautious riders set off eastward towards Aberfoyle. It is evening before they get a glimpse of their secret rendezvous. It is an old half-ruined house. In its day it would have been a grand building boasting twelve rooms, supported by a great room and outhouses, including a mews to house the horses. Now, after forty years of neglect, looting and pillaging, the house is a shadow of its former glory.

At one time the house was the seat of the Clan MacGregor.

In 1745, some members of the Clan MacGregor joined the Young Pretender, Charles Edward Stuart's Jacobite army to fight against the English king. Jacobite was the name given to the supporters of the Young Pretender. Members of the Clan MacGregor who fought for the Jacobite cause were hunted by soldiers of the English king, so the house was abandoned.

The Campbells travel slowly over the drove road towards the house. The young lord can now see a prick of light from a building partly hidden by a stand of rowan trees a few hundred yards ahead. As the riders dismount and slowly walk their mounts towards the partially hidden entrance, fierce-looking clansmen, heavily armed, can be spotted lurking in the shadows. Campbell orders his escort to stand down and wait outside the dilapidated building. Wary of a possible trap, Ross accompanies Campbell inside the building with one hand clutching the handle of his sword.

In the great room of this once noble house, a fire is the only form of light and gives off a piney scent. On the opposite side of the room stands a large round oak table. The table is crowded with many of the chiefs of the Jacobite clans – MacDonalds of Glengarry, MacGregors, MacNeil of Barra, Stewart of Appin, Fraser, Farquharson, Hay, MacLean, Cameron, MacLachlan Robertson, Drummond and several other clan chiefs. The Highland chiefs warily eye the two intruders and then look back at Gregor MacGregor. Some of the chiefs seated at the table reach down to their right leg and place a hand on their skean dhu, a six-inch knife secreted in a small holster tucked in the right leg of their tartan hose. Not a sound can be heard and it feels like an age before Ross speaks.

"Where is the head o' the table?"

No one answers.

Again, in a louder, sterner voice Ross asks, "Where is the head o' the table?"

After a moment's silence a voice in a low tone replies. "Where the MacGregor sits is the head o' the table," states Gregor MacGregor, the clan chief, himself. Gregor MacGregor, grandson of Rob Roy MacGregor, Scotland's great folk hero, has been selected by unanimous accord to take the chair at this meeting and has consented.

Tension fills the air until Campbell steps forward, removes his bonnet and bows slowly and graciously. "I am Thomas Campbell, 6th Duke of Argyll, and this is ma kinsman Sandy Ross."

"You are welcome here, Thomas Campbell. I am Gregor MacGregor, clan chief o' the MacGregors. I guarantee yer safety while you and yer men visit MacGregor lands. Sit doon."

Two chairs are brought forward and the visitors sit. Thomas Campbell removes his bonnet and ushers Ross to follow his lead. MacGregor introduces the clan chiefs. There are fifteen present from Argyll, Perthshire, Stirlingshire and Aberdeenshire and from the great glens to the north and west.

"State yer business," MacGregor says abrasively.

"Thank you for allowing me this audience. My late father, John Campbell, 5th Duke of Argyll, asked me to visit with a proposition from the King to the clan chiefs o' Scotland. For hundreds o' years we have fought each other over lands and old hatreds. Many of oor families perished and many carry the scars o' a long feud. My father's heart was heavy wi' guilt when he lay dying and he asked me to come with a message o' peace amongst the clans and hope for a better future."

"And what kind o' hope do you bring, Campbell?" utters MacDonald, the clan chief, in an accent peculiar to the Clan MacDonald.

"I know from what my father told me on his deathbed that there would be suspicion and a great amount o' mistrust. But if you would hear me out I will explain his message. My father, before he passed away, spoke to King George and they discussed a plan to form a Highland division made up o' three regiments. The soldiers will be allowed to wear the kilt and will be made up o' clansmen, just like you. The soldiers will be paid on a regular basis and the officers will be all Highlanders. You will have yer own army drummers and pipers and you will be known by yer own clan names," explains Campbell.

There is a silence at first, then Lachlan MacDonald of

Glengarry and his followers slowly rise up and begin to leave the room.

"Gregor, you must stop the clan chiefs from leaving," urges Andrew Griffin, who is seated to his right.

"Stop, men, stop – hear the Duke out. Let's at least talk it o'er amongst ourselves," pleads MacGregor.

The clan chiefs stop and look around at MacGregor, who is now on his feet.

"Men," continues MacGregor, "we have endured great hardships with the ongoing feuds against the Clan Campbell and their rich and powerful Sassenach allies o'er the past hundred years. Many of our families have perished fighting to retain our lands and homes. You, MacLachlan, and you MacNeil have lost several o' yer brothers fighting to defend yer homes; and you, Fraser, have lost two sons. We must find a way to stop the bleeding and bring peace back to our lands. Will you at least give Campbell a chance to finish what he's come all this way to share with us?" pleads MacGregor with great compassion.

The clan chiefs have great respect for Gregor MacGregor and some nod, showing their agreement to stay and talk. Others reluctantly follow their fellow countryman's lead.

"I want the Campbell out o' here," shouts Lachlan MacDonald, clan chief, whose family had been betrayed and slaughtered by the Campbells at their home in Glencoe many years earlier.

Thomas Campbell stands up and, full of dignity, says, "MacGregor, I thank you for the time in allowing me to address yer fellow clan chiefs. I also thank MacLachlan, MacNeil, MacDonald and Cameron and all of those other chiefs here tonight for yer patience in bearing with my intrusion. I look forward to what this means for the future o' Scotland. I will return to Rowardennan and wait for three days for yer reply." Turning his head in a great bow, Campbell leaves the hall.

Several conversations break out amongst the clan chiefs and it takes MacGregor several minutes to bring order to the meeting.

"Men, men, we have to decide whether we will accept or reject Campbell's proposal," shouts MacGregor at the top of his voice.

Stewart of Appin is the first to stand and speak. "All of us have fought against the mighty Campbells for many years and we have all paid a heavy price. I side with MacGregor and say let the clans unite and form Highland regiments."

Many of the clan chiefs state their agreement with Stewart of Appin, but Lachlan MacDonald slowly draws his great broadsword from its sheath and bangs three times on the table with the sword handle until silence falls on the room.

"I can hardly believe my ears. Consorting with the dirty Campbells – never while I live."

Macdonald and his men start to leave the meeting.

"Gregor, we must go after the MacDonalds and find a way to change his mind, otherwise this whole initiative will fall apart," states Griffin anxiously.

"Men, men, I beg you all to give me time to speak with the MacDonalds of Glengarry. Let us meet again the day after tomorrow, by which time I will have spoken with the MacDonalds," MacGregor shouts pleadingly.

Agreement is reached amongst all of the clan chiefs to support MacGregor's request.

Two days pass and there is no word from Gregor MacGregor. The landlord of The Mill Inn does his best to entertain his distinguished visitors. On the morning of the third day the innkeeper organizes a boar hunt for his guests. It is well received by the soldiers, who long for some action. The hunting party is taken to thick woods to the north of the village. The landlord's son, Rory MacAlpine, acts as guide. The young MacAlpine is a natural tracker of game and the hunting party soon falls upon boar tracks. Within an hour they locate and kill a fair-sized boar. Rory spots other boar tracks, but Thomas Campbell orders his men back to the village.

The six riders maintain a steady gallop as they make their way north towards Lochearnhead. Gregor MacGregor's plan is to try to intercept Lachlan MacDonald and his bodyguard before they turn to the north-east for Glengarry.

"Have you seen any of the Clan MacDonald on the north road today?" asks MacGregor to a group of merchants resting by the side of the road at the entrance to the town of Lochearnhead.

"Aye, a group of riders wearing the MacDonald tartan passed by here about two hours ago," replies a well-dressed merchant holding a large cup in his hand.

A brief stop in Lochearnhead confirms that the MacDonalds did not rest at either of the two taverns for refreshments, so MacGregor and his men kick on towards the village of Killin. Entering Killin, Andrew Griffin spots eight horses standing outside a tavern.

"Gregor, look, I think we have caught up with the MacDonalds," shouts Andrew with great excitement in his voice.

"Lachlan, dear friend," hails Gregor as he enters the tavern to the total surprise of the MacDonalds who are resting and enjoying a welcome meal and beverage.

"Damn the pair of you – can you no leave a man in peace?" states Lachlan MacDonald as he slams his wine goblet on the table, spilling most of the contents.

Gregor sits down beside Lachlan, placing his bonnet on a nearby chair, and orders more wine.

"If ye think I'm going to change my mind and support Campbell's proposal y'are dreaming, man. I would not trust any Campbells as far as I could throw them," adds MacDonald gruffly.

"I understand Lachlan, I truly do. I know fine well about the massacre at Glencoe and the other atrocities committed over the years by the hand o' John Campbell. But the fact is John Campbell's deceased, and it's his son we are now dealing with."

"Thomas Campbell is his father's son; what makes you believe that things will be any different?"

"I believe this young Campbell when he advocates peace amongst the clans. If he wants to continue in his father's footsteps he would be sending his soldiers to destroy our villages and steal our livestock."

Andrew Griffin approaches the table and takes a seat next to Gregor.

"Lachlan, this is my cousin Andrew frae Port Glasgow. Andrew and I believe Campbell's proposal will be good for oor men and their families. The men will get paid on a regular basis, and be able to wear the kilt and play the pipes. Andrew here is recognized as one of Scotland's finest pipers and, like me, wants the Highland traditions to continue."

"So, Andrew, what makes you think Campbell will keep his word?" asks MacDonald.

"Lachlan, just like you my family have been persecuted over the years at the hand o' the Campbells. When I was a wee lad living in Glenstrae we were hunted by the Campbells and their Sassenach friends from down south. Ma father was forced to flee from his home in Glenstrae and move his family to Arbroath on the east coast o' Scotland and change our family name. Your clan, Lachlan, is one of the biggest in Scotland. If the MacDonalds don't come to Stirling some o' the other clan chiefs will also refuse to come and the whole idea of forming three Highland regiments will be lost. I believe Thomas Campbell will keep his word," states Griffin with great conviction.

Gregor, who has been watching Lachlan's facial expression, realizes that he is still against supporting Campbell's proposal.

"Look, Lachlan, what will it take to change yer mind and join us at Stirling this summer?" asks Gregor forcefully.

Lachlan sits quietly for several minutes thinking, then states, "If Campbell agrees to appoint three lieutenant colonels from members of the clans who supported the Jacobite cause then I may recommend that my clan supports the proposal."

Griffin does not believe for one minute that Thomas Campbell will support MacDonald's request, but quickly realizes that Lachlan in a way has softened his attitude towards the idea of supporting a Campbell proposal of any kind.

"Are there any other conditions, Lachlan?" asks Griffin.

"Aye, there is: the clansmen must be allowed to speak in their native Gaelic if they so choose," replies Lachlan sternly.

"I will take yer proposal back to the other clan chiefs, and if they all agree I will write to Campbell, dear friend," comments

MacGregor as he rises, placing his hand on MacDonald's shoulder.

On the third day, towards evening, two riders approach the village of Rowardennan from the east at full gallop. The riders wear the tartan of the Clan MacGregor and bring a message for Campbell. They are told to wait for a reply.

Thomas Campbell reads the message with great care.

> The clan chiefs will agree to your proposal under the following conditions. The conditions are that you appoint three lieutenant colonels for each of the Highland regiments from clan members who supported the Jacobite cause and that the men be allowed to speak in their native Gaelic tongue, if they so desire.
> Signed,
> Gregor MacGregor,
> clan chief.

Campbell sits down with the letter in one hand and places his other hand on his chin, leaning his elbow on his knee. He thinks on how he can sell this request to the King and the army chief of staff. After several minutes he rises and requests pen and paper.

> I agree to your terms. I will take your request to the King and his senior military officers and let you know their response.
> Signed,
> Thomas Campbell,
> 6th Duke of Argyll.

The two riders swiftly gallop away to the east and Campbell shows a rare turn of emotion, smiling and saying excitedly, "Come, Ross, we must hurry – there is much work to do."

Chapter 3

A CLOSE CALL

Peggy, Campbell's mount, thunders south towards London at full gallop followed by Campbell's full bodyguard of 100 soldiers. The past few days have proved difficult for Campbell, trying to think of a way to convince the King and his generals to support MacGregor's proposal. The generals of the army have been cool on the idea of forming any Highland regiments, never mind the three that Campbell proposed to the King. As he gallops south he decides how he will make his case to the King to get agreement to the clan chief's proposals. If the King can be persuaded to support the idea of appointing three members to lead three new regiments from the clans who supported the Jacobite cause, then the general's support may follow.

Thomas Campbell is led into a large garden where the senior army officers are huddled around the Duke of Essex, Colonel Clypton. As Campbell approaches, the senior army officers suddenly take off in different directions, leaving Campbell and Clypton to themselves.

"Good day, Clypton. How are you?" asks Campbell politely, sensing a conspiracy in the making.

"Well, Campbell, good to see you," replies Clypton awkwardly.

"Are you joining us at the meeting with the King?"

"Yes, I have been invited to attend."

"I'm counting on yer support, Clypton."

"Look here, Campbell, the senior army staff gathered here

today are not in favour of placing the leadership of the three Highland regiments in the hands of former Jacobite supporters. Not on, old chap."

At that moment an announcement is heard ordering all those gathered in the garden to proceed to the palace to attend the meeting with the King. Campbell does not get a chance to respond to Clypton's comments as he rushes off towards the palace.

Everyone stands as the King enters the great hall.

"Please be seated, gentlemen," requests the King.

"Welcome to all. I have called this meeting to discuss Thomas Campbell's proposal regarding senior army officer appointments for the three new Highland regiments. First, I would invite General Marshalsea to make a few remarks."

"Thank you, Your Majesty. As chief of staff of the army, I have discussed Thomas Campbell's proposals with all senior members of my staff. The feeling amongst the officers is that it would not be in the army's best interests to place the leadership of the three new Highland regiments in the hands of former supporters of the Jacobite cause. We concluded, after careful deliberation, that leaders be found and appointed from amongst the general staff of the army. Also, sire, we feel that allowing the recruits to speak in Gaelic would make communication difficult amongst the officers and the men," explains Marshalsea.

"Thank you, Marshalsea. Thomas Campbell, I invite you to respond to Marshalsea's comments."

"Thank you, Yer Majesty. I have met with the clan chiefs o' Scotland. The clan chiefs believe that appointing regimental leaders from members of clans who supported the Jacobite cause would encourage the recruiting of men from all of the Scottish clans. Also, it would have the effect of uniting the clans – something that has not been achieved since the '45 rebellion, Yer Majesty."

There are several comments of disapproval made amongst the attendees.

"Gentlemen, please, one spokesperson at a time. Kindly raise your hand if you wish to speak. General Trimble, you have the floor."

"Thank you, sire. Campbell, is it not the case that there is a great deal of mistrust amongst the Scottish clans towards the Lowlanders, the Campbell's and the British Army?"

"Yes, Trimble, there is mistrust, a great deal o' mistrust. Ma clan has to earn its trust amongst certain clans who in my opinion were badly treated in the past. My goal is to regain the trust o' my fellow countrymen. What better way than to build trust through appointing capable and competent members of the clans who previously supported the Jacobite cause," utters Campbell with confidence.

"The Duke of Essex has the floor, gentlemen," states the King.

"Sire, I feel General Trimble's points are sound. The Clan MacDonald and Campbell are mortal enemies. How can Thomas Campbell expect cooperation from a MacDonald if one of their clan is appointed to the position of lieutenant colonel of one of the three Scottish regiments?"

"Fair point, Essex. Thomas Campbell, can you respond?"

"It is true, Yer Majesty, that the MacDonalds' hatred against my clan is well known throughout Scotland and England. The background to this hatred stems from an incident of betrayal by the Campbells against the MacDonalds of Glencoe. I am ashamed of this betrayal, and my earnest hope is to start to gain back the respect and trust o' the Clan MacDonald. Lachlan MacDonald, clan chief o' the Clan MacDonald, is not requesting that he become one of three appointees of the Highland regiments. His request is that no Campbells or Sassenachs be appointed as lieutenant colonels of the Highland regiments."

The discussion carries on for over half an hour, then the King, as chair of the meeting, brings the discussion to an end.

"Gentlemen, I have listened carefully to all of your comments. It strikes me that with Thomas Campbell as colonel-in-chief and the Duke of Essex as second in command of the Highland division that should be sufficient oversight to ensure that orders are carried out in line with the army's wishes. Campbell, who are you recommending be appointed as lieutenant colonels of the three Highland regiments?"

"Sire, I have here documents listing the names of my recommendations."

Copies of a list of names are passed around the table.

"As you see, sire, I am recommending Gregor MacGregor, chief of the Clan MacGregor, to be appointed as the first lieutenant colonel of the first Highland regiment. MacGregor has acted as spokesman for the clan chiefs of Scotland at meetings which I attended recently. He is a well-respected figure amongst the clan chiefs and has displayed excellent leadership qualities."

Marshalsea raises his hand to speak.

"You have the floor, Marshalsea."

"Sire, if the appointments for the rank of major could be left to me and my staff, with input sought from Campbell, we could agree to this request."

Campbell reluctantly signals his agreement as he sees no other way to get Marshalsea's support.

"On the question of language, Marshalsea, have you any solutions to offer at this time?" asks the King.

"Yes, Your Majesty. If the Highlanders, whose first language is Gaelic, can be taught to speak English as part of their basic army training, I could support Campbell's request."

After discussion on this point it is agreed that the training will include teaching English to those recruits whose native tongue is Gaelic.

The meeting comes to an end and all of the attendees are invited to refreshments of champagne, wine and fruit in the garden.

The Queen hosts her husband's guests and Thomas Campbell is introduced to one of the Queen's daughters, Princess Augusta. Campbell is immediately taken by the young princess.

Chapter 4

ARMY BUSINESS

Situated in the southern wilds of Argyll, near the town of Killean, is the castle of the 6th Duke of Argyll. Within the great hall of the castle, Thomas Campbell has assembled a group of his senior military personnel and business leaders from the many cities of the Lowlands of Scotland. These dignitaries include the Chief of Arms, Major Duncan Campbell of Lochnell, who is directly responsible for the recruiting and training of new volunteers to the Duke of Argyll's standing army and for the purchase and maintenance of all armaments used by the soldiers in battle; His Majesty's representative, Colonel John Clypton, Duke of Essex, who has been appointed by King George III to be Thomas Campbell's deputy commander of the soon to be formed Highland Division; and merchants from the cities of Glasgow and Edinburgh and from the town of Stirling. Other attendees include Big Jock Brown, head of Campbell's household, who faithfully served Thomas Campbell's father, the late John Campbell, for many years.

"Gentlemen, we have some pressing business to attend to. In five weeks I will raise the King's standard at the town of Stirling and recruit a division o' clansmen, three regiments, and 4,500 men in all. To achieve this will take a great deal o' planning. The King has advised me that there is pressing need for a show o' strength in South Africa to remove the Dutch from Cape Town. Also, the French are on the move in Portugal and Spain, so there is lots for the army to do," states Campbell confidently.

Campbell of Lochnell, a career soldier, requests to speak.

"My Lord, the Highland clans will no join us at Stirling. The policies o' pacification o' the clans following the Battle of Culloden in 1746 by the British Government are deeply rooted in the memories o' those Highland families who opted to continue to stay in Scotland. We will be fortunate to form one regiment, let alone the three that the King has settled on," states Lochnell with great conviction.

"Ah, but y'are wrong, Lochnell," replies Thomas Campbell. "There is a strategy that I have in place which will entice even the most firm Highland hearts to join us. We will form companies o' men from the same parish, district, glen and town. The battalions will be led by men from the same areas as the soldiers. They will get to wear the kilt, play the pipes and drums, bear arms, and speak in their native Gaelic tongue if they so choose. It will seem like the old clan days are here again, except now the British Government will be feeding, clothing and paying them wages, instead o' their clan chiefs, and more importantly they'll have no fear o' retribution!"

Clapping instantly breaks out amongst the attendees at the table. Thomas Campbell makes perfect sense to all in attendance; and for a young man of barely twenty years, he has an old head on his shoulders. It is from this meeting that Thomas Campbell, 6th Duke of Argyll, inherits the nickname of Old Tom.

"Gentlemen, I have a letter here from the King. His Majesty has graciously agreed to recommendations made by Colonel Clypton and myself for a name for the new Highland regiments and the tartan to be worn by the soldiers. The new Highland Division will be known as the Argyll and Sutherland Highlanders, or the 98th Argyllshire Highlanders. As for the tartan for the kilts to be worn by the new men of the new Highland Division, the King has settled for the Black Watch tartan, which is a dark-coloured tartan of green with a black stripe," explains Campbell. "Now I will ask the Duke of Essex to bring us up to date on a motto for the new army," adds Campbell.

"Thank you, Campbell. Gentlemen, the King has also expressed an interest in a motto to be placed on the regimental colours of the new Highland Division. After reviewing many suggestion the King accepted the phrase 'Honour and Victory' to be inscribed along the top of the regimental colours. The full motto is 'May honour and victory ever attend you!'"

Clapping breaks out, indicating agreement amongst all present.

"Gentlemen, I must leave you now to attend to some urgent business. His Lordship the Duke of Essex will chair the meeting."

All rise as Thomas Campbell takes his leave.

"Perhaps Mr Pringle can update us on the amount of material required for the making of the kilts?" requests Clypton.

"Thank you, My Lord. I have spoken with all of the weavers from Glasgow, Paisley and Edinburgh and they have started weaving the material for the soldiers' kilts. One question has arisen that relates to the amount of material required for each kilt. Will you need the traditional five yards o' cloth for each kilt?" asks Willie Pringle, a highly regarded and trustworthy Edinburgh merchant who is recognized as the leading supplier of cloth suitable for the making of kilts in Scotland.

"For my soldiers I allow six yards o' cloth," comments Lochnell.

"Could you please explain, Lochnell, why six yards of material is required?" requests Clypton.

"My Lord, the extra yard is for maintenance of the kilts. Kilts do get damaged while fighting in the field, so an extra yard should take care o' the maintenance," suggests Lochnell.

"Excellent point, sir," replies Clypton, who understands Lochnell's reasoning.

It is agreed that Willie Pringle, the highly regarded Edinburgh merchant, will advise all of his weavers and dyers to produce six yards of the Black Watch tartan cloth for each of the 4,500 soldiers.

"Now, on the question of armaments, could you, Mr Templeton, please advise us on what armaments are available?"

Gordon Templeton is a rich merchant from the city of Glasgow. Templeton is a tall, slim man, has a wiry appearance, and although barely thirty years of age he already has silver-coloured hair. In the world of commerce he is known as the Silver Fox.

"Gentlemen, we have a wide variety of armaments in stock, so can we identify the quantities and types o' heavy armaments that will be required?" requests Templeton.

Colonel Clypton starts off the discussion by identifying the artillery needs for the division. "For artillery, we will require approximately forty-nine-pound batteries."

Lochnell supports Clypton's assessment, and the other members signal their agreement.

Templeton passes documents around the table listing all of the smaller-sized armaments currently available. Descriptions of all of the armaments with pictures or sketches of each product help make this discussion move along at a fair clip.

"Gentlemen, as you see from the documents that I have circulated, there is a wide variety of smaller armaments with pictures or sketches for each item displayed. I can offer you a wide selection of black gunpowder, muzzle-loading flintlock and matchlock muskets, rifles and pistols, lead balls, and bayonets," explains Templeton.

"Mr Templeton, where would we find dirks?" requests Lochnell.

"Dirks, sir?" responds Templeton, somewhat puzzled by the question.

"Part of the Highlanders' dress includes a dirk or *biodag* as it is called by the clansmen. It's a long stabbing knife approximately eighteen inches in length and is used by the men when fighting the enemy at close quarters," explains Lochnell.

Templeton agrees to follow up after the meeting and arrange for quantities of dirks to be manufactured at his foundries in Glasgow.

"Lochnell, where would the men wear their dirks?" enquires Clypton with great curiosity.

"My Lord, the dirks are housed in a sheath and hung from the kilt belt," explains Lochnell.

Seeing that Clypton accepts the explanation, the attendees discuss the number of tents, cooks and bottle washers, and a host of other supplies are requisitioned.

After listening carefully to the discussion Clypton feels that all of the key planning for equipping the new Highland army has been covered and asks if there is any other business. Hearing none, Clypton motions to close the discussion.

"Only one other thing missing, gentlemen, from our plan: some good Scotch whisky. Remember that when we recruit a new soldier to the British Army the tradition is that we must seal the deal with a dram o' Scotch whisky and five bright new-minted shillings. As for the shillings, gentlemen, the King has generously provided me with chests full o' shiny newly minted coins. However, we will need to place an order for lots o' good Scotch. What would you suggest, Lochnell?" asks Clypton.

"I suggest 400 bottles o' Scotch from distilleries located at Tobermory and Talisker."

Sensing no objections, Lochnell then makes the following remark: "The king o' drinks, as I conceive it, Talisker, Isla or Glenlivet."

As the meeting comes to an end, Big Jock Brown, head of the household, enters the room with a silver tray containing two bottles of single malt Scotch, and crystal drinking glasses.

"To complete our business of the day, gentlemen, will you join me and raise your glasses and sample the pungent, peaty and powerful taste of a ten-year-old Scotch? I give you, the King!"

And the crowd echoes back, "To the King!"

Chapter 5

A GREAT HONOUR

Thomas Campbell and his bodyguard make their way steadily north towards the town of Tarbet, where he has arranged to meet with Gregor MacGregor and his cousin Andrew Griffin.

"Gregor, it's gone 5 p.m. Do you think young Campbell will come?"

"I hope so, Andrew – we have come a long way for the meeting."

Just after 6 p.m. Campbell and Sandy Ross appear.

"Apologies, gentlemen, for my lateness," comments Campbell as he takes a seat beside MacGregor. "You'll be wondering, gentlemen, what's on my mind, calling this meeting at such short notice," says Campbell as he accepts a glass of wine.

"Yer message sounded urgent," states MacGregor.

"Since our last meeting I have given much thought to who should lead the three Highland regiments. When I updated the King and his generals on our agreement there were a considerable number of comments made by some of the more senior army officers. However, the King is in favour of my plans and I am glad to report that each Highland regiment will be led by a member from a clan who served under the Young Pretender," explains Campbell.

"I sense that it was a bit o' a struggle to get agreement on our terms," replies MacGregor.

"That it was, MacGregor, that it was. Now, the first appointment as regimental leader will be announced soon after the first Highland regiment is in place. I expect that to be mid-July if all goes well. My recommendation to the King and his senior advisors was that you, Gregor MacGregor, be appointed lieutenant colonel of the first Highland regiment. How do you feel about that, MacGregor?"

For the first time in his life MacGregor is speechless.

"Congratulations, Gregor – a great honour!" states Griffin as he throws his arms around his cousin, who is finding it difficult to understand what Campbell just said.

"My Lord, I am – I am overwhelmed with the honour you bestow on me. Thank you, sir, thank you," cries Gregor as he rises to shake Campbell's hand.

"What I ask in return, MacGregor, is yer loyalty as I will be colonel-in-chief of the Highland Division; Colonel Clypton, the Duke of Essex, will be my deputy commander." Campbell, however, fails to mention that officers of the rank of major and below will be hand-picked by Marshalsea, chief of staff of the army.

"Ma Lord, you can count on my complete loyalty and support," replies Gregor, his face flushed, still reeling from the news of his unexpected appointment.

Chapter 6

TROOPING OF THE COLOURS

Soon July comes, and on that warm day in 1794 a large crowd has assembled at the city gates of the town of Stirling in expectation of the raising the King's standard and for the trooping of the regimental colours. The army volunteers memorize the vibrant colours in the flag, so that when the day of the battle comes they will be ready to rally round the colours and fight for the King.

Old Tom stands before a crowd of over 2,000 people, including volunteers, pipers, drummers, sheriffs from nearby towns and villages, tradesmen, merchants, hostlers and local residents. Provost Macpherson represents the town of Stirling and members of his distinguished council are amongst the dignitaries. Other distinguished guests include many of the clan chiefs and nobility of Scotland. Old Tom is clothed in his full ceremonial Scottish outfit, consisting of a feather bonnet, red tunic, Black Watch tartan kilt, large sporran, low-cut shoes with buckles, and a skean dhu placed in the hose of his right leg. He is over six feet tall, and is an impressive figure in his Highland dress.

"My lords, ladies and gentlemen and distinguished guests, on behalf of our noble king I bring you all greetings. Today is another great moment in the history o' bonnie Scotland. For today I have the authority and full support of His Majesty to raise the King's standard. A Scottish division o' three Highland regiments is being raised and will be known as the Argyll and Sutherland Highlanders – the 98th Argyllshire Highlanders. The regimental motto is 'May honour and victory ever attend you!' The division will be comprised o' 4,500 men, all clansmen. The three regiments will be kilted and will be paid by the King himself. As yer commander-in-chief, it will be a great honour to lead you into battle. And now I will ask Lieutenant Colonel Gregor MacGregor to assist me in raising the King's standard and present the colours of our new regiments," shouts Old Tom to the cheers of the large crowd.

At this point, Old Tom leaves the stage and makes his way to a small hill nearby where a guard of honour and Lieutenant Colonel Gregor MacGregor are waiting. Pipers and drummers play 'The Gathering of Lochiel', a stirring bagpipe tune, and amidst all of the pomp and ceremony Old Tom raises the King's standard. It is a magnificent standard, with gold thread and dazzling colours. Balmoral and glengarry bonnets are thrown into the air and the cheering of the large crowd is deafening. Old Tom presents the new regimental colours to Lieutenant Colonel MacGregor and proclaims him as the first lieutenant colonel of the first regiment of the 98th. Inscribed along the top of the regimental colours are the words 'Honour and Victory'. The ceremonies are followed by a march past of the regimental colours, accompanied by 100 soldiers, pipers and drummers from Old Tom's personal bodyguard. The pipers play rousing marches.

It is a great moment indeed for all in attendance and for Scotland. The clan chiefs who have gathered together to observe the proceedings are happy with Gregor MacGregor's appointment as lieutenant colonel of the first Highland regiment.

The recruiting of volunteers commences shortly after the trooping of the regimental colours. By late afternoon over 600 clansmen are assembled at Stirling. Men appear from Ross and Cromarty in the north-west of Scotland who can speak only in Gaelic. Other recruits come from villages along the River Tay and from towns to the north and east, including Inverness, Banff, and Old Aberdeen, and from villages along the shores of Loch Linnhe.

In the early evening, a large contingent enters the camp singing. These men are members of the Clans Bruce, Hay, Lindsay and Farquharson, and have travelled from the kingdom of Fife and lands beyond Dundee. In the gloaming, over 100 clansmen enter the camp in full Highland dress carrying claymores (large two-handed swords) and targes (round shields made from laminated wood and heavily studded in the centre). These men are fierce-looking warriors from the Western Isles who wear their long beards in a flaunting, ostentatious way. Three pipers and a side drummer dressed in the MacLeod of Lewis tartan lead the Western warriors. Even cats and dogs are drawn to the sound of the procession as the wives and children follow behind in carts and wagons, heads held high as the men march to the skirl of the Highland bagpipes. Fellow clansmen leave the warmth of their campfires when they hear the sound of the pipes and drums. Clapping and cheering breaks out amongst all of the onlookers at the magnificent sight of the new recruits.

Colonel Clypton and his aides spend long hours inspecting the volunteers. Some men, unfit for service, are fed and sent home. Those who pass muster are given the traditional half a gill of Scotch whisky and five new shiny shillings, confirming their service into the British Army.

Over 1,000 meals are served to all those in attendance. Pipers, drummers and singers from nearby towns entertain the gathering. Sleep does not come easy to many of the new recruits, who renew old friendships until the wee hours of the morning.

The second day of recruiting volunteers is as hectic as the first. Another 400 volunteers arrive from Northern Scotland. Some of these volunteers are men from the Shetland Islands, who bear a Nordic look about them. They had been visiting the town of Inverness on the northern mainland of Scotland when they heard the news of a new Highland Division being formed and they have come along more out of curiosity than anything else. When the young men arrive there is dancing, singing and piping in progress, and they get caught up in the excitement of the moment and accept the 'wee half o' Scotch' and five new shiny shillings from Colonel Clypton, and soon find themselves members of a newly formed Highland regiment.

Some of the recruits have previous military experience. Many men from Blair Atholl who arrive on the second day served previously as officers in the British Army and are now offered commissions by Lieutenant Colonel Gregor MacGregor in his newly formed regiment. Other volunteers arrive who have served as pipers or drummers with clan chiefs and have been involved in battles of various sizes. These men are made lance corporals, corporals or sergeants. Wherever possible, companies are formed from men from the same parishes. The new recruits are put to work right away. The fields occupied by army volunteers gradually take on a new look.

"Major Percy, advise the other officers that we will tour the campsite," commands Lieutenant Colonel MacGregor. Percy is the first appointment by General Marshalsea, chief of staff of the army. Major Percy is distantly related to Colonel Clypton. Percy has a certain arrogance about him and MacGregor is finding it difficult to communicate with Percy.

A dozen officers of all ranks set off behind MacGregor to conduct their field inspection.

"Percy, when will the latrines be completed?" questions MacGregor.

"I have been assured, sir, that the men will have them completed by tomorrow night."

"The trenches must be completed by tonight. See to it."

"Major Waterworth, do we have enough firewood to cook the meals?"

"Yes, sir. We have six cords of firewood stacked and I have three groups of men out foraging in the woods on the east side of the camp," replies Waterworth nervously.

The Waterworths are a rich English family, having made their fortune in cotton mills located in the Midlands of England. Brian Waterworth had risen quickly in the ranks to major largely as a result of his parents' influence with members of Marshalsea's staff. Major Waterworth has no battlefield experience, having spent most of his army career as an aide to General Trimble.

As the inspection party make their way to the west side of the camp, groups of volunteers can be observed trying to assemble tents. It appears to MacGregor that the army volunteers are having a great deal of trouble trying to assemble the tents.

"Lieutenant MacDonald, go and supervise the assembling o' the tents or we will have no place to house the recruits tonight," orders MacGregor.

Lieutenant MacDonald is the youngest brother of Lachlan MacDonald of Glengarry and appears to have the makings of a good officer.

"Major Waterworth, how many tents do we have?" asks MacGregor.

"I think we have approximately sixty tents, sir," replies Waterworth.

"You think or ye know, Major."

"I will go and check, sir, and report back," replies Waterworth nervously as he hurries towards the west side of the camp.

MacGregor and his officers make their way towards the north side of the camp, where teams of volunteers and local contractors are busily constructing a north–south road through the site.

"Major Percy, is the road construction on schedule?"

"Sir, the road will be ready in four days."

"Major, that's not what I asked. Is the road construction on schedule?"

"No, sir, we are a full day behind schedule," replies Percy sheepishly.

"Well, sir, get over there and get it back on schedule," orders MacGregor abruptly, leaving Percy in no doubt about his expectations.

Colonel MacGregor then dismisses his officers.

On his return to his headquarters, Willie Pringle is waiting to see MacGregor.

"Good morning, Pringle. What brings you here?"

"I had a meeting with the weavers yesterday, Colonel, and was advised that they have fallen behind with the army's weaving schedule for the cloth for the kilts," states Pringle.

"Well, what actions do you recommend, sir?"

"Colonel MacGregor, I recommend that we contract the Selkirk weavers located in the Border country. I know their work, and the weavers can be relied upon to deliver the material to the dyers on time," states Pringle, who appears uncomfortable about coming to MacGregor with this report after he had given the army his assurance that the weavers and dyers' work schedule would be met.

"Pringle, you have a fine reputation so I will agree to yer recommendation provided that you personally oversee the work and that you keep me updated on progress."

"Thank you, Colonel. I will no let you down a second time," promises Pringle as he turns and hurries out of the room.

The Selkirk weavers, at the urging of Pringle, work long hours. Every weaver sees the bold dark-green and black stripes in their dreams as they rush to meet the army's deadline.

Weavers provide seamstresses with over 18,000 yards of the Black Watch tartan material. The seamstresses have been instructed to use only five of the six yards of material assigned to make each kilt. One yard of material for each kilt made is to be kept in storage to repair damaged kilts.

By the end of August 1794, two of the three regiments are brought up to full strength. Lachlan MacDonald and the other clan chiefs are happy with Gregor MacGregor's appointment.

"Gentlemen, I have the honour to advise you that the second Highland regiment will be led by David Murray of Atholl," states Campbell at the officers' morning meeting.

Clapping breaks out amongst the officers assembled.

"Lieutenant Colonel Murray will arrive here tomorrow. As you know, gentlemen, many of the Atholl Highlanders have already joined the first and second Highland regiments. I hope I can count on you to welcome Murray and help him settle in. Now, gentlemen, how is the training o' the recruits progressing?" requests Old Tom.

"Sir, all o' the men's training schedules are in place. Battalion commanders have been appointed and training o' the recruits is in progress. The training consists o' marching in companies, target shooting, battle formation and learning how to fight against mounted horsemen, whom many of the clansmen find intimidating," explains MacGregor.

"Good work," states Campbell, who is pleased with the army's progress.

"Sir, the army pipers' and drummers' positions have been filled, but we are having difficulty with communicating with some of the recruits who can only speak in Gaelic," explains Sandy Ross.

"Sir, I would recommend that we recruit translators to teach the Gaels how to speak in English," recommends MacGregor.

"I agree," states Sandy Ross, who is a Lowlander and does not speak any Gaelic.

"I will leave you to recruit translators, MacGregor," states Campbell.

Ten female translators are hired. The women come from Islay and Kintyre, Oban and Mull, the Spey Valley and Mid Argyll. Some of the women are widowed, and most of them are single, much to the men's celebration. The translators are provided with good accommodation in Stirling on the north side of town, three miles from the Argylls' camp.

Old Tom is pleased with the recruiting progress as he sits down at his desk, pulling paper, quill and an ink horn before him, and drafts the following letter to the King;

Your Majesty,

I trust that this communication finds you in the best of health.

I am pleased to report that the morale amongst your two new regiments is high. The volunteers are making good progress and I have every confidence that they will be ready for a royal inspection in the autumn of this year. As Your Majesty's birthday is in October, may I so boldly suggest that you consider coming to Scotland for a royal inspection of your Highland regiments.

Regarding the recruiting of a third Highland regiment, runners have been dispatched all over the Highlands to try and attract more volunteers.

I will keep Your Majesty informed of the progress made in recruiting a third Highland regiment.

Your humble servant and most affectionate admirer,

Thomas Campbell

The King seizes on Campbell's idea and writes to Campbell requesting that he invite all of Scotland's dignitaries to the royal inspection. The King's official birthday is 15 October, so this is the date set for His Majesty's inspection and for the trooping of the regimental colours.

"Gentlemen, I have here a letter from the King indicating that he will conduct a royal inspection of the two Highland regiments on October the 15th of this year," states Thomas Campbell, who appears very happy that the King is coming to Scotland.

"Sir, if I may speak?" requests Lieutenant Colonel David Murray.

"Please do, Murray."

"The companies of the second Highland regiment are having difficulty at marching in formation. I have changed the drilling sergeants, but the men's marching still has not improved sufficiently for a royal inspection," explains Murray.

"What about the first regiment, MacGregor? Are they faring any better?" Campbell asks.

"The first regiment has made good progress during the past month because most of the men are hand-picked, sir. I am certain that the first regiment will be ready to be inspected by mid-October," replies MacGregor confidently.

"Well then, I will send six of my best officers from my household guard to assist you to improve the soldiers' marching. These six officers, gentlemen, are all Campbells, born and bred in Argyll: Captains Colin, Archibald and John Campbell, and Lieutenants Hugh, James and Duncan Campbell. Between them they have a vast amount of military experience in the training o' new recruits and in marching and battlefield strategies. Several of these officers have been decorated for outstanding service and have received recognition for gallantry by their regimental commanders-in-chief," explains Thomas Campbell.

"When can I expect the officers, sir?" enquires Murray, who is anxious to get the men ready for inspection.

"You can expect them in three days' time, Murray. Make good use of them," adds Campbell, who is anxious to get the men up to standard before the visit of the King.

In the early morning the new officers meet with Lieutenant Colonel Murray to discuss a plan of action.

"Well, men, it looks like we have our work cut out for us," comments Captain John Campbell, the senior-ranking officer of Thomas Campbell's bodyguard, as he reviews the drilling sergeant's reports. John Campbell passes the reports to his colleague, Captain Archibald Campbell.

"Yes, yes, I see what you mean – lots of work to do, and so little time to do it," states Captain Archibald as he scans the drilling reports.

Agreement is quickly reached amongst the new drilling officers and Lieutenant Colonel David Murray that the drilling and marching schedules be intensified.

After the officers' meeting, Lieutenant Duncan Campbell starts compiling new daily drilling schedules, and all officers agree that the daily roll call is to be set an hour earlier. Within a week the companies and battalions of the second regiment of the 98th are taking on a new look.

In the early morning of 8 October, the two Highland regiments are ordered to perform a trial run. The morning air is cool and misty. The Scottish mist lingers in the air well into the day and the sun is unable to break through the heavy cloud cover. Six pipers and three side drummers are on hand to lead the men through their drilling routines. The march formation selected for the 3,000 men is not complex, but relies heavily on precise timing between the company leaders and battalion commanders. The first part of the full dress rehearsal goes well. However, during the second part, some of the companies of the second Highland regiment drift too far on the turns and the main lines break formation. Lieutenant Colonel David Murray stops the parade and orders an officers' call and the men are told to stand down.

"It will no do, gentlemen. It will just no do. The King will be here in a week and the second regiment is still no ready. We have to put on a good show for His Majesty. We will practise for eight hours a day instead of four hours. All other training and leave is cancelled until we get this right. All of Scotland's chiefs and dignitaries will be here, and some o' them are hoping that this whole idea of Highland regiments will fail. I have never been part o' any failure and it's no startin' now. Do you all ken?"

"Aye, sir, we understand," replies the officer.

No one is left in any doubt of what is expected.

The men grumble when they hear news of the revised training schedules. The weather has turned cold with a sharp wind blowing, as grey clouds scud overhead and it is forecast for sleet. For hour after hour the men are drilled in battalions primarily using the quick march, which is 120 beats per minute with a thirty-inch step. The men are paraded in four directions – advance, retire, left and right – hour after hour. The advance is the primary direction of the soldiers' movement, so all battalions have no problem with this marching command. However, the retire command causes problems during the first two days. Several battalions are unable to master the 'retire march' command, so practice continues until the men reach and pass the point of exhaustion. Most soldiers on parade have little difficulty complying with the 'left and right of the advance' commands.

The toughest drilling officer, Captain John Campbell, is assigned to a battalion of the second Highland regiment who are struggling to follow the 'retire' drilling command.

"Here he comes – John the Bastard – for another day o' misery," states Corporal Ross Noble, member of the second company of the second Highland regiment.

"Attention!" is the command from the regimental sergeant major.

"Stand at ease," orders Captain John Campbell.

After days of constant drilling the men have grown to despise Captain John Campbell. He is considered by the soldiers to be mean and a bully.

Conducting his inspection of the men, Campbell stops and places his right foot on the ground between the soldier's legs. On the tip of his right shoe is a small mirror, which he uses on a selective basis to verify that the soldier's dress code is in compliance with the army regulations. The army regulations state no undergarments are to be worn when the soldiers are on parade.

"Laddie, y'are overdressed on parade – fall out," shouts Captain Campbell, referring to the soldier's garment under his kilt.

On cold days, such as this, many of the soldiers take a chance and go on parade wearing warm woolly garments under their kilts. Soldiers who Captain John orders to fall out find themselves on report, which inevitably means that they will be assigned to digging trenches or peeling potatoes for a week.

For eight hours each day Captain John Campbell drills the men to the point of exhaustion. Anyone heard talking in the ranks is punished.

The regimental adjutant, Alan Macpherson, an Oban man, reports drilling progress to Lieutenant Colonel Murray. By the end of the fifth day, Macpherson reports that the men of the second regiment are ready for inspection. On the day before the King's arrival, both regiments are ordered to take to the field in full regalia for a dress rehearsal.

"What a great sight!" exclaims Colonel MacGregor as he and Murray observe the two regiments marching in formation to the skirl of the Highland bagpipes and beat of the drums.

"Aye, it truly is a great sight to behold," comments Murray, who is relieved that his men have mastered the drilling steps and march formations.

"Who would have believed it, Murray! Only this time last

year the MacGregors and Campbells were mortal enemies, and the other clans were fighting and squabbling amongst themselves. Just look at us now," cries MacGregor, who is in jubilant spirits. "Tell Thomas Campbell that we are ready for the King's inspection," shouts MacGregor as he wheels his mount around and gallops off towards army headquarters.

On 15 October skies clear and it is a crisp, cool morning. Lieutenant Colonel MacGregor has ordered a big hot breakfast for the men, and morale is high going into the day.

"I want the men to be on their best behaviour today, Major Percy and Major Waterworth," requests MacGregor as he sits astride his handsome bay waiting for the soldiers to form ranks.

The regimental camp is a few miles from the entrance to Stirling Castle. To access the castle the troops pass over the field of Bannockburn, site of the greatest Scottish victory over the English Army, in 1314. When the Highlanders hear of the marching route to Stirling Castle they are jubilant. Many of their forefathers fought and won a magnificent victory at Bannockburn under the leadership of Robert the Bruce, Scotland's national hero.

His Majesty is in Edinburgh and is expected to arrive at Stirling in the early afternoon. All arrangements are complete and security is tightened. The King always travels with his bodyguard, approximately 200 mounted horsemen who are all hand-picked. On this occasion, Colonel Clypton, Duke of Essex, is the officer in charge and he is leading the King's mounted bodyguard en route from Edinburgh to Stirling Castle.

"Sir, all formations are in place," states MacGregor.

"Thank you, MacGregor," replies Campbell.

"Pipes, drums and colours to the front," orders Campbell.

The regimental colours are carried today by Lieutenant Donald MacDonald, younger brother of Lachlan MacDonald, clan chief.

The officers and the men wear scarlet coats faced with yellow, dark-green tartan kilts with black stripes, black socks, diced hose in red and white, and scarlet garters. On their feet they wear Highland shoes with yellow or gold shoe buckles. Beneath their scarlet coats the soldiers wear white shirts or *leiners*. Dirks and large sporrans are hung from wide black leather belts, which the soldiers wear around their waist. The headdress consists of a plain red-and-white dicing on their black glengarrie's and feather bonnets.

Old Tom takes his position at the head of the line. He is childishly pleased with the two regiments' smart appearance. The blue, scarlet and yellow of the soldiers and the crimson sashes and golden gorgets of the officers make a magnificent sight as the morning sun catches the points of the curved blades of the sergeants' halberts.

"Forward march!" is the command as the pipes and drums usher the army forward to the sound of stirring bagpipe tunes.

It is a magnificent sight. Gone are the old Highland weapons and attire. No broadsword, or clansmen's saffron shirts and belted plaids. The Argylls are armed like any Sassenach regiment. Flintlock muskets, barrels burnished and stocks a cherry brown are now standard issue. Each man carries a hanger on his left side, a short cross-hilted sword in a black leather scabbard. On the right side of his belt is his *patrontash*, a stiff cartridge box containing twelve rounds of powder and ball wrapped in cylinders of paper. On his left buttock hangs a bayonet, the new dagger blade with a hilt that could be locked on the barrel, leaving the musket free for firing. Finally each soldier has a grey knapsack for his ammunition, his spare shoes and coarse linen shirt. The knapsacks are slung over their shoulders, or hung from their muskets while marching. The soldiers, fully kilted, march towards Stirling Castle on a cool and sunny morning. The line stretches far towards the horizon. To the skirl of the Highland bagpipes, the men march in rows of four, their spirits soaring and their heads held high. As they march they realize how proud their forefathers must have felt defeating the mighty English Army to ensure a free Scotland.

Passing the field of Bannockburn great cheers break out amongst the rank and file in recognition of Scotland's finest moment. "Bannockburn, Bannockburn," chant the men of the glens.

Major Percy rides quickly towards Thomas Campbell.

"Sir, the men – shall I tell them to stop their chanting? It's offensive to the English."

"Leave them be, Percy, leave them be," replies Campbell.

As the lead elements of the army approach the entrance to Stirling Castle, large crowds of onlookers assemble. They have come from the towns of Stirling, Perth, Aberfoyle, Callander, Killin and Falkirk, and from villages around Dunblane, Doune and the Bridge of Allan. As the regimental colours pass, the crowds cheer loudly and wave flags. Included amongst the onlookers is Andrew Griffin, who has just been introduced to Sandy Ross, Old Tom's kinsman. The two men take their seats in the stand overlooking the esplanade.

"You must be proud of yer cousin, Griffin, being named first lieutenant colonel of the first regiment of the 98th," comments Ross, who is still not convinced that senior officers should be appointed from the Jacobite leaders.

"I am most definitely proud, Ross – a great honour!"

"Six months ago I could never have imagined such an event as this, Griffin. For as many years as I can recall, the Campbells and the MacGregors have been mortal enemies and now here the two clans are marching side by side united under one banner. Amazing!"

"Certainly is amazing, Ross. Here's hoping that the hatchets are finally buried," comments Griffin, who senses that Ross is not fully supportive of the idea of members of the two clans agreeing to serve in the same regiments.

At that moment two riders arrive from the east with the news that the King and his bodyguard are less than an hour from the castle. The army stands at ease and light refreshments are passed amongst the men.

A fanfare of trumpets signals the arrival of the King.

George III in his regal splendour enters the castle esplanade in a magnificent carriage pulled by six black stallions. The army is commanded to stand at attention and the crowd's roar can be heard above the noise of the trumpet fanfare. Each of the horses' bridles pulling the royal carriage is silver-plated, and valets dressed in red-and-orange outfits with matching caps sit astride each of the six horses. The coach is driven by a man dressed in a long gold-threaded coat with emblems of the King's standard on the front and the back of the coat. Two other valets are seated at the rear of the carriage. The carriage is gold-trimmed, with the royal insignia mounted on the two carriage doors; and the carriage roof has a gold-mounted crown seated on a gold frame. Two gold-trimmed framed lamps are positioned to the right of the two carriage doors.

The carriage comes to a stop in front of a stand where all of Scotland's dignitaries are seated. As the King steps from the carriage he is greeted by Thomas Campbell. The King and Campbell make their way to the centre of the stand, where they are seated by ushers.

After the clapping from the large crowd is over, Thomas Campbell rises from his seat and gives the official welcome.

"Yer Majesty, all of Scotland welcomes yer visit with open arms, and we thank you most sincerely for having graciously consented to form the first division of Scottish Highlanders. Today two of the three Highland regiments stand at the ready to be inspected by Your Majesty," states Thomas Campbell, 6th Duke of Argyll, with great pride.

The King makes his way with Campbell and the Duke of Essex to inspect the two Highland regiments. For half an hour His Majesty walks up and down the long lines formed by men of the 98th, stopping on occasion to briefly talk with some of the rank and file.

"I am indeed impressed, Campbell, with the look of your men. They appear to be of a good sort and are well turned out," comments the King. "I especially like the kilts," adds the King as he takes his seat in the stand.

Before the 'trooping of the colours' ceremony begins the King says a few words to all in attendance.

"Thank you so much for the generous welcome to Scotland on the occasion of my birthday. The trooping of the colours dates back to the reign of King Charles II in the seventeenth century, when the colours of a regiment were used as a rallying point in battle. So every day the regimental colours were trooped in front of the regiment to make sure that every man could recognize those of his own regiment. In the confusion of battle, it is important for our men to recognize their regimental colours," states the King with dignity.

Great cheers and applause are heard as the King returns to his seat.

The trooping of the regimental colours proceeds and Thomas Campbell's pipes and drums lead off the ceremony. The first Highland regiment moves forward to the skirl of the pipes and to the drums beating a ruffle. Senior officers sweep off their hats in salute as the regimental colours pass the stand. Shortly afterwards, the second Highland regiment marches past the King proudly led by Lieutenant Colonel David Murray to the cheers of the dignitaries and visiting public. Both regiments then march around the parade ground, keeping in tight formation to the delight of the senior regimental officers.

The trooping of the colours goes off without a hitch, and the King is impressed with the appearance and the discipline of the army. The day is a huge success for the soldiers, for Thomas Campbell, for the clans and for all of Scotland.

Chapter 7

A NEW SCOTTISH ARMY

In the following weeks, King George III calls a meeting of his army chief of staff. Thomas Campbell and Colonel Clypton, the Duke of Essex, are also invited to attend. The meeting is held at Kew Palace, near London, and is preceded by a lavish dinner. Queen Charlotte, the King's wife, has arranged the seating in such a way that Thomas Campbell is on her left side and on her right sits her beautiful young daughter, Augusta.

Now eighteen years old, Princess Augusta is a stunning young lady with honey-blond hair and green eyes. Augusta is a vivacious and confident young lady, and is endowed with a wonderful personality, able to hold a conversation with anyone. Her many talents include being an accomplished singer and she is proficient at playing the piano. She wears a low-cut green silk dress with gold embroidery, which displays a full figure. Tonight's dinner party is the young princess's first formal event following her recent coming-out. Princess Augusta has been well tutored in the basic principles of upper-class decorum. She has been taught that men and women in the higher reaches of society necessarily operate within a frame of decorum. The tutoring provided to Augusta includes the importance of manners as indices to good character. The Queen believes that manners control character while behaviours determine the impressions others form. Augusta's training was to ensure that she always makes a favourable impression while attending social gatherings and parties.

Having such a beautiful and talented daughter, Queen

Charlotte is naturally anxious for Augusta to marry well. Thomas Campbell's apparent lack of social propriety makes him for the moment romantically unacceptable, despite his rank. However, the King has great hopes for his prospects in the army.

"Tell me, Thomas Campbell, is it really as barren and remote in Argyll as my father tells me?" enquires the young princess.

"Ah, yes, My Lady, it is indeed remote and windswept, but the country holds great beauty and is blessed with wonderful hunting," replies Campbell, trying to put the best face on it. "I take it My Lady rides," continues Campbell, who is intrigued by the beautiful princess.

"Of course, Mr Campbell. I not only ride, but I join my brothers and father on the hunt."

At this point the Queen interjects. "Will you be carrying on the traditions of your late father, Mr Campbell?"

"Traditions Yer Majesty?" enquires Campbell with a confused expression on his face.

"Come along, Mr Campbell. I am referring to the New Year's tradition that Scots so well celebrate," retorts the Queen.

"Ah, you mean Hogmanay, Yer Majesty," replies Campbell awkwardly, though he is not normally so slow-witted.

"Yes, yes, Mr Campbell, Hogmanay," replies the Queen, who is eager for a well-suited match for her daughter; and although Thomas Campbell is not yet wealthy, if the King's plans come to pass, he may be.

"And what on earth is Hogmanay?" enquires Augusta.

"If I may, Yer Majesty – well, it's a New Year's Eve celebration," explains Campbell. "My late father, John Campbell, started the tradition before I was born and it has now become something o' a major Scottish event, My Lady," continues Campbell, who is encouraged by the Princess's interest.

"And whatever do you do at this Hogmanay thing, Mr Campbell?" enquires Augusta.

"Well, My Lady, we have a great feast on New Year's Eve followed by a ceilidh, which is an evening of informal Scottish traditional dancing and also Gaelic singing. All members o' my household staff and also all noble men and women in Argyll are invited to attend," explains Campbell with great enthusiasm. Not wanting to offend the royal family, Campbell immediately follows up with "Of course Yer Majesties are also very welcome to attend."

"Mr Campbell, you amaze me! Hogmanay? Ceilidh? It sounds so wonderful," states the vivacious young princess, who is interested in anything she has not tried before.

"Then Yer Majesty and family are all very welcome to attend this New Year's celebrations," invites Campbell.

"That's settled," replies Queen Charlotte firmly. "More wine, Mr Campbell?"

On the following morning, the King and his guests meet to discuss some pressing foreign-policy matters relating to South Africa. The chief of staff, the Earl of Marshalsea, reports that the Dutch have garrisoned a fort in a strategic location in Cape Town, causing problems for British merchant ships and the Royal Navy. Previously, the navy could anchor at Cape Town and take on provisions. The British trading routes lay inland from Cape Town, so access is now cut off. A long discussion takes place, during which time it is agreed that some military action has to be taken to oust the Dutch. The King listens to the discussion, but has not participated up to this point.

"And what has Thomas Campbell to say?" asks the King.

"I believe, My Lord, that this is a job for the 98th," replies Campbell in a confident manner.

A light laughter and commentary breaks out, suggesting that some members of the distinguished gathering do not consider this solution feasible.

Thomas Campbell quickly interjects.

"Yer Majesty, our regiment is new, I agree, but we need to earn our stripes, our battle honours. What better way than in Cape Town?" pleads Campbell with great poise and confidence.

Marshalsea is not convinced, but the King supports Campbell's idea.

"Well, let's see what these clansmen can do, shall we?" says the King.

Marshalsea can see the King has made up his mind, so it is agreed that Campbell will take one regiment of 1,500 men to South Africa in the spring of 1795 to unseat the Dutch garrison at Hout Bay, Cape Town. The discussion now turns to the recruiting of a third Highland regiment. Thomas Campbell advises the King that there are not enough young men available in the Highlands of Scotland to form a third regiment.

"I would recommend, sire, that the King's standard be raised in the Lowlands o' Scotland to fill the positions for a third Scottish regiment," states Campbell boldly.

Marshalsea is surprised at this recommendation coming from Campbell.

"Mr Campbell, you know better than anyone that the Lowlanders have a poor opinion of the Highlanders. Can you honestly see them fighting side by side in battle?" questions Marshalsea.

"Hear, hear" is the comment from several of the other senior officers in attendance.

"I agree that there is conflict between the Lowlanders and the Highlanders, but what better way to resolve this than by bringing the men together in a common cause!" states Campbell with great conviction.

The King closely observes Thomas Campbell and remembers how his father, the late John Campbell, had participated in the fight against the Scottish clans who supported the Jacobite cause all those years ago. Now the son of the former Duke of Argyll is trying to unite the Lowlanders and Highlanders into one army. Quite amazing, thinks the King.

"It's a very bold move that you propose, Campbell, and has inherent risks," states the King with caution in his voice as he stares into Thomas Campbell's eyes. "What makes you believe that the Lowlanders will want to stand in battle with the sons of those Highland clansmen your father defeated at Culloden?"

There is a moment of silence in the room, during which time Campbell composes himself.

"Yer Majesty is right. The Lowlanders have old hatreds against the Highlanders; I know this for a fact. But my father on his deathbed gave me a mission to unite all of the Highlanders and Lowlanders, to bury once and for all the old hatreds on both sides and create one army, one nation," states Campbell in a strong, confident and passionate voice.

There is silence in the room and all eyes fall on the King. The King stares at Thomas Campbell and for the first time detects greatness in this young man and realizes that a natural future leader of the army has emerged from his officer corps.

"My standard will be raised, gentlemen, at the town of Paisley, ten miles to the west of the city of Glasgow. Colonel Clypton will assist Thomas Campbell in the formation of a Lowland regiment, which will become the third regiment of the newly formed division," commands the King.

On Sunday, with the business of the army complete, Campbell is invited to a garden party to celebrate the mild weather by dining outdoors. The Queen is now anxious for Augusta and Thomas Campbell to get better acquainted. Campbell is delighted to have an opportunity to speak with Augusta in private, although he soon discovers that the young princess is rarely alone with two ladies-in-waiting by her side.

"My Lady, can I take it that you will visit my castle in Argyll this December to celebrate Hogmanay?" asks Campbell pleadingly.

"I would be delighted to accept your invitation, Mr Campbell," replies the Princess gracefully.

"Thank you, My Lady. I will do everything in my power to make it a happy occasion," replies Campbell. "If you will permit me, My Lady, please accept this small token as a reminder of Scotland," adds Campbell with a trembling voice.

Campbell hands Princess Augusta a brooch with a sprig of heather attached to it. Emeralds and small diamonds in the setting of a Scottish thistle surround the brooch. Augusta is deeply touched and accepts the gift under the Queen Mother's distant gaze from the garden fountain.

In other parts of the garden, several of the senior army officers are huddled together discussing Thomas Campbell and the Duke of Essex's chances of success in completing the formation of a new Highland Division. The general consensus amongst this group of officers is that the plan will fail because of the mistrust that obviously exists between the Highlanders and the Lowlanders of Scotland.

November proves a very hectic month for Thomas Campbell. The King's standard is raised at Paisley, a small town known for its shawls and cotton products. The town is strategically located close to the city of Glasgow, with a large population, and also to the town of Port Glasgow, whose shipyards employ many young men. Within the first three days of recruiting, 1,000 men sign up. Many of the men who are recruited are unemployed labourers. Colonel Clypton and his aids work long hours each day to keep pace with the large numbers of volunteers. Glasgow provides several hundred men, and 100 volunteers join from the town of Port Glasgow. The remainder of the recruits come from the towns of Bothwell, Motherwell, Cambuslang, Clydebank, Hamilton and Airdrie, and from villages along the banks of the River Clyde in the Lanark Hills. Some recruits hail from the northern part of Ireland: from Ballymena, from Port Rush and from the city of Belfast.

During the recruiting drive, Lieutenant Colonel Gregor MacGregor visits his cousin Andrew Griffin in Port Glasgow, where he is employed as a manager in the shipyards.

"How are you, man?" enquires Gregor MacGregor, shaking his cousin's hand heartily.

"Wonderful to see you, Gregor. I'm keeping well, thanks," replies Andrew, who is glad of the visit from his cousin.

Andrew and Gregor settle down at a table drinking two pale ales from a local brewery.

"So what brings you south, Gregor?" asks Andrew as Gregor lights up a pipe and starts puffing his favourite brand of tobacco.

"Well, I guess you heard the news o' my formal appointment

52

with a Highland regiment," states Gregor proudly.

"Aye, that I did. Congratulations, Gregor. I wish you the very best o' luck," replies Andrew, patting his cousin on the back.

"Well, I was wondering, quite frankly, about your future, Andrew," states Gregor as he leans forward in his chair and stares straight at Andrew.

"My future's right here in the shipyards, Gregor," replies Andrew with conviction. "Port Glasgow and the city of Glasgow have reputations owing to their position on one of the world's greatest shipping waterways," states Griffin proudly.

"Aye, I do understand, but big things are brewing in Europe. I expect it will no be long before we hear o' a general call to arms from the King himself. As you probably have heard, Napoleon Bonaparte is on the march, and it's only a matter o' time before the British get involved in a big way, Andrew," comments Gregor as he finishes his drink.

"So how does that affect me, Gregor?" asks Andrew curiously as he opens another two bottles of pale ale.

"Well, let's see – y'are thirty years old now, recognized as a top-class piper and piping instructor in Scotland, so I thought it might be the right time for you to join up with the new Lowland regiment of the 98th as head army piper, Andrew," states Gregor as he stares straight into his cousin's eyes to ensure he is getting Andrew's full attention on this matter.

Unknown to Andrew, Gregor has an ulterior motive for recruiting his cousin into the newly formed army. The senior officers of the 98th believe that forming a full pipe band with side, tenor and base drums will help give the 98th a unique identity and raise the morale and spirit of the new recruits.

"This is a big move y'are suggesting, cousin. I need a few days to think about it," replies Andrew cautiously.

"Well, I'm planning to stay in Port Glasgow for the next three days. I'm helping Thomas Campbell and his assistant, Colonel Clypton, recruit new volunteers for the Lowland regiment," states Gregor, who senses that he may have his cousin interested in a new career.

Changing the subject, the two men talk about their families.

"One o' the things I have been curious about as clan chief o' the MacGregors is why have ye still not changed yer name back to MacGregor after our last conversation on the topic, Andrew?" asks Gregor, somewhat confused by his cousin's lack of action on this matter which Gregor, as clan chief, thinks important enough to bring up again.

"Well, the name change has been in my mind since our last visit. My father talked about it when he relocated the family from Arbroath to Port Glasgow, but because my father died so suddenly after our arrival I have not done anything about it," states Andrew sheepishly.

"So what's stopping you from adopting yer clan name now?" asks Gregor.

"Well, it's the men in the Port Glasgow shipyards. I continually hear abusive comments being made by the Lowland tradesmen and labourers against the clansmen, describing how they should all be exterminated. It is because of this hatred by the Lowlanders against the Highlanders that I have not changed my name back to MacGregor," explains Andrew.

It is clear to Gregor that his cousin Andrew is still not yet ready to change his name back to MacGregor; but he thinks getting Andrew away from the shipyards and into the 98th will do the trick, so he turns the discussion to Andrew's immediate family.

"How are yer sister, Isla, and yer brother, Thomas, doing these days, Andrew?" enquires Gregor.

"Isla and her husband are in Ayrshire, south-west o' here, and run a large farm. Isla loves animals, as you know, and breeds dogs. Ever since the time the family lived in the fishing village o' Arbroath Isla has loved every type of dog known to man," says Andrew, laughing. "Now, as for my brother Thomas, he left the Port Glasgow shipyards – oh, let me see, about two years ago – and took employment with a Newcastle shipbuilder in the north-east o' England, and I have na heard one peep from him. In fact," continues Andrew, "I don't even know his mailing address."

"Are you still teaching students to play the Highland bagpipes, Andrew?" asks Gregor.

"Oh aye, Gregor. In fact, I have to request time off work from time to time to teach the bagpipes. Lots of young men are interested in learning to play the pipes these days, and they know from the grapevine that I was classically trained in the pibroch by the McCrimmons o' Skye."

Gregor decides that he'll return one more time to try to convince Andrew to sign up with the 98th as chief army piper with the rank of sergeant major added to the title.

Andrew comes to the realization that he cannot struggle against the fate which is working against him, so he accepts his cousin's offer of employment two days later and joins the Lowland regiment of the 98th as head piper with the rank of sergeant major.

The 98th Argyllshire Highlanders are now comprised of two Highland regiments and one regiment of Lowlanders with some recruits from the northern part of Ireland. Thomas Campbell writes to the King with a recommendation that Sir John Macmillan of the Isle of Arran should become lieutenant colonel of the Lowland regiment. In his letter to the King, Campbell lists the many notable accomplishments of Macmillan during the past ten years while he served with the British Army in North America. Macmillan's service record is impeccable and he has received the King's Medal for bravery for showing great courage in the heat of battle. In addition, Campbell emphasized to the King that Macmillan was well respected amongst his army peers as an honourable soldier. The King discusses Campbell's recommendation with Marshalsea, head of the Army Board, and with other senior military advisors. Some of Marshalsea's staff have served with Macmillan and agree with Campbell's assessment of Macmillan's attributes. With Marshalsea's support, Sir John Macmillan is appointed lieutenant colonel of the Lowland regiment of the 98th.

Chapter 8

ROYAL VISITORS

Old Tom rides toward the grey horizon at the head of 100 of his bodyguard where his castle in Argyll beckons him home after his long travels with the regiments. The galloping horse beneath him was a gift from his father on his eighteenth birthday. Old Tom loves his horse named Peggy dearly. She's a nine-year-old mare, over sixteen hands, and has tremendous shanks. What Peggy lacks in speed she more than makes up for in stamina.

As he gallops across the wide-open expanses of the Mull of Kintyre, his thoughts turn towards the New Year's Eve party. Hogmanay has grown into a great social event in Scotland. The Royal family and their entourage are due to arrive at the castle in Argyll shortly after Christmas, which means that Old Tom and his household staff have little time to prepare for this very important event.

On his arrival at the castle on the evening of 19 December the young duke immediately calls a meeting of all of his household staff and Sandy Ross, his kinsman.

"Ladies and gentlemen, I wish you all well. Soon the Queen and her daughter will be arriving with their travelling companions to visit us for the New Year celebrations. In the past, you all supported ma father, John Campbell, in making Hogmanay a great success for all of Argyll. I am asking for the same support from all of you to make this Hogmanay the greatest ever. Our royal visitors must be treated in the manner which they are accustomed to," states Old Tom.

"You can count on all of us, Ma Lord," shouts Big Jock

Brown, butler and head of all of the many servants.

"Thank you, Jock Brown; and I know you all will do yer very best. Please arrange for extra staff to be brought in. We will need a' the help we can get our hands on," adds Campbell anxiously.

Sandy Ross detects a change in Thomas Campbell. In all the years since Sandy has watched Thomas Campbell grow into the fine army leader that stands before him today, he has never seen so much emotion and excitement come from this young man.

"Is there anything I can do, My Lord, to help with all the preparations?" enquires Ross.

"Aye, there is – come to my library directly and I will go through a few special arrangements," requests Campbell excitedly.

The two men proceed to a warm room off the main hallway. A large fireplace and a life-sized portrait of the 5th Duke of Argyll occupy one wall of the room. A large window and bookshelves occupy the three remaining walls. An oak desk stands in the centre of the room covered in papers, miniature cannons, sketches of regimental gatherings and quills and ink.

Reaching for a crystal decanter shaped in the form of a Scottish thistle, Campbell pours two glasses of Scotch and hands one to his kinsman.

"Talisker, My Lord?" enquires Ross.

"Aye, the very same," Campbell replies.

"*Slainte mhor*," toasts Ross.

Both men empty their whisky glasses as if there is no time to spare.

"The royal visitors have never attended a New Year ceilidh before, Ross, so it's going to be a bit o' a shock to their system when the Scottish traditional dancing gets going, do ye ken?" asks Campbell looking for confirmation that Ross understands that the event may be something of a surprise to the royal visitors.

"Oh, I do," replies Ross, sensing what is to come.

Old Tom refills both glasses.

"What I need is for someone to tutor Princess Augusta in a reel or two. Do you know anyone, Ross, who could teach the Princess some o' the steps in the eightsome reel?" Campbell asks with a cunning look in his eyes.

"Aye, I do, My Lord."

Ross has known where this conversation has been heading for some time. He has been thinking of the names of some of the regimental dance instructors, but they are all male.

"As you know, My Lord, all o' the regimental dance instructors are male, so I was thinking o' bringing my young sister, Heather Ross, over from Edinburgh. She is a lady-in-waiting to the Earl o' Midlothian's wife, and she has associated herself with more cultivated company. Heather is at ease interacting with well-born and -bred men and women. My sister also knows all the steps o' reels, strathspeys and waltzes, My Lord," explains Ross.

"Excellent, excellent! Man, you have saved the day," shouts a relieved Thomas Campbell, patting Ross on the shoulder and then refilling whisky glasses. "Here's a toast to Bonnie Heather Ross. Bonnie Heather!" toasts Campbell.

During the next week the great castle of Argyll is busier than it has been in many years. No expense is spared in decorating and refurnishing the rooms to be occupied by the Queen, the Princess and their companions. Carpenters and other tradesmen from all over Argyll are brought in and the Royal guests' suite of rooms is made like new in short order. Christmas passes as another working day, and the tradesmen are rewarded handsomely for all of their fine efforts. Following 26 December the castle grounds are turned into a magical place, fit for a queen and a princess. Oil lamps and waxen candles are hung all around the grounds along the esplanade, and hundreds of bunches of holly and ivy are decorated with tartan cloth and placed at strategic places within the castle and in the castle grounds. Outdoor fires burn brightly to keep the ground staff warm while working around the castle grounds. A great Christmas tree, a Scots pine, is harvested from pine woodlands located a mile from the castle and brought into the castle grounds by local woodsmen. The pine woodlands supports a rich assortment of wildlife peculiar to this part of Scotland, including capercaillie, blackcock and red deer, so the Duke has placed restrictions on how many Scots pine trees can be harvested in a year. Big Jock Brown's family is asked to decorate the magnificent Scots pine tree.

All arrangements are now in place for the royal visitors. There is an air of anticipation and excitement amongst all of the staff and servants from the nearby villages, most of whom have never seen a member of a royal family let alone the reigning queen and her daughter, Princess Augusta. Campbell orders his kinsman to invite all of the best regimental pipers to the ceilidh on Hogmanay. The best piper in the army, Colonel MacGregor's cousin Andrew Griffin, is to head this group of twenty musicians.

It is still three days before Hogmanay, and dawn arrives with a blanket of gently falling snow. In great splendour the beautiful young princess and her mother, Queen Charlotte, approach the castle in the Royal carriage as the sun rises on the serene landscape. The travellers have been on the road for three days, but despite the cold weather the Queen and her daughter both look radiant as they step out of the magnificent carriage. The King is not well enough to make the long journey north, so he sends his regrets to the host, Thomas Campbell. The entire household is assembled on the castle esplanade and great cheers arise as twenty of Scotland's finest pipers and drummers play the welcome. A sign has been erected above the entrance to the castle. It is in Gaelic and reads, 'Ceud Mile Failte'. Princess Augusta pauses to read the unfamiliar text.

Thomas Campbell observes the Princess's interest in the sign and steps forward. "It means, a hundred-thousand welcomes, My Lady," explains Campbell, bowing graciously.

The Queen and her daughter are overwhelmed with the whole setting, and with tears in her beautiful green eyes Princess Augusta thanks everyone for the wonderful welcome. The Queen graciously thanks Thomas Campbell for such a very warm welcome to Scotland.

In their chambers within the castle the Queen is in discussion with her daughter concerning her conduct during her visit to Argyll.

"Augusta, my dear, I would like to remind you about the practice of good manners while visiting Thomas Campbell. I am specifically referring to the code of behaviour while attending the dance party, or ceilidh as Thomas Campbell calls it. The code involves a set of prescriptions about dancing partners. You must only dance with whomever you have been engaged with for the evening and with no one else – never to someone to whom you have not been formally introduced," states the Queen.

"Mama, I shall only dance with Thomas Campbell and Heather Ross and no one else," replies Augusta.

"Why Heather Ross?"

"Scottish traditional dances, Mama, such as 'The Dashing White Sergeant' require sets of three persons, and Thomas Campbell will ask Heather Ross to provide me with some coaching in the steps which appear in the dance programme for the evening," states Augusta, hoping her mother does not disapprove.

"Very well, my dear – dancing with Thomas Campbell and Heather Ross is acceptable," replies the Queen.

After breakfast on the morning of 29 December, Campbell introduces Princess Augusta to Heather Ross, sister of Sandy Ross. Heather looks well. She always does. Tall, slender, elegant, beautiful, she is dressed in white, her robe soft, flowing, fleecy as a cloud. Her long black hair lies gently on her shoulders and her skin is as white as the new-fallen snow.

"It is my honour," comments the Princess as Heather bows graciously to the young royal.

"I have taken the liberty o' asking this young lady to assist you in learning oor Scottish reels in preparation for the ceilidh," explains Campbell.

"Wonderful," replies the Princess. "I do so much want to participate at your ceilidh." And turning to Heather with an enthusiastic smile, Princess Augusta adds, "I expect that Miss Ross and I will be diligent in our practice."

Heather Ross, Princess Augusta and three ladies-in-waiting

suddenly disappear amidst laughs and giggles, and, excluding meals, this is the last time Campbell spends with Princess Augusta before the New Year's celebrations.

Hogmanay turns out to be a big and lavish affair. All of the nobility of Argyll attend and many of Scotland's clan chiefs accept Campbell's invitation and make the long journey to Argyll. England's Duke of Essex, Colonel Clypton, arrives with the chief of staff of the army, the Earl of Marshalsea, to attend the Queen. All three regimental lieutenant colonels are also amongst the distinguished guests.

There is a great deal of anticipation as a trumpet fanfare signals the arrival of the royal guests. The Queen makes an elegant entry escorted by the Duke of Essex, Colonel Clypton. Following close behind her mother is Princess Augusta accompanied by her escort, the Earl of Marshalsea. To everyone's amazement, Princess Augusta enters the great ballroom with a stunning white pearled evening dress partly covered by a beautiful tartan sash worn over and broached on her right shoulder. It is not the dress that utterly stuns some of the guests, but the fact that the sash she wears so brazenly is that of the Stewarts of Appin, who fought on the side of the Young Pretender, Bonnie Prince Charlie, against the Duke of Cumberland.

"Good God!" exclaims General Trimble, aide to the Earl of Marshalsea. "Did her father or mother not teach her anything? A Hanoverian princess wearing the clan tartan of the defeated pretender to the British throne! Whatever next!"

Many of the clan chiefs who supported the Jacobite uprising are the first to recover from the surprise and start clapping and cheering the young and bold princess with great enthusiasm. Others follow, and soon Campbell is there to rescue the beautiful princess.

"Welcome, Ma Lady," says Campbell, bowing gracefully.

Campbell cannot help but notice that the tartan sash worn by the Princess over her right shoulder is being held in place by the Scottish brooch that he gave her as a gift. Campbell thanks her for wearing the brooch.

"You are certainly full o' surprises, Ma Lady!" he exclaims, taking her hand and introducing her to his guests.

The clan chiefs of Scotland are extremely attentive to Princess Augusta. Campbell finds it difficult during the evening to get near his royal visitor, let alone hold a conversation.

The feast is a great event. The 300 guests, heated by several glasses of the finest Scotch malt whisky, sit down to dine. Campbell gives the toast: to Queen and Princess Augusta. There is a great amount of chatter in the room as the guests eat and drink their fill. The Earl of Marshalsea brings the King's greeting, and Andrew Griffin entertains the guests with some of the finest piping ever heard. Princess Augusta asks to meet the piper and thanks him for the excellent entertainment. While meeting the Princess, Andrew Griffin is introduced to Heather Ross. For Andrew it is love at first sight. As he stands and stares at Heather, captivated by her beauty, her cheeks wear the loveliest carmine flush.

After the meal, the ceilidh begins. The regimental pipers and drummers march into the ballroom and play a set of four stirring Scottish tunes. The first dance on the programme is 'The Dashing White Sergeant', a very popular reel. Groups of three dancers form on the large dance floor. To Campbell's amazement, Princess Augusta and Heather Ross come rushing over and invite him to join them in this dance. The pipers lead off the reel and soon the great ballroom floor is a sea of lively dancers, over 100 in all. With the careful assistance of Heather, Princess Augusta works her way skilfully through the intricate steps of the Scottish reel, keeping in time with the beat of the music. Campbell is delighted. Princess Augusta proves to be a very quick learner and extremely nimble on her feet.

Following two sets of 'The Dashing White Sergeant', three singers from the Hebrides appear. These three young ladies are sisters and often perform at ceilidhs and other social gatherings in the Western Isles. Their songs are unaccompanied and are sung in their native Gaelic tongue. The melodies are haunting and the Princess is extremely moved by the beauty and grace of their singing. Heather is sent to the three sisters after their performance, and they each receive newly minted gold sovereigns, compliments of an appreciative princess.

There is a lot of laughter, as the guests are heated by whisky and traditional Scottish dancing. The evening continues with 'The Gay Gordons', a dance for two people. It is the tradition that the Duke leads off this dance. Campbell nervously requests Princess Augusta to join him. Showing great poise and confidence, she gracefully accepts her host's invitation. Campbell is much taller than his partner. He is over six feet tall while Princess Augusta is barely over five feet four inches. However, the height difference does not seem to matter. Princess Augusta and her partner execute the dance gracefully. Soon other couples join in the dancing.

During the breaks from dancing, Andrew Griffin goes searching for Heather Ross. He finds her talking with one of the ladies-in-waiting.

"If I may have a wee word, Miss Heather?" asks Griffin discreetly.

They find a quieter spot on the far side of the ballroom and enter into an intimate conversation.

"I have no much time, Heather, so I will come straight to the point. I would very much like to see you again. I have some time off in January and I was wondering if we could meet if I come to Edinburgh," he says hesitatingly.

"I would like that, sir," replies Heather gracefully.

Instinctively Griffin holds her hands and as their eyes meet she trembles. Griffin gently embraces Heather, and his heart swells and his face flushes. He finds difficulty in breathing. At that moment the master of ceremonies for the evening announces 'The Stronsay Waltz', and Andrew holds Heather in his arms and they dance to this beautiful Highland melody.

When all of the Scottish traditional dancing is complete, the remaining guests form a large circle around the dance floor and hold hands for the singing of 'Auld Lang Syne'. A young Ayrshire farmer, Robert Burns, has become famous since the publishing of his poetry and songs in the Kilmarnock edition of his works. Included in his publication is a song named 'Auld Lang Syne', which Campbell's father, the 5th Duke of Argyll, had taken a great liking to – so much so that prior to his death he ended Hogmanay celebrations with the singing of 'Auld Lang Syne'. The young Duke is determined to continue with this tradition. Many of the soldiers in attendance are familiar with the song and start the singing. The evening ends with three great cheers of 'Hip hip, and hurrah'. Campbell thanks all of his guests for attending the New Year celebrations and extends an invitation to all present to come again next year.

On New Year's Day Campbell arranges to show the Queen and Princess around his estate. After lunch, a party of twenty board four large sleighs. Each sleigh is drawn by two horses, and the party set out to tour the grand estate of the 6th Duke of Argyll. The snow has stopped and the sky is now clearing from the west. Warm blankets and hot drinks are provided by the servants to keep out the chill. Travelling south of the great castle, the tour guides point out two eagles circling in the sky high above. Ospreys are also spotted on top of some very tall trees. The Princess is thrilled. Further on, a herd of red deer appears in the distance, foraging on the snow-covered ground for food. The land is rugged, vast and windswept, thinks Princess Augusta, but there is a great beauty and serenity about it.

It is dusk before the party returns to the castle. After refreshments, Thomas Campbell gives the Princess a private tour of the castle. The Queen declines her host's invitation and retires to her rooms to rest after the tour.

Princess Augusta soon learns a great deal about Clan Campbell. They laugh, giggle and joke at some of paintings of Thomas Campbell's ancestors. They make fun of some of their clothes and the very serious facial expressions so well captured by the artists in many of the large canvases hung in the great rooms of the castle.

Campbell is amazed at the Princess. She is so full of life, and she is not only a beautiful young lady but she possesses a great spirit, which Campbell so much admires.

The conversation turns to South Africa and Campbell's departure.

"How long will you be gone?"

"I'm no sure, My Lady, but I am hoping I will be home by July," Campbell replies softly as he looks into her beautiful green eyes.

"My Lady, may I write to you during my travels to South Africa?" requests Campbell nervously.

"You may, Thomas Campbell," replies the Princess with the prettiest smile and blush ever seen.

Sensing it is now or never, Campbell gently holds the Princess's hands. She responds with a nervous smile, and for a few precious moments they gently embrace; then he releases her as Big Jock Brown suddenly appears with an urgent message for the Princess. It is distressing news coming so soon after such a happy and intimate moment.

"Is it bad news, My Lady?" asks the Duke anxiously.

"It's my father – he is ill and I must speak with Mama immediately," states the Princess who excuses herself and rushes off to speak with the Queen.

At first light on the following morning, the Queen and her daughter wish everyone goodbye and thank their host for the excellent hospitality as they enter the royal coach. In the cold of the early winter morning, the entire household turns out to say goodbye to the royals. Singing breaks out amongst the servants – a Jacobite song written in memory of the Young Pretender, Charles Edward Stuart:

> Will ye no come back again?
> Will ye no come back again?
> Better lo'ed ye canna be,
> Will ye no come back again?

Campbell feels so sad and his heart is heavy as the great carriage pulls away followed by a military escort into the early morning mist, and within a few minutes the Princess, her mother and their military escort are gone.

Chapter 9

A PROPOSAL OF MARRIAGE

Andrew Griffin rides east from Port Glasgow towards Edinburgh, Scotland's capital city, on a cool, damp January morning, thinking of what he will say to his bonnie Heather. He comes bearing the gift of love and with a stunning ring as a proposal of marriage. Andrew's deep feelings for Heather repeatedly lead him towards an immediate proposal of marriage.

The road surface between the cities of Glasgow and Edinburgh has recently been improved. Thanks to John Macadam, the forty-three miles between the two cities can now be completed in less than six hours. Previously, the journey took almost twelve hours by coach because of the poor quality of the road surface.

It is evening when Griffin approaches the town. He has arranged to meet his newly found love the following day for lunch at a discreet tavern, the Crown and Anchor in Prestonpans, a village to the east of Edinburgh, close to where Heather resides.

A few years ago, Griffin stayed at the tavern when he was teaching piping to some young army recruits and remembers the place as hospitable and clean. It is quiet when he arrives, and a welcoming fire and a jug of the landlord's best ale greet him. The ale is brewed locally and has a sweet velvet taste with a nice head. After dinner, Griffin makes his way to his room. He has arranged accommodation at the rear of the tavern overlooking a quiet wooded area.

That night Andrew tosses and turns and dreams of his love. At mid-morning on the following day a coach carrying Heather Ross and her companion Sheilah Little arrives at the tavern.

Heather wears a long red cloak, and her dark hair falls gently over her slender shoulders. Her dazzling complexion and elegant walk turn the heads of many of the local men, who stop and stare at her and her equally attractive companion as they enter the tavern.

Andrew is waiting in the hallway, and when their eyes meet they gently embrace. Heather introduces her companion and friend Sheilah to Andrew, and they proceed to the restaurant. The restaurant is quiet – only a few local businessmen sit in a corner smoking their pipes. Heather chooses a seat by the fire and they order a meal and wine. Sheilah, observing that Andrew appears shy, launches into a conversation about her friend Ian, who is a side drummer, and that gets Andrew and Heather involved in a lively conversation.

After lunch, Sheilah discreetly excuses herself and Andrew and Heather continue to get to know one other. Later, Sheilah returns and suggests that all three go for a walk. The landlord has advised Sheilah that there are gardens located a short distance from the tavern so all three bundle up and go for a stroll. The day has warmed and the wind has dropped, so walking in a strong winter sun proves pleasant. Heather talks about her brother Sandy Ross and how concerned she is about the upcoming war with the Dutch and French. Andrew tries to reassure Heather, easing her fears for her brother's safety. Sheilah walks ahead of her companions and Andrew takes the opportunity to advise Heather that he plans to stay at the Crown and Anchor tavern for a few days as he has arranged to visit some family and friends who reside in Edinburgh.

"Andrew, I would like to invite you to my home for dinner. Will you have time during this visit?" asks Heather.

"Oh yes, I would very much like to meet yer family," replies Andrew, who is delighted at Heather's invitation.

So it is arranged that Andrew will visit the Ross family on the following evening.

* * * * *

The dinner party includes six guests and the host and hostess, Major Lachlan Ross and his wife, Shauna Ross. In addition to Heather and Andrew, the guests are Sheilah Little and her friend Ian Macrae (a barrister-at-law in Edinburgh and a champion side drummer), Colonel Macrae and his wife, Lady Eilean Donan Macrae. Heather's father, Major Lachlan Ross, now retired from a successful military career, proposes a toast of welcome to his guests.

During the meal, Shauna Ross is seated next to Andrew. Shauna engages in deep conversation with Andrew and, before the men retire to the lounge for a nip of brandy, Mrs Ross is thoroughly taken by Andrew Griffin.

Andrew soon discovers Heather's father, Major Ross, is up to date with the political situations in South Africa, Spain and Portugal.

"Will you join the regiment for their campaign in South Africa, Andrew?" asks Ross.

"Aye, that I will, sir," Griffin proudly replies.

Colonel Macrae explains that his regiment has some very promising pipers and invites Andrew to Edinburgh Castle to listen to the band practice. Andrew agrees and sees this as a perfect opportunity to get to know Major Ross's close friend.

Riding up the esplanade at Edinburgh Castle, which is mounted on a great rock, is an amazing experience for Andrew. He has read many articles about the castle, but up until now could never have comprehended the sheer magnificence of the place. The setting and the view of the surrounding medieval Old Town are stunning. The town comprises a warren of medieval cobbled streets snuggling on to the spine of the volcanic rock, which travels east from the castle esplanade to Holyrood Park with its palace and ruined abbey. After dismounting, Andrew is led across the expansive esplanade to an inner gate, then up a steep set of steps referred to by the locals as the Lang Steps, and as he approaches a large brick building he and his escort can hear the sounds of pipers tuning their bagpipes.

"In here, sir," ushers the escort.

As Andrew enters the room where the pipers are tuning their bagpipes, Colonel McCrae's adjutant, Captain John Macrae, approaches him and advises Andrew that the Colonel will join him later. Andrew is seated on a stage overlooking the pipers. Soon, the pipers form a circle and the pipe major puts the band through their paces, playing a selection of reels, marches, strathspeys and jigs. Later, Colonel Macrae joins the piping practice and is anxious to hear Andrew's opinion of his pipers.

"The Pipe Major is very experienced, sir. He appears very skilful in changing the timing o' the pipers' play as they move from a slow march to a reel," comments Andrew cautiously, not wanting to dampen Macrae's enthusiasm.

At the end of the practice, the Pipe Major asks two of his younger pipers to stay behind. Andrew is introduced to Piper Hamish Macrae and Piper Ian MacDougall. Andrew soon discovers that these two young men are the Colonel's favourite pipers, and Andrew is asked to critique their play. Hamish Macrae begins well and starts playing a reel which Andrew knows very well. When Macrae is finished Ian MacDougall launches into a strathspey. It quickly becomes clear to Andrew that both young men have talent and with the right tutoring can become very competent pipers.

"Colonel, could I spend an hour with the two lads and go over some techniques which may help improve their playing?" offers Andrew.

"Go right ahead, Griffin," replies a delighted Macrae.

The Pipe Major requests to stay and it is agreed that Andrew will share some of his knowledge with all three men.

Just before lunch the Colonel reappears.

"Well then, lads, how did you fare?" enquires the Colonel enthusiastically.

The Pipe Major advises his Colonel that all three have learned some new piping techniques which not only will help them improve their playing but will also be a benefit to the other pipers in the regimental band. The men are asked to play a reel and Macrae immediately notices the improvement.

"Thank you, Griffin, for mentoring my lads – much appreciated, much appreciated," shouts the Colonel heartily. "Now for lunch!"

Two days later the perfect opportunity arises for Andrew to discuss his intentions towards Heather with her father.

"Sir, since I met Heather I have been absolutely captivated with Heather's charm and grace. I realize we have known one another for a short time, but the fact is that I love Heather dearly and I would respectfully request yer permission to ask for Heather's hand in marriage."

Ross has anticipated this request because his wife, Shauna, is captivated by Andrew.

"Yes, Andrew, it would make my wife and myself very happy if you become part of o' the family," replies Ross, offering his hand on the matter.

The following day Heather and Andrew meet for lunch. As he converses with Heather, he finds himself moved by aspects of her personality such as her spontaneous kindness and empathy towards her friends, and he feels overwhelmed by his recurrent desire to guide and protect her. After eating, Andrew reaches into his pocket and places a little box in Heather's hand.

"My darling, I realize that we have known each other for a short time, but since the moment I first set eyes on you I have been deeply in love. Heather, will you marry me?" asks Andrew with great tenderness.

"Oh yes, my love," replies Heather gently.

Heather slowly opens the little blue trinket box. Inside is a diamond ring. The ring is beautifully set with a large ruby surrounded by brilliant diamonds.

"It's so beautiful, Andrew, so dazzling," continues Heather as she closely examines the ring.

Andrew gently places the ring on Heather's finger and the two lovers kiss.

"This ring has been in our family for three generations and I dearly want you to have it as a token of my undying love. You have made me the happiest man on earth," adds Andrew as he holds both of Heather's hands close to his chest and gently kisses Heather on the lips.

"I must leave soon. I have to return to my work. I will be missed," says Heather softly as she reaches for her cloak.

Andrew leans closer to Heather and covers her face with his warm kisses. Heather looks at him with the prettiest of smiles and blushes ever seen.

When Andrew returns to the tavern from his visit with Heather, the landlord introduces him to three gentlemen who are playing cards in the dining room. One, a Hamish MacKenzie, is a local merchant who trades in pottery and haberdashery. The other two, Tam MacBride and Johnny Souter, are gentlemen farmers from local villages.

"Would you like to join us for a wee game o' cards, Andrew?" asks Hamish in a welcoming tone.

"Oh aye, Hamish, cards are my favourite pastime," replies Andrew, drawing up a chair and rubbing his hands together.

Since Andrew began working at the Port Glasgow shipyards he has learned to play cards with his shipyard companions. Over the years, Andrew's card-playing skills have improved, and the more he has played the more addicted he has become. Unlike fellow shipyard companions, who frown when bad hands are dealt or bite their lips, Andrew never displays any emotions or unusual mannerisms no matter what kind of hand he is dealt. Since Andrew started playing cards he has won more often than he has lost, and when he wins a reasonable sum of money at cards he buys himself a new kilt or jacket, or another set of Highland bagpipes for his students to practise on.

The three locals have established rules for their card games over the years and Andrew agrees to abide by these rules. The four men play until after midnight. Andrew has been dealt some losing hands earlier in the evening, but is now on a winning streak.

"Och, yer no quitting, gentlemen, just as I am getting going!" jokes Andrew.

"Early rise, sir," replies Johnny Souter.

"You are welcome, Andrew, to join us another time," states MacBride, pulling his balmoral bonnet over his balding head.

The next evening Andrew, Heather, Sheilah and Ian meet for dinner. There is great excitement as plans are made for a wedding.

"I want a June wedding at my father's home here in Edinburgh. Sheilah has agreed to be my bridesmaid, Andrew. My older brother, Sandy, kinsman to the Duke o' Argyll, and my younger brother, Jamie, who lives at home, are my only immediate family. On my mother's side I have two cousins," continues Heather.

"For my part, darling, I am a MacGregor. Rob Roy MacGregor was my grandfather," explains Griffin proudly. "I have many other relatives scattered throughout Scotland. Some of my family went abroad after the Highland clearances," adds Andrew thoughtfully. "Ma father changed the family name from MacGregor to Griffin because the Campbells were persecuting members of our clan over land titles. The family made a hasty move from Glenstrae in the Highlands to Arbroath, a wee fishing village on the east coast of Scotland. It was a very difficult time for the family to make ends meet. Finding a job was a challenge and we endured some hard times. Eventually my father heard about jobs in the shipyards in Port Glasgow. We scraped enough money together and made our way south to Port Glasgow situated on the River Clyde. My father got a labouring job in the shipyards on the Clyde and worked long hours. One day Dad came home and suddenly dropped down on to the kitchen floor and died. Dad's death was so sudden – it happened without any warning. I started working in the shipyards in Port Glasgow to support the family. After ten years I was promoted to manager," continues Andrew.

Heather detects a change in the tone in Andrew's voice as he recounts hardships borne by his family.

"It must have been a very difficult time for you and the family, Andrew, following the sudden death of yer father," comments Heather sympathetically and holding Andrew's hands in hers.

"It was indeed a terrible time for my mother and for my sister Isla," replies Andrew with his head bowed low.

"But, Andrew, you have done so well, becoming manager of the shipyards and tutoring many fine young men in the art of playing the Highland bagpipes."

"Aye, y'are right, Heather, y'are right. Both Isla and I have been very fortunate during the past few years. We have been able to support our mother and she lives a comfortable life after many years of toil," agrees Andrew, whose attitude is becoming a bit more positive. "I just hope I am making the right decision in accepting my cousin's offer to join the Lowland regiment o' the 98th," continues Andrew.

"Oh, I am certain you'll do very well in the army, Andrew," comments Heather in a reassuring and supportive tone of voice.

"Why do you no change yer name back to MacGregor?" continues Heather with a great deal of curiosity in her voice.

"Aye, well you may ask," replies Andrew. "I am a truly proud MacGregor; oor clan has a great history and we MacGregors are descended from ancient kings o' Scotland, but the people I worked with in the Port Glasgow shipyards hate the Highlanders and I never let on I was a Highlander or my real name was MacGregor," explains Griffin sheepishly.

"You got to hold yer head high and be proud o' who you are, Andrew, and let folks know what you believe in," states Heather in a strong and forceful manner.

"Aye, y'are right, my love, y'are right," agrees Andrew, holding her two hands in an embrace.

"What about yer sister Isla? Are you close?" asks Heather, anxious to get to know more about Andrew's family.

"When we lived in the town of Arbroath we went to school together and spent a lot o' time playing with animals and sailing. Isla loves animals. We had a cat and dog when we were young," replies Andrew happily.

"What were the animals' names?" enquires Heather.

"Let me remember. Oh aye, the cat's name was Billy and the wee dog's name was Busby," replies Andrew.

"I love animals too," comments Heather.

Heather's positive manner is beginning to encourage Andrew to share happy family memories.

"When I was a wee lad I used to work part-time at weekends in a local bakery delivering cakes, bread, biscuits and bridies to our customers in a horse and cart. After a few months, old man Beattie, the baker, let me go because I ate most of his biscuits before I delivered them to his customers," explains Andrew, laughing at the memory of his youth.

"Are you very fond of biscuits, Andrew?" enquires Heather curiously.

"Oh aye, I love biscuits, especially oatmeal, tea biscuits and shortbread. My dad used to call me Andy Biscuit," says Andrew, laughing.

"Are you serious, Andrew?"

"Oh aye, very serious," replies Andrew, maintaining a poker face.

"What caused the sudden death of yer father, Andrew?"

"Well, we could not afford to pay a doctor, but our landlord was a doctor and he thought it was something to do with ma dad's heart. It was a great blow to the family because up until my father's sudden death he enjoyed good health and was very active."

"And where do you live, Andrew?"

"I live at Braemar Gardens in a large house overlooking the River Clyde in Port Glasgow," replies Andrew.

"What made you choose such a large house, Andrew?"

"Well, I won the house during a game of cards, Heather."

"Won a large house playing cards? That's amazing," comments Heather, who is wondering how someone could lose their home, and a large one to boot, playing in a card game.

The conversation continues into the wee hours and all of the plans are made for a June wedding.

The next day Andrew bids farewell to his new-found family and friends and rides away to the west to rejoin his regiment at Stirling with wonderful memories of his time with his bonnie Heather Ross.

Chapter 10

A SEA VOYAGE

Lieutenant Colonel MacGregor and Thomas Campbell are standing on the pier in Port Glasgow making a final decision on their travel arrangements to South Africa. The weather has been unfavourable for the past week, but it is now moderating.

"We will leave now, MacGregor; the tide and the weather are right. Assemble the men," orders Campbell.

It takes four hours for all of the clansmen to board the three great sailing ships. The frigate *Pathfinder*, a ship of the line, is the largest and fastest of the three seagoing vessels, and because it is equipped with eighty guns it is given a classification of third rate by the Royal Navy. Modifications were made to *Pathfinder* to enable troops to be housed below decks. The other two sailing vessels, *Valiant* and *Waverly*, are full-rigged merchantman vessels possessing forty guns and given a Royal Navy classification as fourth rate. It is the first sea voyage for most of the Highlanders. Many of the young soldiers are in fear of the sea.

At high tide, the three ships set sail down the River Clyde without much fanfare. The three vessels make their way west down the Clyde to the 'Tail o' the Bank'. *Pathfinder* passes Greenock and Gourock, turns south and navigates the waters between the Isle of Bute and Millport closely followed by the other two merchantmen. Soon, the three ships pass the Isle of Arran and are steered windward by the helmsmen. They pick up speed as they sail towards the Isle of Man.

The captain of the frigate *Pathfinder*, James Munro, aged fifty-six, is a veteran seaman. As a teenager he was press-ganged into the British Navy and has sailed with some of Britain's greatest sea heroes. In July 1776, Munro sailed with Captain James Cook as master's mate. Captain Munro entertains his guests with many amazing adventure stories over dinner and praises the great courage and bravery of seamen on long voyages, some of which last three years. Old Tom admires Munro as a great mariner and also for his courage and fortitude and hopes that some of his clansmen have the same mettle.

The first few weeks of the voyage are a time for adjustment for many of the clansmen, including Thomas Campbell and Gregor MacGregor. Campbell and MacGregor strike up a friendship, being in such close contact with one another on board *Pathfinder*. Amongst the topics they openly discuss are the feuding between the Campbells, the MacGregors and other local clans. Both men commit to promoting harmony and cooperation amongst the Clans Campbell and MacGregor in an attempt to unite the army and the country.

As the ships continue southward the weather improves, the seas grow calmer and the vessels enjoy fair winds. The soldiers on board soon find their sea legs.

"My Lord, the conditions below deck are cramped, I would recommend that the officers devise daily schedules to allow companies of men to go on deck at regular intervals," comments Dr. Graham Moncrieff, the ship's surgeon, at the officers' morning meeting.

"Very well – MacGregor, please make the arrangements and advise the other two ships' captains," orders Thomas Campbell.

Lieutenant Roy MacGregor is given the task of preparing a daily schedule for the soldiers on board *Pathfinder* to allow the soldiers to stretch their legs on deck.

"Sergeant Griffin, I have prepared a daily schedule for you and the pipers and drummers to come on deck each morning and practise," explains Lieutenant MacGregor. "Rifle practice will be held each afternoon," adds MacGregor.

"Thank you, sir. I will advise the men," replies Griffin.

The pipers and drummers are happy with Sergeant Griffin's news and welcome the chance to breathe some fresh sea air and enjoy the warm sun.

"My Lord, I have noticed a change in my men since the pipers and drummers started practising on their pipes and drums," comments Captain Munro as he and Thomas Campbell stand by the helm watching Sergeant Griffin put the men through their paces on the lower forward deck.

"And what type o' change would that be, Captain Munro?" enquires Campbell.

"Well, during long sea voyages the men like to hear music and sing, dance and play the penny whistle. Hearing the bagpipe music during the past week has perked up my lads, and a happy crew is a good crew, wouldn't you agree, My Lord?"

"I would indeed agree with your comments, Munro. So are you planning for the ship's crew to entertain us during this voyage?" asks Campbell, sensing that Munro is anxious for his sailors to show off their stuff.

"Aye, I'll have a wee word with the ship's mate and see what can be arranged," replies Munro, who is happy with Campbell's interest.

The next day Captain Munro meets with the ship's mate, Davy Johnstone, a twenty-year veteran seaman.

"Davy, I would like you to organize some singing on deck – some sea shanties, ye ken. Who is the lead shanty man on board, Davy?" continues Munro.

"That would be old Salty Brown – he's yer man, Captain," replies Davy.

Salty Brown is only too happy to organize singing on deck. During his twenty-plus years at sea Salty has learned a wide repertoire of songs of the sea and has a good singing voice. The sea shanties include hauling and heaving songs and anchor-raising tunes.

The ship's decks are packed with young soldiers eager to hear the songs of the sea. Salty has arranged for six of his close mates to accompany him. Salty's sea mates bring their fiddles, penny whistles and accordions. Salty has a loud singing voice that is capable of being heard above the noise of the waves, wind, birds and general clatter of the ship while at sea.

Captain Munro introduces the entertainers.

"Gentlemen, the shanty man tonight is Salty Brown. For those of you who do not know, the shanty man sings the lead in each song accompanied by six musicians, and the ship's crew follows with the refrains," explains Captain Munro.

Salty Brown leads off the singing with a halyard shanty called 'A Hundred Years' followed by 'The Saucy Sailor Boy' and 'What Do You Do with a Drunken Sailor'. Soon the soldiers are clapping and joining in the singing. The songs sung so well by Salty Brown, the shanty man, have a simple melody, repeated over with different words so the audience finds it easy to join in the boisterous singing. The evening is a great success and Old Tom thanks the ship's captain for the excellent entertainment. The morale amongst the soldiers on board *Pathfinder* is high following the entertainment so Captain Munro arranges for the other two vessels to provide similar entertainment.

The three ships continue to enjoy fair winds and good weather during the second week of the voyage south. Each afternoon the training on deck continues. The officers lead the soldiers in firing and loading their rifles. Campbell continually reinforces the requirement for the battalion commanders to teach the clansmen how to load their rifles quickly and be able to fire off three rounds in a minute. Only a few of the men in the Highland regiment are able to achieve this loading-and-firing speed, so the battalion commanders make the men practise for longer hours during the sea voyage. Campbell anticipates that he will be outnumbered during the upcoming campaign so he wants his riflemen to have the advantage of being able to fire off more shots than his enemy to even the odds.

The journey south takes the three great ships past Portugal and the Canary Islands. All three ships stay in view of each other and are in regular contact by hand signals using flags. Dress code for the soldiers is relaxed on board the sailing vessels.

Kilts are removed and the men wear trews, a form of trousers, as the weather becomes warmer.

"Land ho on the port bow," is the cry heard from *Pathfinder*'s lookout located on the topmast.

"It's the coast of Africa, Campbell," shouts Munro, peering through his spyglass.

There is great excitement amongst the soldiers who are engaged in rifle practice on the upper deck. For the clansmen, it is an amazing sight and no one can comprehend the sheer size of the African continent. Compared to their homeland of Scotland, it is an intimidating sight.

The weather becomes much hotter now and many of the men report to sickbay aboard the three ships. The surgeons and their staff on board the vessels are kept busy attending to the men in sickbay who suffer from fever and heat exhaustion.

At the beginning of the third week at sea the weather changes and the waves start running in huge swells. A tropical squall develops quickly and wind gusts batter the vessels with considerable force. Munro orders the helmsman to bring the bow nearer the wind. Sails are trimmed and everything on board is tied down. The weather seems to have taken an ill-natured fit and to be favouring the journey with nothing but storms of heavy rain and high winds which last for twenty-four hours. The flagship, *Pathfinder*, survives the storm with only minor damage to the bowsprit. However, the other two ships, *Valiant* and *Waverly*, sustain some major damage. *Valiant* loses her rudder and the crew work on making a jury rudder, a makeshift arrangement to give *Valiant* the ability to steer. The mizzenmast is disabled on board *Waverly* and the crew works for several hours and make a jury mast, which is a temporary makeshift mast.

Emergency officers' meetings are convened on board *Valiant* and *Waverly*. The captains of *Valiant* and *Waverly* signal to the flagship that they must go ashore and make repairs to both of their ships before proceeding to Cape Town.

"My Lord, we must perform repairs to *Waverly* and *Valiant* before we engage the Dutch garrison at Cape Town. Both ships' crews have made temporary repairs, but we cannot engage the enemies until the damages to both ships are properly repaired," advises Munro at the morning officers' meeting on board *Pathfinder*.

"Well, Munro, there's nothing to be done but make proper repairs to the damaged vessels. How long will it take, Captain?"

"I estimate about two days, assuming we locate the right type of wood, ye ken," replies Munro thoughtfully.

"Where would we land to make the repairs, Captain?" asks Campbell anxiously.

Munro rises from his seat and points to the map of South Africa which has been placed on a wall of the cabin.

"Right here, just south of the town of Saldanha, and north of Cape Town," replies Munro, using a ruler to pinpoint the landing area.

"Do you know the waters around Saldanha, Captain?" enquires Campbell, who appears concerned with the sudden change in plan.

"Aye, My Lord, I know the waters well enough to navigate a safe passage," reassures Munro, who senses Campbell's anxiety at the change in plan and the requirement of not being spotted by the enemy.

"Munro, please proceed with plans to anchor and form work parties. Speed is essential. MacGregor, arrange for three companies of your men to go ashore to secure the area. Our position must not be spotted by any Dutch grenadiers. Understood?"

"Yes, sir, understood," reply all in attendance.

The three ships silently enter the waters south of Saldanha under cover of darkness. The weather is warm and humid and there is no sign of any Dutch or French frigates. Old Tom puts his men on full alert in case enemy ships are sighted. Munro's men measure the depth of the water as they near land.

"Twenty fathoms," shouts a crew member on board *Pathfinder.*

"Anchor!" is called and the crew slowly releases the heavy ship's anchor.

It is a moonless night as four longboats are launched and make their way to shore. The plan is for the soldiers to secure a landing area then deploy some of their men to forage for water and fruit. Later, work parties will collect wood to assist the carpenters repairing the two damaged ships. Landfall is about five miles south of the town of Saldanha. The sea is now calm and the clansmen come ashore in rowing boats. By first light the soldiers are deployed and the water and fruit parties go inland to forage. Munro has learned from Captain Cook that, to avoid scurvy amongst the sailors, lots of fresh fruits should be eaten on longer voyages.

After an hour, three of the four work parties return with fresh water and fruit. There is no sign of the fourth work party. A company of clansmen is sent out to search for the missing eight men. Working their way inland through thick brush, the clansmen come across a small village. Soon local tribesmen come into view. It appears that the water party has been ambushed and some of the soldiers are feared dead. Others are captured and lie on the ground tied to stakes.

The officer in charge of the company of clansmen is Lieutenant James MacGregor from Aberfeldy, who previously carried the regimental colours. Lieutenant MacGregor deploys the men and advises them to wait for his signal. Sergeant Andrew Griffin is a member of the company of men. Griffin is ordered to devise a diversionary attack on the village to draw the tribesmen away from the area where the prisoners are being held. Lieutenant MacGregor will then rescue the captive soldiers.

The villagers are startled at first by the screams of the advancing clansmen and the sound of rifle fire. Some of the younger men of the village rally and counter-attack, drawing most of the male villagers away from the prisoners. Sergeant Griffin and his men retreat in good order followed by the charging male warriors. This action allows Lieutenant MacGregor and a company of his men to enter the village. Some tribesmen who remain in the village engage in hand-to-hand fighting with the Scottish invaders. The soldiers make good use of their bayonets and dirks. Within a few minutes the four soldiers held prisoner are rescued.

The clansmen and the four prisoners make their way to the beach area where the remaining Highlanders are deployed. After a few minutes, rifle fire can be heard and retreating soldiers suddenly appear from the bush, hotly pursued by an angry mob of village tribesmen carrying long spears. Lieutenant MacGregor quickly forms the soldiers into line and, once the retreating Highlanders are safe, Lieutenant MacGregor orders his soldiers to fire at the oncoming tribesmen. Within a few minutes, more than thirty of the natives lie dead or wounded on the beach. The remaining tribesmen flee in the direction they had come. Lieutenant MacGregor orders his men to pursue the retreating villagers because he does not want their position reported. Led by Sergeant Griffin, a company of soldiers take off at the quick step in hot pursuit of the fleeing tribesmen.

Within half an hour, all resistance comes to an end. The 98th occupies the village and prisoners are rounded up and locked in a compound and guarded. Pickets are deployed around the village to ensure no one enters the area while repairs are being made to the two damaged ships.

Ships' carpenters work all night effecting repairs. By late afternoon on the following day, Munro receives reports that the repairs to the two ships have been completed. Munro is very pleased with the speed at which the work has been completed by his men. To show his appreciation Captain Munro orders a casket of rum to be shared amongst all of the men who worked on the repairs to *Valiant* and *Waverly*.

The next morning at an officers' meeting on board *Pathfinder* Campbell informs the assembled officers of a report prepared by the chief of staff, the Earl of Marshalsea. The intelligence report states that the Dutch garrison at Hout Bay, Cape Town, numbers about 600 regulars. Munro is familiar with the fortress occupied by the Dutch.

"Could ye describe the location and size of the fortress, Munro?" requests Campbell.

"The waters surrounding Hout Bay are deep enough for our ships to enter. The fort is located above the bay. The problem is that the fortress has large guns pointing out to sea and commands a clear view o' any ship that dares come within a mile of the shoreline," explains Munro.

"And the Dutch guns? Is their range greater than ours?" asks Old Tom.

"Oh aye, My Lord, much greater," replies a cautious Munro.

"And what, then, would you recommend, Captain?" requests Old Tom.

"I have two crew members that were imprisoned in the fortress about ten years ago and escaped, ye ken. They made their way north to Saldanha and boarded a ship bound for Port Elizabeth," explains Munro.

"Well then, Lieutenant Colonel MacGregor, what do you say to that?" asks Old Tom.

"Looks like we have the makings o' a plan, sir," replies MacGregor.

Further discussion follows and a plan of attack is devised. Success now depends on good timing, and the ships getting into range of the fort without being discovered by the Dutch defenders.

Early the next morning the three sailing vessels move cautiously south towards Cape Town. Munro is an excellent pilot. He knows the waters around Cape Town well. Preparations are made to land a battalion of soldiers north of Cape Town. Lieutenant Colonel MacGregor selects Major Jamie MacLeod, an officer from Callander, in the Trossachs area of Scotland, to lead the assault on the fortress and take out the Dutch guns. Captain Munro's two guides are introduced to Major MacLeod. Their names are Davie Wallace and Ally Steele. Both sailors have over twenty-five years' experience at sea and have fought in many skirmishes. Steele has two scars, one on his neck and the other on his right forearm. Wallace lost a finger through frostbite sailing with Captain Cook in search of the North-West Passage. Both men agree that the assault on the fort can be made as planned.

* * * * *

Two days later, *Pathfinder* approaches landfall under cover of darkness. The other two ships sail south and lay off shore in wait, out of sight of the fortress at Hout Bay. *Pathfinder* anchors and 300 clansmen and their two guides prepare to disembark. Soon the men start climbing down the ship's ladders to the longboats. The first longboat makes its way towards the shore. It is a dark, cloudy and muggy evening. The clansmen are armed to the teeth and wear trews in case they have to swim the last part of the journey to shore. The two guides, Wallace and Steele, carry pistols and knives and sit at the front of the boat with Major MacLeod. MacLeod orders his men to raise oars and soon the first longboat makes its way to shore. Quickly the clansmen disembark and move forward and form a picket line a few hundred yards inland. The two guides, Wallace and Steele, go ahead to scout the lay of the land accompanied by two soldiers. The scouting party makes its way south along the rugged coastline.

The other longboats start to load the rest of the landing party. Soon all of the longboats are packed with Highlanders and start rowing towards the shore. One boat has difficulty coping with the ocean swell and some of the clansmen get their first taste of the South Atlantic Ocean. Within an hour all of the men are crouched on the beach awaiting orders to advance. The longboats return to the flagship.

There are no roads – only sand dunes and thick underbrush, which slows the advance of the scouting party. As the four men stealthily make their way up a rough pathway, the undergrowth changes to dry, thick grass in sandy soil. About two hours before dawn the four men rest.

Steele and Wallace move slowly and silently forward, leaving their two companions. Steele estimates the fortress is less than half a mile away. Crossing a stream, the two seamen come to a sharp turn, which leads them on to a small bluff offering a clear view of the bay. Just enough light seeps through the overhanging cloud for Steele to see that the bay area is free of Dutch ships. The fortress is situated on hills above the bay and less than a quarter of a mile inland. There is no sign of any activity in the fortress. Steele remains at the vantage point to observe while Wallace and two soldiers head back to the landing area to update the officers. Major MacLeod orders his column to come to attention. The soldiers stand up, form columns of twos and make their way slowly up from the beach to a rugged trail which leads the men to higher ground. The roaring surf has soaked many of the men's trews, socks and shoes. Pools of water start to form on the trail from the incoming tide, slowing the soldier's advance.

Daylight is breaking to the east behind the fortress as the last of the Highlanders reaches the scouting party and the men are ordered to rest.

"Thank God for small mercies," comments one soldier as he removes his shoes and soaking socks.

Wallace, who is standing nearby, turns to his shipmate Steele and says, "Some of the men look like drowned rats!"

Major MacLeod orders companies of clansmen to move forward in crouching positions as they enter the bay area from the undergrowth. It takes about twenty minutes for the men to make their way up and along the shoulder of the hill to the entrance to the fortress. Scouts who had gone ahead signal the positions of the Dutch guards on the four turrets of the fortress. Soon the Clansmen are positioned, ready to attack, staying out of sight of the Dutch guards.

MacLeod and his men start their ground attack on the Dutch stronghold. Marksmen of the 98th take out the guards on the fort's turrets.

Captain Munro and the three sailing ships move closer to the shoreline with their guns trained on the fortress. Soon the ships open up a steady bombardment on the fortress. The attack comes as a surprise to the Dutch garrison, who are caught unprepared. For ten minutes the three ships pound the fortress and breach the walls in two places. Lieutenant Colonel MacGregor and the remainder of the army start to disembark from the ships. They climb into small boats and row quickly to shore. At this point the Dutch defenders start to return cannon fire on the three ships. Munro orders the remainder of the small boats to be launched and the soldiers to board and quickly row for the shore. Minutes later, *Pathfinder* takes a direct hit from Dutch cannon fire, so Munro orders the three ships to put to sea and move out of reach of the Dutch artillery.

All of the longboats are now closing in on the shore. Two of the boats are hit by fire from the Dutch gunners and several men are killed, drowned or wounded before they reach land. Meanwhile, MacLeod and his men begin assaulting the outer walls of the fortress in several locations. The Dutch garrison is now mounting a more coordinated defence of the fort. As clansmen breach the outer walls of the fort damaged by cannon fire, hand-to-hand fighting breaks out in several pockets. At first, the clansmen have the advantage and are able to get several of their companies up and over the fortress walls and also through some of the breaches in the defences caused by the ships' cannon fire. The Dutch defenders regroup and push many of the clansmen back. MacLeod commits more men at this point and fierce fighting rages all along the outer walls of the fortress, and inside the fortress where the walls have been damaged. Initially the clansmen are unable to silence all of the Dutch cannon on the fortifications, but the Dutch fire slows due to hand-to-hand fighting around the cannons.

Major MacLeod has now committed all of his men to the fight for possession of the fortress. Clansmen make the best progress where the walls have been breached, and a company of men from the Isle of Skye is able to take possession of two of the Dutch cannons on the west wall.

The Argylls who are now landing on the beach form into two lines, and pipers and drummers lead the advance on the fortress playing stirring marches. The men keep in good order and both lines quickly advance towards the fort. The Dutch cannons are not effective at close range, so the Dutch soldiers use their muskets and rifles to slow the attack on their positions. The pipers and drummers are the first to take the brunt of the Dutch fire, and four pipers and drummers fall under a hail of bullets.

The officers order the 98th regiment to fix bayonets and charge forward. Meanwhile, a company of men from the Isle of Skye who captured two of the Dutch cannons enter the fortress and fight their way towards the main gates.

The soldiers of the 98th are met by a resolute defence in the form of companies of Dutch grenadiers, who have been held in reserve. The Clansmen and the Dutchmen rain rifle fire on each other and casualties quickly mount. Both sides stand their ground. The clansmen begin to gain an advantage, and some of the men from the Isle of Skye reach the main gates and throw open the doors to the fortress.

The charging Highlanders on the beach see the gates to the fort open and instinctively rush forward into the fortress, screaming and yelling. The Dutch abandon many of their defensive positions along the outer walls and retreat to the inner fortress and form new and stronger defensive positions.

MacLeod and MacGregor meet and quickly weigh up the situation. It is agreed that the Dutch defences will be attacked from two sides at the same time. MacLeod attacks from the left and Lieutenant Colonel MacGregor from the right. The remaining elements of the Dutch garrison are tightly packed in a courtyard in the inner fortress. The defenders have four small three-pounder cannons, which have been rushed into position. After sustained attacks from both sides the Dutchmen hold their ground. Lieutenant Colonel MacGregor orders his best marksmen to take positions above the courtyard and fire down on the Dutchmen below. Soon it becomes clear that this strategy is proving effective as the marksmen pick off many of the Dutch defenders. The Dutch officers order a white flag to be raised and the fighting soon comes to an end.

Great cheers are heard all around the fortress walls and from inside the stronghold as clansmen taste their first victory in a major battle. Lieutenant Colonel MacGregor orders the Dutch flag to be taken down and the Union Jack to be raised above the fortress. It is a great moment for the men of the glens to witness.

* * * * *

The clean-up of the fortress takes three days. The remaining Dutch medical staff assist with the wounded. All of the captives are imprisoned. The dead are buried in graves behind the fortress. Captain Munro assesses the damage to *Pathfinder* and ships' carpenters work on repairs to the masts and rigging.

At an officers' call, Old Tom is advised of the heroics of two young officers, Lieutenant James MacGregor and Lieutenant Donald MacDonald. Lieutenant Colonel MacGregor recommends that James MacGregor and Donald MacDonald be decorated for bravery and that men under their command be mentioned in dispatches. Included in the dispatches is Sergeant Andrew Griffin, who led the pipers and drummers' charge on the main gates of the fortress. The spirit of the army is high despite losses sustained during the assault on the fort.

Chapter 11

HOMEWARD BOUND

In May 1795, *Pathfinder* sets sail from Cape Town for Scotland accompanied by *Valiant* and *Waverly*. All of the wounded men who are pronounced fit to travel are taken on board. A battalion of the 98th remains behind to defend the fortress at Cape Town and will stay in South Africa until the Earl of Marshalsea sends a relief garrison.

The journey home is a period of reflection for Thomas Campbell. His thoughts turn to the beautiful Princess Augusta. During the long, quiet evenings of the voyage home he composes passionate love letters to the Princess. He knows within his heart that she is the right person for him for the remainder of his life. Campbell longs to hold Augusta and make love to her. She is witty, full of life, and fun to be with as well as a beautiful woman. What more could a man want? His thoughts also turn to the King's health. Campbell decides that he will visit the King on his return and if he finds His Majesty in good health, he will ask for his daughter's hand in marriage.

"Gentlemen, my orders today relate to our fallen soldiers. I want you all to write letters to the families of those soldiers killed in battle during this campaign. I will sign all of the letters," adds Campbell, who appears sombre and somewhat subdued by his fellow officers at the daily briefing meeting.

Below deck, Sergeant Andrew Griffin is sitting reading to two of his pipers who received gunshot wounds when charging the main gate of the fortress at Hout Bay. Corporal Andy Fraser is more seriously wounded than his fellow piper, Ian McLachlan. During the reading Fraser constantly falls in and out of sleep, and when he slumbers he cries out for help. This sleeping pattern continues for three days until on the morning of the fourth day Fraser is pronounced dead by the ship's surgeon. Corporal Andy Fraser is buried at sea and as a mark of respect Captain Munro arranges for the ship's bell to be rung. Fraser's sergeant, Andrew Griffin, plays the lament on his Highland bagpipes as the body of his fallen comrade wrapped in sailing canvas is given up to the sea.

The three great sailing ships enter the harbour at Port Glasgow. The weather on the return trip has been favourable. After the ships are safely docked in the harbour, special couriers are dispatched with letters to Princess Augusta, the King and the chief of staff. The army is to be billeted at Stirling Castle, which is located over thirty miles to the north, so the men disembark from the ships and make ready for the march.

Old Tom issues an order to his senior officers stating that the men be given a leave of absence on a rotational basis over the next three months. Orders are also drafted for replacements to bring the regiment back up to full strength. The Duke returns home to Argyll with his trusted kinsman, Sandy Ross, to await word from his beloved Augusta.

Within a week Campbell receives letters from Princess Augusta. The news is extremely disturbing. Her father, King George, has been stricken with a mysterious illness that turns him from a healthy, upright, honourable man into a ranting, raving lunatic almost overnight. The first seizure experienced by the King lasted a month. Doctors try various treatments, but none are effective. By the middle of May the King appears to have made a modest recovery and the family hopes and prays that his health will continue to improve. This news causes Campbell extreme grief. The King supported his commission in the army. Also, Thomas Campbell has received encouragement from the Queen to develop a relationship with her daughter, Augusta.

The Princess's letters are full of love and she expresses her utmost desire to see Thomas Campbell at 'the earliest possible date'.

Other letters, from the Earl of Marshalsea, indicate that William Pitt the younger has been appointed prime minister. Pitt is raising taxes to stop the spread of the French Revolution in Belgium, and war in Europe with the French appears inevitable.

It is a sunny morning as Sergeant Andrew Griffin makes his way towards Edinburgh to visit his bonnie Heather Ross. After his arrival at the Ross residence Andrew discovers that wedding preparations are well advanced. Heather and her friend Sheilah Little appear to have made all of the necessary wedding arrangements. Heather is very happy and relieved that Andrew has returned home to her unharmed.

"I am so pleased you're home, Andrew," says Heather as she and Andrew embrace one another. The sight of Andrew home safely and unharmed sends her blood coursing through her veins and brings her a rapturous bliss. The touch of Andrew's embrace thrills her every fibre. For Andrew, Heather is his first true love. After years of waiting he has finally met the love of his life.

Shauna Ross, Heather's mother, is extremely happy that her daughter has found true love and prays for a sunny June wedding day.

Thomas Campbell and Sandy Ross head south to London at full gallop accompanied by their bodyguard. The royal family is in residence at Kew Palace, near London. When Campbell and his beautiful princess meet there are tears of joy, and long and passionate embraces. The King is still unwell and not receiving any guests, so Queen Charlotte gives the young couple her blessings. The wedding is planned for Westminster Cathedral in the autumn.

During this visit to Kew Palace, Thomas Campbell is introduced to Augusta's oldest brother, George Augustus Frederick.

"Mr Campbell, this is my eldest son, Frederick," states the Queen as Campbell bows graciously to the future King of England. Frederick is twenty-nine years old, good-looking, intelligent, and well educated. He is also charming and has a great love of music and the arts.

"Very pleased to meet you, sir," said Thomas Campbell.

The Prince enters into conversation with Campbell, wishing him happiness for his upcoming marriage to his younger sister, Augusta. Campbell is impressed with the Prince's talent for making him feel at ease and for welcoming him into the royal family.

Queen Charlotte takes a leading role in the wedding plans and Campbell's mother comes out of mourning to assist the Queen with the wedding arrangements.

King George is feeling well enough to meet with his future son-in-law. He gives them both his blessing and promises he will attend the wedding in the autumn. His Majesty orders Campbell to have the battle honours of Cape Town mounted on the Argylls' colours, below the regimental motto, 'Honour and Victory'.

Politically, the marriage between Princess Augusta and Thomas Campbell is a great match. The Campbells are the strongest and most powerful clan in Scotland and Princess Augusta, through wearing the Stewarts of Appin tartan at the New Year's Eve ceilidh, has won over the most hardened of Gaelic hearts in Scotland. The King knows that war with France is inevitable. The French are trying to spread revolution throughout Europe and the British Army will need to be strong to stop the French. King George and the Earl of Marshalsea hope that Thomas Campbell can give the country a victory against a mighty and well-led French Army.

Chapter 12

TWO WEDDINGS

Fortunately, 21 June is a bright sunny day in Scotland's capital city. Heather Ross and Sheilah Little have risen early and are almost ready to join Heather's father downstairs for the short journey to the local Kirk, where an anxious groom awaits.

"Y'are so beautiful, Heather!" exclaims the proud father. "You look so much like yer mother the day we wed."

Heather is stunning in her wedding dress, which her mother helped design. She wears her thick black hair up and it is held in place by two diamond-mounted hair clasps, a gift from her mother. Her shoes are white with a gold trim and the flowers she carries are tied together with the Clan MacGregor tartan cloth.

Soon the wedding barouche rolls over cobbled streets with the clatter of the carriage wheels jolting over the uneven paving. The barouche passes into a beautiful archway decorated with flowers and stops at the entrance to the church. Sandy Ross, Heather's brother, has agreed to be best man, and Thomas Campbell is one of many distinguished guests. Andrew has been fortified for the wedding ceremony thanks to Sandy Ross, who concealed a wee flask in his large kilt sporran filled with a single malt Scotch. Andrew is dressed in his MacGregor tartan kilt and a Bonnie Prince Charlie dress jacket, waistcoat, white shirt, black bow tie and black brogue shoes. Tucked in between Andrew's stocking and his right leg is a skean dhu, or black knife. It is a small knife with its curved handle protruding above the stocking top some two or three inches. The knife is held in place by a garter band.

The church is packed – standing room only. Many members of Clan MacGregor have made their way to Edinburgh from all parts of Scotland. The service is simple, as requested by Heather, and when the minister says, "You may kiss the bride," two pipers appear and lead the adorable couple down the aisle playing a selection of Andrew's favourite bagpipe tunes, including 'Mairi's Wedding'.

The wedding reception is a grand affair. Heather's parents have gone to great lengths to decorate the house and a caterer has been engaged to attend to the distinguished guests. A tent is assembled in the backyard of their home to accommodate the large number of house guests.

"Congratulations, Mr and Mrs Griffin. I wish you great happiness," states Thomas Campbell to the newlyweds with great conviction.

"It will be your turn soon, My Lord," replies Griffin, shaking the Duke's hand.

"Ah yes, in a few short months I will be an old married man," replies Campbell jokingly.

Later, in the garden, Andrew's cousin Lieutenant Colonel MacGregor advises him that he has received a commission.

"Congratulations, Lieutenant Griffin," states Gregor, shaking his cousin's hand vigorously.

Andrew and Heather are thrilled with the news of a commission and thank Gregor. The newlyweds cut the wedding cake and, after visiting with their guests, say their farewells and leave on their honeymoon to spend a few quiet weeks in the Isle of Skye in North-West Scotland.

London is abuzz with talk of the wedding of the year. All of London's leading society will be at Westminster Cathedral to witness the wedding of the Princess. Queen Charlotte has scrutinized the wedding invitation list, and only the King's most loyal supporters are to attend. Old Tom invites 100 of his family and friends. In total, 600 people will attend the service at Westminster, although only 400 are invited to the reception at Kew Palace, near London.

Princess Augusta has chosen three bridesmaids. Her older sister, Louisa, is the maid of honour, and Augusta's two closest friends, Lady Sarah Jane Brougham and Lady Anne Marie Percival, make up the wedding party. Prince Frederick has graciously agreed to act as Thomas Campbell's best man. At the request of Princess Augusta, Lieutenant Andrew Griffin will be the wedding piper.

The crowds gather early in the morning along the route that the wedding party will follow to Westminster. The Earl of Marshalsea, chief of staff of the army, has arranged for Colonel Clypton, the Duke of Essex, and four regiments of fusiliers to form lines along the wedding route to control the crowds. It is a beautiful autumn morning as the royal carriage travels towards Westminster Cathedral.

Although the crowd is very large, they are well behaved and clap and cheer as the magnificent carriage, pulled by four great white stallions, carries the beautiful princess down The Strand towards Westminster. The King feels well enough to attend the wedding and he proudly sits beside his daughter in the great carriage.

On arriving at Westminster, the three bridesmaids greet the radiant princess. She wears a magnificent white silk-and-satin dress with a plunging neckline, which displays her full figure. Her honey-blond hair is held in place by a stunning tiara, given to her by her grandmother for her wedding day. The tiara is surrounded by clusters of large diamonds and gives off a brilliant light as the autumn sun strikes the headpiece. The Princess exits gracefully from the royal carriage carrying a bouquet of flowers spattered with sprigs of white and purple heather and surrounded by ribbons made from cloth of the Clan Campbell tartan. The crowds who gather outside Westminster Cathedral cheer loudly as the young royal turns and graciously waves. The service lasts for one and a half hours. It is a great ordeal for Princess Augusta and Thomas Campbell.

* * * * *

The wedding reception is held later that day at Kew Palace. Amongst the guests are the King's cousins from Germany, who bring disturbing news about Napoleon Bonaparte and the French Revolution. Queen Charlotte discourages talk about the European wars and changes the subject to the wedding whenever Bonaparte's name is mentioned.

The newlyweds are sought out by all 400 guests, who are anxious to wish them joy and happiness. The King is not feeling well enough to attend the reception, so it is left to Queen Charlotte and their son Frederick, Duke of York, to see to their guests. The young couple enters the Great Hall at Kew Palace for the formal reception. Lieutenant Griffin, chief piper of the regiment, leads the newlyweds to the pipe tune 'Mairi's Wedding', which Princess Augusta has chosen. Guests clap in unison to the pipe music.

The clan chiefs and other dignitaries from Scotland are delighted with the bride, and from their discussions at the wedding it appears that they have accepted Thomas Campbell despite the old hatreds and wars with Clan Campbell. The clan chief of the MacDonalds is the only one still expressing a dissenting voice against the Campbells of Argyll.

The evening is a wonderful success and the guests continue to celebrate well into the night. After thanking their guests for the many tributes, good wishes and gifts, the young newlyweds say their goodbyes and leave on a three-week honeymoon to the wilds of Cornwall, in South-West England. The King gives the newlyweds a gift of a large home in Kensington beside Hyde Park, in Central London, in the hope that they will make frequent use of it.

Chapter 13

SASSENACHS AND TEUCHTERS

In November 1795 Thomas Campbell arranges for all officers of the Highland and Lowland regiments to meet at Stirling to discuss the divisions' upcoming campaign to Portugal. The French are spreading revolution throughout Europe, and the Germans and Austrians have reported fighting with the French.

"Gentlemen, the army will be leaving for Portugal in early May o' next year. The French Army is in Portugal and in Spain. Our orders from the chief of staff of the army are to drive the French from Portugal. King George has signed an alliance with Prince Jao of Portugal, ruling monarch, so the Portuguese will provide support during the upcoming campaign. Make no mistake, men: the French are a formidable foe and Napoleon Bonaparte is making a name for himself as a worthy adversary," states Old Tom to all of his senior officers.

After the officers' address, Campbell meets with his three lieutenant colonels of the Highland and Lowland regiments.

"Gentlemen, give me an update on the morale amongst the men under yer command," requests Campbell.

MacGregor is the first to speak.

"Sir, the new recruits for the first Highland regiment are settling in well and the veterans are giving them the support they need. However, there is still conflict between the Highland and Lowland regiments. They treat one another with disdainful suspicion. I read reports of fights and brawls almost every week," states MacGregor.

Murray and Macmillan also talk about fist fights and violence over gambling between members of the Lowland and Highland regiments. Campbell listens carefully.

"Gentlemen, it's important that we work hard at promoting harmony between the regiments. We need to form these men into one army, united and strong. Aye, we'll need to be strong to defeat the French. I want you to flush out the ringleaders and make an example o' them," orders Campbell.

The Lowland regiment of the 98th camp on the south side of Glasgow in fields at Pollockshaws. Pollockshaws is considered by the locals as a fashionable area of the city. The two Highland regiments are camped a mile to the west of Pollockshaws. The battalion which Lieutenant Andrew Griffin is a member of is comprised of several companies of men from Port Glasgow and from the city of Glasgow.

The soldiers from Glasgow call themselves 'Glaswegians' and are a bunch of rough, tough and rowdy men. Many of these men come from the infamous east end of the city of Glasgow, where to survive you have to carry a knife or razor and rely on your wits. These men are mean-hearted; many are orphans and most have been imprisoned at one time or another. The Lowlanders hate anyone who comes from the Highlands of Scotland and refer to them as 'Teuchters', 'Kilty Calbums' or worse.

The meanest men in Griffin's company are Dougie Reid, Billy Porter, Andy Laurie and Davie Tosh. These four men cause more trouble than all of the other men in the battalion and have been punished on several occasions for fighting with the Highlanders, gambling and stealing. The ringleader is Dougie Reid. He is an orphan and has grown up stealing and fighting on the streets of the Gorbals, an area in the south side of Glasgow which is known for extreme poverty and crime.

Many members of Griffin's battalion are suspicious of him. During card games Lieutenant Griffin often talks a lot about the Highlanders and gives the impression that he is sympathetic to their cause. Griffin tells stories about the MacGregors and how great a hero Rob Roy MacGregor is in Scottish folklore.

Grudgingly, Griffin wins acceptance amongst the soldiers from Glasgow because when he gambles with the Glaswegians Griffin never complains when he loses money in a card game. When card games are organized, usually by Reid or one of his three cronies, the question often arises, "Is the MacGregor playing with us tonight?" Over time, Griffin earns the nickname of the MacGregor by the men of his Lowland battalion.

The Highlanders, for their part, refer to the men from the Scottish Lowland regiment as Sassenachs. English soldiers are also referred to as Sassenachs by the clansmen.

Life at Pollockshaws consists of constant drilling, inspections, rifle target practice and other routine duties such as digging latrines, which the Glaswegians perform on a regular basis, because of their general lack of discipline. The only excitement the soldiers from Glasgow can hope for is a game of cards or visiting local brothels and taverns, which they make a habit of.

A Mademoiselle Louise, who claims to be French, operates the local brothel in Pollockshaws. Mademoiselle Louise is in fact the illegitimate daughter of a French nobleman who had a romantic encounter with a local girl while serving in Bonnie Prince Charlie's Jacobite army. Mademoiselle Louise – or Mary Smith, as she was christened – is a product of the love affair. Mary's mother, Louise Smith, was given a large home in the fashionable area of Pollockshaws, in Glasgow, as a gift by the French nobleman on discovering that Louise Smith was pregnant with his child. Louise found it difficult to run such a large house, so she turned it into a high-class brothel. Louise's daughter Mary grew up watching men from all walks of life come and go. When Louise died, Mary continued on with her mother's chosen profession. To add some flare to the business, Mary became known as Mademoiselle Louise.

Mademoiselle Louise has taken a shine to Dougie Reid because he regularly visits the brothel. On some occasions he is not charged for services provided. However, when Dougie refuses to pay his drinks bill, he is barred from visiting the establishment. When Dougie is drunk, he and his buddies try to force their way into the brothel; but after he and his mates receive several beatings from the security guards, they stop frequenting this house of ill repute.

The MacGregor tries to humour Reid and his three cronies, but they are difficult to control and only respond to severe punishment. In order to improve discipline amongst the men serving under him, Lieutenant Griffin arranges meetings with Reid to try to improve his behaviour.

"Corporal Reid, every week I get reports of your poor behaviour. As a soldier of the 98th, I expect you to stay out o' trouble and set a good example to your men," states Lieutenant Griffin.

"It's no my fault, Lieutenant, if I try to defend myself. I'm no the one who starts the fightin'," replies Reid.

"Look, Reid, my orders are to stop the fighting, and if you continue to pick fights with the Highlanders I will have no option but to take disciplinary action against you. Do you understand?" asks Griffin, who is now on his feet staring straight into Reid's dark eyes.

"Aye, sir, I understand," replies Reid with little or no conviction in his voice.

Despite further warnings by Griffin, Reid continues in his wayward and violent ways, and Griffin has no option but to formally reprimand Reid. Corporal Reid loses his stripes for a second time and is confined to barracks for two weeks as a punishment for disobeying his officer's warnings.

As May 1796 approaches, the battalion commanders offer the men a three-day pass to visit their families. The regiments have been advised that they might be abroad for almost a year.

Andrew Griffin hastens home to Braemar Gardens, Port Glasgow, where his beloved Heather resides. Their first baby is due in September. Heather is very upset because her husband will be abroad at the time of the baby's birth.

"I know how you feel, Heather, and I am so sorry that I will no be here to comfort you when the baby is born, my love."

"What if you get killed? Then the baby will never know the

father," cries Heather, who is very emotional.

"Look, Isla will be coming to stay with you before the baby arrives, and my mother will visit every day, my dearie," replies Andrew, trying to comfort his distressed wife.

"I want my mother here when the baby arrives, Andrew. I need my mother," replies Heather with tears flowing from her beautiful eyes.

Andrew does not have the courage to tell Heather that he may be abroad for a year.

During the next two days Andrew and Heather stay indoors and become intimate. Heather senses a foreboding that she may not see her husband again and this intensifies her passion. Time passes quickly and, before Andrew departs, Isla, Andrew's sister, arrives from the wee town of Ayr; Mary MacGregor, Andrew's mother, also visits her distressed daughter-in-law. On the day before the men are ordered to return to camp, Heather's brother Sandy Ross visits his sister, and this has a calming effect on Heather.

With heavy heart, Andrew mounts his horse and carefully places a small portrait of Heather inside his army blouse and rides away to the east to join his regiment, which is camped in the city of Glasgow.

Thomas Campbell is subdued as he kisses his beloved Augusta goodbye. The last few days have been wonderful and their love for each other is greater than ever before. The young newlyweds stay in their suite of rooms and meals are brought in and served at their bedside. The Princess is very upset at being parted from her husband after such a short and happy time. She pleads with him to return home when the army is not engaged in battle. Campbell promises his wife that he will write frequently and try to come home for Christmas, if at all possible.

Chapter 14

PORTUGESE CAMPAIGN:
Ten Ships to Portugal

Wretched as the weather has been with its strong winds and heavy rain, the sun shows itself just before its setting on the last day of April 1796. Its slanting beams fall on the ten great sailing ships moored at the Port Glasgow docks. The following day, 1 May, a great fleet of ten magnificent sailing ships make their way out of Port Glasgow heavily laden with sailors, soldiers, artillery, horses and provisions. Compared with the trip to Cape Town, this is a shorter voyage and a landing in Portugal is expected within a few weeks.

The flagship *Seaforth* is the first of the fleet of ships to dock at the port of Figueira da Foz north of Lisbon. The other ships arrive later that day. Over the next two days the soldiers disembark and all of the provisions are brought on shore. Old Tom's first orders are for two battalions of Highlanders to march north to the town of Aveiro to set up a defence against a possible French attack. The French are stationed at Porto and also have garrisons at Braga and Chaves, on the border with Spain.

The remainder of the Highlanders camp on the west side of the road to Aveiro and the Lowlanders on the east side. Maria, Queen of Portugal, has stepped down from the Portuguese throne and her second son, Joao, who is Prince of Brazil, also acts as King of Portugal. Because of the threat from France, Portugal signs treaties of mutual assistance with Britain and Spain.

Prince Joao is naturally relieved to see the Argylls arrive on

Portuguese soil to oust the French. French frigates have been capturing Portuguese ships from South America laden with spices and precious metals and confiscating the ships' cargoes. This is why Portugal has signed a treaty with Britain, which boasts a large and powerful fleet of man-of-war vessels.

The Prince invites Campbell and his senior officers to dinner at a residence in Figueira da Foz. The dinner is a most lavish affair. The Prince wants the British to stay in Portugal until the French withdraw their troops. Portugal is a great seafaring nation and trades all over the world. With French frigates at the city of Porto, other Portuguese seaports along the Atlantic coastline may also be threatened. Prince Jao is concerned that French frigates may put a stop to Portuguese trading, which would have a devastating impact on the Portuguese economy.

"Yer Highness can be assured that the British ships are staying in Portuguese waters and will take on any French frigates which venture this way," states Old Tom in a most reassuring manner.

Reassurance from Campbell pleases the Prince.

"Also, Yer Majesty may be interested to know that Sir Arthur Wellesley and Colonel Clypton, the Duke of Essex, are in Belgium with their fusiliers."

The Prince is impressed and he becomes even more attentive towards his new allies. It is agreed that the Portuguese will initially provide 1,000 infantry and 300 horsemen to assist Thomas Campbell in the upcoming campaign against the uninvited French intruders.

Chapter 15

PORTUGESE CAMPAIGN:
Aveiro

"Gentlemen, the news from Aveiro is disturbing. The French grenadiers have attacked the two Highland battalions under the command of Lieutenant Colonel Gregor MacGregor. MacGregor has pushed back the French assault, but is having difficulty dealing with the French cavalry," states Campbell anxiously at the officers' morning briefing meeting.

The clansmen are inexperienced in fighting attacking horsemen at full gallop. At Bannockburn, in 1314, Robert the Bruce trained the clansmen to fight mounted English knights in 'schiltron' formations using long spears, and this strategy proved very effective. Now that the clansmen use rifles, it is more difficult to defend against a charging French lancer or dragoon. If the first rifle shot misses the target, the chances are that the riflemen will have insufficient time to reload and discharge a second volley before being assaulted by a French lance or sword.

"Major Carvaliho, can you provide cavalry support to Lieutenant Colonel MacGregor?" requests a disturbed Thomas Campbell.

"Yes, My Lord. I can arrange for three companies of Portuguese horsemen to leave this afternoon with guides," replies Major Carvaliho, cousin to Prince Jao and spokesman for the Portuguese Army.

"Thank you, sir, for your country's support," states Old Tom, relieved by such an immediate and positive response.

Training against attacking horsemen is increased and Old

Tom has all the men practising loading and firing off three rounds in a minute each day.

The Lowlanders enjoy the warm weather, but complain about the amount of drilling, the frequency of rifle practice and the food.

"The bloody food is rubbish," swears Private Dougie Reid. "Give this shit to the Teuchters – they'll eat anything," adds Reid as he throws the contents of the plate away.

"Och, it's not that bad," comments Billy Porter, trying to humour Reid, who is a nasty piece of work.

"We have had worse than this stuff," chips in Davie Tosh as he deals the cards.

Three-card brag is the game in progress. Andrew Griffin has joined the card game despite assurances to his wife, Heather, that he will not participate in gaming of any kind. The kitty for this card game has grown to £2 and an edge is creeping into the game. Griffin has a pair of queens and a king and has just raised the bet. Reid has two aces and a ten and he thinks that he has a winning hand.

"I'll raise you two shillings," shouts Reid.

"Too rich for me," says Tosh, throwing in his hand.

"And me," adds the MacGregor reluctantly as he has already expended all of his cash.

Everyone looks at Porter and Laurie, who both sit quietly thinking of what to do.

"I'm foldin'," states Laurie, who has a pair of sixes.

"I'm in lads," shouts an excited Porter and adds another florin to the growing kitty. Porter has three jacks.

"See ya," shouts Reid, placing a florin on the table.

"Three jacks," says Porter loudly as he spreads his cards out on the table and motions to collect the winnings.

"Why, ya cunning wee cheat," screams Reid as he reaches over and punches Porter in the face.

At this point a fight breaks out and Reid pulls a knife from under his coat and cuts Porter on the arm. There is blood all over the card table. Two passing sergeants stop the fight and drag Reid and Porter away, kicking and screaming.

An investigation follows and Private Reid is placed into solitary confinement for a week. Porter receives medical treatment for the wounds inflicted on his arm. Gambling is prohibited amongst the men. Lieutenant Griffin and the other soldiers involved in the card game are also reprimanded.

The soldiers of the Lowland regiment continue to pick on the Highlanders. The Lowlanders' and the Highlanders' camps have been separated but there are still reports of fighting amongst the soldiers.

"The men need action, My Lord," states Sandy Ross.

"Aye, y'are right, Ross," replies Campbell. "Call an officers' meeting for tomorrow morning and invite the Portuguese," orders Campbell with a stern look on his face.

The officer corps gathers in a large tent early the next morning.

"Men, the French frigates at Porto will be attacked by our ships in five days. The attack on the French frigates at Porto will take place at first light in conjunction with a coordinated ground attack. The Highland regiment will leave tonight under cover o' darkness and then march north to join the two battalions o' the 98th and Portuguese horsemen at Aveiro. From there the combined forces will move towards Porto. The French intelligence will no doubt hear o' the attack and send reinforcements from Chaves. Three battalions of the Lowland regiment will be waiting for any French reinforcements north-east of Porto and hopefully catch them by surprise; 100 Portuguese horsemen and 500 foot soldiers will accompany the Lowlanders. The rest o' the army will stay here to protect our flank," explains Old Tom.

There is silence. The first to speak is Major Carvaliho.

"It is a very bold plan, Colonel. I salute you," comments Major Carvaliho as he smokes a cigar.

Other officers are less confident, but Carvaliho advises the meeting that he has excellent scouts who are volunteers, know the country well and are good fighters on horseback.

Preparations begin and the Lowland regiment is the first to depart, accompanied by twenty pipers and drummers led by the MacGregor, Lieutenant Andrew Griffin. The column advances north towards Chaves to the skirl of the Highland bagpipes. Later, the remaining battalions of the first Highland regiment march off in the direction of Aveiro with their Portuguese allies to link up with the advanced party.

The Lowlanders make good progress and arrive three days later at a rendezvous point twenty miles south-west of Chaves at the Alforino Crossing. The Portuguese guides recommend this spot because it is the junction of the main roads from Braga and Vila Real. Lieutenant Colonel John Macmillan likes the ground and orders the men to start digging trenches on either side of the road. A trench line 400 yards long is dug and hidden nine-pound batteries are placed in nearby woods, blocking the advance of any French army moving south toward Porto. Pickets are posted a mile north in the shape of an arch on high ground looking towards Chaves.

Chapter 16

PORTUGESE CAMPAIGN:
Porto

By early morning on the fifth day, the Argylls and their Portuguese allies are in position east of Porto. At first light, the British frigates raise their battle flags and approach the seaport of Porto and open fire on the anchored French ships. Two French frigates are sunk within half an hour. The other French ships engage the British and a dogfight erupts. The British ships take two direct hits.

As the sea battle continues, the clansmen and their Portuguese allies attack the town of Porto from the east. The defendants are not prepared for this attack, so this allows the 98th and their Portuguese allies to advance quickly towards the centre of the town without a great deal of opposition. As the allies approach the town square, they come under heavy fire from companies of French infantrymen and cannot make any further forward progress. Seizing the advantage, the French officers order drummers to beat the *pas de charge* and companies of French grenadiers pour out of their defensive positions on to the streets and assault the 98th and Portuguese positions. The clansmen and Portuguese are pushed back and have to form a new defensive line amongst the houses lining the narrow streets. It is not until the Portuguese cavalry attack the French soldiers that the Argylls and their allies regain their forward momentum.

The sea battle is still in progress and three of the remaining four French frigates have taken direct hits, so the speed of their return fire is slowing diminishing. The French ships hoist white flags indicating surrender and soon the sea battle comes to an end. Three of the British ships are damaged, one seriously.

On land, the French reinforce their new defensive positions in the centre of Porto and the allies are unable to break the French lines. The battle rages on into the afternoon, and by early evening there is stalemate. Unknown to the allies, three members of the French cavalry escape from the city under cover of darkness and gallop off to the north towards Chaves. The three French horsemen avoid the main roads in fear of being spotted. Their route towards Chaves bypasses the Lowland army's positions at Alforino Crossing. After fifteen hours of riding and resting the French horsemen arrive at the town of Chaves.

On the second day of the battle, elements of the 98th attack the French lines from the south. This action results in the French splitting their forces. Sensing that the battle may develop into a house-by-house affair, Old Tom coordinates his attacks from the south and the east. The French feel the intense pressure from this renewed allied effort and slowly give up ground on the south and east sides of the city and take up defensive positions on the north side of Porto. These tactics are effective in wearing down the French, but the allies' losses are mounting. During the second day of the battle the allies sustain 200 casualties, wounded or dead.

Early on the third morning, it appears that the French are making efforts to withdraw from Porto to the north. A company of horsemen is dispatched to the north-west towards Alforino Crossing to warn Lieutenant Colonel Macmillan. By the time the company of horsemen arrives at their destination, a battle is in progress. French reinforcements from Chaves make contact with Lieutenant Colonel Macmillan's Lowlanders and their Portuguese allies. The fighting is spread out over a large area. The French try to outflank Lieutenant Colonel Macmillan. Fortunately for the 98th, the Portuguese foot soldiers join the fight and push back the flanking attacks. Fierce hand-to-hand fighting follows and the losses are high on both sides.

As the battle progresses the French grenadiers mount a concerted attack against the Argylls' centre. The Lowlanders hold their positions, but the French continue to push hard on the centre and break the Argylls' lines in two places. Lieutenant Colonel Macmillan has Portuguese foot soldiers in reserve and they rush in to close the gaps along the centre of the allies' line of defence. It is a very close call, but Macmillan's defensive line holds steady and the French are gradually pushed back.

A few hours later the French regroup and continue their attack against the Lowlanders' centre. Gaps begin to appear in the French lines, but are quickly filled by supporting companies of grenadiers who have been held in reserve. The French resolve shakes the confidence of the defenders and it soon becomes clear that the 98th and their Portuguese allies are in a life-or-death struggle, with no quarter given or asked.

Davie Tosh and Andy Laurie of the Lowland regiment soon realize that life in the army is no easy ride. Their two mates, Dougie Reid and Billy Porter, are back at headquarters. Reid is in confinement and Porter is in a field hospital recovering from knife wounds sustained at the hands of his so-called friend.

Lieutenant Colonel Macmillan, sensing that the centre of the Argylls' line is again close to the breaking point, brings up his pipers, who play in an effort to raise the flagging spirits of his exhausted men. The fighting continues and casualties continue to mount on both sides. Gradually the Lowlanders' training pays dividends. Many of the soldiers of the Argylls have learned how to load their rifles and fire off three rounds within one minute. The centre of the French infantry lines begins to thin out as a result of the rapid return fire. The French trumpeters sound the retreat and the brave French soldiers begin to leave the field in good order in the direction of Chaves. Lieutenant Colonel Macmillan wants to pursue the retreating French and finish them off, but his orders are to move west towards the coast and engage the retreating French soldiers at Vila do Conde.

The next morning the Lowlanders and their Portuguese allies bury their dead. The stark reality of the battle has shaken many of the young men of the 98th Lowland regiment and their brave Portuguese allies. The wounded are sent back to Figueira da Foz under the escort of Portuguese horsemen. The main body of the army rests for another day then moves west accompanied by their allies.

Scouts are sent ahead to locate the French. At a village six miles to the south-west of Vila do Conde the scouting party, made up of Portuguese volunteers and Argyll horsemen, discover that the village is deserted. Campfires are still burning, but there is no sign of any of the inhabitants of the village. Further on, towards Vila do Conde, the scouts notice wagon tracks. Some civilian bodies lie dead at the side of the road. Riders are sent back to advise the advancing army, and the remaining horsemen push on towards Vila do Conde. Two miles from the town of Vila do Conde, the French ambush the scouting party and they are all killed.

Chapter 17

PORTUGESE CAMPAIGN:
Vila Do Conde

It takes Lieutenant Colonel Macmillan three days to reach the outskirts of Vila do Conde. His men are tired and the officers are cautious. After the fight with the French at Alforino Crossing, the 98th and their allies realize that the French grenadiers are a formidable adversary and Macmillan's men will be severely tested during this campaign.

Reports provided to Macmillan indicate that approximately 1,000 French foot soldiers and horsemen are encamped at Vila do Conde. It appears that the French are hoping to be rescued by sea by French frigates. Lieutenant Colonel Macmillan deploys his men around the town. Portuguese officers recommend a frontal attack on the town, but Macmillan adopts a more cautious approach after his recent experience with the French. Riders are sent south to Old Tom with reports of the Battle of Alforino Crossing and the current siege at Vila do Conde.

Thomas Campbell is delighted with news of the great victory at Alforino Crossing, which is a worthily won battle honour to be placed on the regimental colours beside 'Cape Town'. Porto will also be a battle honour. Reports of the army's progress are dispatched by Campbell to Earl Marshalsea in England, and to Sir Arthur Wellesley and Colonel Clypton, the Duke of Essex, who are in Belgium. Included in dispatches to England are letters to his beloved Augusta whom Campbell misses desperately.

Old Tom is becoming a good army strategist. He clearly understands that the only way the French forces at Vila do Conde can escape is by sea. The garrison from Chaves got their noses blooded at Alforino Crossing and it will take time for them to regroup. Campbell does not want to risk another attack from the French garrison at Chaves, so he sends two battalions of Highlanders to camp at Alforino Crossing. He hopes that this will deter the French from any renewed advance towards Vila do Conde in an attempt to rescue the trapped French grenadiers.

Prince Joao is very happy and excited with the news of two great victories over the French, especially the sea battle. The Prince provides Old Tom with 4,000 additional Portuguese foot soldiers and 500 horsemen to drive the French from Portugal. Provisions are also made available to the 98th by the Portuguese in the form of food, medicines and ammunition.

The new Portuguese infantry are sent north to join the siege at Vila do Conde.

Two weeks pass and the stalemate at Vila do Conde continues. The French are well dug in and the 98th are unable to dislodge them from their stronghold. No activity is reported from the allies' detachments at Alforino Crossing.

News arrives that the French are attempting to break out from their position at Vila do Conde to the north. Heavy fighting is reported and the Argylls push back the French. Lieutenant Colonel Macmillan places his men on full alert. The next morning the French do break out. The Portuguese soldiers who have been held in reserve become engaged. The fighting lasts all day and the French sustain heavy casualties. Despite their losses, the French keep attacking. Two battalions of Lowlanders enter the fighting and by dusk most of the French soldiers are killed or taken prisoner. The 98th capture the French colours. The French colours are those of the 2nd Bordeaux Grenadiers and they have proven that they are a formidable foe. In winning the battle, the allies' losses are heavy. The Portuguese report over 400 casualties and the Lowland regiments sustain almost 200 soldiers dead or wounded.

Thomas Campbell arrives at Vila do Conde three days after the battle. Lieutenant Colonel Macmillan is congratulated and Campbell addresses all of the troops on parade.

"I'm proud of you men," shouts Campbell. "You have done Scotland and Portugal proud."

There is a great amount of cheering and then Campbell takes the salute for the march past of the regimental colours. The morale of the army is high, despite the loss of so many officers and young men from the ranks.

Chapter 18

PORTUGESE CAMPAIGN:
Alarming News

Dispatches arrive from England during July from the chief of staff of the army. The news is alarming. Seemingly, the French are infuriated by the defeats by unknown Scottish and Portuguese regiments. The news from army headquarters is that the French general Bruno Cisse is concentrating his troops at Madrid in Spain and is planning to move west against the 98th and their Portuguese allies. Estimates of the enemy's strength range from 15,000 to 20,000 men. Cisse is expected to join the French garrison at Chaves and then drive south to defeat the combined Argylls and Portuguese Army. Rumours indicate that elements of the Spanish Army stationed at Madrid may also be joining Cisse's upcoming campaign against the combined Scottish and Portuguese forces.

Old Tom is told to expect the French by the beginning of September. Colonel Clypton is being urgently dispatched from Belgium with 5,000 fusiliers and 300 horsemen to reinforce Old Tom's army. Clypton is expected to arrive at Porto during August. Meanwhile, Sir Arthur Wellesley is staying in Belgium to fight the French, who are encouraging revolution amongst the locals.

The news of General Cisse's entry into the war comes as an unwelcome surprise to the officers at their morning meeting.

"Sir, we should withdraw," states Lieutenant Colonel Macmillan. "Cisse has a great reputation as being one of Napoleon's most capable generals. The French under Cisse have been fighting throughout Europe and have won all of their campaigns. Even with Colonel Clypton's fusiliers we will be outnumbered," pleads Macmillan.

"Aye, y'are right, Macmillan – we will be outnumbered, but we can choose the ground," states Campbell with great confidence. "The other thing is that we cannot retreat. We have to hold on to the ground we have won so dearly. If we are pushed out o' Portugal, we will also be run out o' Belgium. Our orders are clear, gentlemen: hold on to the ground we've won, and drive the French out of Portugal," repeats Campbell.

Campbell senses fear amongst his officer corps as the men break into conversation. He decides at that moment to give the officers some encouragement.

"Men, up to now we have proved that the 98th are a great fighting force. With the help o' our brave Portuguese allies we have defeated all that have come before us. Dispatches from England indicate that the French and Spanish have signed a secret treaty and are at this very moment organizing a large force to send against us. Our troops have prevailed up till now and I am confident we can continue to prevail. Colonel Clypton will be here soon with his fusiliers, who have been fighting in Belgium. The famous Scots Greys, all 300 horsemen, are also being dispatched to support us in the upcoming battle. Our Portuguese allies – God bless them – have promised thousands more foot soldiers and additional horsemen. Portuguese volunteers under the leadership of Juan Carlos will act as our guides. These volunteers know the country well and are great horsemen and fighters. I know we can stop Cisse's advance and send him, and his grenadiers, home limping. The spirit o' oor forefathers is in our men, I know it! What do you say? Are you ready for the fight o' yer lives?" shouts Campbell.

"Aye, aye, we're ready," reply the officers, standing, clapping and shouting their support for Old Tom.

Chapter 19

PORTUGESE CAMPAIGN:
Fife and Drums

Colonel Clypton's arrival during August 1796 is a great relief to the army. The sight of the fusiliers marching from the dockside, to the sound of the fife and drums, is a morale booster for the men of the 98th and their Portuguese allies. Clypton is a confident and slightly abrasive man, and his officers both fear and respect him. He is a stickler for detail and for his orders to be carried out without fail or question at all times. Clypton also recognizes the need to keep moral high amongst the men and takes every opportunity to decorate and praise his men when they excel in battle.

"I like the cut o' yer men, Clypton," comments Campbell as they march through the town towards their camp.

"Yes, they are a good sort," replies Clypton confidently as he sits astride his horse.

Clypton, as second in command of the army, is updated on the current situation and is introduced to his Portuguese allies. Major Richardo Carvaliho of the Portuguese Army is Prince Jao's spokesperson. Carvaliho has a good command of the English language and is a relative of the Prince. Carvaliho has been appointed by Prince Jao to be the liaison officer between the British and the Portuguese. Plans are in progress to organize the men for the upcoming battle against the French and Spanish forces. In total, Old Tom has 15,000 men at his disposal.

At an army planning meeting Major Carvaliho explains where the French and Spanish forces might advance into Portugal from Spain.

"There are two possibilities where the roads and terrain can allow for such a large force to advance into Portugal, with heavy cannon and supply columns," explains Major Carvaliho. "One route is the road from Spain to Chaves, where the French garrison is currently stationed, and the other route is to the south. The southern route is more difficult and requires the French and Spanish forces to negotiate a steep pass and long stretches of uneven ground," continues Major Carvaliho, using a large map to help his fellow officers follow what he is saying.

Under questioning from Old Tom, Major Carvaliho explains that he grew up close to the southern route and knows the land well.

"In yer opinion, Major Carvaliho, do you think that the enemy will try to negotiate the southern route?" enquires Old Tom.

"My Lord, the northern route is faster and less dangerous, and also allows Cisse to join up with the French garrison at Chaves, so it seems that the northern route is more obvious," explains Major Carvaliho.

"Thank you, Major Carvaliho," says Old Tom.

Colonel Clypton has been silent up until this point of the meeting.

"Major Carvaliho, knowing the land so well, are there any other avenues open to Cisse?" asks Clypton.

Looking closely at the map of Portugal, Major Carvaliho explains: "The northern coastal road has not been repaired for many years, and is under constant threat from falling rocks when water comes cascading down the mountainside."

"So there are three possibilities, gentlemen, we must consider," sums up Old Tom. It is agreed that Juan Carlos will split his volunteers into three groups and set up watch posts at each of the three locations.

The next morning Juan Carlos and his volunteers ride off to the north and south-west. Another group of men from Lieutenant Colonel Macmillan's regiment gallop towards Chaves accompanied by six scouts from Major Carvaliho's command to monitor any movement of the French garrison.

In the meantime, the men's training has been intensified and the Portuguese allies have also been put through their paces. The Portuguese Ambassador in Madrid has been sending regular dispatches to Prince Joao, but recently these dispatches have stopped.

Four days pass and no word comes from any of the scouting parties. The officers and the men become uneasy. Old Tom orders special meals to be served over the next two days in an attempt to improve the morale of the army. The meals are well received by all of the men. Even the Glaswegians in the Lowland regiment appreciate the variety and quality of the food. Entertainment is arranged by the local town mayor in the form of dancers and singers accompanied by local bands. Soldiers of the 98th and the Portuguese Army welcome and appreciate the entertainment – especially the local dancers.

Another three days pass and still no word. Before dawn on the next morning, two riders approach the army encampment at full gallop. Their horses are saturated in sweat and the riders are covered in sand and dust. Old Tom and Colonel Clypton are awakened. The riders are ushered into Old Tom's tent. The reports are alarming. A combined force of French and Spanish, estimated in excess of 20,000 men, are advancing into Portugal along the southern route.

A detachment from the French garrison at Chaves is also reported moving south. Their strength is estimated at 2,000 men. Based on the progress of Cisse's army, scouts estimate that they will be here in five days. Campbell and Clypton meet in private.

"We must attack the Chaves garrison before they join up with the main body," states Clypton sternly.

"I agree. It's our only chance if we are to defeat the might o' a combined French and Spanish force," replies Campbell with a serious facial expression.

Chapter 20

PORTUGESE CAMPAIGN:
Lippeto Hills

A plan is quickly drawn up. A combined force of Argylls and Portuguese will attack the soldiers from the Chaves garrison, who are reported moving south-west along the Old Lopez Road. Lieutenant Colonel Macmillan and his regiment of Lowlanders, supported by the Portuguese soldiers and Juan Carlos volunteers, move out of the camp under cover of darkness. The column turns to the north and marches off at a quick pace to stirring bagpipe tunes played by Lieutenant Andrew Griffin and his pipers and side drummers.

The volunteers led by Juan Carlos move ahead of the army column and act as scouts. Most of the volunteers come from villages located in Northern Portugal. Juan Carlos was born across the border in Spain. His father was Spanish, but his mother was Portuguese from the village of Vila Flor, located to the east of Vila Real. When Juan was three years old his parents returned to live in the village of Vila Flor, so Juan knows the northern part of Portugal very well. Juan and his volunteers fear being ruled by the French, so they have formed themselves into a gorilla group to fight the intruders from France. Since the French entered Portugal they have plundered and killed Portuguese families and taken all their food. Juan Carlos's volunteers are accomplished horsemen and good fighters, so they can be relied upon in a skirmish or battle.

The column of volunteers turns towards the north-east, taking a faster route. They continue until late that evening and find a secure camp at the foot of the Lippeto Hills. No fires are allowed in case they are detected by the enemy.

At dawn, the next morning, they break camp, and soon move towards the north-east with the Lippeto Hills covering their flank. At noon they stop, hide their horses in nearby bushes and trees, and form a picket line along the north-east edge of the Lippeto Hills. From there they can observe the land to the north and east.

In the early afternoon some of the Portuguese scouts spot large clouds of dust to the north. Two scouts carefully move forward to get a closer sighting of the dust columns. Sure enough, it is the leading element of the French garrison from Chaves. Riders are sent back to Lieutenant Colonel Macmillan, who is about a day's ride behind. The riders make good progress and reach Macmillan's camp early the next morning.

"Senhor, the French garrison from Chaves has been spotted on a road to the north. They are two days' march away from this position," explains Juan Carlos.

"Thank you, sir, thank you," replies a grateful Macmillan, who appears to be relieved at hearing the news.

"Please advise me of the best ground on which to engage the French column," requests Macmillan.

Juan Carlos feels very good that he is being asked to pick the ground for such an important battle.

"Ten miles to the north the road runs through a valley. The slopes of the hills in the valley contain trees and bushes on both sides, and offer cover for your men. If the soldiers occupy both sides of the valley, and your horsemen are placed under cover at the southern exit, I will take my men and guard the north entrance in case the French try to return the way they came," explains Juan Carlos.

"Excellent plan, sir," replies Macmillan enthusiastically.

The Argylls and their allies move to the north at daybreak led by their pipers and drummers playing John Mackenzie's 'Farewell to Strathglass', a stirring march. Speed is the important factor. By early afternoon, after a forced march, the weary column arrives at their destination. The soldiers are deployed along each side of the hills overlooking the valley. Juan Carlos rides to the north end of the valley to rejoin his men and brief them on the plan. The French are less than five miles away and the lead elements of their columns can be seen from where Juan Carlos stands.

The plan is for the scouts to hide in the woods until the French pass their position at the north end of the valley. The Scots Greys take up a position at the southern end of the valley and wait under cover in nearby woods.

In the late afternoon, a company of French lancers enters the valley. The French column is spread out over half a mile. At the rear of their column is a second company of French dragoons. As soon as all of the French enter the valley, Macmillan gives the signal to open fire. The noise of a great crackle of muskets and rifles crescendoes against the valley walls. The French are taken completely by surprise as they are not expecting any attack. The 98th and Portuguese soldiers keep up a steady volley of shots and the French grenadiers and horsemen take a real pounding. The French lancers in front of the column try to attack by charging up the slopes of the valley, but their horses stumble because the grades of the slopes are too steep for mounted horses to advance. The French grenadiers finally form two lines and keep up a good return fire against the 98th and their Portuguese allies. General Henry, the senior French officer, orders the lancers to try to break out to the south end of the valley. No sooner have the lancers entered the southern end of the valley than the Scots Greys launch a surprise attack. The French lancers are outnumbered, but they put up a good fight. Seeing that they cannot break through, the remaining French horsemen retreat back into the valley.

By late evening more than half of the French soldiers have been killed or wounded. General Henry now tries the northern escape route and orders the lancers to charge through the valley in a desperate bid to break out of the trap. The French horsemen try to fight their way out of the trap, but Juan Carlos and his men appear firing their muskets on the lancers. Soon the Portuguese volunteers overwhelm the remaining elements of the gallant French horsemen.

Lieutenant Colonel Macmillan, sensing that the French grenadier's resistance is coming to an end, orders a bayonet charge down the hills into the valley below. The allies come thundering down the steep slopes, smashing into the defending Frenchmen. The Scots Greys on horseback also attack from the south end of the valley. Hand-to-hand fighting ensues and soldiers of the 98th use their bayonets and dirks to good effect, killing many of the enemy soldiers. By dusk all serious resistance comes to an end and General Henry is taken prisoner together with 200 of his men. Ninety Portuguese soldiers are killed or wounded and fifty soldiers of 98th are lost in the fight. Twenty horsemen of the Scots Greys are reported dead or wounded.

Juan Carlos and his men move off to the south-west under cover of darkness. Their objective is to locate Old Tom and deliver dispatches outlining the battle at the Lippeto Hills.

Chapter 21

PORTUGESE CAMPAIGN:
Battle of Vila Real

Portuguese scouts indicate that the main body of the combined French and Spanish armies is about ten miles away. The 98th and their allies are camped by the El Torrino river. Pickets are deployed on the other side of the river in a wide radius. Juan Carlos and the remainder of his volunteers arrive at the Argyll's camp late in the evening. A meeting takes place, during which time Juan Carlos presents dispatches to Campbell and Clypton from Lieutenant Colonel Macmillan. All of the men are delighted with the news of the victory at the Lippeto Hills. Campbell thanks Juan Carlos for such a skilful plan.

"When will Macmillan and his men arrive here?" asks Clypton.

"They will march all night and be here late tomorrow afternoon," Juan Carlos replies.

"Excellent! We will prepare to give them a good welcome," states Campbell, who is in high spirits.

Reports from Major Carvaliho confirm that the French and Spanish troops are camped less than ten miles to the east, near the town of Vila Real. It appears that General Cisse is waiting for the arrival of toops from the Chaves garrison. Clypton estimates that Cisse will wait another day or two then will move his troops against the British and Portuguese forces.

"That, gentlemen, gives us some breathing room," states Old Tom.

"Certainly does," agrees Clypton.

"Gentlemen, when the Lowland regiment arrives they will be exhausted and in need o' a rest. I am planning to keep Lieutenant Colonel Macmillan's men in reserve when the battle commences with Cisse," explains Old Tom.

All agree on this strategy.

Lieutenant Andrew Griffin accompanied by pipers and side drummers leads the column of Lowland and Portuguese soldiers proudly into Old Tom's camp playing 6/8 marches. A great roar erupts and men throw their glengarry and balmoral bonnets high in the air. Although Macmillan and his men are exhausted, they keep in good order as they march past Old Tom. The heroes of the Lippeto Hills are greeted with a rifle salute from an honour guard of two companies of men.

"It is indeed a great pleasure, sir, to shake yer hand, Macmillan," states Campbell with great emotion.

The two men embrace and the army cheers and celebrates. It is another fine moment to be savoured by the Argylls and Portuguese allies.

Later that night, at dinner, Old Tom and his officers discuss the plan to fight General Cisse.

"Gentlemen, up until now we have been indeed very fortunate. We have defeated the French in several engagements and now they are sending one of their best generals against us with battle-hardened troops. Make no mistake, gentlemen, the French grenadiers are a formidable fighting force. They have been campaigning in Europe and have been victorious in all o' their battles and skirmishes. The facts are these: the combined French and Spanish armies outnumber us. If we let them attack us, we may be in for a real hiding. It's important that we choose the ground and we attack them," states Campbell with great poise and conviction.

There are several loud comments of disbelief and anguish amongst the officers. It is Major Carvaliho, a well-known diplomat amongst his people, who comes to Old Tom's rescue.

"Again, My Lord, you have chosen a bold plan which even

General Cisse will not expect," comments Major Carvaliho in a cool, calm and reassuring voice. "The element of surprise is an advantage which may offset our lack of numbers," adds Major Carvaliho with great poise.

Other officers speak, suggesting that the plan is too risky and will fail. At that point Colonel Clypton, the Duke of Essex, takes the floor.

"Gentlemen, if we lose the coming battle against the combined French and Spanish forces, Cisse will turn to the north and march on Belgium and attack Sir Arthur Wellesley and his fusiliers and push us out of Europe. Then you can expect a French invasion, gentlemen – yes, an invasion on our very own soil," warns Clypton with great passion.

There is a stunned silence broken eventually by Lieutenant Colonel MacGregor.

"The Highlanders stand to the ready, Campbell. Just say the word."

"That's the stuff, MacGregor, that's the stuff," shouts Clypton.

The next day the scouts from the east report that General Cisse has not changed his position. As the darkening hour of night approaches, Old Tom orders the wheels of the artillery carriages to be greased, and the men are ordered to maintain complete silence. The soldiers break camp under cover of darkness, and with muffled drums the army moves silently towards the El Torrino river crossing and a new dawning.

All of the army crosses the El Torrino river and is quietly moving to the east, towards Cisse's encampment under cover of darkness. Juan Carlos and his volunteers ride ahead of the army to scout the land, which they know so well. As a boy, Juan Carlos hunted in the surrounding hills and is familiar with all of the villages, river crossings and roads. The French and Spanish are camped near the town of Vila Real. From his vantage point, Juan Carlos observes the enemy encampment.

The French and Spanish are camped in the shape of the letter L. Their main encampment runs west to east on a line of gently rising ground. At the end of the west side of the encampment the camp turns to the north for about half a mile. The French lancers and dragoons are located on the east side of the main encampment. Sentries are placed all along the west–east line of the camp, and also along the north–south line. Fires burn brightly and there is a high level of activity in the encampment. It appears that the French may be getting ready to break camp.

Juan Carlos and his volunteers move cautiously towards the French camp. The French sentries pace slowly up and down, muskets carried at the ready, keeping a wistful eye open through the half-light of the approaching dawn. When the volunteers come in sight of the French sentries, they dismount and make their way forward, crouching silently in groups of four. Soon, the Portuguese volunteers silently kill French sentries.

Shortly after dawn, Campbell receives a report from Juan Carlos that the French sentries have been eliminated. Campbell's heavy artillery is camouflaged behind bushes and deep undergrowth out of sight of the French. The weather is dry and warm, and a gentle breeze blows out of the west. The sky is slowly clearing and it promises to be a beautiful day.

The Scots Greys and the Portuguese horsemen stand at the ready. The roar of Campbell's nine-pounders is the first to be heard this day. Forty-nine-pounder heavy cannons fire round shot and shells, which rain down on the French encampments, destroying tents, soldiers and French artillery. Wounded horses scream and run off in different directions. Fires break out in many areas of the camp and columns of smoke fills the air as flames comes into contact with munitions, causing explosions and adding to the general confusion. After two full rounds of missiles have been fired by Campbell's artillerymen, the Scots Greys and Portuguese horsemen charge Cisse's main camp. Hundreds of horsemen, screaming and yelling and waving their long swords and lances, charge at full gallop towards the enemy encampment. The allies are on the enemy before they can mount a proper defence. Horses smash their way through the French camp, killing and wounding all in their wake. Riders cut and slash at French grenadiers, dismounted lancers and dragoon officers who are trying desperately to rally their horsemen. Some dragoon officers start firing their carbines at the invaders. When the Scots Greys and the Portuguese horse reach the far end of the camp they turn and charge back.

In the meantime, several French lancers and companies of French dragoons have saddled their horses and meet the charging allies head on. The horsemen collide in a sudden bloody melee. The clash of horse and steel is ferocious. Riders are unseated and thrown from their mounts, horses fall down and some horsemen are trapped and crushed by the weight of their mounts. More French lancers and dragoons join the fray and the fight is on. The officers of the Scots Greys use their flintlocks against charging French lancers. As the French grenadiers begin to form lines to block the Scots Greys and Portuguese horsemen's escape, officers order their buglers to sound the retreat. It is a good decision, because given a few minutes more the French would have cut off the only escape route of Campbell's charging horsemen.

As soon as the Scots Greys and the Portuguese horsemen reach the safety of their lines the fusiliers and Portuguese foot soldiers advance against the main French defences. Clypton's 5,000 fusiliers move forward, supported by two regiments of Portuguese foot soldiers on their left, commanded by General Deco. Artillery fire precedes the advance and is concentrated on the French main west–east lines. As the 8,000 men move forward the French grenadiers quickly form their defensive lines and bring up their artillery. Six-pounders open fire on the advancing fusiliers and brave Portuguese foot soldiers.

It is now the allies' turn to taste the carnage caused by French artillery. Iron balls explode in a burst of smoke, ripping holes in the advancing allied lines. Gaps appear all along the advancing lines, but to their credit the fusiliers fill the gaps and keep their formation and continue their forward progress. The two Portuguese regiments also feel the sting of the French cannon as missiles cut through their ranks, exploding in men's faces and creating carnage and death amongst the companies of foot soldiers. Still the men come on at the urging of their officers. At 100 yards from the French lines the allies stop and a great crackle of rifles and muskets can be heard all over the battlefield. Clypton's artillery is silent now and the advancing fusiliers and Portuguese come bravely forward to meet the might of the French veterans.

Over on the far left of the battlefield the two Highland regiments, 3,000-strong, are in place to advance against the enemy's north–south line of defenders, comprising Spanish and French regulars. On the Highlanders' right are 2,000 Portuguese foot soldiers under the command of Colonel Pepe. Old Tom's cannonade leads off the attack. Twenty-nine-pound batteries rain their deadly loads on the enemy's lines. The Spanish and French have 8,000 men forming a north–south line of defence. After several rounds of heavy artillery fire, the pipers and side drummers lead the army forward. The pipers play stirring marches and the young men's blood tingles as the 98th advance with their kilts swaying and their bonnet tassels and glengarry feathers fluttering in the stiffening breeze. On the far left of the Highlanders' line are the men of Atholl. In 1778 the young Duke of Atholl raised a regiment of 1,000 men. Colonel James Murray, son of Lord George Murray, had trained these men and they had become a formidable fighting force. The Atholl regiment was disbanded three years later, so many of the soldiers who had served under Colonel James Murray signed up with the 98th. The men of Atholl anchor the Argyll's line on the far left opposite the Spanish defenders.

Two long lines of the 98th and their Portuguese allies advance, keeping their formation and supported by Old Tom's deadly cannonade. The two lines of soldiers enter a dip in the land and temporarily lose sight of the enemy. As the allies march out of the dip led by the pipers and side drummers, the order is to halt. The front line kneels and the soldiers cock their rifles.

"Fire!"

A great crash of muskets and rifles pours a hail of bullets into the enemy lines, quickly followed by a second volley from the standing line of soldiers. Quickly the men reload and the two lines advance at the quickstep against the defending Spanish and French soldiers. French batteries open fire, smashing round shot down into the advancing columns. Screams and cries are heard as knots of soldiers are splattered with exploding shells and are hurled skyward. Large holes begin to appear in the front line of the allies' attack. Young men from the Western Isles of Scotland let off cries of despair as they witness many of their friends and comrades falling to the ground under heavy fire from the enemy's cannon and musket fire. On the far left of the advance, the men of Atholl make good progress against the Spanish defenders. On the right of the line, the brave Portuguese foot soldiers come forward now at the quickstep as they take heavy fire from the defending Frenchmen.

The Parisian Guard, who were involved in the French Revolution from the beginning, respond by pushing hard against Clypton's fusiliers. The struggle in the centre of the line becomes desperate. Officers of the fusiliers urge their men on and a titanic struggle develops. Slowly the fusiliers are pushed back. Cisse's gamble of putting his veterans in the centre of his defensive line is paying off. The French general now commits another two battalions of French regulars to join the centre of his line and break the fusiliers' centre. The Portuguese, sensing their comrades are losing the battle, begin to fall back in good order.

The Highlanders try to continue to advance, taking heavy losses. The Portuguese progress on their right is stalled – they have formed firing lines, but cannot make any further forward progress. Soon the Highlanders' advance comes to an abrupt stop in the centre of the line and only sporadic fire is now being made against the French lines of defence. All of the pipers, with the exception of one young cadet, Rory MacPherson, have been killed or are so badly wounded that they are unable to play their bagpipes. The young cadet, Rory MacPherson, from the village of Tomintoul, has taken some shrapnel to the side of the forehead and is bleeding from his wound. Rory is in shock. The constant bombardment of the French artillery and the loss of his fellow pipers and drummers has shaken him to the core and he is terrified. It is only on the far left of the 98th's line of attack that the men of Atholl have reached the end of the Spanish lines and are now trying to outflank the Spanish defenders. Heavy hand-to-hand fighting is in progress.

Clypton sends urgent dispatches to Old Tom asking for reinforcements. Clypton's bold charge looked initially as if it would succeed, but now the French, having reinforced the centre of their line of defence, have halted the progress of Clypton's gallant men. The fusiliers start to give ground back to the French. The Portuguese soldiers on Clypton's left are now in an orderly retreat.

Cries of *"Vive la France! Vive la Republique!"* can be heard above the din of battle.

Campbell, who is observing the battle from his vantage point, knows that Clypton's charge on the French centre has failed by a whisker to break the defendants' lines. Cisse's reinforcements have done their job and saved the main French line of defence from breaking. Campbell is reluctant to commit reserves at this point, until he has a clear understanding of what the outcome of the battle will be between the Highland regiments, their Portuguese allies, and the French and Spanish defenders.

A dispatch is hurriedly written by Campbell responding to Clypton's urgent pleas for reinforcements. Sandy Ross, Old Tom's trusted kinsman, is asked to deliver the message personally. Ross sets off with two other riders, but as the three men gallop towards Clypton's lines a French artillery shell explodes directly in front of the three riders, who are all unseated from their horses. Ross falls unconscious to the ground with a shrapnel wound to the head. His horse also is struck by shrapnel and rolls over on the ground, and the horse's legs end up on top of the unconscious Ross. One of the two other riders is instantly killed and his companion is wounded in the arm. The wounded man retrieves the dispatch from Sandy Ross and continues on foot towards Clypton's field position as the French shrapnel has also killed the other two horses.

The Highland regiment's line gradually breaks in the centre and the men start to fall back in confusion. The Spanish and French firepower has taken its toll on the centre of the Argyll's line and large gaps appear. Panic begins to creep in – especially amongst the young men from the Western Isles, who have never experienced such carnage and terror.

As the soldiers fall back, a great hulking man, over six feet two inches tall, with long black whiskers, dark flashing eyes and great biceps, shouts, "Stand, men! Stand yer ground!"

Some soldiers hear the shouts and cries of Sergeant Douglas over the din of the battle. Sergeant Ewan Douglas, better known by the sobriquet of 'the Black Douglas', is a blacksmith by trade from Cromarty in North-West Scotland. He joined the Argylls after the regiment's return from the South African Campaign. Some soldiers rally around their sergeant holding the regimental colours. Young Rory MacPherson is one of the men to respond. The Black Douglas, seeing he is a piper, orders him to play.

"I cannae, sir – I cannae play," cries young Rory, who is in shock and bleeding from his wounds.

"Play, for God's sake, man – play a tune," orders the Black Douglas, who now holds the regimental colours above his head.

Young Rory picks up his pipes and starts to play 'The Lonach Gathering', but at first the drones of the pipes cannot be heard above the noise of battle.

"Louder, man! Louder!" screams the Black Douglas.

The young piper takes strength from the great hulking sergeant and plays as loud as he can. Highlanders, hearing the sound of the bagpipes, instinctively move towards the piper and regimental colours through the thick veil of gunpowder smoke. Soon over 200 men form two lines behind the piper and all of the soldiers crouch down in a long hollow in the ground to avoid the French and Spanish artillery, which continues to bombard the allies' lines.

Some distance away Lieutenant Colonel Macmillan and

his Lowland regiment stand by watching this carnage. The Sassenachs cannot believe the tremendous courage and fighting spirit shown by the Teuchters, whom they so often mock. Even Porter, Tosh, Reid and Laurie are moved by the great courage shown by the Highlanders in battle. Most men would run away if exposed to such ferocious artillery and rifle fire, they all think.

The honour of carrying the Lowland regimental colours has been given to Lieutenant Andrew Griffin. The colour party, accompanying the MacGregor, includes six soldiers and two young ensigns from Port Glasgow and Northern Ireland.

The MacGregor weeps openly as he witnesses his fellow Highlanders being cut to pieces. He wonders why Old Tom does not sound the retreat to save the men from total destruction. The officers of the Lowland regiment make no move to recall the Argylls and their brave Portuguese allies. Shifting and muttering sounds start to emerge from the long rows of sullen men of the Lowland regiment, who stand and watch the carnage of the battle. The Sassenachs in the Lowland regiment start to become more unsettled and shout out abusive language at their officers.

"Stand fast in the ranks!" shouts the officers.

"Steady in the ranks," call the officers all along the line of the Lowland regiment.

The more the carnage continues, the more unsettled the men in the Lowland ranks become. No one pays any attention to the officers' warnings and the men continue to shout obscenities. Even the hard-hearted Reid, who despises the Highlanders, shouts for the officers of the line to call for the retreat, or for the Lowland regiment to advance.

Lieutenant Griffin's heart is heavy and tears run down his face as he observes the death of so many men of the Highland clans of Scotland. He recalls the stories his father told him of the Battle of Culloden and the countless number of deaths after the battle at the hands of the Duke of Cumberland. Finally, something inside Griffin snaps and before he knows what is happening he motions forward the regimental colours.

Instinctively, the colour party follows the regimental colour bearer. Officers nearby, realizing what is happening, order the colour party to return to the ranks, but the orders fall on deaf ears. Suddenly, the whole Lowlanders' line starts to advance behind the colour party. The officers continue shouting at the men to return to their original positions, but the officers are swept along in the great tide. The whole regiment, 1,500 men, now come forward steadily towards their fallen comrades – the first time in the history of the British Army that a regiment advances without a direct order.

Old Tom views the advance through his telescope from a nearby hill and is in shock. Clypton has repeatedly requested reinforcements because he senses that the French are planning a counter-attack against the centre of his line.

The MacGregor moves forward at the quickstep now with the eight men of the colour party following close behind. A wind from the west catches the regimental colours and they flutter in the steady breeze. The MacGregor is oblivious to the artillery and rifle fire which rains around him, and also to the shouting of the officers from behind. Soon the MacGregor and the colour party come into view of the Black Douglas, who remains crouched in a long hollow in the land with his men.

When the Black Douglas sees the colour party and the long line of Lowlanders advancing at the quickstep behind them, he shouts, "Look, men, look – the regiment's advancing."

The MacGregor, the colour party and the Black Douglas charge into the abyss with the rest of the army following closely behind. The MacGregor is the first to fall under a hail of bullets from French muskets and rifle fire. One member of the colour party picks up the regimental colours and the charge continues straight at the centre of the French and Spanish lines. Soon the flag bearer falls and a young ensign picks up the colours, and dashes forward towards the enemy's lines. The Portuguese on the right see what is happening, regroup, and charge straight at the French and Spanish guns.

The whole north–south line of Cisse's defences is now under a renewed and ferocious assault. On the far left, the men from

Blair Atholl turn the defensive line of the Spanish, who are now falling back in panic. The Spanish have committed all of their reserves, so they are unable to reinforce their line of defence. The Argylls smash into the French and Spanish lines and hand-to-hand fighting develops. Teuchters and Sassenachs fight side by side – one army, one nation, united against the combined might of the French and Spanish forces. The Glaswegians from the east end of the city of Glasgow, who were raised amongst street gangs using their knives and razors, are now in their element. This is their type of fight. Using their bayonets, swords and dirks they cut and slash their way through the French and Spanish defences.

The French officers, realizing that their lines are breaking join their men in the front lines shouting encouragement: "*Vive la France! Vive la Republique!*"

The French grenadiers, who fought their way through Europe, respond to the calls of their officers and start to push back against the ferocious Argylls' assault. Nearby, the Black Douglas waves the regimental colours and continues to rally and encourage the men; and young Rory MacPherson blows the bagpipes as hard as he can, which spurs on the remaining Highlanders and their fellow countrymen from the Lowlands of Scotland.

On the far left of the enemy's lines, the Spanish retreat turns into a rout and the men of Atholl pour into the gaps. The French, sensing they are being outflanked, fall back in good order and try to form new defensive lines. Most of the brave French and Spanish officers lie dead or wounded on the front lines, so there are no officers remaining to direct the French defence. Lieutenant Colonel Macmillan and Lieutenant Colonel MacGregor sense victory and force their men on.

"On, laddies! On, laddies!" shouts Lieutenant Colonel MacGregor at the top of his voice as he charges on his mount straight at the retreating French and Spanish soldiers brandishing a sword.

Within minutes the whole French north–south line is in a general retreat.

"They're on the run," shouts Lieutenant Colonel MacGregor. "Forward, men, forward!"

Clypton observes what is happening on his far left and orders the fusiliers and the Portuguese soldiers to advance against the French east–west line. General Cisse, sensing he is losing the battle on the north–south defensive line, rushes in a reserve regiment to form a new defensive line at right angles with his main east–west line of defence. The regiment is the 2nd Nantes Grenadiers – veterans from Cisse's home town of Nantes in France. These Frenchman have fought in many campaigns and will stand their ground. Cisse orders his mobile artillery to be rushed to the front lines. Soon four- and six-pound batteries are hurriedly positioned. French artillerymen now pound the oncoming English fusiliers and their Portuguese allies.

In a desperate move to try to ensure that he is not outflanked, Cisse orders companies of French lancers and dragoons to gallop to the positions held by the Spanish and stop the advance of the Argylls. Old Tom observes the French horsemen galloping towards the Highlanders' left flank and orders the Scots Greys and Portuguese horsemen to rush to engage the French lancers and dragoons.

The Scots Greys are the first to engage the French before they can reach the positions now held by the Atholl Highlanders. Swords, sabers and lances clash as horsemen on both sides try to gain an advantage. Soon the Portuguese horsemen join the fray and horses tumble; riders are unseated and trampled to death. The French horsemen outnumber their enemy and fight desperately to stop their army being outflanked. As the fighting continues, Thomas Campbell is urged by Major Carvaliho to send in Juan Carlos and his volunteers to even the odds. The order is given and Juan Carlos and all of his horsemen join the battle. Within an hour the French lancers and dragoons take heavy losses and the pealing of the French trumpets sounds the retreat.

It is now approaching midday and the battle has been raging for many hours. Lieutenant Colonel MacGregor halts the advance of the Argylls and forms two long lines; he then continues his assault on the new French regiment from Nantes which has taken the field. The two lines of Highlanders and Lowlanders, now one army, pour rifle fire on the French defendants. The French return the fire and rip holes in the Argylls' lines, which are less than 100 yards away. Screams of pain and terror are heard all along the Argylls' lines, but to their credit the men stand their ground. The men of Atholl, who have been placed in the front and centre of the line, shout encouragement to the young Highlanders and Lowlanders. Sensing the Highlanders may retreat, the officers serving with the Atholl Highlanders start singing to raise the confidence of the young crofters, farmers and fishermen from the Western Isles, who are clearly in distress at this ferocious encounter. All of the men of Blair Atholl join the throng, and soon the two long lines of soldiers steady.

The order to form firing lines is shouted down the line, and the front line of soldiers assumes the kneeling position. Then both lines pour fire into the enemy. Most of the soldiers fire off three rounds in a minute. The rifle training now begins to pay off. Large holes appear in the French lines, but still the brave French grenadiers stand their ground. Lieutenant Colonel MacGregor, realizing that the French soldiers will not leave the field, orders a bayonet charge. Fix bayonets! Advance! At the quickstep the two lines of soldiers advance, intimidating the French defenders who display great courage. Losses are now mounting on both sides, and Lieutenant Colonel MacGregor marvels at the courage of his foe. The sound of French trumpets signals the retreat and the French grenadiers from Nantes leave the field to the Argylls and their Portuguese allies.

Clypton's men come on at the quickstep with their Portuguese allies on his left against the French east–west line of defence. Soon the two adversaries are facing each other and both sides return rifle fire. A desperate struggle is in progress because the battle is now in the balance.

"Bayonets!" an officer shouts; then "Charge!" is the

command as the fusiliers come forward at the quickstep with their Portuguese allies in tightly packed lines on their left. Soon, both sides become locked in hand-to-hand fighting all along the east–west line of the French defence. The French grenadiers now begin to fall back and Cisse orders a general retreat, in fear of being outflanked. Clypton's men, to their credit, pursue the enemy.

By mid-afternoon, the long and bloody battle finally has come to an end. The French leave the field all along the east–west line of defence. Great cheers can be heard from the Teuchters and their Sassenach countrymen. The Portuguese allies who fought with such valour to protect their native soil also join in the celebrations. Bonnets are tossed high in the air. The pipers who escaped being killed or wounded play their bagpipes and the soldiers cheer, shout and dance for joy. It is a great moment to savour, especially for the soldiers from the Western Isles. The Highland regiments of the 98th sustain fifty per cent casualties, the Lowlanders thirty per cent, and the Portuguese about forty per cent, dead or wounded. Half of the Portuguese horsemen are killed and the Scots Greys lose almost a third of their strength.

Old Tom orders Juan Carlos and his remaining volunteers to monitor the French retreat to ensure that they do not try to regroup and counter-attack.

Finally, the last rifle volleys of the battle are fired. As Old Tom crosses the smoke-filled battlefield with his personal bodyguard, he is aghast at the devastation. Dead bodies, hundreds of wounded men, some trying to crawl back to the safety of their lines, dead horses, broken and abandoned artillery batteries and other armaments, smashed and abandoned artillery carts, torn banners, broken lances, and drums are strewn across the width and depth of the battlefield.

Amongst the dead and wounded Old Tom finds his kinsman Sandy Ross. Sandy lies unconscious on the ground. Medical staff confirm that Ross is still alive, which is welcome news to Campbell. Ross is taken to a nearby field hospital. Further on, Old Tom observes Lieutenant Griffin being attended to by some of the medical aids. A bloodstained bandage circles Griffin's head, and there are bloodstains on his collar from the scalp wound left by a French bullet. Bandages are also wrapped tightly around his shoulder and his right leg. French bullets have penetrated his shoulder and also his leg below his knee and a musket ball is lodged in his leg, causing him a great amount of pain. Medical aids are trying to stop the bleeding from his wounds. Old Tom dismounts from his mount, Peggy, his great white mare, kneels down and holds Griffin's bandaged head on his lap.

Griffin slowly opens his eyes and sees the gaze of his commanding officer with a naked honesty.

"Ye did not follow ma orders today, Lieutenant Griffin," states Old Tom quietly. "I realize what you did was from the heart and the charge you led turned the whole tide o' the battle in our favour. We've won a great victory here today – one of the greatest in our history. The Highland and Lowland regiments are now truly united – one army, and one nation. I'm going to forgive you for moving forward without my command and because yer act o' bravery won the day you are now a captain," says Old Tom, staring into Griffin's eyes.

Griffin feels extremely groggy. He grasps the Duke's arm and thanks his commander for his understanding and great compassion.

Beside Captain Griffin lies Corporal James Brodie from old Aberdeen, who has just died of his wounds. Some of the other members of the colour party who followed the MacGregor's charge also lie nearby, bleeding from their wounds.

The moon rises huge and fast this evening as the men of the 98th sit silently by their campfires. For many it is a time for deep reflection. Those soldiers who survived this ferocious encounter rest in their camp beds, mentally and physically exhausted, and mourn the loss of so many of their family, friends and colleagues. Some companies of the 98th have been completely destroyed. Hundreds of wounded men are housed in nearby field hospitals, thinking of their homeland and families.

Pipers who were fortunate enough to survive the charges against the enemy's lines play laments on their chanters in memory of those beloved clansmen who fell during this bloody battle. Some of the men from the Western Isles sit silently by their campfires on this foreign field and remember their glens, the shining lochs and the smell of peat burning on the home fires. These men have never before strayed far from their homes and loved ones, and yearn to return to their crofts, cottages and shielings, and dream about seeing once again the mist-covered mountains of their homeland.

Old Tom, accompanied by his bodyguard, walks round the camp congratulating the men on such a great victory. At the Lowlanders' camp, where the Northern Ireland contingent is billeted, the sound of the uillean pipes fills the air. Old Tom approaches the camp with his bodyguard and speaks with a young lieutenant, Tommy Best, from Ballymena, in Northern Ireland.

"Sir," says the young lieutenant, "what's the name o' the place we fought at today?"

"Vila Real," replies Old Tom. "This battle will be known as the Battle of Vila Real."

Old Tom then visits the field hospital where his kinsman Sandy Ross is still lying unconscious. He speaks with one of the army surgeons and discovers that Ross's condition is very serious. This news distresses Campbell. In another part of the field hospital, Campbell is advised that one of his personal bodyguards, Captain Colin Campbell, is in serious condition and not expected to live.

Old Tom approaches the makeshift bed of his dear friend and comrade and kneels down. Colin Campbell's father served Old Tom's family for many years and young Colin has continued with the family tradition. He holds Colin's hand and thanks him for his loyal service. Colin, recognizing his lord and master, tries to get up but falls back on his makeshift bed and moments later passes away peacefully.

It takes Old Tom several minutes to compose himself.

Campbell's bodyguard, seeing their leader is distressed, step back. Campbell is not a religious man. His father took him many times to the local kirk in Argyll when he was a child, but Campbell never did feel a strong calling for prayer until now. After several minutes of reflection and prayer Campbell slowly rises and salutes his fallen comrade. He places a large brooch with a boar's head surrounded by emeralds and silver on the chest of his fallen and faithful comrade. Old Tom's bodyguard stands at attention for a few minutes.

"See that this broach is included with Captain Campbell's personal belongings and sent home to his family," orders Old Tom softly.

James Arthur, regimental surgeon; Alexander Donald, adjutant; and Alexander Chambers, the chaplain, along with many wounded officers and soldiers watch silently, witnessing this fine moment.

Captain Griffin is sitting up in bed with bloodstained bandages around his head, shoulder and leg as Old Tom approaches.

"Are you feeling any better, Captain Griffin?"

"Aye, My Lord, I feel a wee bit better," replies Griffin, who is still in great pain but no longer feels so groggy.

"They are shipping you home," explains Old Tom. "I wish you a full recovery, Captain."

"Ma Lord," says Griffin softly, "would you see tae my pipers and drummers and the survivors o' the colour party? Would you see to the wounded?" pleads Griffin, clutching his commander's arm.

"Aye, I will sir, that I will," promises Old Tom as he places his hand on Captain Griffin's shoulder in a gesture of reassurance.

Old Tom is better than his word. The surviving wounded men from the colour party and all of the wounded pipers and drummers are taken care of, and those who die of their wounds are given full military honours. In his dispatches to Marshalsea, Old Tom specifically mentions the heroics of the regimental pipers and drummers, and the colour party, many of whom made the ultimate sacrifice to earn this great victory. Also named in dispatches are Captain Andrew Griffin, the Black Douglas, Rory MacPherson, the young piper, and several of the Highland officers who stood their ground against ferocious enemy fire. Dougie Reid and Billy Porter, the rough and rowdy Glaswegians who slashed their way across that deadly battlefield at Vila Real, demonstrating outstanding courage in the face of the enemy, are also mentioned in Old Tom's report of the battle. Lieutenant Colonel Macmillan and Lieutenant Colonel MacGregor are recommended for the King's Medal for their great and unwavering courage and leadership. Colonel Clypton, the Duke of Essex, is also recommended for the King's Medal for bravery in the face of the enemy. A separate letter is sent to Prince Jao relating the bravery of the Portuguese horsemen and foot soldiers during this great encounter to free the Portuguese from the French and Spanish invaders. Juan Carlos is recommended for a special honour for his military advice, intelligence reports and outstanding bravery in the face of the enemy.

The news of the victory at Vila Real is sent to the King and the Earl of Marshalsea. There is great joy and excitement. Queen Charlotte orders church bells to be rung throughout the kingdom, and in Scotland there is a great amount of celebration amongst the clans. Dispatches indicate that the wounded soldiers and officers will be returning home soon. The main body of the army will follow in October 1796.

Heather Griffin receives word from the army that Andrew is recovering from his wounds. Heather is so thankful that her darling Andrew has been spared. However, the army report also advises Heather that her brother Sandy Ross has still not regained consciousness, and this is a cause of great concern to her.

Chapter 22

BOYS OF BLUEHILL

During the voyage home of the wounded soldiers from Portugal, Captain Griffin stays close to his unconscious brother-in-law Sandy Ross. Sandy is constantly examined by Dr. James Arthur, the army surgeon. Old Tom also visits the ship's cabin, which Sandy occupies on a daily basis, but there is no change in Sandy's condition.

After a week at sea, Dr. Arthur examines Sandy and pronounces him dead. Captain Griffin and Thomas Campbell are stunned and shaken by the news.

"I have lost my most loyal friend and companion, Captain Griffin," states Campbell as he sits down on the bed occupied by his late kinsman. "Sandy served my father for ten years and was as loyal a man as there ever was. He will be sorely missed," states a heartbroken Thomas Campbell as he bows his head in grief.

It is Sunday morning on board *Seaforth* and Thomas Campbell spends time writing letters to the families of his deceased fellow officers. A knock on the door and in walks Gregor MacGregor.

"Guid morning, sir. You smell o' candlewax and ink. Have you been writing?"

"Yes, Gregor. I have been writing to the families o' the fallen officers."

"Sir, the funeral service is ready to begin on the main deck."

Campbell flips shut his writing desk, reaches for his hat, and taking some deep breaths, makes his way on deck.

Captain Kidd and the full ship's crew are waiting on deck together with some of the less seriously injured soldiers. The army chaplain, Alexander Chambers, conducts the service. A lament is played on the Highland bagpipes by a surviving piper as all those on deck hang their heads in sorrow. Sandy Ross is buried at sea on a warm Sunday morning to the sound of the ship's bell.

It takes Andrew Griffin several days of grieving before he can come to terms with the death of his brother-in-law. Andrew thinks of Heather and her parents and how they will react to the sad news of Sandy's death.

In the officers' dining room during the third week of the voyage home, one of the wounded officers', Captain Stuart Fraser, talks about his plans when he returns to Scotland.

"Aye, I am planning to travel north wi' several o' the other wounded officers to the village o' Bluehill to recover from our wounds," explains Captain Fraser, who was shot in the leg and arm during the charge on the French lines at Vila Real.

"I have never heard o' the village o' Bluehill, Stuart," comments Captain Griffin as he eats his evening meal.

"Ma father first told me about it when I was a lad, Andrew. It's a beautiful spot. I visited the village one summer with ma father and was taken by the beauty o' the place. The views from the village are truly memorable, Andrew. Scottish bluebells grow in great profusion all along the west side o' the hills surrounding the village. On a clear day, looking to the west, you can see fishing boats sailing between the Western Islands. The Lord o' the Isles built a summer home at Bluehill in 1737 and several local folk settled nearby," explains Stuart, who is obviously very taken by the place.

"Is the summer home still standing, Stuart?" enquires Andrew.

"Well, after the 1745 Jacobite rebellion the house was abandoned, ye ken, and fell into disrepair. In 1767, soldiers returning from the war came upon this place and decided to restore it and use it as a place for war veterans to recover from their wounds. Several o' the residents o' the place agreed to turn the building into a piping and drumming school. Many o' the wounded soldiers who visited the building in Bluehill were army-trained pipers or drummers," explains Stuart enthusiastically. "So the reputation o' Bluehill for piping and drumming instruction is becoming better known, Andrew. I'm surprised you have not heard o' it," continues Stuart as he sips on a glass of Madeira.

"Sounds like an interesting place, Stuart. Are you thinking o' staying over at Bluehill?" enquires Andrew.

"Aye, when we disembark at Port Glasgow some o' the wounded lads are heading north with me to Bluehill. We plan to stay at Bluehill for a while until we recuperate from our wounds and to brush up on the piping, ye ken," replies Stuart, who appears to be committed to his plans. "What about yerself, Andrew?" enquires Stuart.

"For my part, Stuart, I am anxious to return home to ma wife, Heather, and our newborn son, wee Grieg," replies Andrew with an anxious tone in his voice.

When the ship carrying the wounded soldiers docks at Port Glasgow, six of the wounded are transported north towards Inveraray and the village of Bluehill to convalesce. Among the officers who accompany Captain Stuart Fraser to Bluehill is Donald MacDonald, who distinguished himself in the South African Campaign and who has been promoted to the rank of captain. MacDonald was wounded early in the Battle of Vila Real and is now recovering from shots to his chest and leg. The other members of the party consist of Lieutenant Roy Cameron from Inverness, Sergeant Hughie MacDougall from the village of Stromeferry in North-West Scotland, and Corporal Ross Noble from a small fishing village located on Calgary Bay on the island of Mull in the Inner Hebrides. Two brothers from the Isle of Lewis, Donald and Shaulto Stewart, who both carry the rank of corporal, make up the remainder of the party who travel to Bluehill. The Stewart brothers rallied behind the Black

Douglas in their final assault on the French and Spanish lines at Vila Real. With the exception of the Stewart brothers, all of the men in their company were killed. The two wounded Stewart brothers are fine pipers.

Waiting at the pier in the Port of Glasgow is Heather Griffin and her newborn son, wee Grieg, to welcome Andrew home. Because of the nature of his wounds, Andrew is amongst the last of the wounded soldiers to leave the ship. Accompanied by a fellow officer, Andrew is assisted down to the pier.

"Andrew, Andrew, my love, how are you?" cries Heather as she runs to meet her wounded hero carrying wee Grieg in her arms.

Andrew embraces his wife with one hand while placing his other hand firmly on a cane which supports his stance.

"So this is my wee son, Grieg. He's a fine wee lad, Heather," cries Andrew, who is so happy to be home with his family.

"Andrew, where is Sandy? I have not seen Sandy disembark. Is he well?" asks Heather anxiously.

"Heather, let's go to the barouche and we can have a wee talk."

The Griffin family make their way slowly to an awaiting barouche.

"Heather, Sandy never regained consciousness," said Andrew softly with his hand on her shoulder. "He was pronounced dead at sea and given a sea burial by members of the ship's crew. I'm so sorry for yer great loss," continues Andrew as he embraces Heather and wee Grieg.

"You mean – you mean he's dead – my brother Sandy's dead, Andrew?" stutters Heather in disbelief.

It is dusk when the coach carrying the six wounded soldiers arrives at the village of Bluehill. Chanters can be heard above the sound of cooks preparing the evening meal. As he steps out of the coach, Captain Stuart Fraser senses a certain serenity about the place. The long lush green plateau, which stretches north for a mile, the sweetness of the Highland air, and the soft cries of the distant herring gulls that fly above the sea to the west, add to the allure of this small village.

Major Jimmy Reynolds greets Stuart and his fellow officers. Reynolds is the senior ranking officer in residence at Bluehill. He fought in India before returning home to Scotland after being seriously wounded in battle. Reynolds is a founding member of the piping and drumming school and has stayed on to teach the chanter and piping. He warmly welcomes the newcomers to Bluehill.

"Good evening to you, friends. Come inside and have a wee nip," invites Reynolds to his six new visitors in a hearty manner.

Glasses of Scotch whisky are poured and all of the men get to know one other quickly. Jimmy Reynolds is a real live wire and entertains his guests with jokes and interesting stories about his escapades in India. There are fifteen soldiers in residence at Bluehill.

"All six of you can stay at Bluehill. The terms are simple. If you agree to teach pipin' and drummin' the stay is free while y'are here. The students' fees pay for the running o' the household. If you do not teach piping or drumming the cost of the stay is two shillings, or a florin a week," explains Jimmy.

All of the six visitors have played the pipes and drums for many years and are capable of teaching drumming or piping, so they all agree to Jimmy's terms while they recuperate from their battle wounds.

After a few days, one of the new piping instructors catches Major Reynolds' eye. Captain Donald MacDonald from Glencoe has a great piping technique and is very good at coaching the students. The other two soldiers that impress Jimmy are Lieutenant Roy Cameron and Shaulto Stewart.

Every other day a doctor visits Bluehill from the nearby town of Inveraray and tends to the men's wounds. If the wounds are serious, the patients are taken to Inveraray and stay in a small hospital, which the local townsfolk support.

Captain Stuart Fraser has a wound to the chest and damage to his upper left thigh, so he has to stay at the local hospital in

Inveraray. There he meets Jeannie MacQueen, a local nurse. Jeannie is a widow. Her husband, Gordon, was killed while serving with the British Army in India, and she has taken up nursing to support her family. Jeannie has a son named Malcolm who is eleven years old and Stuart and Malcolm quickly become friends. Stuart tells an impressionable young Malcolm stories about the great battles in Europe while he recuperates from his wounds in hospital. Young Malcolm is very interested in piping, and Stuart shows the lad how to play the chanter during his hospital stay. Jeannie takes a liking to Stuart, but he is shy with the women.

Hughie MacDougall, from the village of Stromeferry, also requires a stay at the hospital in Inveraray for a couple of weeks following surgery. The other men just need rest to allow their wounds to heal so that they can make a full recovery.

After being released from hospital, Captain Stuart Fraser spends time socializing with Major Jimmy Reynolds. Stuart considers Jimmy to be an amazing character. Jimmy's bravery and his long and distinguished army service are reflected in all of the memorabilia and medals on display in the officers' mess at Bluehill.

"It looks like you have had a very busy life serving yer country, pipe major," comments Stuart as he scans his eye around the room.

"Aye, it's been an event-filled army life, that's for sure," replies Jimmy as he remembers all the campaigns he fought in over the years. "My father and grandfather were soldiers and damn fine pipers, you understand," continues Jimmy, who appears to be in a very relaxed and talkative mood.

"I was seventeen years old when I left ma home in bonnie Dundee and joined the army as a piper. I was indeed fortunate enough to be decorated several times for leading the men in charges against enemy lines. Before I got shot, I received several promotions and field commissions during major engagements on the Afghanistan border," explains Jimmy thoughtfully.

"Who taught you to play the Highland bagpipes so well?" enquires Stuart, who is very interested in Jimmy's army life.

"Well, when I was barely thirteen years old, ma father arranged for me to be trained in the classical music o' the great Highland bagpipes, the *piobaireachd* or pibroch. In Gaelic it means pipe music and it is sometimes referred to as *ceol mor*, or the great music. Aye, I remember ma father checking on me every night to see if I had done my two hours on the chanter," recalls Reynolds, smiling at the memory of his youth.

"What was life like for you during yer time in India, Jimmy?" enquires Stuart.

"I served in India for over twenty years, Stuart, and I worked my way up to major o' the regiment during all that time in India. It was a good life. I made lots o' friends and we spent oor social time in the officers' mess. The stories we shared would make you laugh yer head off, Stuart. The English serving officers would drink their gin and tonics or chota pegs, as the local Indian servants called them. As for me, I stuck to the good old Scottish whisky and never had any bother wi' my health, unlike some of the English officers. Aye, life was good until I got badly shot up in an ambush. Come to think o' it, I was the only survivor of my company, Stuart. They shipped me home after that episode and I came here to Bluehill," recounts Jimmy as he pours himself another drink.

"Did you ever find time in yer busy army life to get married, Jimmy?" asks Stuart with a certain amount of curiosity in his voice.

"Between the fighting and teaching the local soldiers how to play the pipes in India, there never seemed time enough to develop a lasting relationship with a young woman, ye ken, although I did have several affairs o' the heart, Stuart," remembers Jimmy, smiling. "Three years ago I met a lovely lassie from the port o' Oban, on the north-west coast o' Scotland. She owns and operates a tavern called The Sailor's Hornpipe. It's a lively tavern and is located on George Street, close to the North Pier," explains Jimmy.

"And what's the lady's name," enquires Stuart, who is intrigued by this conversation.

"Maggie Morrison, or Big Maggie as she is known to the

locals," replies Jimmy. "Aye, she is a lovely lady, Stuart, and there is never a day that goes by when she's not in my thoughts," comments Jimmy, smiling as he remembers Maggie's long blond hair, pretty face and bright blue eyes and the steamy relationship they have enjoyed during the past three years.

"I see that there is a Gordon Morrison on the list of students currently being trained here at Bluehill. Any relation, Jimmy?" enquires Stuart curiously.

"Aye, Gordon is Maggie's son. Gordon is only eighteen years old and shows great promise in piping. He has the makings of becoming a top-class piper," states Jimmy with great conviction. "Maggie has arranged for Gordon to be articled with a law firm in Inverness – a town at the north end of Loch Ness, where a mysterious sea monster lurks in the dark depths o' the water," laughs Jimmy, who is in great form. "Young Gordon has been given the best education that money can buy, so here's hoping he becomes a solicitor. His mother has her heart set on it," continues Jimmy.

"Where do the other piping students come from?" enquires Stuart.

"Well, with the exception of Gordon Morrison, the piping students at Bluehill are young men from local crofts, villages and towns. The students receive three hours' tutoring four days a week, and are required to practise each day on their chanters. Teaching of the chanters is the key ingredient to achieving excellence in piping," states Jimmy forcefully. "We teach oor students using the Highland bagpipes, which consist of a bag, blowpipe, chanter and three drones (one bass and two tenors). The pibroch is taught on the chanter using the *canntaireachd*; and while the sound of the classical pipe-band music on the chanter is not exactly exhilarating, we have discovered that the pipers who follow this line o' teaching are amongst the very best pipers in Scotland. To the ear o' the general public, music played on the Highland bagpipes sound much better, but the best pipers prefer the pibroch because it is more of a challenge and allows them to start with the basic theme, embellish it, then return to the original theme, Stuart," explains Jimmy. "I believe, Stuart, that it takes seven years o' practice to become a top-class piper. At Bluehill we monitor the students' progress on the bagpipes, and several students who are not able to make the grade are released. This way, only the best and most dedicated students graduate from oor piping school."

"How about the drumming, Jimmy?" enquires Stuart.

"Drumming standards are also demanding," states Jimmy. "The drumming programme takes two years to complete, and graduating drummers are offered positions in the army or are recruited by the clan chiefs o' Scotland. To keep the level o' instruction high, we have developed programmes for the instructors that they are required to follow. Part o' the requirement is for the instructors to practise for two hours a day on their drums," explains Jimmy with pride.

Captain Stuart Fraser is impressed with the whole piping and drumming programme at Bluehill and praises Jimmy for developing and maintaining such high piping and drumming standards.

News arrives at Bluehill that the main body of the army will arrive in Port Glasgow in three weeks from Portugal.

"From what you say, Fraser, yer victories in Portugal really put us Scots on the map," comments Reynolds enthusiastically.

"Aye, they did that, Jimmy – truly great victories against a formidable foe, ye ken," replies Fraser proudly.

"Wouldn't it be a nice idea to formally welcome back oor heroes?" suggests Reynolds as he sips his Scotch whisky.

"What are you getting at, man?" enquires Fraser with a quizzical look on his face.

"Well, say we organize twenty pipers and drummers to march to Port Glasgow to welcome home our heroes, and along the way we recruit some new piping and drumming students. Wouldn't that be good for all o' us?" questions Reynolds.

Fraser is tickled pink with the idea and agrees to Jimmy's plan to recruit new students.

A meeting is called of all of the residents of the piping and drumming schools. Reynolds and Fraser explain the idea of marching to Port Glasgow to welcome the 98th home and recruit some students along the way.

"Some o' us canna walk that far, Reynolds," states Big Dougie Kidd, a Dunnodian, over six foot three inches tall, who has lost a leg in battle.

"Aye, I ken," agrees Reynolds sympathetically. "But you could tend to the wagons and take care o' the booze and all of our gear on the way down."

"Aye, I could, but some o' us will have to stay behind and mind the shop while you lot are away enjoying yerselves," replies Big Dougie in a sarcastic manner.

It is agreed that at least half a dozen residents of the house will stay at Bluehill and the rest will go to Port Glasgow. A newsletter containing details of the plans to march to Port Glasgow is prepared by one of the local printers, and runners carry the message to local towns and villages. Copies of the newsletter are given to the students to distribute, and some find their way into the hands of fishermen who spread the news to residents of the Western Isles.

Discussions centre around the route the pipers and drummers will take. It is agreed that the piping and drumming instructors will be transported to the town of Arrochar in the south, which will be the marshalling point. From there, the Boys of Bluehill will march down the Garelochhead road, stay overnight at the villages of Shandon and Rhu and the town of Helensburgh, then march to Cardross and take the ferry across the River Clyde to Port Glasgow. It is estimated that the march will take six days and the best part of a day to cross the River Clyde on the ferry. To prepare for the march, Reynolds organizes daily practices. For seven days pipers, tenor, side and bass drummers practise their reels, marches and strathspeys. Reynolds agrees to be pipe major on the march to Port Glasgow, and Captain Malcolm MacDonald is appointed deputy pipe major.

Things do not go well during the first two days of practice. Reynolds is trying to teach the men a common combination of tunes, which consists of a march, a strathspey and a reel and which is referred to as *ceol beag*, the Gaelic term for light music. Arguments break out about some of the standards of playing, especially amongst the pipers. It is clear early on that playing in a band is much more challenging than playing as individuals.

After the third day of practice, Reynolds gathers the men together and serves them a glass of Scotch. The Scotch is named Oban. It is from the port of Oban, located to the north-west of the village of Bluehill. The Scotch is fifteen years old and has a delicately peaty aroma. Piping students whose parents own the distillery where the Scotch is distilled have donated the whisky to the piping and drumming school.

After the second bottle of scotch is consumed, Stuart Fraser, who is feeling no pain, raises one of the bottles above his head and says, "Fifteen-year-old Scotch, lads – old enough to be out on its own!"

Everybody has a good laugh and the party continues into the wee hours of the morning. Band practices are much better after this and there is a lot less argument amongst the instructors.

Several of the piping and drumming students want to march with the Boys of Bluehill to Port Glasgow. Reynolds restricts the number of band members to sixteen, which leaves vacancies for three pipers and a drummer. The competition amongst the students for the chance to play with the pipe band is fierce for the four vacant positions. Ten pipers and drummers compete for the four positions. Three judges are drawn from a hat from amongst the Bluehill piping and drumming instructors. Captain Stuart Fraser's name is drawn along with that of Corporal Ross Noble and Captain Malcolm MacDonald.

It is a cloud-covered day with the promise of rain, but people from local villages and hamlets turn out nonetheless, more out of curiosity than anything else, to see the competition. Maggie Morrison makes a rare visit from the port of Oban to hear her son Gordon play. Maggie is dressed soberly, but richly, in a full-length silk dress in a fashionable style. She carries an umbrella and her face is covered with rouge and powder in an attempt to mask her advancing years. A small grandstand has been assembled in a nearby field for the judging, and an area is roped off for the pipers and drummers. Each piper is given one reel, a jig and a march to play. A mist hangs in the air and it is an eerily cool day for the time of year. Despite the weather, Maggie Morrison and 100 other folk attend the event.

The first round of competition narrows the field down to four pipers and two drummers. The final four pipers are Gordon Morrison from the port of Oban, Willie Wilson from Aberfoyle, Johnny Urqhart from Balladeer, and Geordie McAllister from Dalwhinnie in the Grampian Mountains. These four young men are good pipers – they have been well tutored, and a few come from a long line of piping families. All pipers give their best performance.

After hearing from all four pipers, the three judges retire to a small nearby tent.

"As for myself, I canna separate the four," states Captain Stuart Fraser.

"Neither kin I," adds Corporal Ross Noble.

Captain MacDonald listens to the comments and agrees that the four men are almost equal in tone, technique and knowledge of the pipe tunes. All three judges agree that the four competitors will march with the Boys of Bluehill to Port Glasgow. When the announcement is made everyone is happy except Pipe Major Jimmy Reynolds.

"What are you thinking o', men!" exclaims Reynolds abruptly as he knocks back his beer.

"Well, if someone drops out you will still have your original twenty," explains Captain MacDonald.

Maggie Morrison is delighted that her son Gordon has been selected and shows her gratitude to Reynolds during her visit. Gordon Morrison is also very happy at being selected to play with such fine pipers and drummers. The side drummer selected is Finlay Currie from the town of Perth.

"Thank you, Pipe Major Reynolds. I'm awful glad I made the

grade," comments Morrison with great sincerity. "Can I take it I was selected for my playing, Pipe Major?" enquires Morrison, who is well aware of the love affair between his mother and Reynolds.

"On yer piping abilities, Gordon – and do not get any other ideas into that head o' yours, do you understand?" replies Reynolds sternly.

"Aye, I understand," replies Gordon, who is surprised at the Pipe Major's forceful response.

After a moment Jimmy Reynolds says, "You'll do just fine, laddie, just fine. The only thing you need to remember when you play in competition is just do what you have done in practice, no more," adds Reynolds as he places a reassuring arm on Gordon's shoulder.

"I was thinking, Pipe Major, about the piping school here at Bluehill. As you know, I am an articled clerk with a law firm in Inverness and hope to be a solicitor one day. I have gained a good grasp o' Latin, you ken," explains Morison.

"*Amo, amas, amat*," replies Reynolds quickly, wanting to show Morrison that he too has had some decent schooling.

"Aye, that's right. Well, I was thinking the other day that maybe the piping school should have some sort of motto to attract new pipers and drummers and to let them know about the high standards you are setting here at Bluehill," explains Morrison.

"Well, have you come up with anything, laddie?" asks Reynolds with great curiosity.

"That I have," replies Morrison, who now has Pipe Major Reynolds' full attention.

Morrison produces a piece of paper from underneath his tunic. It reads:

Boys of Bluehill
Motto

'*Altiora Peto*'

"And what exactly does this mean, son?" asks Reynolds, whose Latin does not extend this far.

"It means 'I am striving for the highest'," replies Morrison.

Reynolds looks at the lad and for the first time since the start of his relationship with Gordon's mother he sees an opportunity to bond with this young man.

"Aye, I like it – I like it very much. I'll tell you what, son: I'll get a big plaque made up in Port Glasgow and it will be placed right above the entrance to oor building," promises Reynolds.

From that moment on, Reynolds and Morrison are like father and son.

Sure enough, one of the original pipers gets sick the day before the band is due to leave for Arrochar, so twenty pipers and drummers assemble in the courtyard on the day of departure. Local merchants donate coaches, wagons and carts to transport the men to Arrochar. From there, other merchants arrange transportation to carry all the band's gear, which includes twenty-four bottles of Oban Scotch whisky, compliments of the distillers at the port of Oban. Farewells are said and the convoy, consisting of four coaches, wagons, carts and horses, heads south. On the road to Arrochar, the Boys of Bluehill are joined by other groups of Highland folk, who are also making their way to Port Glasgow. By the time the band approaches the town of Arrochar almost eighty people have joined the group. Some of these are drummers and pipers; others are relatives and friends of the soldiers of the 98th Highland regiments. As they march behind the pipe band, singing breaks out amongst the Highland folk.

Nothing is to prepare Pipe Major Reynolds for the reception at Arrochar. As the pipe band and their followers enter the town, over 300 folk line up along the road, standing beside tents and makeshift shelters. These people heard of the return of the 98th to Scotland and the Boys of Bluehill's march to Port Glasgow.

That night, Pipe Major Reynolds leads a practice session on the pipes and drums and everyone turns out to hear them play. The evening develops into a ceilidh, with volunteer singers, fiddlers and dancers joining in. The next morning the Boys of Bluehill line up to march south. Members of the Argyll regiments dress in their Black Watch tartan kilts – this is the regimental tartan chosen by the King. Other band members, who are not affiliated with the Argylls, wear their own clan or regimental tartans. Playing 'The Black Bear', Pipe Major Reynolds marches off, leading the Boys of Bluehill towards the village of Garelochhead. Over 300 people now follow the band as they march south. The plan for the march south is for the band to play for fifteen minutes, and then take a fifteen-minute break while the drummers play on their own. Every hour they will stop and rest for ten minutes and take refreshments. On the first day this works fairly well. Approaching Garelochhead at dusk, a great roar goes up as the pipe band and their swelling entourage enters the village. Over 400 people stand at the roadside and cheer on the Boys of Bluehill. Some of the welcoming committee are dressed in army outfits, while others are dressed in civilian clothes and wear packs on their backs; others are dressed in kilts representing most of the clans of Scotland. Reynolds and the other band members are astonished. The residents of the village organize a big meal in a nearby field. Tents are set up and the evening develops into another ceilidh. Local Highland dancers provide entertainment. Singers from the islands of Colonsay, Jura and Islay, sing Scottish lilts in Gaelic.

Corporal Ross Noble, one of the band members, visits with his two sisters, Morag and Lindsay, and his brother Robbie, who has come over from the Inner Hebrides to join the march south. Accompanying the two sisters is a friend from the Isle of Bute, named Fiona Campbell. Fiona is high-spirited female with red hair, green eyes and a dazzling smile. Ross Noble is immediately attracted to Fiona. As the evening progresses, Fiona and Ross spend time talking and getting to know each other. Fiona sings two beautiful lilts in Gaelic, and Noble is totally captivated by this ravishing young woman.

"Why don't you come with my family to Port Glasgow, Fiona, and welcome home the soldiers of the 98th," suggests Noble.

"I will join yer family, Ross Noble," replies Fiona, who is excited by the moment.

It is early morning before the campfires are finally doused and the last wee drams of Scotch whisky are consumed amongst the locals.

The pipe band assembles the next day at mid-morning. All of the band members are tired and welcome the later start to the day. Over 600 people follow the Boys of Bluehill as they make their way south towards the village of Shandon. The drummers are holding up well, but the pipers are having more frequent breaks. As they march down the road many of the followers sing Scottish songs, which they bring with them from different parts of Scotland. These songs have been passed down from one generation to another and tell of the hard lives of the Scottish crofters, weavers and fishermen, their work and families.

At the town of Shandon, another 300 people await the arrival of the band and their followers. Entering the town, folk cheer and clap as the pipers blast out their tunes of glory. The people at Shandon provided over twenty-five recruits to the Highland regiment of the 98th. Friends and relatives of the soldiers who fought at Vila Real wait by the roadside to show their appreciation to those members of the band who also fought side by side with their friends and loved ones. It is proving more and more difficult to provide food for such a large group of people. Deer and rabbit stews are served to over 700 people by volunteer families of the town. A local choir performs Scottish songs in Gaelic and English.

The following morning Pipe Major Reynolds meets with his band members.

"It's getting out o' hand!" exclaims Reynolds.

"It cannot go on like this," adds Captain Donald MacDonald.

All of the members of the pipe band agree that, if things continue the way they are, the whole affair will get out of control. They also agree that the crowds have been well behaved and there has not been any report of fighting. Over 100 or so pipers and drummers, whom Reynolds and MacDonald recently met on their journey south, are very good prospects for the piping and drumming school at Bluehill. Captain MacDonald has compiled a list of the names and addresses of pipers and drummers who have shown an interest in attending the piping and drumming school at Bluehill.

As Reynolds stands chatting with MacDonald at the side of the road, a large body of riders appears from the south. They are local militia from the town of Helensburgh. A Captain Glen Grant introduces himself to Pipe Major Reynolds.

"Good morning, sir. Captain Glen Grant from Helensburgh, come to provide an escort to you and yer followers," said Grant politely.

"Aye, you are a welcome sight, Grant," replies the Pipe Major, feeling somewhat relieved.

Grant advises Pipe Major Reynolds that over 500 people have assembled at Helensburgh, and the local provost, Willie Ferguson, is concerned about the size of the parade.

"We share yer concern, Grant," states Captain MacDonald.

"We never thought for one minute it would come to this," adds MacDonald, who is amazed at the turn of events.

"Well, the followers are Teuchters and Sassenachs alike, and they all want to be at Port Glasgow to welcome home their heroes," explains Grant.

Over a thousand people march behind the Boys of Bluehill as they enter the town of Helensburgh and are greeted by a large crowd of locals who line the streets cheering and waving the Scottish lion rampart and St Andrew's flags. The provost of Helensburgh has organized a formal reception for the Boys of Bluehill in honour of the great victory by the 98th at Vila Real.

"My lords, ladies and gentlemen, on behalf o' the folks o' Helensburgh I bid you all welcome to our fair wee town. As yer provost for the past ten years, I canna think o' a finer moment to toast oor native Scotland. No since Bannockburn have we seen such a victory to celebrate. Some o' our own local lads joined up with the Highland regiment o' the 98th and fought at Vila

Real against the French. We are proud o' all o' them. Please join me in a salute to the 98th," requests the provost.

"The 98th!" shouts the large and boisterous crowd.

Chanting and cheering breaks out as Scottish flags and banners are waved in the air.

The march is ahead of schedule so the Boys of Bluehill decide to stay another day at Helensburgh and set out the following morning for Cardross and the ferry crossing over the River Clyde to Port Glasgow. News from Cardross is that over 1,000 people have already arrived and extra ferries have been scheduled.

Captain MacDonald adds local Helensburgh folk to his list of pipers and drummers who show an interest in attending the piping school at Bluehill. Almost 200 names of potential piping and drumming students have now been recorded since the band left Bluehill.

As the pipe band departs from Helensburgh over 1,500 people march behind them as they make their way to the Cardross ferry. The provost assigns another twenty local militia horsemen to escort the large column south to Cardross. As the pipe band marches and plays, people sing and clap. Folks from all over Scotland now assemble behind the band. All of the clans of Scotland are represented in the march south to Cardross for the ferry crossing.

As the large column approaches the town of Cardross, two other pipe bands stand waiting at the side of the road to welcome the Boys of Bluehill and their followers. One of the bands is from the Earl of Dumbarton's Light Foot Regiment and the other band has travelled from the town of Kilcreggan. The Kilcreggan band comprises former soldiers and men who served with militia groups located in the Cowal Peninsula in Argyll. Almost 1,000 people wait in a light rain as the Boys of Bluehill and their large following enters the wee town of Cardross. A great cheer erupts as Pipe Major Reynolds salutes the waiting crowds by throwing his mace high into the air and then rotating it clockwise and then counterclockwise.

The local dignitaries are assembled in the town square and the Earl of Renfrew has come over on the ferry from Port Glasgow to welcome the Boys of Bluehill and all their followers.

Speeches are made and Captain MacDonald is asked to say a few words on behalf of the 98th.

"On behalf of the Boys o' Bluehill and soldiers who fought at Vila Real in Portugal I thank you most sincerely for your wonderful welcome on this cool day. The army's victory at Vila Real will go down as one of the greatest in Scotland's history. As at Bannockburn, the 98th was outnumbered, but like Bannockburn every man stood their ground and sent General Cisse and his French grenadiers packing!" shouts MacDonald with great conviction to a cheering and appreciative crowd.

"Thank you, Captain MacDonald, thank you. It's a great day for Scotland, ladies and gentlemen, and I welcome you all to Port Glasgow. In three days from today we will welcome home our heroes and fellow countrymen," states the Earl of Renfrew to the chanting, cheering and clapping of this large and boisterous crowd.

During the next day, celebrations take place in the fields to the west of Cardross. Tents are assembled and fires burn throughout the night. Dancing, singing and piping continue until dusk. On the morning of the second day over 3,000 people are ferried across the River Clyde to Port Glasgow. A large area close to the ferry landing has been set up for all of the people who accompany the pipe band. An additional 2,000 visitors have arrived from Lowland towns to the east and south to welcome home their heroes. The ferries run non-stop to ensure that everyone is transported across the River Clyde to Port Glasgow before their heroes arrive from Portugal.

On the morning of the ship's arrival from Portugal, over 6,000 people gather near the docks. Thousands of others line the streets of the town of Port Glasgow. The Boys of Bluehill have been given a spot on the pier to welcome home the soldiers. Captain

Andrew Griffin has recovered sufficiently from his wounds and has assembled a local pipe band consisting of sixteen pipers and drummers, and they are located in the town square. At mid-morning, soldiers begin disembarking from ships which stand moored in the docks at Port Glasgow.

The first five companies to step on to the pier are men from one of the Highland regiments. Great cheers are heard all the way into the town square. The colour party directs the men on to the docks and they line up in good order. The Black Douglas, who distinguished himself at Vila Real, carries the regimental colours. The Boys of Bluehill play 'The Gathering of Lochiel' for the men of the glens. When the regiment is assembled, Old Tom appears mounted on his great white steed, Peggy, and leads his men down Shore Street into the town centre.

The second Highland regiment follows shortly afterwards. The Lowland regiment, under the leadership of Lieutenant Colonel Macmillan, brings up the rear. The parade takes the men through narrow side streets and into the town square, where they form ranks. Dignitaries wait to greet the 98th. By midday all of the men of Old Tom's division are assembled in the crowded square. The regimental colours include many battle honours and they are displayed for all of Scotland to see. To Old Tom's utter surprise, Princess Augusta and the Earl of Marshalsea, chief of staff of the army, are amongst the dignitaries. Heather Griffin and her baby son, Grieg, are also seated close to the stand. Old Tom dismounts from Peggy and makes his way to the centre of the stand. His beautiful wife, Augusta, embraces him, and the Earl of Marshalsea gives his greetings.

The Earl of Renfrew is the master of ceremonies and welcomes the royal visitor, the dignitaries, the army, and all of the people from all over Scotland who have assembled.

Several speeches are made and the Earl of Marshalsea makes the following comments: "Ladies and gentlemen, His Majesty George III is deeply indebted to the 98th for their magnificent victories in Portugal and for the great personal sacrifices that all of the ranks made in driving the French out of Portugal.

To show his appreciation, the King has instructed me tell you that his son-in-law, Thomas Campbell, 6th Duke of Argyll, will become my deputy, second in command of all the British armies," states Marshalsea eloquently, to thunderous applause from the large crowd. "As for the men who performed heroic deeds during the battle, they will receive the King's Medal for bravery. I have also a list of commissions and promotions for men of the Highland and Lowland regiments," says Marshalsea.

The awarding of the medals and announcing all of the promotions amongst the officers and men last for over an hour. This event is followed by the march past of the regimental colours, and Old Tom takes the salute. The 98th are a magnificent sight to the eyes of the locals as company after company of men march in tight formations, shoulder to shoulder, with their kilts swinging, to the skirl of the Highland bagpipes led by Captain Griffin and his pipes and drums.

The Earl of Renfrew entertains Thomas Campbell and his wife, Princess Augusta, at his castle located near Port Glasgow. The young couple retire early to their rooms.

"Darling, my father is very ill and has been confined to his rooms at Kew Palace. Many doctors are in attendance, but no one seems to know the cause of his illness," cries the Princess, who is distressed at her father's failing health.

"I am so sorry for yer father's suffering, my dear. I truly hope that the doctors can find a way to improve his health," replies Campbell, embracing his wife.

Discussion turns to Campbell's new job with the army.

"Does this mean that you will spend more time in England, Thomas?" enquires Augusta, and she composes herself.

"Yes, my love. I will be based in London for most o' the time, and we can be together," Campbell reassures his grief-stricken wife. "I will relinquish my position as colonel in chief of the 98th soon, my darling," he adds.

This comment brings a smile to Augusta's face as she wipes away the tears from her bloodshot eyes.

"My brother, the Duke of York, advised me today that he will be campaigning in Europe next year with the army," comments Augusta, who is concerned for her brother's safety.

Heather and her husband, Andrew, are in a loving embrace at their home in Braemar Gardens in Port Glasgow.

"I missed you so much, Heather, so very much," states Andrew as he embraces his wife.

"Andrew, I do not want you to continue with the army if it means we will be parted for long periods of time. I just cannot cope with you being away for months on end, especially now that wee Grieg has arrived," comments Heather.

As they rest in bed talking and caressing each other, Andrew agrees to speak to Lieutenant Colonel Macmillan to try to get a different job with the army, which will keep him closer to home.

That evening, Heather's family arrives from Edinburgh. It's the first time that they have all been together since the passing of Sandy Ross. The next few days are spent in quiet reflection, in memory of Sandy and for Heather's parents to get to know their grandson, wee Grieg.

Later in the week the family attends a christening at a nearby church. The baby is christened Grieg Andrew Griffin. Andrew's sister Isla attends the christening of her nephew. After the christening service is over, the family say their goodbyes and return to their homes.

Later, Heather arranges a dinner party for their friends. Included amongst the guests is Andrew's friend Captain Stuart Fraser, accompanied by Jimmy Reynolds and Ross Noble, who has now been promoted to the rank of sergeant. Sergeant Noble, who comes from a small village situated on Calgary Bay on the island of Mull, talks about the march from Arrochar and the thousands of people who followed the pipe band.

"Have you any family, Sergeant Noble, in these parts?" Heather asks.

"My two sisters came over from the isle o' Mull to greet me," replies Noble.

The women talk about Heather's newly born son, Grieg, while the men are in deep discussion about Sandy's death and the war in Europe. Jimmy Reynolds updates Andrew on the success of the piping and drumming school at Bluehill. Andrew advises his friends of his plans to talk to Lieutenant Colonel Macmillan about a different job in the army.

"Why don't you try and be appointed as chief piping instructor for the 98th, Andrew?" suggests Jimmy Reynolds. "That will keep you posted in Scotland."

"Great idea, Jimmy. I'll bring it up with Lieutenant Colonel Macmillan," replies Griffin enthusiastically as he refills his guests' whisky glasses.

After everyone leaves, Heather talks to Andrew about her deceased brother. Andrew tells Heather that Sandy was held in the highest regard. He also confides in her the words spoken by the Duke of Argyll at Sandy's passing. Andrew's comforting words help Heather get through this very difficult period of her life.

Chapter 23

FIRST COWAL GATHERING

Thomas Campbell meets with all of his officers. The army is camped just outside Port Glasgow. Over 5,000 people are also camped about a mile away and visit with their family members and friends. The local militia is having a hard time controlling such large numbers of people, and although most of the visitors are friendly there have been several reports of fighting through drunkenness, and some family quarrels have resulted in violence. The town provost is nervous and the officers of the 98th agree that the situation will need to be defused.

Old Tom is advised by his staff that fourteen pipe bands have been keeping the visitors entertained, but there are ongoing arguments about which band is the best and the pipe majors have got themselves involved in brawls with one another in the local taverns. Old Tom realizes that the brawls cannot be allowed to continue and makes a suggestion to his assembled officers.

"Gentlemen, it's very obvious that the people o' Scotland are very interested in piping and drumming. The piping school at Bluehill has been a great success. Pipe Major Reynolds o' the Boys of Bluehill tells me that he has 200 students waiting to be accepted at Bluehill. What if we organize a Highland gathering and invite all o' the pipe bands visiting Port Glasgow to come and compete against one another? That way we can settle who the best band is," suggests Old Tom.

"But where would this competition be held, My Lord?" enquires Lieutenant Colonel Macmillan.

"Well, it just so happens that I have the very place. Cowal Field, overlooking the wee town o' Dunoon, has 200 acres o' good flat land and I can provide the tents, and all the service folk to attend to the meals," replies Old Tom enthusiastically.

"And what about the judging?" asks Macmillan.

"Aye, well, we will do the same as the Boys o' Bluehill – we will appoint judges for the piping and drumming, and for the Highland dancing and singing, and I will donate the prizes," adds Old Tom enthusiastically.

"These proposals should get the thousands of folks out of Port Glasgow, and the local provost will be delighted," comments Macmillan.

All in attendance support Old Tom's proposal as a means of defusing the current situation.

The next morning the announcement is made that the first Highland gathering will be held at Cowal Field near the town of Dunoon in four days' time. It will be a two-day event and tents and meals will be provided. The announcement is of great interest to many of the folks who have come to visit the 98th, and most of them decide to make their way west, along the coastal road through Greenock and Gourock, to catch the ferry over to the town of Dunoon.

Riders are sent to the Duke of Argyll's castle, and all of the household servants and people from local villages are rounded up and taken in a great convoy to Dunoon. Big Jock Brown, Old Tom's butler, organizes the servants. Many tents are erected and latrine pits are dug. Cooks are hired and wagonloads of food are delivered to Cowal Field. The militia round up 100 local folk to act as stewards during the Highland gathering. A programme is developed for the two-day event which consists of piping and drumming (band and individual piping and drumming competitions), Highland dancing, singing competitions and field events, including a tug of war and caber tossing to get rid of some of the excess energy of some of the overzealous Sassenachs and Teuchters. Judges are appointed for all of the competitions. Each competition has three judges and their decisions are not subject to appeal.

On the first morning of the Highland gathering over 3,000 spectators arrive. The stewards guide them to their tents and each is given meal tickets for the two-day event. The weather is cool, but dry and breezy. Open pit fires are monitored to prevent fire spreading to local woodlands. At mid-morning, Old Tom formally opens the Highland gathering and asks for everyone's cooperation to make these games a success.

The first event is a preliminary round of the Highland dance competition for lads and lassies. The age groups are from five to fifteen years, and sixteen years of age and over – 100 children and youths are competing. The judges are Fiona Moffat, Sandra Magee and Grant MacKinnon. As teenagers, Fiona and Sandra danced in local competitive events for several years and now are instructors of Scottish Highland dancing. Grant MacKinnon is a sergeant with the Argylls and has taught Scottish traditional dancing to the men of the regiments. As a youth, Grant was trained in Highland dancing techniques at his home in Inverness. The first round of the Highland dancing is in progress and a large crowd is in attendance.

Individual and choir singing competitions are in progress in one of the large tents. The individual competition is for youths under eighteen and for adults. Two songs are selected for the youths aged fifteen to eighteen penned by Scotland's poet Robert Burns. These are 'My Love Is Like a Red, Red Rose' and 'My Heart's in the Highlands'.

For the adults the two songs selected are 'Mhairi's Wedding' and 'Braes of Balquhidder'.

Four adult choirs have entered the competition. The choirs sing unaccompanied. All four choirs sing in Gaelic – two Gaelic songs are to be sung by the choirs. The songs selected by the judges are 'Tha Mi'N Duil Gun Dean Mi Banais' (a quick, catchy tune) and 'Co-Eismealachd' (a slower song with a beautiful melody).

* * * * *

On a different part of Cowal Field contestants can be seen assembling for the individual piping competitions. The individual piping competitions are divided into two age groups: under eighteen years of age and over eighteen years.

Over 100 entries have been received and judges for the under-eighteen-years-old competition are Hamish Macbeth (a retired pipe major), Angus Campbell (Laird of Portmahomack) and Ally Buchan (son of Sir James Buchan of Strathmore). For the older pipers, the judges are Bill Fyffe of Shotts and Dykehead (a former army piper), Roy MacGregor (cousin to Lieutenant Colonel Gregor MacGregor), and Geordie Drummond of Kintai (an experienced piper).

The preliminary rounds of the individual piping competition run all day and the finals will take place on the following day. There is a great deal of interest in this competition and an audience of over 1,500 gathers to listen to Scotland's finest pipers. In the event of trouble, the game organizers assign additional stewards.

The pipe band competitions are scheduled to take place on the east side of Cowal Field. The ground on the east side is flatter and a large stand has been erected for the audience. By mid-morning the stand is full and many people arriving later have to settle for sitting on the damp grass. Twenty stewards are assigned to the pipe-band area of the field to ensure that there is no fighting. Arguments amongst the pipe majors have been reported in the local press and the game organizers are concerned about the behaviour of some of the spectators, who appear to be spoiling for a fight. Although alcohol is not on sale at Cowal Field, many of the spectators seem to have brought their own supply of alcohol with them.

The first morning passes without incident. The Highland dancing is very competitive, especially amongst the Campbells and MacDonalds, who have a long history of feuding.

In the individual piping and drumming competitions, the

audience is very appreciative of the high standards demonstrated by all of the competitors.

At lunchtime on the first day, Fiona Campbell, along with Morag and Lindsay, sisters of Sergeant Ross Noble, go off in search of the Boys of Bluehill pipes and drums. After a time, the three ladies find Sergeant Ross Noble and other members of the band practising behind a large tent. The band is due to compete in the mid-afternoon and is in the process of practising the three tunes assigned to all of the bands in the preliminary rounds. Ross is delighted to see the beautiful Fiona. Major Reynolds is happy with the band's practice sessions and allows the band members a one-hour break to have lunch.

"Before ye all disappear, lads, it's a dry lunch today – no drinking. Do ye all ken?" asks Pipe Major Reynolds.

"Aye, aye," is the response.

Ross introduces his two sisters to Captain Donald MacDonald. Lindsay is a tall, elegant young lady of sixteen years, with blue eyes and long blond hair. Morag, on the other hand, is shorter, with dark hair and stunning black eyes. Within minutes Lindsay and her older sister Morag are in deep conversation with Captain MacDonald.

Fiona and Ross slip away and find a quiet wooded area where they kiss and embrace. Fiona is a ravishing young woman and Ross cannot control himself, such is his passion for the vivacious Fiona. They find a secluded area under a large tree and for half an hour Ross makes passionate love to the beautiful and vivacious Fiona.

As they rest quietly on the grass, Ross realizes that it is time to return to the practice session, but Fiona is deeply aroused and does not let him leave. It takes all of Ross's strength and willpower to resist Fiona's advances.

Major Reynolds is annoyed when Noble comes running back across the field to join the band.

"Y'are late. I suppose you have been drinking, Noble," states Reynolds sarcastically.

"No, no, Pipe Major, I was visiting my sisters," replies Noble sheepishly.

The results of the preliminary rounds of the Highland dancing are well received by a knowledgeable audience. Ten youths, male and female, are selected for the second round from the younger participants. In the sixteen-years-and-older category, twelve dancers progress to round two of the competition.

Over at the individual piping competition, twenty pipers in the under-eighteen age group have been selected for the second round of competition. In the over-eighteen-years age group, twelve pipers advance in the competition.

The pipe-band contest is split into two groups. The draw places the Boys of Bluehill in group two with six other bands on the east side of the stands. The bands assigned to group one play on the west side of the stands. The competition starts in the mid-afternoon and continues until dusk. Later, the judges will announce four bands from each of the two group, who will move forward to the next round of the competition. Shotts and Dykehead Caledonia, from the first group, move ahead accompanied by Dumbarton Light Foot, Kilcreggan Pipes and Drums, and the Port Glasgow Shippers, led by Pipe Major Andrew Griffin. In the second group the four successful bands are the Boys of Bluehill, the Isle of Skye Pipes and Drums, Sons of Edinburgh, and Ballymena Pipes and Drums.

The results of the singing competitions are announced. In the individual youth category the winners are Flora MacDonald from Glencoe and Robbie MacFarlane from Stirling. In the adult category Heather Moncrief from Perth is awarded the female prize and Geordie MacKay from the nearby town of Largs wins the male prize.

The judges assigned to picking the best choir, however, cannot agree, so a tie is announced. The prize is shared by Aberfeldy & District Gaelic Choir and Largs Gaelic Choir.

On the first evening, over 6,000 meals are served. Fiddlers, singers, accordionists and drummers entertain the large crowds by brightly burning bonfires. Glaswegians who come down to Dunoon for the fun, and to play cards, find their way to one of the many tents where card games are in progress. Dougie Reid and his three cronies get themselves involved in these card games. Captain Andrew Griffin has promised his wife that he will stay away from playing cards with the rough Glaswegians.

Griffin has no desire to socialize with Reid and his friends after his promise to his wife. However, Griffin does meet up with officers from Northern Ireland who are assigned to the Lowland regiment of the 98th and Griffin is talked into joining their card game.

The first evening passes without any major trouble. The local militia escorts some intoxicated soldiers back to their billets.

The weather is sunnier and warmer on the second day of competition. The finals of the Highland-dancing competition are in progress by mid-morning.

The individual piping competition commences in front of a large crowd in excess of 2,000 spectators. The finals of the pipe-band competition are scheduled to start at midday. The eight pipe bands draw straws to settle the order in which they will play. Ballymena Pipes and Drums are drawn first followed by Kilcreggan, Isle of Skye, Dumbarton Light Foot, Port Glasgow Shippers, Boys of Bluehill, Shotts and Dykehead and Sons of Edinburgh.

Thomas Campbell and the game organizers appear at the pipe-band competition after lunch. The number of spectators has now risen to over 3,000. Each band plays three pipe tunes and the judges rate the bands on general appearance, technique and quality of the sound. When the Port Glasgow Shippers take the field, a great roar is heard from the spectators. Many of the spectators are from the Port Glasgow area and personally know several of the pipers and drummers playing in the Port Glasgow Shippers band.

* * * * *

The first winners of the Highland gathering are announced in the late afternoon. The Duke of Argyll presents the gold medals for Highland dancing to Ewan Macpherson from the Mull of Kintyre and Shauna Stewart from the outer Hebrides for the under-fifteen competitors. In the sixteen-years-and-older competition, the gold medals are awarded to Jeannie Campbell from Portmahomack and Donald MacGillivray of Fort William.

In the field events, the tug-of-war competition finals are in progress and many people move to see the final two teams compete. The finalists are two heavyweight teams from Glasgow and Edinburgh. The men from Glasgow are mostly shipbuilders who work on Clydeside as riggers, millwrights and carpenters. All of these men weigh in at over sixteen stone and half of the men are over six feet tall. The men from Edinburgh include blacksmiths, hostlers, coalmen and brickies. The best of three pulls wins the competition.

The first pull almost results in a tie. Both teams appear evenly matched, but after a heroic second effort the Glasgow team prevails. In the second pull, the men of Edinburgh redeem themselves and tie the match. Just prior to the start of the third and final pull, a sudden rain shower starts to fall, which makes the ground a bit slippy. The anchorman for the Edinburgh team finds himself on a slope with wet ground, which makes his footing difficult. The Glasgow anchorman has flat stony ground to work with and this proves to be the difference between the two teams. The Glasgow team is victorious, much to the delight of the soldiers of the Lowland regiment, whose home town is Glasgow.

The individual piping competition is reaching a climax. The judges in the under-eighteen competition all agree that Donald Lindsay from Killin is the best overall piper. In the over-eighteen categories, the judges find it difficult to decide between two of the very best pipers heard at the competition, Captain Andrew

Griffin and Angus McCall from Tomintoul. Both of these pipers play perfect tunes and the judges cannot agree who is the better piper. Pipe Major Reynolds is consulted and a discussion takes place on how to proceed.

"I recommend a tiebreaker, gentlemen," suggest Reynolds.

The judges agree that a tiebreaker will be held. The two pipers are given a jig, a reel and a strathspey to play. Two additional judges are added to the pool of judges: Pipe Major Reynolds and Hamish McLeod from the Isle of Skye Pipes and Drums. A large crowd assembles to hear the tiebreaker. The spectators for the run-off between the two pipers include all of Angus McCall's family and most of the residents of the village of Tomintoul, who shout encouragement to their local hero Angus McCall. On a toss of the coin, Angus McCall plays first. McCall has played for ten years and teaches piping on the chanter. His forefathers were pipers and the legacy of piping excellence has been passed on to McCall. He has played at several small town galas and fêtes, but has never played before a crowd in excess of 4,000 people and is nervous, especially having to go first. However, he rises to the occasion and the crowd shows their appreciation.

Griffin comes from a long line of MacGregors who pride themselves on their piping. The occasion does not bother Captain Griffin and, despite suffering from pains from his army wounds, produces such a display of piping as has never been heard before.

When Griffin finishes, Pipe Major Reynolds realizes that he had just witnessed the finest individual pipe playing he has heard in his thirty long years of piping. The judges agree with Reynolds' assessment and Old Tom is delighted to present Captain Griffin with the gold medal for finest piper in Scotland – a great honour. Angus McCall receives the silver medal and is congratulated for his outstanding display of piping.

"Andrew, Andrew, you were wonderful," cries Heather as she hugs her husband for winning the gold medal.

Soon Isla, Andrew's sister, is congratulating her brother for his fine win.

The visitors from the village of Tomintoul believe that their piper should have won and a scuffle breaks out amongst some of the spectators. Other bystanders get drawn into the fighting and it takes the stewards over fifteen minutes to contain and remove the troublemakers.

Meanwhile, soldiers from the Lowland and Highland regiments of the 98th attending the games give Griffin a standing ovation. Billy Porter and Andy Laurie, the tough and rowdy Glaswegians, are amongst the Lowland regiment spectators who congratulate the MacGregor for his fine achievement.

As evening approaches, the final pipe-band event is well under way. After all bands play their assigned pipe tunes, the judges retire to a nearby tent to rate the performers. The consensus is that the best three bands are the Isle of Skye, the Boys of Bluehill and Shotts and Dykehead. The judges agree to have the bands play three more tunes to decide the overall winner. The pipe tunes selected are 'John MacColl's March to Kilbowie Cottage', 'Tulloch Gorm' (strathspey) and 'The Duke of Richmond' (reel). These are formidable pipe tunes and will challenge any pipe band. The order of playing is the Isle of Skye, Shotts and Dykehead and the Boys of Bluehill. The three bands compete before a large and partisan crowd. As dusk approaches, the weather cools and a light wind blows out of the west.

The Isle of Skye Pipes and Drums start to play and give a terrific display of piping and drumming. Shotts and Dykehead follow, and their performance also thrills the crowd of onlookers.

Pipe Major Reynolds speaks to his band members before playing.

"Lads, all I want ye to do is to imagine y'are in Bluehill and this is just another wee practice session. That's all, lads."

"OK, Pipe Major," reply the members of the band.

The younger band members, who joined as students, worship the veterans and follow their lead. Wee Willie Wilson from Aberfoyle is one of the newcomers to the pipe band and is extremely nervous. Pipe Major Reynolds recognizes Wilson's nervousness and has a word with the eighteen-year-old prior to the start of playing to settle the young man down.

"You'll do just fine, laddie. Just follow my lead," reassures Reynolds as he pats Wilson on the back.

The master of ceremonies introduces the final band and the Boys of Bluehill march proudly on to the field. Pipe Major Reynolds is a master at giving direction to band members and handles his mace with precision, which instils confidence to all of the members of the pipe band.

When the Boys of Bluehill complete their set, loud cheers are heard over the din of the crowd of onlookers in response to a display of piping-and-drumming excellence. The judges are unanimous. Placed first is the Boys of Bluehill; second is the Isle of Skye; and third place is given to Shotts and Dykehead Caledonia. It is a very popular decision and Old Tom is thrilled that half of Reynolds' band members have served with the Argylls.

When the trophy is presented to Pipe Major Reynolds, soldiers in attendance shout, "98th! 98th!" in recognition of those soldiers who have served with the Argylls.

Old Tom closes the first Highland gathering at dusk. The games have been a success and, to everyone's delight, Old Tom announces that he will sponsor next year's gathering, which will again be held at Cowal Field during the month of August and will be open to all of Scotland.

Chapter 24

OLD TOM'S FAREWELL

"Well Andrew, have ye made up yer mind about meeting with Lieutenant Colonel Macmillan about a new posting in the army?" asks Heather anxiously.

"Aye, my dear, I have requested a meeting for this week to talk to our regimental leader."

A few days later Captain Andrew Griffin meets with Lieutenant Colonel Macmillan of the Lowland regiment to discuss his request for a new position in the army. After the battle of Vila Real, the 98th has recruited a large number of new recruits, several of whom have some piping experience, but it is evident to Macmillan that a considerable amount of tutoring will be required to keep the regimental piping standard up to par.

"Sir, I am requesting being posted to a different job in the army. As you know, Heather's brother Sandy Ross died after the battle of Vila Real, and my wife is very unhappy with me staying in my present position with the army," explains Griffin.

"I understand, Captain. As you know, the army wants to keep the piping and drumming standards high. The senior officers of the 98th feel it's very good for morale if we have top-class pipers and drummers in our regiments. So what I can do for ye, Griffin, is offer you a new position teaching piping and drumming at Port Glasgow Barracks. You will retain your current rank as captain," adds Macmillan, who does not want to lose Griffin.

Griffin is delighted with the new arrangement and thanks his colonel. Then he rushes home to tell Heather the news of his appointment.

"I am so happy," says Heather as she embraces her husband and feels a great weight of worry fall from her shoulders.

With the passing of her brother and Andrew's serious battle wounds she feels she cannot bear another loss in the family.

A piping school for new army recruits is to be set up in Port Glasgow Barracks. The barracks are part of a gift donated by the Earl of Renfrew and consist of a series of older buildings located in the west end of the town. The Earl of Renfrew agrees to renovate the buildings, which are to be used as a training facility for the new army recruits. The renovations will provide sleeping accommodation for up to 150 men, a large mess, rooms for training new recruits and ten acres of flat land to act as a parade ground for drilling the recruits. The renovations will be ready in the New Year and a Major Ronnie MacKinnon will be the commanding officer. MacKinnon fought side by side with Lieutenant Colonel Macmillan in Portugal. After MacKinnon's arrival, Griffin will officially become the chief army piper for the 98th and retain the rank of captain.

A meeting of senior army officers is held in London to discuss who will be appointed as the Duke of Argyll's successor as colonel-in-chief of the 98th. The two names on the shortlist are Lieutenant Colonel Macmillan and Lieutenant Colonel Gregor MacGregor. Both officers are described as competent and capable of performing the job. Macmillan has the seniority with the army, but other considerations are tabled for discussion. One of the points made by Thomas Campbell is the importance of improving the relationship between the soldiers of the two Highland regiments and the Lowland regiment. Campbell recommends the job be given to Lieutenant Colonel MacGregor, who is older than Macmillan, and when MacGregor retires from the army the leadership should pass to Macmillan. After a lengthy discussion the senior officers vote, and on a split decision Lieutenant Colonel Gregor MacGregor is nominated as colonel-in-chief of the 98th. The King approves the recommendation made by senior officers of the army.

Lieutenant Colonel MacGregor is formally appointed as Old Tom's successor as colonel-in-chief of the 98th, and the change in command is scheduled for the New Year. Major Archie Robertson will become lieutenant colonel of the first Highland regiment of the 98th. Robertson fought in the American colonies for several years and has just returned home to Scotland to finish off his career in the army before taking retirement. The news is well received amongst the clan chiefs of Scotland, including Clan MacDonald.

"We expect great things of you, Captain Griffin," states Lieutenant Colonel Macmillan. "You proved at Cowal Field that you are the best piper in all of Scotland. Your challenge now is to train the new men to the same standard. Winning at Cowal Field is our objective," continues Macmillan.

"I'll do my very best, sir," replies Griffin, who is very happy with the new job and the location of the army barracks, which is close to his home in Braemar Gardens.

Heather is delighted with the news and relieved that her husband will not have to travel abroad with the army. She advises Andrew that they have been invited to the Duke of Argyll's Hogmanay party at his castle in Argyll on 31 December 1796.

Princess Augusta is extremely excited as she greets her husband at their castle in Argyll.

"My love, my love, I have wonderful news," she says with great joy. "We are having a baby."

Campbell is so happy that he picks up his wife and spins her round a few times before gently placing her feet back on the ground.

"My wee darling, I am so happy," cries Campbell.

The young newly-weds dance around the room and when Big Jock Brown enters to announce dinner is ready Campbell tells his trusted butler the news.

"Tell the staff, Brown, and have a wee celebration tonight. Feel free to break open a few bottles o' my best Scotch and have a toast with the staff," says Campbell excitedly.

"I thank you, My Lord – we'll do just that. And congratulations on behalf o' all the staff," replies Jock Brown.

It is a joyous Christmas for the Campbells. Princess Augusta is a very happy young lady and she celebrates Christmas by giving all of the servants special gifts. The young princess is kept busy making arrangements for the ceilidh on Hogmanay – 200 guests are invited, and to her amazement her older brother, Prince Frederick, agrees to come up from London with the Earl of Marshalsea. Thomas Campbell keeps busy before Christmas completing all of his duties as colonel-in-chief of the 98th. It has been a glorious year for the men of the 98th and the regimental colours tell the story of all of the battle honours won. The 98th under Campbell's leadership have become famous.

The King has formed other Scottish regiments. The Cameron Highlanders and the Gordon Highlanders have been raised. Allan Cameron of Erracht, who served in America, has returned home and helped raise the Cameron Highlanders. The Gordon Highlanders are also formed with the assistance of Jane, Duchess of Gordon, and the regiment marches to the pipe music 'The Gordons' March'. By the beginning of 1797, the Scottish Highlanders are becoming a significant part of the British Army, and it is against this setting that Old Tom assumes his appointment as deputy chief of the army.

The celebration on 31 December 1796 is a Hogmanay to remember. Princess Augusta invites all of the senior officers of the 98th and the lower ranks who received medals for bravery in the Portuguese Campaign. During the banquet, Campbell, who is dressed in Scottish garb, gives an emotional farewell dinner speech to the members of the 98th who are in attendance.

"You will be in good hands, men, under the capable leadership o' Colonel Gregor MacGregor, who fought by yer side in Portugal. I know you will no let him down when the fighting starts again," says Old Tom confidently. "Many of you distinguished yerselves at Vila Real and won the King's Medal for bravery. I am proud of all of my soldiers. It has been a great honour to have served with you. Highlanders and Sassenachs fought shoulder to shoulder – one army, one great nation," states Old Tom, who is now very emotional and has tears in his eyes.

The Argylls give their departing colonel-in-chief a standing ovation and shouts of "Old Tom, Old Tom," can be heard all throughout the great hall.

The Earl of Marshalsea addresses the gathering and introduces Prince Frederick, heir to the throne. Prince Frederick gives a toast to his brother-in-law, the Duke of Argyll.

After the meal and formalities complete, Scottish traditional dancing commences. Because there are so many of the officer core in attendance from the 98th, eight male officers from the 98th dance many of the eightsome reels together and there are some wild scenes on the dance floor. Participating in one of the reels is Captain Andrew Griffin and his wife, Heather, Sergeant Ross Noble and Fiona Campbell, Princess Augusta and Old Tom, and Colonel MacGregor and his wife, Mary. Ross Noble advises the dance party that he and Fiona are engaged and will marry early in the New Year. The dance party offer their congratulations.

After the reel is finished a waltz is announced. Thomas Campbell and his wife take to the floor and lead the dancing to the beautiful melody of 'Lovely Stornaway', a personal favourite of the Duke's.

The ceilidh lasts until well after midnight. When the last reel has been completed the remaining guests assemble around the dance floor in a large circle to close out a wonderful evening. Guests join hands and sing 'Auld Lang Syne', written by Robert Burns, the poet. Those officers from the 98th in attendance are in full voice, and the evening finishes with three great cheers of "Hip hip and hurrah!" Hogmanay, in Scotland, continues to be a major social event.

Chapter 25

BIRTHS AND DEATH

The opening of the army barracks on the west side of Port Glasgow gives the town an added importance. By 1802 the barracks in Port Glasgow can accommodate over 150 soldiers in training. Andrew Griffin is now in his fifth year as chief army piper of the 98th at Port Glasgow Barracks. He has been promoted to the rank of major at the recommendation of Ronnie MacKinnon, the barracks commander. MacKinnon, for his part, has been elevated to the rank of lieutenant colonel as a result of additional responsibilities associated with the running of Port Glasgow Barracks. During his five years at Port Glasgow Barracks, Griffin has trained hundreds of army pipers. Because pipers and drummers lead the army's assaults during battles, the number of deaths reported amongst army pipers and drummers is very high. Some of the army pipers and drummers who survive their wounds in battle end up at Bluehill.

Heather Griffin has given birth to two additional children, Roy and Annie. Roy is three and wee Annie is one year old, while their older brother, Grieg, is now six years old. Grieg shows a great interest in ships and constantly makes requests to go down to the Port Glasgow docks to see the great sailing ships, which bring cargoes from all over the world for the British public. Because Andrew teaches piping during the day and also gives private lessons in the evenings to some students, or is at The Tickled Trout Inn playing cards, Grieg's requests fall to Heather. Grieg's younger brother, Roy, enjoys hearing his father play the bagpipes, while wee Annie, like her Aunt Isla, loves animals.

For the past year Andrew's mother, Mary, has been unwell, and this is a great cause of concern to Andrew and Isla. Andrew visits his mother whenever he can and Isla travels from Ayrshire to Port Glasgow to visit her sick mother while living at the Griffins' home at Braemar Gardens. The family physician, Dr. Purdie, advises Andrew and Isla that their mother may not have long to live.

On 5 May 1802, Mary Griffin dies peacefully at a hospital in Port Glasgow. Andrew arranges a funeral service for his deceased mother. The funeral is held on a sunny afternoon in May. The service is led by a friend of the family, the Reverend Donald Macbeth. Many members of the Clan MacGregor attend, including some of Mary Griffin's old friends from Glenstrae in the Highlands of Scotland, where Mary grew up. Isla, Andrew's sister, is heartbroken at the death of her mother. At the wake following the funeral service, Isla is so distressed that she has to retire to bed. Heather does her best to comfort her sister-in-law. Out of respect for Major Griffin and Colonel Gregor MacGregor, the Duke of Argyll attends the funeral. Thomas Campbell has been visiting Inveraray in the north and has donated a large sum of money to the local hospital to increase the number of beds. The number of wounded soldiers visiting Bluehill has been on the rise, and this has put a great strain on Inveraray Hospital, where most of the more seriously injured soldiers seek a bed and services of the local surgeon.

"Please accept my deepest sympathies, Major Griffin, on your great loss," said Thomas Campbell with great empathy.

"Thank you, Ma Lord; ma mother will be greatly missed by the family," replies Griffin. "I understand that you are sponsoring a new wing at Inveraray Hospital, and the new wing will be named after yer wife, Princess Augusta," comments Griffin.

"Yes, Dr. Ronald Sinclair, resident surgeon, was very kind to make this recommendation to the local committee who run the hospital," replies Campbell.

The discussion then turns to piping.

"The Boys of Bluehill pipes and drums, Andrew, have won

the pipe-band championship during the past five years at Cowal Field. I'm hoping your army pipers and drummers can reverse that trend, Andrew," says Campbell, who is anxious for a victory for the 98th.

"We have an excellent pipe band this year, sir. I'm sure our boys will win gold this time round," replies Andrew with confidence.

While Andrew and Thomas Campbell exchange their news, Heather has excused herself and returns to her home at Braemar Gardens, where Isla is resting.

"How are you, Isla my dear?" enquires Heather as she enters Isla's bedroom.

"Thanks, Heather. I'm feeling a wee bit better. My mother's passing was a great shock," replies Isla, crying into her handkerchief.

"Can I get you anything to help comfort you, Isla."

"No thanks, Heather. Mrs Beattie has been in several times with cups o' tea and handkerchiefs." After a while Isla sits up in her bed and advises Heather that she is feeling better. "How are your guests, Heather? You will be missed."

"Gregor and Andrew are looking after them. You've not to worry – everything is under control," replies Heather reassuringly.

"And how are you doing, Heather? You look tired," comments Isla, holding Heather's hand. "It must be a strain with the three children to look after, Heather?"

At first Heather looks away from her sister-in-law, not wanting to cause her any more concern.

"Is everything OK, Heather?" asks Isla, sensing that something is bothering her sister-in-law.

"Well, it's – it's, Andrew, Isla," replies Heather with a stammer, not wanting to make eye contact with Isla.

"Is Andrew not keeping well, Heather?"

"Isla, I have been anxious to talk to someone for some time," replies Heather softly with tears in her eyes.

"Do you feel like talking to me about it now?" asks Isla gently, holding Heather's hand.

"For some time now I have been unhappy, Isla," says Heather hesitatingly, trying to gather enough strength to continue. "Over the past few years Andrew has spent more and more time away from home. Wee Annie always asks for her daddy. If it's no piping, it's The Tickled Trout Inn, where Andrew spends hours playing at cards and gambling. Our boys need their dad at home and I have tried so many times to discourage card playing, but I am afraid it's become an obsession with Andrew, Isla," says Heather, now openly sobbing.

"There now, don't distress yourself, Heather," said Isla, sitting up in bed and holding Heather, whose tears are now rolling down her beautiful face.

"What should I do, Isla? What should I do?"

It takes Isla almost half an hour to assist her sister-in-law in gaining her composure.

"Look, what if I stayed on for a few more days and we can have a proper talk?" suggests Isla.

"Oh, thank you, Isla – thank you so much," replies Heather, hugging Isla.

Chapter 26

FAMILY SUPPORT

The guests depart from the wake and Andrew and his cousin Gregor return home to Braemar Gardens. Gregor stays with the Griffin family for another day then departs to attend to pressing army business.

Andrew Griffin returns to work, which enables Heather and Isla to spend some intimate time together.

"It was when Andrew returned from Portugal that I really began to notice that he spent very little time at home. As I was nursing Grieg I did not think about it too much, but after the births of Roy and wee Annie I was having trouble coping with the three children on my own, Isla," explains Heather.

"I have Mrs Beattie and her sister-in-law to help around the house, but I soon realized that I needed Andrew to spend time with the boys. Grieg hardly knows his dad, and Roy is so keen for his dad to teach him how to play the chanter. Wee Annie cries going to bed at night, asking for her dad to tuck her in," continues Heather sadly.

"Have you had a talk with Andrew about the children, Heather?" asks Isla, who is surprised to hear Heather's comments as she never suspected her sister-in-law was unhappy.

"I've tried several times to talk to Andrew about the children's needs, but he is so preoccupied with his piping and cards."

"When was the last time that the family had a holiday?" enquires Isla.

"The only family holiday that we have had was visiting

my mother and father in Prestonpans for my dad's birthday," replies Heather.

"Well, look here, it's about time that you all had a holiday in the country, and I know the very place," says Isla excitedly.

"Where would that be, Isla?" enquires Heather as she uses her sodden handkerchief to dry her eyes.

"At my farm in Ayrshire, of course. The children will love spending time with the animals and we could go swimming," replies Isla.

"That's so very kind of you, Isla, and such a good idea for Andrew to spend uninterrupted time with the family," replies Heather, who has now broken into a smile with the thought of a holiday.

"That's settled. I will talk to my brother and convince him that a holiday is a good idea," states Isla in an assertive tone of voice.

Chapter 27

FAMILY HOLIDAY

The next day Isla and her brother Andrew have a talk and after a few minutes Andrew reluctantly agrees to his sister's invitation.

The children are very excited when they hear the news about the holiday. Arrangements are made and Andrew's request to his colonel for time off work is approved.

At the end of May 1802, the Griffin family takes a well-earned holiday and travel by coach to the south-west of Scotland by way of the coastal town of Largs to visit Andrew and Ross's farm. The farm is located just south of the town of Ayr, on the south-west coast of Scotland. As the coach enters the farm the children notice a large sign: 'Applecross Farm'. The farm covers an area of over 800 acres of excellent farmland, rich in fertile soil. Half of the land is under the plough and produces high-quality potatoes and several types of other vegetables. The remainder of the land is used by Isla to breed dogs and horses and also to train the animals. Isla likes all breeds of dog, but specializes in breeding West Highland terriers and sheepdogs. She named the property 'Applecross Farm' after the Applecross Hills in the far north-west of Scotland, where she has a cottage and fifty acres of land. The cottage is her and her husband's hideaway when things get too stressful.

The Griffin children, Grieg, Roy and wee Annie, marvel at all of the animals that roam freely around the farm. The coach comes to a halt outside a large house with tall windows and two statues guarding the entrance.

"Welcome – welcome, everyone," says Isla as the children are the first to exit from the coach.

"Auntie Isla, you have lots of pets," cries Grieg as he tries to pet two scraggly-looking dogs, which are crouched by Isla's side.

Isla's guests are taken to their rooms on the upper floor of the large house, which has eight bedrooms – four upstairs and four downstairs.

The next morning the children rise and quickly eat their breakfast, which consists of hot porridge and scrambled eggs, compliments of the cook, Mrs Brodie, from the Border country of Scotland.

Isla takes her guests for a tour around the farm. It's a bright sunny morning and everyone is in high spirits. On their tour the children chase chickens, rabbits, dogs, cats and swans, which make use of a large man-made lake.

"We have trout in the lake, Andrew. I could arrange for fishing rods for you and the boys," offers Isla.

"Good idea, Isla. It will be the boys' first chance at trying to catch a fish," replies Andrew, who remembers his time in Arbroath when he and his father would be taken out on a fishing trawler by local fishermen for some deep-sea fishing.

When the children are taken to the horse stables they immediately volunteer to help feed and groom the horses. Isla has several different breeds of horses.

"What breed are these big horses, Isla?" asks Heather curiously.

"These are Clydesdales, Heather. The Clydesdales are bred in the Lanark Hills," replies Isla.

The dogs which Isla breeds are kept in kennels, and the children are thrilled at seeing so many cute and well-groomed dogs.

On their return to the house the children come across cats and chickens as well as rabbits and other wild animals that venture on to the farm from time to time, and have fun chasing and petting the animals.

"How many people do you employ, Isla?" enquires Andrew,

who is impressed at the size of Isla's operation.

"Well, let me see – ah yes, Ross and I have six regular employees who help pick the potatoes, weed the many vegetable gardens and perform clean-up work in the horse stables and kennels. Then there's our cook, Mrs Brodie, a lady from the Scottish Border country who makes the best puddings, and our handyman, Danny Waddell from Glasgow, who fixes everything and anything," explains Isla. "To maintain our home we have two maids, who do the house cleaning and washing, attend to the fires and assist Mrs Brodie," adds Isla.

Isla's husband, Ross, appears late in the evening when the children are tucked up in bed. Ross is an animal doctor and gets called out by local farmers at all hours to attend to sick animals.

"Good evening, Andrew and Heather. Sorry I am so late – it's the job. I just don't know how long the visits to examine the animals will take," explains Ross as he joins Isla and her guests by the fire.

"Isla and I are so glad you could make it down here to visit us. Ayrshire is a beautiful place and the soil is excellent for growing potatoes and many other types of vegetables. While you are here you will taste some of the best meals at the hands of our cook, Mrs Brodie," says Ross proudly as he pours his guests a glass of wine.

In the late evenings, when the children are in bed, tired after their early morning rise to feed the animals, Ross suggests that he and Andrew ride over to a local tavern which is located almost four miles from the farm. The inn is appropriately named The Ploughman. As Andrew and Ross enter the tavern they immediately notice a heavy medley of smells, consisting of ale, pipe tobacco and smoke, the latter coming from damp wood burning on the fire. The ceilings of the tavern are low; the windows are closed, so the heavy odours are more pronounced. Locals gather at a table beside the fireplace with their sheep dogs by their side and play card games. The new landlord, Lefty Brown, who just purchased the tavern, is a retired prizefighter.

He will take over the running of the tavern at the end of the month. Lefty spends so much time at The Ploughman that he has decided to buy the place from the original owner, Old Man Souter, who built the tavern thirty-five years ago. Souter is something of a legend in these parts, but he decided to sell the tavern and move back east to Edinburgh, his birthplace.

"Good evening, gentlemen. What is yer pleasure?" asks Old Man Souter, a short, stout man, with balding head, ruddy cheeks and large silver-grey sideburns.

"Jug of your finest ale, Landlord," replies Ross.

"Are ye new to these parts?" asks Old Man Souter as he pours two glasses of ale from a large brown-coloured jug.

"No, I live at Applecross Farm, about four miles from here, Landlord, but my brother-in-law is visiting from Port Glasgow," replies Ross as he passes a glass of ale to Andrew.

"You must be the animal doctor my locals talk about," states Souter.

"I am indeed, Landlord."

"Y'are very welcome, sir. This drink is on the house," states Souter as he wipes the counter clean of drips from pouring the ale.

Andrew and Ross start to move away to find a table, but the landlord continues his conversation with Ross, who feels obliged to listen. Andrew returns to Ross's side.

"I'm packing my bags, gentlemen, and going home to Auld Reekie after thirty-five years serving drinks to my loyal customers," recounts Souter.

"Why are you leaving?" asks Andrew, who is trying to politely wrap up the conversation between Ross and Souter.

"Well, do ye see that gentleman over there in the blue jacket standing by the fire? That's Lefty Brown, the new owner of The Ploughman. Lefty's offer to buy the tavern and the land was so very generous I just could not refuse him, ye ken," replies Souter, placing a bar towel over his right shoulder and smiling.

"By the way, gentlemen, did I ever tell ye how I came to build the tavern?"

"No, no, I don't believe you did," replies Ross, hoping that this is going to be a short explanation so that he and Andrew can start their visit.

"Well, thirty-five years ago, almost to the day, I was ploughing the fields where the tavern now stands when I came across a large metal box buried a few feet beneath the surface. With the help of Jock Stevenson, the local blacksmith, we took the large metal box back home on a horse-drawn cart. Jock and I then tried to open the metal container, but try as we might, it just would not budge. Finally, Jock located metal drill bits and drilled a series of holes in the container, then prised it open with the help of large metal cutters. Inside the box were two pairs of old silver-and-brass candlesticks, some ladies' jewellery and a well-worn and half-rotted document. I took the old document into my home and over the next few days cleaned it up. The half-rotted paper turned out to be a map of the south-west coastline of Scotland and identified the location of the town of Stranraer and caves to the south. It had the appearance of a treasure map, but Jock was very sceptical and I was not sure. Eventually curiosity got the better of us, and after a couple of weeks both of us decided to travel down the west coast to Stranraer and try and locate the caves shown on the map. For three days we searched the coastline to the southern end of Stranraer for caves, but no caves could be located along the shoreline. Well, we almost gave up the search, but one evening we decided to go further down the coast and it is then that we discovered a series of caves. The half-rotted map was not to scale. The location of the caves was in a remote peninsula. For two days we explored the caves and eventually we came across the remains of a shipwreck. Well, we got so excited and decided to stay and continue the search. Jock and I started digging and after two days, to our utter amazement, we discovered a few gold coins imbedded in the sandy floor of one of the caves."

"So what did you decide to do?" interrupts Andrew, who is wondering when Old Man Souter will get to the end of this tale.

"Well, we couldn't give up and just leave. No, no! Jock and I kept on digging over the floor of the caves, and shortly afterwards I really lucked out, gentlemen," states Souter, whose face is turning a bright red and his eyes are almost popping out of his head. "We dug faster and faster until we reached a depth of almost five feet, when we hit something metal. A small-sized metal box, no less," states Souter, who is now so excited that he has difficulty breathing, and is shuffling his feet with great excitement.

"And what was in the metal container?" asks Ross, who is anxious to hear the end of Souter's story.

"Well, gold coins, sir – lots of gold coins," replies Souter, who starts rubbing his hands in glee. "Jock and I were so happy – so happy. So we took our treasure to the town of Stranraer and stayed at The Thistle Inn on Dalrymple Street for a couple of days and got very drunk. The gold coins netted Jock and I 2,000 pounds each. I bought the land we are standing on and built The Ploughman."

"Whatever happened to your friend, Jock Stevenson?" asks Ross curiously.

"Jock went north to the city of Glasgow and started a successful ironmonger's business in the Trongate area of the city. Over a period of time, Jock bought several other shops and turned them into ironmongers," recounts Souter, who seems to become calmer as he rubs his chin and stares at the ground.

"Do you ever see Jock?" asks Andrew.

"Aye, I have visited Jock in Glasgow a couple of times over the years. He has now become a very wealthy businessman, my friend Jock Stevenson," replies Souter.

"Well, that's quite a story – quite a story," comments Ross. "We wish you a happy life in Edinburgh," adds Ross as he and Andrew quickly move to a table close to the fire.

"What do you make of that story, Andrew?" asks Ross, who is so glad to be sitting away from Old Man Souter.

"I'm sure he did find treasure, but from the way he told the story and his facial expressions he must have recited it hundreds of times to other locals," replies Andrew, laughing.

"Well, the next time we visit The Ploughman maybe Lefty Brown will be the landlord and Old Man Souter will have left for our capital city," states Ross, smiling.

As Andrew and Ross enjoy their ale a man approaches their table.

"Gentlemen, can I interest you in a wee game o' cards?" asks Johnny Findlater, a local farmer who is a regular visitor to the pub.

"No, thank you, sir – I will just watch," replies Andrew, who really does want to join in the game but remembers his commitment to Heather.

Ross also declines Findlater's offer. Ross is not a card player and Isla has not confided in her husband about Andrew's addiction to card playing and gambling.

A few days later in the evening Ross receives an urgent message from Stewart Herriot, a local farmer who has a lame hunter requiring Ross's immediate attention. Although Ross is good at curing the ailments of sheep and cows, his speciality is treating horses, for which he has a great passion.

After Ross departs, Andrew decides to revisit The Ploughman on his own. When Andrew enters the tavern, Johnny Findlater waves him over to his table.

"On yer own? Why not join us for a wee game of cards to pass the time?" suggests Findlater, who appears to be a very amiable type of person.

"Well, just a few hands, then, Findlater," replies Andrew as he takes a seat at the card table.

Time passes quickly and before long the landlord calls closing time. It is after midnight when Andrew returns to find Heather, Isla and Ross sitting out on the verandah drinking tea.

"Hello, Andrew. Sorry I could not join you this evening. Herriot's horse hurt himself by getting tangled up with an old rusted fence and caught the end of a rusted nail," explains Ross. "How was your visit to The Ploughman?"

"Oh fine, Ross. I enjoyed a jug of the locally brewed pale ale," replies Andrew, avoiding mentioning his games of cards with Findlater, and not wanting to upset Heather.

"Was Old Man Souter at the tavern?" asks Ross, smiling.

"No, he finally left yesterday to pack up all his belongings then head north," replies Andrew with a smirk on his face.

The weather is warm and sunny, so Andrew and Heather ride out after breakfast while the children help their Auntie Isla groom the horses and feed the dogs and chickens. Their riding takes them along the rugged west coast of Scotland, where the winds come gusting off the Irish Sea. After an hour's riding they find a quiet spot, where they rest and enjoy the breathtaking scenery. Although Andrew's war wounds still cause him some pain, he is glad to be on holiday spending time with his beloved Heather and the children. It is their first proper family holiday together and offers a welcome break and a chance for Heather and Andrew to get to know each other again. As they rest beneath a large pine tree Heather enjoys the feel of the warm sun on her face and the westerly breeze brushing gently over her body. Heather caresses Andrew and she begins to feels the passion that she had experienced with her husband when they first met. For over an hour they kiss and caress each other and become intimate.

As they rest peacefully beneath the pine tree Heather talks about the children.

"Andrew, I am so happy that you are spending time with the children. It's so important for them to have this time with you away from the demands and pressures of your work," says Heather softly.

"Yes, my darling, it is wonderful to be with the children. The boys love the fishing – and did you notice how happy Grieg was when he caught his first trout?" asks Andrew.

"Andrew, do you know what would make me really happy?"

"What's that?" replies Andrew.

"If you would give up yer card playing and gambling and spend more time with the boys. You can see how happy Grieg and Roy are just having you around them and really getting to know you better," says Heather.

"I really love playing at cards with the lads, but if it makes you happier, Heather, I will give up my card playing," replies

Andrew, who realizes that he had been neglectful with the boys during the past few years.

As the two lovers lie on the grass looking up at the cloudless sky, Andrew speaks about changing his name back to MacGregor.

"Are you now really in a mind to change our name back to MacGregor?" asks Heather gently.

"After talking to my cousin Gregor, I have made up my mind, darling: I will change our name to MacGregor," replies Andrew with a great deal of commitment in his voice.

"Well, in my opinion MacGregor is a far better name than Griffin," comments Heather sarcastically.

"Griffin was our taken name, Heather. We were given three choices, according to my dad: Gray, Grieg or Griffin," explains Andrew, somewhat curious that his wife has never mentioned this before.

"Well, being named after a fabulous monster with an eagle's head and wings and a lion's body is no exactly flattering, Andrew," replies Heather, laughing.

"I had no idea, Heather. And when did you discover this information?" asks Andrew with a great deal of curiosity in his voice.

"After you proposed to marry me, I checked out yer family name at the museum in Edinburgh," states Heather, who can see how surprised Andrew is with this piece of news.

"Well, well, you learn something new every day," comments Andrew, who is amazed that his wife has kept this piece of family information to herself all of these years.

"We'd better get back, Andrew – we'll be missed," said Heather as she rises and dusts the grass off of her clothes. She makes her way towards the horses, feeling very happy with the outcome of the morning.

It is after the lunch hour when the two lovers arrive back at Applecross Farm.

"Where have you been, Mummy?" asks wee Annie, youngest of Heather's three children.

"Yer daddy and me went for a long ride on Auntie Isla's horses and explored the coast," replies Heather, tongue in cheek.

"Mummy, can we go swimming this afternoon?" asks wee Annie. "Auntie Isla knows a nice place."

"All right, my wee dearie, we will get a quick bite to eat and then we'll all go swimming," promises Heather.

Isla has two great Clydesdale horses, one stallion and the other a mare that she purchased from a horse dealer in the Lanark Hills who specializes in breeding Clydesdales. Both horses are enormous – over eighteen hands – with bay-coloured coats and four white feet. Their faces are also white. Their names are Bill and Lady.

The children love Bill and Lady and spend a lot of time in their barns standing on boxes, brushing the coats of the two great workhorses. Bill and Lady are hitched up to a large hay wagon and Andrew and Ross load the wagon with food, drinks and towels and off they go singing songs in the early afternoon sun accompanied by Isla's two dogs. As puppies, the dogs' original owners abused them. Isla took them into her care and nursed them back to health. The dogs' appearance is deceiving. Both dogs look undernourished and lean, but they are both in good health and are very loyal and obedient to Isla, who loves them both dearly.

The hay wagon travels south-east with the sea at their back, and they pass through meadows laden with fern and bracken and cross several small streams before they reach a gently flowing river. Ross, who has guided the party to this beautiful spot, jumps off the hay wagon.

"All out," shouts Ross.

Soon the hay wagon is unloaded and towels are set on the ground, and before long the children and dogs are splashing around in the river.

"It's a grand wee spot, Isla," comments Andrew.

"Aye, that it is; we come here often for a swim. It's nice and quiet – nobody bothers us," replies Isla as she leans back in a chair and enjoys the warm sun on her shoulders and face.

"The children took swimming lessons at the Port Glasgow baths a few years ago, so they are at ease in the water, Isla," says Andrew.

As the afternoon wears on, another family unexpectedly arrives in a horse-drawn cart. Ross and Isla are surprised by the arrival of the party, who come dressed for swimming.

"Hello. How are you folks the day?" shouts a tall man with sandy-coloured hair.

"Oh fine – aye, very fine," replies Ross awkwardly with his hands in his pockets.

The newcomers consist of one man, two women and two young girls. The man introduces himself as Dr. Alistair MacLeod. MacLeod explains that his family and his sister Helen are on vacation and are staying at the town of Girvan, located to the south of Ayr. Their home is in Argyll, where MacLeod is a local doctor. They have been exploring the countryside and heard from some locals that there was a safe river for swimming.

"Y'are very welcome to join us," invites Isla.

The MacLeods unload their cart and soon the two young MacLeod girls, Kiely and Shauna are playing in the water with the Griffin children.

Dr. MacLeod introduces his wife, Margaret, and his younger sister, Helen. Andrew recognizes Helen but cannot remember where he first met her, so he introduces himself to this beautiful young woman.

"Aye, we have met before, Major Griffin. I brought some Highland dancers to yer army barracks in Port Glasgow several years ago," explains Helen.

"Aye, I do remember. Nice to meet you again," replies Griffin, who is glad that Helen remembers their previous meeting.

Andrew introduces Helen and Margaret to his wife, sister and brother-in-law.

"I'm delighted to meet you, Helen and Margaret," says Heather.

Heather, Helen and Margaret talk for over an hour while Andrew and Dr. MacLeod get to know each other. Ross and Isla prepare food and drinks for the kids, who are having fun in the river. The children try to persuade Andrew to join them for a swim; but his war wounds still bother him, so he does not accept the children's offer.

It is late afternoon when the two families say their goodbyes. Wee Annie starts crying when Kiely and Shauna get ready to leave, so Isla suggests that the MacLeod family visit Applecross Farm in two days' time, which makes wee Annie very happy.

Each day during their holiday the Griffin children receive riding lessons from Auntie Isla. She is patient with the children and grows to love them dearly. By the time the MacLeods arrive from Girvan, Grieg, Roy and Annie are comfortable in the saddle. Kiely and Shauna have been taught to sing in Gaelic and are also accomplished Highland dancers. Helen operates a dance school in Argyll, which has produced several champion Highland dancers at the Cowal gathering.

"Will you be going to the Cowal gathering this year, Helen?" asks Heather.

"Aye, I will. Kiely and Shauna will be defending their gold medals in the girls' Highland-dance categories," explains Helen proudly.

"Andrew will be there with the 98th Pipes and Drums, hoping to beat the Boys o' Bluehill," comments Heather.

"Yer reputation has travelled far and wide, Major Griffin," states Dr. MacLeod. "Will you be competing for the individual piping championship, Major,"

"I am planning to compete at Cowal, assuming my health holds up," replies Griffin.

Andrew agrees to play the pipes while Kiely and Shauna dance. The two sisters show their skills in Highland dancing by performing the sword dance and the 'Sean Trews'. Isla has two old swords which she bought at an antique store in the town of Ayr, and these are placed on the ground in the shape of a cross for the sword dance. Wee Annie marvels at the girls' great skill and agility and asks her mother if she can take Highland-dance lessons.

"If you like, Heather, I could take wee Annie for a few weeks and give her lessons in Highland dancing," offers Helen.

"That's so kind of you, Helen, so kind," replies Heather, grasping Helen in an embrace. "What do you say, Andrew?" asks Heather.

"Wonderful idea," replies Andrew enthusiastically.

Wee Annie is thrilled and finds it difficult to sleep that night. The MacLeod family stay overnight at Applecross Farm at the invitation of Isla; and before leaving for their return journey to Girvan the following day, Helen arranges for her nieces to sing two beautiful Gaelic songs. As a parting gift, Isla offers a West Highland terrier puppy to Dr. MacLeod. The gift is accepted and Kiely and Shauna name the wee puppy 'Snowball' because of the dog's white fluffy coat. The Griffin and MacLeod families say their goodbyes and agree to meet at the Cowal gathering at Dunoon at the end of August.

The long warm days pass quickly, and all too quickly the Griffin family are packing their bags and getting ready to return home to Port Glasgow. During their stay, wee Annie develops a strong attachment to one of the new puppies in the dog kennels. The puppy is three months old and is very perky, always sticking its nose into everything. Annie names the puppy 'Totty' after listening to Auntie Isla's farm labourers conversing in the fields while picking and bagging their 'tatties'.

The night before the Griffin family's departure Heather and Isla go for a walk around the farm and Heather confides in Isla about Andrew's commitment to give up playing cards and gambling and spend more time with the children.

"I am so happy for you, Heather, so happy," replies Isla as she embraces her sister-in-law.

"Auntie Isla has a wee gift for you, Annie," says Heather as she hands Annie a basket with the lid closed. Annie opens the lid of the basket and out jumps Totty, who licks Annie's face and cuddles up to her. Annie is ecstatic. Auntie Isla will always be her favourite aunt.

The journey home to Port Glasgow turns into a happy event for the Griffin children, who play with their newest family member, wee Totty. For Andrew and Heather it is a time to reflect on the beautiful memories and the intimacy they shared during this happy holiday. Andrew's commitment to Heather about giving up card playing and gambling and spending more time with the children makes Heather very happy.

Chapter 28

UGLY MESS DINNER

"Well, gentlemen, this staff meeting is to complete our planning for the fourth annual recognition dinner," states Lieutenant Colonel MacKinnon, officer in charge of the Port Glasgow army barracks.

"I have a wee list o' four names, gentlemen, for yer review," says Captain Andy Menzies, drum instructor. "As you see from the list, Ronnie Reid from Glasgow won the individual drummin' contest for the over-eighteen age group at Cowal Field this year. Ronnie graduated from barracks training only last year," adds Menzies, looking around the table for comments.

"Any relation to the infamous Corporal Dougie Reid o' the Lowland regiment?" enquires Major Griffin.

"Aye, Ronnie is Dougie's younger brother. Unlike Dougie, who grew up on the streets o' the east end o' Glasgow, Ronnie was adopted and spent his teenage years with a well-to-do family on the west side of the city of Glasgow," explains Menzies.

"Do we all agree, gentlemen, that Ronnie will receive the barracks drumming trophy this year?" asks MacKinnon.

"Aye!" is the collective response.

"Then, it's unanimous," states MacKinnon.

"There are two nominations for the piping trophy," explains Major Griffin. "Tommy and Geordie Ross. These two lads are twins and hail from Shotts and Dykehead. They are also two fine pipers," adds Griffin enthusiastically. "Tommy and Geordie graduated from the army barracks training two years ago and were separated. Tommy went to the first Highland regiment and Geordie plays with the Lowland regiment. Both brothers have won three trophies since leaving Port Glasgow."

"How can we separate the two brothers?" questions Lieutenant Laurie MacCallum, one of Griffin's assistants. "They appear very evenly matched?"

"It's no easy. Both brothers have excellent piping techniques and, from what the regimental Lieutenant Colonels tell me, both are among the regiment's best pipers," explains Griffin.

"This is tricky, gentlemen; we do not want to offend either one of these lads. I recommend we call it a tie and put both o' their names on the damn trophy," suggests MacKinnon.

All agree.

"For the 'best soldier' trophy whom do we have, lads?" asks MacKinnon.

Major Griffin places a list of three names on the table.

"We have Charlie MacNab from Aviemore; Hamish Macnicol, who hails from the village o' Broadford, Isle of Skye; and Jimmy Hay, who comes from Old Aberdeen," explains Major Griffin. "Captain Fergus, who is in charge o' drilling the men, said that he knows all three soldiers and only Hay has previously been placed on report for lateness," continues Griffin.

"Well, it's between Macnicol and MacNab, gentlemen," states MacKinnon firmly.

"Macnicol is from a part o' Scotland that sends many o' its men to the 98th recruitment camps and to other Scottish regiments. For a wee village in a remote part o' the Isle of Skye, it's amazing how many men have served as soldiers," adds Griffin.

After further discussion it is agreed that Macnicol will receive the trophy for the best soldier.

The army mess is full on the evening of 7 November 1802. Wives and sweethearts attend, so it is standing room only. A young up-and-coming soldier, Sergeant Bill Campbell, of the Lowland regiment, pipes in the head table. The head table consists of Lieutenant Colonel MacKinnon and his wife, Flora;

Major Griffin and Heather; Captain Andy Menzies accompanied by his wife, Shauna; Captain Rory Ferguson and his wife, Isobel; and guest speaker Colonel Gregor MacGregor and his wife Mary.

There is a great excitement amongst all of the guests. The morale of the men is very high following the 98th's victories in Europe. The master of ceremonies for the evening is a Gourock man, Jack Glenney, who works with Customs and Excise in Greenock House. In his younger days, Jack was a soldier and fought in India. After returning from service in India, he became a customs officer and has a reputation as a fine speaker with a great sense of humour.

After the introductions, a local preacher, Willie Telfer, gives the Selkirk Grace. The meal is then served. The bill o' fare consists of Scotch broth, steak-and-kidney pudding, 'champit tatties', 'weel-bashed neeps', and 'clootie dumpling' for dessert. On each table is placed a bottle of wine and a bottle of Scotch whisky. The Scotch is Auchentoshan, ten-year-old malt, soft-bodied Scotch with a touch of fruit and a sweet aftertaste. The Scotch is triple-distilled for smoothness and subtlety of aroma. The distillery where the Scotch is made is located near the city of Glasgow, overlooking the shipbuilding yards at Clydebank. During the meal, Scottish Highland dancers entertain the guests. A beautiful young lady named Helen McLeod is the dance instructor. She has been a champion Highland dancer. Now she teaches young children in the intricate steps of Highland dancing. Helen's dance group consists of four boys and four girls between the ages of ten and sixteen years. Tommy and Geordie Rose play the Highland bagpipes while the young dancers thrill the audience with their dancing skills. When the sword dance is complete, the audience show their appreciation with a standing ovation.

Other entertainment comes in the form of Gaelic singers from the Outer Hebrides in North-West Scotland and from a local youth choir who sing traditional Scottish songs, some penned by Robert Burns, the poet.

The guests are a noisy bunch and there is none more

boisterous than Corporal Dougie Reid, who has come to see his younger brother, Ronnie Reid, receive the 'best side drummer' award. Dougie Reid married a Glasgow woman named Jeannie Robertson, whom he met in a tavern in the rough east end of the city of Glasgow. Both are well suited. Jeannie is a barmaid at The Saracen Head, a rowdy tavern where all of the local hard cases visit. Jeannie is a bit of a tough nut herself. She is one of eight children who grew up in a single end tenement building in the Parkhead district of Glasgow, where survival is the name of the game. Jeannie is the eldest of the eight children. Five children survived and entered the workforce as soon as they became teenagers. Jeannie is used to fighting; it is all she has known during her life. Although only five feet two inches in height, she can handle any lout who gets out of control through consuming too much alcohol. Jeannie served Dougie Reid many jugs of ale during his frequent visits to The Saracen Head while on leave from the army. After a few months Dougie began to court wee Jeannie. Dougie waited for Jeannie to finish work late in the evening, and then escorted her home. Usually he had a bottle and off they went to some quiet spot and got drunk, followed by lovemaking. This pattern continued for almost three years, and then one night Jeannie told Dougie that she was pregnant with his child. Dougie had no way of knowing if the bairn was his, but he took Jeannie at her word and they got married. Dougie's army buddies, Tosh, Laurie and Porter, all attended the wedding and it ended up in a drunken brawl with two people being taken to a local hospital suffering from knife wounds.

Dougie and Jeannie are having a great time of it at their table in the officer's mess. When free booze is on offer, Dougie and Jeannie are in their element. Three other couples that are seated beside Dougie and Jeannie try to distance themselves from the two 'loudmouths'. Jeannie is wearing a low-cut dress which displays her handsome breasts. A blond wig partly conceals scars on her neck. Her face is thickly covered with make-up and deep-red lipstick. For a young mother, her language is inexcusable. As the evening wears on, Jeannie and Dougie get drunk and their behaviour is quickly getting out of control.

Colonel Gregor MacGregor gives a short speech and congratulates everyone for choosing the army as a career. The presentations take less than half an hour. When it comes to the 'best drummer' award, Ronnie Reid steps forward to receive the trophy. From the back of the room Dougie Reid starts shouting, "Good on yerself, son! Greatest wee fella, ma brother."

Colonel Gregor cannot be heard above Dougie's shouting. Meanwhile Jeannie, who is also intoxicated, stands on the table and starts screaming her head off. Major Griffin commands two sergeants-at-arms to calm Dougie and Jeannie down, but the more they try the uglier the scene becomes. One of the sergeants-at-arms, an Ayrshire lad, over six feet two inches tall, takes Dougie by the arm and tries to escort him out of the room, but Dougie's first instinct is to belt him on the jaw. A fight erupts and the whole table gets involved. Jeannie goes for the sergeant-at-arms, picks up a glass and strikes him on the head. The glass breaks and blood streams from the sergeant's head wound. It takes ten minutes to settle things down. Dougie is dragged from the room and placed in custody and Jeannie is taken outside and sent home. Ronnie Reid, who witnesses this ugly scene, is embarrassed and apologizes to his commanding officer for his brother's bad behaviour.

The evening ends with a large circle being formed around the mess hall and the remaining guests join hands and sing 'Auld Lang Syne'.

Corporal Dougie Reid is sentenced to two weeks in the brig and loses his corporal's stripes. It is the third time in his years of service in the army that he has lost his stripes because of drunk-and-disorderly behaviour and brawling. When Reid is released from detention he leaves the army the following month and gets a job in the shipyards in Port Glasgow.

Chapter 29

CANADIAN VISITORS

"We'll have to consider increasing the size o' the buildings or add a new wing to the existing building," states Pipe Major Jimmy Reynolds at a meeting of the piping and drumming school instructors at Bluehill. "There is just no enough space to cater for the number o' applicants," adds Reynolds.

"But where will the money come from?" asks Big Dougie Kidd.

"Aye, ye well may ask," replies Reynolds, tapping his fingers on the table.

"What if we ask Thomas Campbell for some money?" suggests Jimmy Patterson, a new arrival at Bluehill. "After all," continues Patterson, "I hear that Thomas Campbell funded the new wing of the hospital in Inveraray."

After some discussion Major Reynolds agrees to write to Thomas Campbell, deputy chief of the army, and request financial support. Some building estimates are obtained from local contractors, and this information is sent to Thomas Campbell. There are now over 100 piping and drumming students attending at Bluehill and thirty-five residents, twenty of whom are instructors. There is also a list of over 200 people anxiously waiting to be accepted at Bluehill. The fame of the piping and drumming school travels far and wide.

Graham MacGregor, son of Rob Roy MacGregor, emigrated to Cape Breton, an island adjacent to Nova Scotia in Eastern Canada. Before dying in 1781, Graham taught his son Stewart

MacGregor how to play the Scottish Highland bagpipes. Stewart has learned of the reputation of Bluehill from army pipers who were instructed by Pipe Major Reynolds and who are now stationed at the port of Louisbourg on Cape Breton Island, Nova Scotia. Stewart is anxious to raise the standard of piping amongst the residents of Cape Breton, most of whom are descendants of Scottish immigrants. He has a vision of a Canadian piping and drumming school located on Cape Breton. Stewart decides to write to Pipe Major Reynolds and ask if he and a friend, Colin MacDonald, can spend a summer at Bluehill to learn advanced piping and drumming techniques. The letter comes as a pleasant surprise to Reynolds – all the more reason to request funds from the Duke of Argyll to expand the piping and drumming building at Bluehill.

A subcommittee of the army board reviews Pipe Major Reynolds' request. Old Tom is the chair and he considers the request to be reasonable. Most of the subcommittee members concur, but one senior officer, General Trimble, thinks that a per diem allowance should also be paid during the time army officers are recuperating from their wounds at Bluehill to help offset the operating costs of the building. Old Tom takes the modified request to the full army board, which supports the request for funds. A one-time-only payment of £3,000 is paid to help erect a second building or expand the existing building at Bluehill. In addition, a per diem allowance will be paid to the piping and drumming school for wounded officers during the period of their recuperation.

"Well, lads, we got what we asked for and then some," comments Jimmy Reynolds as he completes reading the army's generous response for additional funding to his building committee. "Next step is to prepare detailed building plans and get some accurate building cost estimates," adds Reynolds, who is very pleased with the army's response.

Plans are drawn up, building cost estimates are received and a construction contractor is selected to build an extension to the existing building, which is less costly than erecting a new building. Within a month most of the exterior framing of the extension is in place. Three months later the extension is complete. An additional fourteen rooms are added for the residents, and four larger rooms for piping and drumming instruction.

Reynolds writes to Colonel Gregor MacGregor and Major Andrew Griffin about Stewart's request to visit Bluehill and enrol in the piping classes. Colonel MacGregor thinks it is a great opportunity to arrange a Clan MacGregor reunion, and he discusses the matter with his cousin Andrew, who is very supportive.

By the spring of 1806, Bluehill is taking on a very different look. The new extension to the main building is complete and fully occupied and the landscaping gives the area a whole new look. Local merchants have also built a tavern named The Drum and Monkey Tavern, which is located less than half a mile from the modified army facility. In addition to a tavern and a restaurant, the new inn has six guest rooms for rent. The rooms are constantly occupied. Visitors come from all over the country and also from abroad to be taught piping and drumming, such is the reputation of Bluehill.

Stewart MacGregor and Colin MacDonald arrive at Port Glasgow from Canada in May 1806. The journey had been long and tedious and Stewart is delighted to be greeted by his two cousins Colonel Gregor MacGregor and Major Andrew Griffin. It is a very emotional reunion. The Canadians accompany Andrew and Gregor to The Tickled Trout Inn, which is located on Shore Street, near the dock area and within five minutes' walk of Griffin's residence in Braemar Gardens, Port Glasgow. The tavern is packed with Andrew's friends and acquaintances. Some of Andrew's friends, whom he has played cards with over the years, are in attendance in a small room behind the main area of the tavern.

The landlord, Ben McQuarrie, greets Andrew and his friends with great enthusiasm. Ben is a retired fisherman from Tobermory on the island of Mull. He bought the tavern fifteen years ago and renamed it The Tickled Trout Inn because of his love of fishing – especially freshwater fishing, which Ben can talk about for hours on end. On the wall in the tavern hangs a large plaque with the image of a large freshwater trout and below is an inscription penned by Robert Burns, the poet, which reads:

The trout in yonder wimpling burn that glides, a silver dart,
And safe beneath the shady thorn, defies the angler's art.

Over some fine ale and a hearty lunch, the MacGregors catch up on their family history during the past fifty years. Stewart is now sixty years old, and this is the first occasion that he has visited Scotland. He married Morag MacBean from the town of Halifax, Nova Scotia, Canada. Morag's father left Scotland shortly after the Battle of Culloden. Stewart and Morag have a son named Neil and two daughters, Morag and Isobel. Neil received tutoring in the bagpipes as a lad and he has shown great promise playing the pipes. Colin MacDonald, Stewart's close friend, was born in Glencoe, Scotland, but his family left for Canada in 1760, and settled in the town of Sydney on the island of Cape Breton, located close to Nova Scotia. Colin is a side drummer and he wants to learn more about drumming techniques from the instructors at Bluehill so that he can raise the drumming standards amongst the residents on the island of Cape Breton.

Stewart and Colin are accepted as students at Bluehill for a period of three months. Andrew Griffin promises to arrange accommodation for his Canadian cousin and his friend in rooms above The Drum and Monkey Tavern at Bluehill.

"We have planned a Clan MacGregor reunion, Stewart, and would like you and your friend to attend. The reunion is to be held at Aberfoyle at the beginning of August 1806, just before you and Colin return to Canada," said Gregor enthusiastically.

"Sounds like a wonderful chance to meet members of our clan," replies Stewart cheerfully.

* * * * *

Colonel MacGregor sends invitations out to all known members of the Clan MacGregor, including the family of his deceased brother David, who relocated to France after the Battle of Culloden. David has two children, Charles and Louise.

"And how many of the clan do you expect to attend the reunion?" asks Stewart with great interest.

"About 200," replies Colonel Gregor.

"It's wonderful to meet you, Stewart," says Heather hugging her Canadian visitor.

"Thank you for providing Colin and I with accommodation, Heather. It is very kind of you and the family," replies Stewart.

After two days visiting the Griffin family Stewart and Colin set out from Port Glasgow for Bluehill by way of the Cardross ferry across the River Clyde then travel north on the Arrochar Road, which the Boys of Bluehill traversed a few years earlier. The Scottish countryside is all that Stewart's father had described. Beautiful hills covered with white and purple heather, shimmering lochs, and majestic snow-tipped mountains.

On their arrival at the village of Bluehill, Pipe Major Reynolds gives the two Canadians a warm welcome and offers them the traditional wee nip of Scotch before touring the piping and drumming school.

Chapter 30

GATHERING OF THE CLAN

For over 300 years MacGregors have assembled at the town of Aberfoyle in early August. It is truly a great tradition. This year, over 400 MacGregors travel from all over Scotland, England, Ireland, France and Canada to attend the gathering. There are very emotional scenes as Gregor MacGregor, the clan chief, gives the welcome in Gaelic and English. Tents are assembled for sleeping accommodation on the outskirts of the town, and Gregor borrows ten army cooks to help feed all of the guests. The weather is dry and there is piping, dancing, singing and games arranged for the children. Campfires burn late into the night, and many of the relatives meet for the first time; several lasting friendships are made during this clan reunion.

Children are introduced to their first and second cousins. Each family member has exciting stories to relate and the discussions go on for the full three days of the reunion. Charlie MacGregor, son of David MacGregor who had gone to France after the Battle of Culloden, talks to his relatives about the French Revolution and the Napoleonic Wars, which are in progress. Charlie's dad, David, died in France in 1775. Charlie now resides in Normandy, France, and has married a local lady named Lyse. Charlie and Lyse have two children, Robbie and Lyse. Because young Robbie was born on 25 January his full name is Robbie Burns MacGregor, after the poet Robert Burns, with whom Robbie shares the same birthdate.

"I plan to return to Scotland with my family to live," states Charlie.

"Well if you need any help settling in, just say the word, Charlie," replies Gregor.

"The French Government has introduced conscription to the army so now is the time for the family to leave France," states Charlie.

Stewart MacGregor tells stories of the vastness of Canada, the beauty of Nova Scotia and of the island of Cape Breton and the size of the Scottish settlements. Many of the Clan MacGregor are surprised that so many exiled Scots chose Nova Scotia, and the island of Cape Breton to live on and some of the families attending the gathering express an interest in moving to Canada to start a new life.

"Because so many Scottish families settled the area and worked the land, it became known as New Scotland, or Nova Scotia," explains Stewart to a captive audience.

Colonel MacGregor talks about the history of the Clan MacGregor, especially Rob Roy MacGregor, famous in Scottish folklore.

"As clan chief o' the MacGregors, I would like to quote a few lines from a poem written by a famous Englishman, William Wordsworth, during his visit to Scotland in 1803. The English have their great folk hero Robin Hood, but we Scots have Rob Roy MacGregor. Wordsworth, in his poem 'Rob Roy's Grave' wrote the following lines about our grandfather:

> *"And thus among these rocks he lived,*
> *Through summer heat and winter snow:*
> *The Eagle he was lord above,*
> *And Rob was lord Below.*
> *And, far and near, through vale and hill,*
> *Are faces that attest the same;*
> *The proud heart flashing through the eyes,*
> *At sound of Rob Roy's name."*

Gregor MacGregor recites the poem with great conviction to the cheering and chanting of all of those present as Rob Roy is widely regarded as a great hero in Scottish folklore.

"Ladies and gentlemen, boys and girls, I wish to announce here tonight that I have reached the ripe old age of sixty-five," states Gregor to the clapping of the clan members. "I will be retiring my commission from the army at the end of this year, but I plan to continue to be clan chief of the MacGregors. My family and I will still reside here in Aberfoyle," continues Gregor to the cheering of all in attendance.

"Gregor, that was a surprise announcement," says Andrew Griffin, taking his cousin's arm and walking to a quiet spot beneath a tree.

"Aye, I have written to Thomas Campbell and advised him of my plans, Andrew. I have talked it over with Mary and the family, ye ken, and they support my plans," replies Gregor confidently.

"I wish you the very best, Gregor, in yer retirement," states Andrew, embracing his favourite cousin.

The family reunion finally comes to an end with tears of joy from all of the attendees. Many of the families exchange addresses and promise to keep in touch. Several of the young men speak to their clan chief about joining the 98th and some ask if they can be enrolled at the piping and drumming school at Bluehill.

A few days after the family reunion, Stewart and Colin make their way back to Port Glasgow and stay with Andrew and Heather Griffin for one week, prior to their departure to Canada.

"How was the piping and drumming school, Stewart?" enquires Andrew.

"The tutoring provided by Pipe Major Reynolds and his staff is exceptional, Andrew. Everyone made us welcome, and Colin and I learned so much during these past eight weeks, which just have flown by," replies Stewart enthusiastically.

Andrew and his two guests visit the Port Glasgow army barracks and are also given tours of the Port Glasgow docks and shipyards, where they meet many of Andrew's former work colleagues, who give the Canadians a warm welcome.

During the remainder of their stay with the Griffin family, Stewart and Colin are whisked away to The Tickled Trout Inn for a drink of pale ale. While Stewart and Colin are describing their experiences at Bluehill, some of Andrew's card-playing friends approach him.

"Andrew, how are you? I have not seen you for some time. Where have you been?"

"Hello, Tommy. I have been busy with the job and family," replies Andrew.

"Well, the lads would like to see more of you. We miss your company at the card table," states Tommy.

Andrew introduces his friend Tommy Bruce to Stewart and Colin and tells Tommy he may see him later.

Shortly after Tommy Bruce leaves, Andrew suggests to Stewart and Colin that they return home to Braemar Gardens. Andrew is anxious to leave the tavern. He feels a great temptation arising within him to play cards and break his promise to Heather.

"Let's grab our coats and bonnets and head home, gentlemen," says Andrew with an anxious tone in his voice.

Major Griffin and his family and friends give the Canadians an emotional send off as Stewart and Colin board the great sailing ship *Voyageur* that will take them home to Canada. A large crowd has gathered at the dockside to wish their families and friends a fond farewell. As the great sailing ship *Voyageur* slips away from the pier, singing breaks out amongst the locals standing on the pier and the Griffin family joins in:

> *"For yer no awa to bide awa*
> *For yer no awa to leave us*
> *For yer no awa to bide awa*
> *Ye'll aye come back and see us."*

In December, Colonel Gregor MacGregor retires from the army. MacGregor is sixty-five years old and has distinguished himself in several army campaigns. The army arranges a retirement party for Gregor for the beginning of December. Thomas Campbell and his wife, Princess Augusta, plan to attend the retirement party along with dignitaries from Scotland and England. Many members of the Clan MacGregor also commit to attend.

Over 300 people appear at the retirement party. Many tributes are paid to Gregor and he is amazed at the number of gifts and good wishes he receives. The tributes paid to Colonel MacGregor include messages from King George III, the Duke of York and many other distinguished leaders. Tributes are also received from the soldiers of all three regiments, from clan chiefs of Scotland and also from Major Andrew Griffin, who thanks his cousin for persuading him to join the 98th. Colonel MacGregor is held in the highest regard by his army peers for superb victories in Europe and for assisting in forming one Scottish united army of Teuchters and Sassenachs.

Chapter 31

BELL, THE INVENTOR

To Heather's surprise, the next few years are in many ways amongst the happiest of her life, aside from the first year of her marriage. Andrew is true to his word to Heather: no gaming and gambling. He spends all of his free time with the children, to the delight of his wife. Grieg is achieving good grades at school and Roy takes chanter lessons from his father every week and shows a great deal of interest and promise. Wee Annie loves her pets. In addition to a dog, Annie has two hamsters and a cat. Heather is happy with family life and writes to her sister-in-law Isla, telling her how wonderful things are at home.

Heather spends more time in her garden, which she loves dearly. The briar rose that she planted after her marriage had grown into a great sprawling, tangled lattice on the outside wall of the house.

Andrew teaches piping to a student one night a week; and after the tutoring is complete he has been coming straight home, avoiding dropping into The Tickled Trout Inn, located on Shore Street. However, on this particular evening his student, Allan Munro, has completed all of his lessons and insists on buying Andrew a drink. Andrew does not want to offend Munro, so the two men drop into The Tickled Trout Inn.

"Andrew, great to see you, my friend," shouts Big Ben McQuarrie as Andrew and Allan sit chatting at a table in the tavern.

"Nice to see you, Ben. How is business?"

217

"Can't complain, Andrew, can't complain," he replies as he places a jug of his finest ale on the table. "Compliments of the house, Andrew," states Big Ben in his usual loud voice, which can be heard above the din in the tavern.

"Thanks Ben – much obliged," replies Andrew.

Allan and Andrew talk about Allan's future plans concerning joining the army as a piper. Andrew encourages Allan to complete his plans which could result in Allan competing at the Cowal gathering within two years.

At that moment, Big Ben approaches Andrew and introduces him to a distinguished gentleman from Glasgow, Henry Bell. Bell is an inventor and he is in Port Glasgow visiting a local shipbuilder, John Wood, regarding a project to build a new boat.

"Pleased to meet you, Andrew," states Bell. "I have heard from Ben that you are Scotland's number-one piper," adds Bell, shaking Griffin's hand.

"Pleasure to meet you, Henry. This is a friend of mine, Allan Munro," replies Andrew.

"May I join you for a few minutes, Andrew?" requests Bell.

"By all means – pull up a chair. Are you visiting Port Glasgow, Henry?" enquires Andrew, trying to make Bell feel comfortable.

"Yes, I am working with a local shipbuilder, John Wood, on a research project, Andrew. In fact, I am expecting John at any moment," adds Bell, who sports a grey beard, has long grey thinning hair swept back away from his face and wears a black coat, white shirt and dark-grey trousers. To Andrew, Bell looks more like someone who would lecture at a university.

"In my spare time I play my chanter, Andrew, and at New Year I give the pipes a really good blow," laughs Bell, who has a likeable nature.

"Have you taken any piping lessons, Henry?" enquires Andrew.

"Yes. When I started playing the chanter about five years ago I met up with a piper who had learned to play the Highland bagpipes in the army, and he spent time teaching me the basic fingering techniques, and not to overblow into the bag."

Just at that moment John Wood approaches the table where Bell is seated.

"Good evening, Henry. Sorry I am late – urgent business," states John Wood.

Bell and Wood shake hands and Bell introduces Wood to Andrew and his student, Allan Munro.

"Delighted to make your acquaintance, gentlemen," says Wood, shaking Andrew and Allan's hands.

"We were just talking about my piping skills, John, which are close to zero. Andrew here is rated as Scotland's best piper," comments Bell.

"Oh yes, I know about Andrew's reputation as a piper, having lived in Port Glasgow for the past twenty years," replies Wood as he sips his glass of Scotch. "I also know that Andrew was involved in shipbuilding here on the River Clyde and held a management position," adds Wood, who gets an immediate reaction from Griffin.

"I'm flattered, John," says Andrew with a surprised look on his face.

"The shipbuilding owners here in Port Glasgow are a tight bunch, and anything to do with shipbuilding or the people involved in shipbuilding is shared amongst us owners," states Wood.

"I'm hoping that Wood will build the hull o' the first commercial steam-powered paddleboat to grace the River Clyde, Griffin," explains Bell.

"And how far along are you, Bell, in the design o' the commercial steamboat?" enquires Griffin with great curiosity.

"Well, I have changed the original design several times, but the latest presentation to the Clyde Trustees has been well received," replies Bell enthusiastically. "A prototype is being built under Wood's direct supervision, and if it works out we are on our way."

"Aye, it will indeed be a great day for Scotland if the prototype proves a winner and commercial steam-powered travel takes off," comments Bell.

A round of drinks appears, compliments of Big Ben, who is listening intently to this conversation.

"Here we are, laddies – on the house. Looks as though we are on the verge o' great changes here on the Clyde," comments Big Ben.

Bell downs a double measure of Scotch without even tasting it, and thanks the landlord.

"Cheers, Ben," says Wood as he also empties his whisky glass in a big hurry.

"If we can get approval for the financing, steam-powered shipping will take off and folks will travel all o'er the world by steam-powered vessels rather than sailing under canvas. I've been working on this project for four years and we are close, lads – aye, we're close," says Bell with great conviction. "Wood here will construct the hull o' the paddle steamers, and John Robertson will build the engine."

"What about the boilers, Bell?" enquires Griffin, who has a keen interest in this important shipping project.

"Well, I think Davie Napier o' Glasgow will build the boilers. He's the best boiler man in the business," replies Bell confidently.

"It sounds like a very ambitious project, Bell," comments Griffin as he sips his pale ale. "I wish you every success, Bell," adds an impressed Andrew Griffin.

"Thanks," replies Bell, who notices Griffin's keen interest in his project.

"How did you like your shipbuilding days here in Port Glasgow, Griffin?" enquires Wood.

"I enjoyed working on the Clyde. Those were good days," replies Andrew.

"If this commercial steamship project goes ahead as planned, would you be interested in joining my company, Griffin? We could use a really good general manager," adds Wood invitingly.

Griffin is initially caught off guard by this sudden and unexpected job offer.

"I've – I've never really given much thought to coming back

into shipbuilding, Wood, but yer project sounds very exciting and, if successful, should put an end to the great sailing ships on the Clyde. I'll sleep on it," adds Griffin, who inwardly is very excited about the project and wants to keep his options open.

After a few more of Big Ben's pale ales, Bell suggests a game of cards to finish off the evening. Wood is keen and Griffin feels obliged to join his colleagues, even though he realizes that by doing so he will break his promise to Heather. The three men proceed to a smaller room adjacent to the main area of the tavern and are joined by a friend of Andrew's, John Johnstone.

It is close to midnight when the card games are complete and the players prepare to exit from the tavern.

"Say, Andrew, how about some private piping lessons while I am here in Port Glasgow?" asks Bell.

"The timing of your request is good, Henry. My student, whom you met here earlier tonight, Allan Munro, just completed his final piping lesson, so I can accommodate your request," replies Andrew, who sees this as an opportunity to stay in touch with Wood.

It is after midnight before Andrew returns to his home in Braemar Gardens.

"Where have you been, Andrew?" asks Heather with a concerned tone in her voice. "Young Grieg waited up for you to show you his model ship."

"I'm sorry, Heather, I am so late getting home. I met some very interesting shipbuilders tonight and I got caught up in some discussions about commercial travel on the River Clyde," replies Griffin, turning away from Heather to avoid eye contact.

"Andrew, ye have no been gambling again?" asks Heather as she folds her arms and feels a sudden shiver pass through her body.

"Aye, I got caught up in a game with some shipbuilders and felt that I couldn't let them down," replies Andrew, staring down at the carpet.

"Let them down, Andrew! You let me and our family down.

221

Ye have broken yer promise to me again," cries Heather, and she moves away from Andrew and slouches into a chair. "You promised so faithfully that you would stop gambling."

She sits back, her eyes dilated and her countenance one living horror. She feels betrayed, grief-stricken, powerless.

Heather's words, her tone, her petulant gestures, her look of revulsion, take Andrew by surprise. He kneels down by his wife, silent, too completely shattered to offer even a whisper of an apology.

Griffin receives a letter from John Wood advising him that the Clyde Trustees have arranged for the financing and building of a prototype steam-built commercial paddle steamer, which will carry passengers. The Clyde Trustees have faith in Henry Bell and support and encourage his development of commercial steam navigation. The boat is to be built in Wood's shipyard at Meadowside and will be forty feet long and ten feet wide.

"Heather, would you listen to this?" requests Andrew, and he starts to recite a passage from John Wood's letter:

> "I would like to offer you the position of general manager at the Meadowside Shipyard in Port Glasgow with special responsibilities for overseeing the building of the first ever steam-powered commercial boat. . . ."

"It's a fine offer, Andrew," agrees Heather as she prepares the evening meal. "If this project is successful we will see many steam-powered boats on the River Clyde and, more to the point, on the Atlantic Ocean during our lifetime. Who would have believed it!" states Heather in wonderment.

"Aye, my dear, y'are right. If Bell's project is successful the River Clyde will become the centre o' a new generation of commercial steamships," replies Andrew excitedly. "We're on the verge o' great things happening, Heather, and to think that we may be part o' it," adds Andrew with the type of excitement in his voice that he displays when winning a gold medal at the Cowal gathering.

"But what will become of yer piping, Andrew? You can't give up yer piping," states Heather pleadingly as her eyes scan the many piping trophies placed all around the living room.

"Aye, I have given this much thought, my dear – much thought. Piping is a big part of my life – it's in my blood, ye ken," says Andrew thoughtfully. "If there is some way to keep my piping going I will jump at the chance to accept Wood's generous offer," continues Andrew, holding Heather's hand.

Chapter 32

FAMILY WEDDING

Andrew Griffin and his family visit Aberfoyle in November to attend a wedding. Colonel Gregor MacGregor's youngest daughter, Mary, is to be married. Mary is thirty-three years old and is a schoolteacher in one of the local parish schools in the town of Aberfoyle. Colonel MacGregor had resigned himself to the fact that Mary might be a spinster for the rest of her life. Mary is a plain-looking woman, tall and slim with long, dark hair. Over the years men had shown little interest in her, and as a result Mary had dedicated herself to her chosen profession in teaching. Mary also spends much of her free time volunteering at the local hospital in Aberfoyle, and it is there that she befriended an older man, Dr. Major Buchanan, who is a retired army surgeon. Major Buchanan is twenty years older than Mary. He retired from the army after serving in India. He is a patient man, a good listener, and has fallen in love with Mary. Mary and Buchanan appear to be a good match.

Andrew Griffin and Major Buchanan have become friends quickly. They have some things in common. Both have the same army rank, and Major Buchanan played the pipes in the army in his early days and has maintained a decent level of proficiency in piping over the years.

Griffin takes the opportunity at the wedding to speak to his cousin Colonel MacGregor about the job offer from John Wood.

"It's a handsome offer, Andrew, and to think that you would be in on the ground floor o' commercial travel on steamships on the River Clyde and eventually on the entire network of major rivers and oceans around the world," states MacGregor with great enthusiasm.

"Aye, I agree, Gregor, but I would not be able to teach the army pipers at the barracks and I would have to give up my commission in the army," replies Griffin in a sullen tone of voice.

"Have you spoken to Lieutenant Colonel MacKinnon yet, Andrew?" enquires his cousin.

"No, I have not got around to it yet," replies Griffin, unsure of how to proceed.

"My advice, Andrew, is to first speak with the Colonel and see if anything can be worked out," suggests his cousin forcefully.

The wedding of Mary MacGregor is another opportunity for a Clan MacGregor reunion. Many of the MacGregor clan accept the wedding invitations, and for those that attend the wedding it is an opportunity to renew old friendships and to exchange information.

Stewart MacGregor and his wife, Morag, travel to the wedding from Cape Breton, Nova Scotia. It is the first occasion that Morag has met all of her husband's family. Stewart advises his clan chief that he organized a small Highland gathering in the town of Sydney, on the island of Cape Breton, last year. Because it was so well attended by the Cape Breton folk and other exiled Scots from Nova Scotia, another event is being planned. Most of the families of the clans who left Scotland and settled in Nova Scotia and Cape Breton attended the gathering. Notable amongst last year's attendees were the MacLeods, McCraes, MacDonnells, Mathesons, MacDonalds, Murrays, Lovatts, Mackays and McGillivrays. The MacGregors organized the event and received some financial assistance from the British Army stationed at the port of Halifax. Many of the soldiers and officers in the Halifax garrison are Scots. Four pipe bands played at the gathering in Cape Breton. Also included in the event were displays of Highland dancing, Gaelic singing and some field events. About 500 people attended over a two-day period.

"Congratulations, Stewart. I am proud of you, man – keep up the good work," said Colonel MacGregor, patting Stewart on the back.

"Thanks, Gregor. I'm on my way to Bluehill to visit Pipe Major Reynolds. I'm hoping to convince Reynolds to visit the island of Cape Breton in the summer with his Boys of Bluehill pipes and drums."

Charlie and Lyse MacGregor also attend the wedding. Charlie advises his relatives that he has moved his children, Robbie and Lyse, from France to Port Glasgow. Charlie is hoping to find work at one of the shipyards in Port Glasgow. Andrew Griffin commits to helping his cousin in any way he can.

There are several surprise guests at the wedding. Andrew's sister Isla attends the wedding with her husband, Ross MacBride, much to the delight of Heather Griffin.

Chapter 33

NEW CAREER

On his return to Port Glasgow after attending the wedding in Aberfoyle, Griffin meets with Lieutenant Colonel MacKinnon.

"I've received a very good offer of employment from John Wood, shipbuilder, who will start building the first commercial steamships next year," says Griffin enthusiastically. "I am really keen on this offer, but I would dearly miss my piping, ye ken," adds Griffin.

"You would be a big loss to the 98th if you left," replies MacKinnon, who holds Griffin in the highest regard. "Why don't you leave it with me, and I'll see what can be done?" suggests MacKinnon.

Lieutenant Colonel MacKinnon meets with the regimental colonel-in-chief, Sir John Macmillan, who has taken over the running of the regiments.

"Aye, I know a wee bit about this matter," says Macmillan, filling his pipe with his favourite thick black tobacco. "I had a few words with Colonel MacGregor at an officers' reunion recently and he spoke about Griffin's situation. I was thinking that we could support Griffin's shipbuilding offer on the understanding that he keeps the position o' pipe major with the 98th."

"But how will this work, sir?" enquires MacKinnon.

"Well, we will set up a contract with Griffin and he will have to agree to be pipe major o' the 98th and spend a minimum o' eight hours a week with the pipe band and attend the Highland gathering at Cowal Field every year," explains Macmillan thoughtfully as he puffs his pipe.

"Aye, I see, sir. I'll meet with Griffin and discuss the terms, sir," replies MacKinnon, who thinks that this solution may be a way of satisfying the army's needs and also Griffin's desire to return to the shipyards.

Andrew and Heather are delighted with the army's offer. Andrew immediately sets up a meeting with John Wood at his premises at Meadowside, Port Glasgow. Wood is very pleased to hear that Griffin has accepted his offer of employment and also about the arrangement with the 98th.

"I'm hoping that the piping will not interfere with my work at the shipyards," states Griffin.

"I'm sure we can accommodate both, Andrew," answers Wood, who is willing to be flexible in order to make Griffin a member of his management team at Meadowside.

It is Andrew Griffin's last day with the 98th as a full-time soldier. Almost sixteen years have passed since Andrew's cousin Colonel Gregor MacGregor, the clan chief, persuaded Andrew to join the Lowland regiment of the 98th as a piper with the rank of sergeant. A party has been arranged by Colonel MacGregor to celebrate Andrew's retirement from the army as a full-time soldier. Stirling Castle is the venue for the party and over 200 people attend. Friends, colleagues, Clan MacGregor relatives and dignitaries from all over the British Isles are in attendance, including Colonel Clypton, the Duke of Essex, and his wife.

The master of ceremonies is Pipe Major Jimmy Reynolds from Bluehill, who has brought his pipes and drums to entertain the guests. A great rivalry has developed between the pipes and drums of the Boys of Bluehill and those of the 98th during the past five years. This is one of the reasons why Sir John Macmillan has offered Griffin the part-time position of pipe major with the 98th. Macmillan believes that Griffin can lead the 98th Pipes and Drums to glory with wins over their great rivals, the Boys of Bluehill, and so keep the morale high amongst the rank and file.

The head table for the evening includes Sir John Macmillan, Lieutenant Colonel Archie Robertson, Lieutenant Colonel MacKinnon, Colonel Gregor MacGregor, Thomas Campbell, the Duke of Argyll, and his stunning wife, Princess Augusta, provosts of Stirling and Port Glasgow and Major Andrew Griffin and his beautiful wife, Heather.

The regimental colours are proudly displayed, showing all of the battle honours won by the 98th since the regiment was formed in July 1794, almost sixteen years ago, here at Stirling Castle, the gateway to the Scottish Highlands. Pipe Major Jimmy Reynolds is in fine form and introduces the head table.

A five-course meal is served and the 98th provide all of the cooks, waiters, dishwashers and stewards for the evening. Big Ben McQuarrie, landlord of The Tickled Trout Inn in Port Glasgow has visited four whisky distilleries in Western Scotland, and they generously donate 100 bottles of Scotch for the many toasts and tributes to Major Griffin.

During the meal, the Boys of Bluehill pipes and drums, seven times champions at the Cowal gathering, entertain the guests under the expert direction of Pipe Major Reynolds. In introducing the many speakers for the evening, Pipe Major Reynolds says that he has played the pipes for more years than he can remember, but has never heard anyone play better than Major Andrew Griffin. Colonel Gregor MacGregor heaps praise on his cousin Andrew and talks about how Clan MacGregor has endeavoured over the centuries to keep the standard of piping high amongst the clan members. Colonel MacGregor's glowing comments also extend to the army pipers and drummers who demonstrate great courage in battlefields throughout the world.

Sir John Macmillan presents Andrew with a plaque containing a list of names of all the graduates from the piping school at the Port Glasgow army barracks. Eight of the graduate pipers on the list have won first place in the individual piping competitions in all grades at the Cowal Highland gathering.

Sir John goes to great lengths to point out how Major Griffin has won the individual piping competition on five separate occasions at the Cowal gathering and is the only piper to win first place in Grade 1 piping competition on two consecutive occasions. The guests give Griffin a standing ovation for his excellence in piping and for coaching eight other pipers who went on to win gold medals in various piping grades at the Cowal gathering.

Thomas Campbell, deputy chief of the British Army, gives a glowing tribute to Griffin, whom he has known for fifteen years; he considers Griffin and his family as friends. Campbell provides a descriptive account of the Battle of Vila Real, with Griffin's key part in it, to the guests. He describes the 98th as the heroes of Vila Real for the way they stood against the veteran French grenadiers. The guests are told how important the pipers and drummers are in battle and how young army pipers trained by Griffin over the years helped turn the tide of many battles through motivating the soldiers and rallying the men around the colours, even in the darkest moments when all seemed lost.

"The pipers' tunes of glory have been heard in foreign fields in South Africa and all over European battlefields," cries Old Tom to the cheers of the guests. "The 98th Pipes and Drums, under the leadership o' Pipe Major Griffin, have won three Grade 1 pipe-band competitions at the Cowal gathering," boasts Campbell to more cheering and chanting from the guests, who are now fired up by the oratory and also with the effects of strong Scotch whisky. "Although Major Griffin is leaving the regiment, he will be contracted by the army to be Pipe Major o' the 98th Pipes and Drums. In recognition o' his contribution to the army over the past sixteen years, he will retain the full rank o' major during his time as leader o' the 98th Pipes and Drums," states Old Tom.

There is a two-minute standing ovation and chanting by the young men from the barracks at Port Glasgow, who hold their major in awe. "Griffin, Griffin, Griffin" is the chant that resounds around the great hall by the young army officers, cadets and soldiers. It is an emotional scene and one that Andrew and Heather will cherish for the rest of their lives. Andrew's three children, Grieg, Roy and wee Annie, who are sitting with their Auntie Isla, instinctively come rushing over to their dad and hugs and kisses are the order of the day.

After completion of all of the formalities, Major Griffin and his family visit with family members, friends and Griffin's old army buddies, who shower them with gifts and tributes. It is well after midnight when the last toast is made and the remainder of the guests make their way home.

The news of Major Griffin's replacement at the army barracks in Port Glasgow is anxiously awaited. On 2 January 1811, Lieutenant Colonel MacKinnon announces that Captain Donald MacDonald will be Griffin's replacement. Captain MacDonald comes well recommended. He has been a piper for over twenty years, and his forefathers, MacDonalds of Clanranald, have championed piping over the past 100 years. MacDonald's grandfather, whom he is named after, fought with Charles Edward Stuart, the Young Pretender, at Prestonpans in 1745 and at Culloden the following year. MacDonald's grandfather died from his wounds a few weeks after the defeat of the Jacobites at Culloden. Captain MacDonald's father served in India with the British Army and taught piping for over fifteen years. In the South African Campaign, Captain MacDonald distinguished himself and was awarded a medal for bravery. Pipe Major Reynolds was requested to provide a report to Sir John Macmillan on the excellence of Captain MacDonald's piping skills and Reynolds' assessment clinched his appointment to the position of chief piping instructor of the 98th at the army barracks in Port Glasgow, with the rank of major. Major MacDonald, who is now thirty-eight years old, is delighted with the honour bestowed on him.

In February 1811 Major MacDonald starts his new job at the Port Glasgow army barracks. He is introduced to all of the army instructors who teach piping, drumming and drilling of the men at the army barracks. Amongst those whom he meets is Staff Sergeant Major Ross Noble.

MacDonald and Noble were members of the Boys of Bluehill band and marched together from Arrochar to Port Glasgow in the summer of 1796.

"How are you, Noble?" asks MacDonald, who is delighted to renew acquaintances after such a long time.

"Just fine, sir," replies Noble, shaking MacDonald's hand heartily.

"I look forward to working with you again, Noble," says MacDonald enthusiastically. "How is yer sister Lindsay keeping?"

"Very well, sir. She married, but soon afterwards her husband was killed in battle, so she has been a widow these past five years and lives with Fiona and me here in Port Glasgow," explains Noble.

"I would very much like to meet her again if you can arrange something," asks MacDonald politely, remembering the beautiful young lady at Cowal Field all those years ago.

"I'll speak to my wife, Fiona, and maybe you can join us for a meal one night," suggests Noble.

Fiona Noble celebrates her thirty-seventh birthday a few weeks later. Sergeant Noble invites Major MacDonald to the birthday party. Amongst the other guests are Ross's two sisters, Lindsay and Morag, and Heather and Andrew Griffin. Lindsay is now thirty-one years old, but has the appearance of a woman in her early twenties. Morag, who is older, is married and has two children who also attend the party. Morag's husband, Alistair Moncrief, is a doctor and has been called away to a local village, but is planning to join the birthday party later in the evening.

Lindsay and Major MacDonald are attracted to each other and are soon deep in conversation, reminiscing about the past. They remember their first meeting at the first Cowal Highland gathering.

"You never married, Major – how come?" enquires Lindsay, who has a very direct and somewhat combative manner.

"I've devoted all my time to the army and have served abroad," replies MacDonald, who feels extremely attracted to Lindsay.

"Have you no hobbies, sir?" asks Lindsay in a sarcastic manner.

"I love horses and often go riding in the Pentland and Grampian Hills," replies MacDonald. "What about your interests, Lindsay?"

"I teach piano and have taken up quilt making. I also sing a little too, ye ken," she adds modestly.

"Perhaps you could find time one day to play the piano and we could sing together, Lindsay," suggests MacDonald.

Before MacDonald knows what is happening Lindsay whisks him into another room, where a large piano stands in one corner.

"Now, Mr MacDonald, are you familiar with the works o' Robert Burns, the poet and songwriter?" asks Lindsay assertively.

"Aye, I know some o' Rabbie Burns' songs," replies MacDonald, who is feeling a bit uncomfortable.

He accepts another Scotch from the lovely Fiona who has been observing the couple for the past five minutes.

"Good. Then let's try this one," suggests Lindsay as she plays the first few bars of a beautiful ballad called 'The Banks o' Doon'.

MacDonald feels uncomfortable at being put on the spot, but his great desire for Lindsay brings him courage and he breaks into song. Guests, hearing the music, begin to crowd into the room to witness a fine tenor do justice to a very beautiful song. As he sings Lindsay's eyes and his meet and both feel great joy and happiness. The guests are delighted with such a fine and unexpected treat. Fiona Noble is stunned at the talent of her husband's new boss, and she and her husband, Ross, demand an encore; so Lindsay and Donald oblige their hosts. If the guests liked the first song, the second is even better. Donald's selection is the Robbie Burns song 'My Luve Is Like a Red, Red Rose'. MacDonald, feeling more confident, and having downed his third Scotch, sings his heart out. While singing,

Donald directs glances at Lindsay, who for the first time in many years blushes. The party ends with the singing of 'Auld Lang Syne' and Lindsay and Donald slip away quietly to be on their own.

As Heather and Andrew make their way home in a gig from the birthday party, Heather asks Andrew if they have just witnessed another forthcoming marriage.

"Well, the way MacDonald looked at Lindsay Noble tonight, I would not be a bit surprised," replies Andrew.

Chapter 34

MEADOWSIDE DOCKS

Andrew Griffin starts his new job as general manager at the Meadowside Docks in Port Glasgow during February 1812. Griffin's first week on the job is, to say the least, eventful. John Wood's order books are full, but the project which is attracting everyone's attention is the building of the first commercial steam-powered boat. Reporters from local and national newspapers are constantly hanging around the shipyard, trying to pick up any gossip or opinions on the building of the world's very first commercial steam-powered boat.

Griffin's first task is to maintain tight security in the part of the shipyard where the work is in progress on the steam-powered boat. His second task is to recruit the best tradesmen available in the parish to construct the boat.

To Griffin's astonishment, he soon learns that Dougie Reid was recruited as a rigger at Meadowside shortly after Reid left the army. Before joining the 98th, Reid served his apprenticeship as a rigger in the shipyards in Clydebank near Glasgow. After four years, Reid gained journeyman status. When Reid's army cronies, Porter, Tosh and Laurie, find out that he has left the army, they meet and discuss seeking employment in the shipyards. Only Tosh has a trade, while the other two worked as labourers before joining the army. Porter has been promoted to sergeant with the 98th and Laurie has made a corporal, so neither is willing to give up the army at this time. Tosh follows Reid into the Port Glasgow shipyards and gains employment as a master carpenter. Reid is still married to Jeannie and has only the one child, named Ricky.

Tosh is happily married to a Molly Thompson, whom he met at a dance in Clydebank. Molly is a big woman with large breasts and hips, and red hair – just the type that Tosh adores. They have two children, Jimmy and Sheanna.

"I noticed that Dougie Reid is employed as a rigger," states Griffin.

"Aye, when he first came looking for work I didn't like the look o' him. I told him I couldn't use him, but he kept coming back – three, maybe four times – so I took him on a temporary basis. He got into an argument a couple o' times, but his work is good – very good, according to his foreman, Sammy Walton. Sammy is a big, tough man and quickly got Dougie sorted out. We havena heard a peep out o' him for a few months," explains Wood.

"I know quite a bit about Dougie Reid," replies Griffin. "We both served in the same company with the 98th. He is a nasty piece of work and was on report more times than you have had hot porridge breakfasts," adds Griffin sternly.

"Well, if he steps out o' line, Sammy Walton will belt him and send him packing," states Wood confidently.

On Griffin's third day on the job, a delegation arrives from the board of the Clyde Trustees. Included in the party is James Munro, a retired sea captain who sailed with the 98th to South Africa in the spring of 1795. Munro is now seventy-one years old. Other members of the delegation include the provost of Glasgow, Big Willie Meicklejohn, who is a large-ruddy faced man, over six feet three inches tall, with a loud voice and has a habit of slapping people on the back with his oversized hands. Accompanying Meicklejohn is the chairman of the Clyde Trustees, Gordon Templeton, who is a wealthy and powerful merchant from the city of Glasgow, having made his millions through trading in the Caribbean and Asia. Accompanying Templeton is his solicitor, Gordon Morrison, son of Maggie

Morrison, landlady of The Sailor's Hornpipe Tavern in the port of Oban.

John Wood has set up a reception area in one of his warehouses situated at the dockside. Wine, Scotch and lots of fine finger foods greet the distinguished guests.

After an hour the party is whisked off on a tour of the Meadowside Shipyard. It is a fine day and the guests are shown two sailing ships under construction, but clearly the delegation has come to view the construction of the first commercial steam-powered boat. A separate fenced-off area has been set up around the building where the work on the steamship is in progress. Access to the area is restricted. No one is allowed to enter without a pass authorized by John Wood. The work on the hull of the prototype steam-powered boat is well advanced. Tradesmen have been assigned on a full-time basis to the construction of the hull.

"What about the boiler and the engine?" enquires Gordon Templeton, known amongst the Glasgow business community as the Silver Fox.

"Well, the boiler is being built in Glasgow and will be ready in ten weeks. The steam engine is being built in a highly secure area adjacent to this building," replies Wood.

"We would like to take a wee peek," says Big Willie Meicklejohn in a loud voice.

The party is led to an adjacent building by two tough-looking security guards, who are armed with batons. They also carry rifles over their shoulders.

"Would ye be expecting trouble?" enquires Munro curiously.

"You canna be too careful. There are lots of people from all over milling around the yard and we want to keep access to this area as secure as possible," stresses Wood.

The delegation enters a large warehouse with a high ceiling. The work on the boat is divided into three separate parts. The majority of the workforce is working on the construction of the engine. Design and assembly drawings are hung on the walls of the warehouse. Men are busy testing flywheels, valves and other key engine parts. No one looks up as Wood and his guests enter the work area. Guard dogs are their only greeting. Four large guard dogs bark and growl at the visitors.

"When the entire component parts o' the engine have been assembled and tested, the boiler will be brought down from Glasgow," explains Wood.

"What are the plans for the launching?" asks Big Willie Meicklejohn, who sees this as an opportunity to have his photograph taken and displayed in the newspapers.

"We are planning to launch in May," replies Wood. "As for the name o' the first commercial steamer, that is top secret," adds Wood, who has anticipated the next question.

After many other questions the visitors are taken back to the reception area, where members of the national press are lurking.

"McBane of the *London Gazette* – can I ask you a few questions, Mr Munro?" asks a young well-dressed Englishman wearing a suit and a black bowler hat.

"Aye, go ahead," replies Captain Munro.

"As a former sea captain, do you believe that steam-powered commercial ships are the way of the future?" asks McBane.

"Aye, I think this project will be a success, ye ken; and if it is, the days o' the great ocean-going sailing ships that I have sailed in all these years will be numbered," replies Munro thoughtfully.

The newspaper reporters are ushered out of the shipyard and Wood arranges to escort his guests to The Tickled Trout Inn for a meal and a beverage. The tavern is very busy, but fortunately Andrew Griffin has reserved a room for Wood's guests. The landlord, Ben McQuarrie, has hired a few extra staff to attend solely to Wood's distinguished guests. During the meal Gordon Morrison and Andrew Griffin, who are seated next to one another, have a conversation about piping.

"I will be spending quite a bit of time in the Port Glasgow area, Andrew. I have been practising my piping whenever I have any free time," said Gordon.

"Your job as a solicitor must take a great deal of your time, Gordon," comments Andrew who has taken a liking to Morrison.

"The job demands on me are heavy," acknowledges Morrison. "I was fortunate in having finished first in my graduating year at Edinburgh University and was offered employment with Scotland's oldest and most famous law firm – Ogilvie, Urqhart and Donaldson of Edinburgh. My law firm's clients include most of the wealthy merchants of Glasgow and of Port Glasgow, who trade in sugar, spices, tea, brandy, timber and other goods highly sought after by the British public. Gordon Templeton is one of our wealthiest clients, so working for Gordon is very demanding. The Templetons own factories in Glasgow and have business interests in all of the leading trade routes to the East and merchant ships sailing down the River Clyde. Gordon Templeton is one of the leading investors in commercial steam-powered shipping. Henry Bell has impressed Templeton and convinced him that steam-powered commercial shipping is the way of the future."

"Tell me, Gordon: how are Pipe Major Reynolds and the Boys of Bluehill pipes and drums?" enquires Andrew.

"It's been two months since I last visited Pipe Major Reynolds at Bluehill. When last we met he was in his usual fine form and we enjoyed a few wee nips," replies Gordon cheerfully.

"I was wondering if you would do me the honour of a private piping lesson, Andrew, while my client and I are in Port Glasgow?" enquires Gordon.

"Certainly, Gordon. How is tomorrow night at 8 p.m. at the army barracks?" suggests Griffin.

"Just fine," replies Gordon, who is pleased at being tutored by Scotland's finest piper.

After two weeks of teaching piping to Bell and Morrison, Heather begins to complain to Andrew about his being away from home and not spending enough time with the children. With Henry Bell insisting on visiting The Tickled Trout Inn for a drink and a game of cards after his piping lessons, Andrew soon realizes that he has overcommitted himself. He has again broken his promise to Heather about playing cards and gambling. Andrew feels trapped. On one hand he made a promise to Heather to give up playing cards and gambling and to spend more time with the children, and on the other hand he wants to stay in touch with Bell because he believes Bell's invention will revolutionize the shipping industry in Scotland and around the world. Also, Andrew believes that Morrison can become an outstanding piper if he receives the proper coaching and encouragement. However, what Andrew fails to recognize is that he has an addiction for cards and gambling. This addiction is causing him to deceive his wife and also himself.

During Gordon's fourth piping lesson a man on horseback, wearing the uniform of the postal service, comes galloping to the gate of Andrew's home with an urgent message for Gordon. The message is from Bluehill and it reads:

> Come immediately. Your mother is seriously ill.
> Signed,
> Pipe Major Jimmy Reynolds

Chapter 35

PASSING OF MAGGIE MORRISON

Andrew Griffin assists Gordon Morrison in choosing a fast horse and helps him on his way from Port Glasgow to Bluehill. Morrison mounts his steed and, peering into the murky darkness, turns up his collar and rides north into the damp cold night. The rain, which has fallen steadily for the past six hours, now turns to snow, which forms a dirty white blanket that smothers the road to Bluehill. As the snowstorm worsens, a fog appears and lingers low in the hills. Morrison is now partially blinded, being unable to read signs to Bluehill, causing him to veer off the road. It takes Morrison almost two days of travel to reach Bluehill, because of the heavy snow and poor road conditions. It was a hellish journey for horse and man. As he approaches the village of Bluehill a light snow falls and he feels the deep chill of the cold winter evening. His horse is totally spent and he himself is near exhaustion. Gordon is greeted by Pipe Major Reynolds. Reynolds assists Morrison as they enter the new building, where a large sign hangs over the entrance: '*Altiora Peto*'.

"Aye, I see you remembered," acknowledges Gordon, pointing to the sign above the entrance to the building.

A warm welcoming fire greets the two men as Gordon removes his wet topcoat, hat and muddy boots. Gordon sinks into a chair by the fire and Jimmy hands Morrison a glass containing half a gill of malt Scotch whisky.

"Get that down you, laddie. You look all in," comments an ashen-faced Reynolds.

"Where's my mother, Jimmy?" he replies, anxiously looking around the room.

Jimmy places his hand on the young man's shoulder.

"I'm so sorry, laddie – yer mother passed away earlier this afternoon," says Jimmy with great empathy.

"What? What? You mean she's dead?" asks Morrison in a trembling voice.

"Aye, laddie, she died mid-afternoon," replies the pipe major with tears in his eyes.

"But – but what happened? What happened?" asks Morrison with tears running down his face.

"Yer ma travelled down to Bluehill for our annual dance five days ago, and while she was here she had a heart attack," explains Reynolds softly.

Gordon drops his glass of Scotch whisky on to the floor and leans over and breaks into tears. He cries like a small boy who has just fallen and hurt himself for the first time. For over five minutes the tears flow freely. Jimmy tries to console this young man whom he has always considered as a son. Reynolds is also heartbroken, for the love of his life experienced a severe heart attack in his arms on the dance floor while performing a Scottish reel.

There is a long silence. The only sound is from a chanter playing in the upper floor of the building. After what seems an endless amount of time Morrison sits up.

"Can I see my mother, please?" requests the young man.

Jimmy takes Gordon into a dimly lit room where eight mourners sit in a corner. These mourners are Maggie's staff from the tavern in the port of Oban. After they closed the tavern, the staff travelled down together from the port of Oban to Bluehill shortly after Maggie had her first heart attack and are staying at The Drum and Monkey Tavern.

"It was the second heart attack this morning that took yer mother," says Reynolds gently. "Dr. Ronald Sinclair of Inveraray came immediately to Bluehill right after yer ma had her first heart attack. Because yer ma could na be moved, Doctor Sinclair stayed here in Bluehill tending Maggie," explains Reynolds.

"The Doctor was at her bedside when she had the second heart attack, but he could na do anything for her," adds Reynolds, now sobbing.

Everyone leaves the room and a devoted son approaches his mother's deathbed. She was a handsome woman, and even in death her beauty stays with her. Gordon sits by her bedside and holds his mother's hand. He remembers how his mother had wanted nothing but the best for her only son, and she spent large sums of money ensuring Gordon Morrison had a first-class education. As Gordon sits beside his mother, he recalls the elaborate ceremony in Edinburgh when he was inducted to the Bar and how his mother and Jimmy Reynolds were present to share the moment. How thrilled his mother was at the first Highland gathering all those years ago when he proudly marched on to Cowal Field with Scotland's greatest pipers and drummers. Other wonderful memories come to life in his mind and thoughts as his head gently slumps backwards into the chair and he nods off into a deep sleep.

A hand on his shoulder wakens Gordon.

"What? What time is it, Jimmy?" asks a bleary-eyed Morrison.

"It's gone 9 a.m., laddie. I've made a wee bit o' breakfast for you."

The funeral service follows the next day. Over 200 people attend. It is a cold, raw February winter's day with a sharp wind blowing out of the north. The funeral attendees include the staff and regulars from The Sailor's Hornpipe in the port of Oban, all of the residents of Bluehill, some officers from the 98th who were students with Gordon at Bluehill, and all of the partners from Gordon's law firm in Edinburgh. Andrew and Heather Griffin attend along with Sir John Macmillan, colonel-in-chief of the 98th. It is a moving scene. The minister who conducts the ceremony is a friend of Maggie's from the port of Oban, the Reverend Irwin Cunningham. He has been friends with Maggie for twenty years and helped her through her grieving period when her husband died. Pipe Major Reynolds, Maggie's best friend and lover, gives the eulogy.

"I can only tell you a' that Maggie Morrison meant the world to me. For the life o' me I canna understand what she saw in me. But of a' the women I met in my lifetime there was nobody who could touch my darling Maggie," says Reynolds with great conviction.

Major Griffin then plays the lament on his Highland bagpipes.

Maggie is laid to rest in a small graveyard in Bluehill facing towards the Western Isles of Scotland, which gave her so much pleasure and joy during her lifetime. The owners of The Drum and Monkey Tavern in Bluehill host a wake following the funeral service. Maggie has no surviving brothers or sisters. Her mother and father died several years ago, so Gordon, now aged thirty-two, is very much on his own.

In a quiet moment at the wake, Pipe Major Reynolds takes Gordon aside.

"I have a letter for you, Gordon, from yer ma," says Reynolds, placing a large envelope into his hands. "After yer ma's first heart attack she dictated this letter to me. I wrote down her words just as she spoke them to me."

Gordon opens the envelope and reads his mother's last words:

My darling son, I only wish we could have spent a few precious moments together so I could tell you how much you meant to me. Over the years, you have brought great joy and happiness to me and made me the proudest mother that Scotland ever had, and for that I am eternally grateful.

I know that your interests and talents are in the law and piping and I truly hope that you excel in your chosen fields of endeavour. My lawyers in Inverness will tell you that I have left The Sailor's Hornpipe Inn to you. Also my three houses in the port of Oban and all my investments in shipping with Gordon Templeton. I invested £3,000 in Henry Bell's commercial steamship venture, so I hope it is a success. Henry Bell seems like a clever man.

I have bought you a partnership in your law firm in the hope that you make a career out of practising law.

I have left some of my personal belongings to Jimmy

Reynolds, whom I loved dearly. Jimmy is a fine man, and my only regret over the years is that I did not accept his proposals of marriage.

Take care of yourself, son, and know that you are my pride and joy.

Your loving mother
Maggie

That night Gordon Morrison cries himself to sleep. It is mid-morning before he appears. As Gordon enters the kitchen Jimmy is sitting in a seat looking out of the window.

"Would you join me, Jimmy, in a wee walk?" asks Gordon.

The two men put on their overcoats and hats and walk to the west towards the sea and find a spot with a magnificent view of the Hebrides. Although it is a cold day the winter sun begins to break through broken clouds and the northerly wind moderates. Not a word has been said since the two men set out on their walk.

Gordon is the first to speak.

"I've been thinking about my future, Jimmy, and I know it lies in practising the law and piping. My mother invested many years o' her life building up her clients and goodwill at The Sailor's Hornpipe Inn in the port o' Oban. I would like to think that her investment would continue," comments Gordon, looking straight at Jimmy.

"What do you mean, Gordon?" asks Reynolds, who is wondering what Gordon is getting at.

"I spoke with the senior partner o' my law firm, Stuart Ogilvie, at the funeral and he is drawing up a deed o' title for The Sailor's Hornpipe with your name as owner," states Gordon.

For the first time in his life Jimmy is speechless. He is unable to respond.

After a few minutes Jimmy says, "Gordon, I'm overwhelmed, but how can I accept such a gift?"

"I would not have it any other way; please say you will accept my gift," pleads Gordon.

Jimmy knows that this means the end of his time at Bluehill. He was a founding member of the piping and drumming school and over the years he has put all of his time and talent into making it a place of excellence for up-and-coming pipers and drummers. People from abroad visit Bluehill knowing they will receive the best piping and drumming instruction. Reynolds has promised Andrew Griffin's cousin Stewart MacGregor that he will bring the Boys of Bluehill pipes and drums over to Cape Breton, Canada, in June to attend their Highland gathering then return to prepare for the Cowal gathering in the town of Dunoon in the autumn. After some reflection, Jimmy, with tears in his eyes, embraces Gordon and accepts his offer. The two men sit on rocks overlooking the sea and the Western Isles for over two hours quietly remembering the woman they both loved.

Chapter 36

MACGREGOR, DESPITE THEM

Colonel Gregor MacGregor receives some disturbing news on a cool evening in early October at his home in the town of Aberfoyle. Gregor's younger brother Roy died very suddenly at his home in Newtonmore, located to the north in the heart of the Scottish Highlands.

Roy and his wife, Maren, moved north to Newtonmore from the town of Callander in 1801. Roy was attracted to the village of Newtonmore when he first saw the place. The River Spey, which flows beneath the village, is renowned for its freshwater fishing and abundant salmon, and Roy had a great passion for freshwater fishing.

Gregor immediately contacts his cousins Andrew Griffin and Charlie MacGregor, advising them of his brother's death and invites them to accompany him to Newtonmore to attend a memorial service in honour of Roy MacGregor. The plan is for Gregor and his two cousins to travel north together to Newtonmore. All three men agree to meet at Aberfoyle and then head north-west on horseback on the road to Callander, following the north shore of Loch Venachar.

By the time all three cousins meet in Aberfoyle to start their journey north, the weather has turned cool, but dry, and the skies are cloudless. The air is still and the midday autumn sun shines as the travellers move to the north-west.

"Beautiful autumn weather, Charlie," comments Gregor as he pats his mount and savours the views of the craggy mountaintops painted with shadows of scudding clouds as they slip up and down the steep-sided glens.

"Aye, it's a grand day," replies Charlie as he breathes in deeply, lovely fragrances of flowers, grass and the cool, crisp mountain air.

Gregor goes on ahead of his two companions and searches for a camping spot for the night. It is late afternoon as Andrew and Charlie reach the outskirts of the town of Callander. Meanwhile Gregor, who has gone ahead, dismounts from his horse on hills outside a small and sleepy village and starts to make camp beside a shieling – a small shelter where farmers spend their summer nights while grazing their cattle. Being late into autumn, the shieling is now unoccupied.

An hour later, Andrew and Charlie locate Gregor. Andrew and Charlie start collecting some dry timber in nearby woods for a fire. Soon an evening meal is being prepared on a brightly burning fire. Charlie is in high spirits as he attends to the three horses. He marvels at the songs sung in nearby trees by linnets and thrushes, and larks circle high above the wooded fields. As he feeds and waters the horses he sings songs taught to him by his father as he goes about his business. Andrew collects drinking water from a fast-running stream and spots silver-bright herring swimming close to the bank of the river. After an enjoyable meal, Gregor smokes his pipe and Andrew offers his relatives a glass of Scotch whisky.

"Play us a wee tune on the bagpipes, Andrew, to cheer us up," requests Charlie.

"Do you have a favourite tune, Charlie?" enquires Andrew, who is now tuning his Highland bagpipes.

"Can you play the pipe tune called 'The Banks o' Allan Water'?" asks Charlie.

"No bother, Charlie," responds Andrew enthusiastically.

"It's a beautiful melody," comments Gregor as Andrew finishes playing.

"I was wondering if you know 'The Black-Haired Maid'," asks Gregor.

"That I do Gregor. Here we go," says Andrew as he swings his pipes over his shoulder.

The three men talk for some time about their families and the history of Clan MacGregor. Andrew tells his cousins about his father's very sudden death. Later they all take cover in the shieling and fall fast asleep wrapped in their warm blankets.

Early the next morning, Gregor is awakened by the sounds of horses. As he gets up and looks out of the door of the shieling he catches a glimpse of two young men leading off their horses towards the village of Strathyre. Gregor quickly wakens his two cousins, who grab their swords and muskets and chase after the horse thieves. Gregor shouts at the thieves, but they ignore his calls.

"Andrew, fire a warning shot," commands Gregor.

Andrew, who is a good marksman, fires a shot above the heads of the two horse thieves. The rifle shot hits an overhanging branch of a large Scots pine tree and branches fall on the horses and the two thieves. The horses bolt off in a panic and the horse thieves run for their lives in opposite directions. Charlie pursues one of the villains and Andrew takes off after the other. Gregor goes in search of the horses.

An hour later, Charlie returns to the campsite with a scrawny, dirty-faced youth who looks as if he has not had a square meal for some time.

Gregor greets his cousin.

"Meet Rory Robertson," says Charlie, who is panting and short of breath after the chase through the bracken. "Any sign o' Andrew?"

"No, I have not seen him yet," responds a worried-looking Gregor. "I did manage to track down the horses though."

As the two cousins question young Rory, Andrew emerges from the woods looking worn out.

"Any luck, Andrew?" asks Gregor.

"I chased the thief for over an hour, but lost him in thick woods to the east," replies Andrew, wiping sweat from his brow.

Gregor questions Rory, but the lad tries to break free from Charlie's grasp. Andrew gives the lad a light cuff over the ear.

"Behave yerself, Rory, or the next one will be more painful," shouts Andrew.

Soon young Rory starts to cry and Charlie releases his tight grasp on the lad. After several minutes Rory starts to talk to his captives.

"My brother, Jamie, made me do it," utters Rory. "My mother and father died last year and we are starving," continues a distressed Rory.

Gregor suggests that they feed the lad and then decide what to do.

After a hearty breakfast consisting of bannock, oatmeal and hot tea, Andrew has a talk with their young captive. Andrew quickly discovers that Rory is a decent lad who has been led astray by his older brother, Jamie. Seemingly Jamie has committed several crimes and is wanted by the local sheriff. Rory was badly advised by his older brother and said that he regretted trying to steal the horses. Gregor and his cousins agree that they should take Rory along with them and turn him over to local authorities in Newtonmore.

Rory rides beside Gregor as they push on towards the village of Killin by way of Lochearnhead. The shining lochs and the splendour and majesty of the autumn colours and mountains all around them are stunning reminders of the natural beauty of the Scottish Highlands. After a brief stop at Killin, to water and feed the horses, the four travellers ride on towards Aberfeldy and Pitlochry. As they ride along, Gregor gets to know young Rory Robertson. Rory is sixteen years old and left school shortly after the death of his parents, who were both killed tragically in an accident. Rory has no family other than his brother, Jamie, who has settled for a life of crime. The young lad seems genuine and sincere to Gregor, who takes a liking to him.

Their journey north takes them along the shore of beautiful Loch Tay with Ben Lawers towering 4,000 feet above them. Approaching Aberfeldy, Andrew spots deer drinking at the edge of Loch Tay. The travellers decide to eat at a local inn called The Stag's Head then continue their journey towards Pitlochry. Young Rory eats three portions of beef stew and almost a full loaf of bread.

"It's the first hot meal I've had in over a week, Gregor,"

states young Rory as he begins to lick his plate.

"What are we going to do with the lad?" asks Charlie, who is also taking a liking to young Rory.

"I don't know," replies Gregor, shaking his head.

It is evening as they approach the village of Pitlochry. Gregor suggests they take advantage of the remaining daylight and kick on towards the Pass of Killiecrankie, where the River Garry flows through a wooded gorge, forming part of the natural corridor linking the Scottish Highlands and Lowlands. Young Rory tells Gregor that he knows the land around Killiecrankie. When Rory was a young boy his father was employed as a ghillie to a local clan chief.

"Aye, I know a good campsite, with fresh water, lots of wood and some game tae hunt and kill," claims Rory excitedly.

The horses travel down a drove road, which narrows then eventually opens up into a clearing surrounded by a stand of oak trees.

"This is the spot, Gregor," says young Rory as he jumps off Gregor's mount.

"Let's stop here, lads, and have a bite to eat. I'm saddle-sore and need to stretch my legs," shouts Gregor as he starts to dismount from his bay.

In the darkness of a cool crisp evening, camp is set up with the help of Rory, who is trying very hard to gain the confidence of all three cousins.

"Where are we?" enquires Charlie.

"This is the Pass o' Killiecrankie," replies young Rory.

The weary travellers settle down on the ground wrapped in the warmth of their woollen blankets. The sky is clear and as Andrew lies on his back he gazes at the starry canopy of heaven. Whatever cares he might have, whatever sources of trouble or anxiety, are all cast away to the wind as he falls into a peaceful slumber.

Early the next morning Gregor cooks a large breakfast with the help of young Rory. Charlie is amazed at the amount of food Rory consumes.

"It's a bottomless pit, Gregor," comments Charlie, laughing at young Rory's huge appetite for food.

"Aye, I know what you mean," replies Gregor as Rory shovels down yet another bowl of oatmeal.

The beauty of the land astonishes Andrew as he explores the area. The deep river gorge is cloaked in ancient woodlands and has unique plants growing all around. All four men explore the spectacular gorge, which is renowned for a plentiful supply of trout and salmon, as well as an extraordinary array of wildlife. Rory spots wood warblers, dippers, buzzards and a Scottish crossbill, the only bird unique to Britain. Further on, Andrew follows the river's edge through cherry and willow bushes, elderberry and briar and is excited as he discovers otters, pine martens, dotterels, ptarmigans, ospreys and red squirrels. But it is Charlie who gets the prize of the day as he sights and shoots a large roe deer. Two thin trees are chopped down, then the branches are stripped off and the legs of the deer are tied to the two trees and the four men carry their prize proudly back to camp. Young Rory volunteers to butcher the dead animal. Gregor watches the lad carve up the deer with great skill.

"And where did you learn this skill?" asks Gregor in a manner suggesting disbelief.

"My father taught me as a boy. My dad was a ghillie on a large estate and worked with other ghillies, gamekeepers and stalkers culling deer each autumn," replies Rory as he starts 'gralloching' the stag.

"And what are ye up to now?" asks Gregor.

"I'm gralloching – I'm cleaning out the guts o' the animal," explains a confident young Rory.

The three cousins stand by with amazed looks on their faces watching Rory as he skilfully carves up the deer.

During the meal, Andrew recounts stories of the Battle of Killiecrankie, which was fought in July 1689 on the very spot where his cousins and young Rory are eating their venison stew.

"When I was a wee lad my father told me that our grandfather Rob Roy and his father, Lieutenant Colonel Donald MacGregor, fought with the Jacobites on this very spot in July 1689. General

John Graham of Claverhouse, known to his men as Bonnie Dundee, defeated the forces supporting the government," recounts Andrew to a very attentive audience.

"What does Jacobite mean?" asks a curious young Rory, who has been listening intently to the conversation.

"Jacobites were the supporters of King James. The Jacobites get their name from a Latin word, Jacobus, which means James in Latin," explains Andrew.

"There is a standing stone around here somewhere which was erected by the locals to commemorate the Battle o' Killiecrankie," explains Gregor.

After eating their fill of venison stew all four men go searching for the standing stone. It is Andrew who spots the stone, partly hidden in the deep growing bracken.

"Here it is!" shouts Andrew.

"It was a bloody battle by all accounts," states Gregor.

"Aye, my father told me many good men fell at this very spot," adds Andrew thoughtfully.

After feeding and watering the horses, the four travellers continue north towards Blair Atholl on roads built by General Wade.

That evening the riders make their way to the village of Calvine, where they stay the night at a local inn.

Early the next morning they eat breakfast and set out for the forest of Blair Atholl and the village of Dalwhinnie.

"If we keep going lads we can make our destination by dusk," shouts Gregor, who is anxious to get to Newtonmore.

Sure enough, the horsemen approach the outskirts of the village of Newtonmore towards dusk and come upon The Creag Dubh Inn, which is situated beside the River Spey. A large sign hangs over the entrance to the inn: '*Ceud Mile Failte*' (100,000 welcomes). The landlord is Roddie Currie, who greets the weary travellers with a large jug of his finest ale.

"Ye'll have come a long way?" enquires Roddie, a ruddy-faced man with a bald head and long sandy-coloured sideburns.

"Aye, we have, landlord," replies a tired Gregor MacGregor.

"We're here to attend the funeral o' my brother, Roy MacGregor," explains Gregor.

"What a shock that was, gentlemen. There was Roy standing large as life at the bar talking away and the very next moment he goes crashing to the ground," explains Roddie with tears in his eyes. "We thought he stumbled, causing the fall, but when we examined him he was gone – gone, poor lad," adds Roddie, visibly shaken by this event.

There is silence in the room.

"Yer brother was one o' my best customers," explains Roddie as he composes himself and wipes the tears from his eyes. "After a day's fishing on the River Spey, Roy would drop by for a wee brew and I would fry up his catch o' the day," remarks Roddie, shaking his head at the passing of a dear friend.

The guests sit by a large, warm fireplace and Roddie's wife, Jessie serves up a big meal consisting of a five-pound salmon, tatties and two veg. Dessert arrives soon after accompanied by a large pot of hot tea. Andrew and Gregor find that they cannot finish their meal, so young Rory does the honours by devouring all of the leftovers.

Being October, the inn is fairly quiet, so Roddie draws up a chair and continues his conversation with his guests.

"Would you ken any o' my other guests?" asks Roddie.

"And who might they be?" enquires Gregor.

"Weel, let me see, there's Murray MacGregor and his wife, Sadie, in room number three, and one o' Roy's army friends from Callander in room number five," explains Roddie.

At Colonel MacGregor's request, Roddie goes to room three and returns with Murray MacGregor and his wife, Sadie. What follows is a very emotional reunion. Gregor has not seen his brother Murray for over ten years. Andrew and Charlie have never met Murray, who has just turned sixty years of age. Gregor introduces everyone. Murray and Sadie arrived earlier in the evening from the town of Inverness to attend the memorial service for Roy MacGregor.

The visit goes on well into the late evening and Roddie brings out a bottle of his finest malt Scotch whisky from the

Glenlivet distillery located to the north-east and situated close to the town of Tomintoul. During the family reunion, a Major MacLeod appears. Colonel MacGregor is astonished to see his old comrade from the South African Campaign in 1795. Major MacLeod retired from the Argylls a few years after the South African Campaign and moved to the town of Callander. During his stay in Callander, MacLeod befriended Roy MacGregor and his wife, Maren.

It is late into the night before everyone retires to their rooms. The memorial service is scheduled to take place the following day after lunch. Gregor arranges with Roddie for young Rory to assist him at the tavern during the memorial service.

At the service for Roy MacGregor, Gregor MacGregor as clan chief gives a eulogy and some of Roy's friends say a few words of comfort for Maren. Roy MacGregor, grandson of Rob Roy MacGregor, is buried in a quiet churchyard at the foot of a cluster of white birch trees whose leaves lie scattered around the small graveyard. At the request of Maren, Andrew plays a lament on his bagpipes called 'Beaumont Lodge'.

Maren, Roy's wife, is very glad to see Gregor, Andrew and Charlie at the memorial service.

Following the service, a wake is held at The Creag Dubh Inn, and Roddie and his staff provide a large amount of food for the fifty guests who are in attendance. Maren's two children, Eilean and Keith, are introduced to all of their relatives. Eilean is married to a merchant and resides in Grantown-on-Spey, a town to the north of Newtonmore. Eilean has two children, Grieg and Robbie. Keith, Eilean's younger brother, is training to be a minister of the church in Inverness. Maren catches up with all of the news of Clan MacGregor and promises to attend the next clan reunion.

"Have ye any plans for the future?" asks Charlie MacGregor.

"Roy's death was so sudden, ye ken, that I have not been able to think about anything except my poor Roy," replies Maren, who takes the arm of her daughter and is visibly shaken at suddenness of her husband's death. "The doctor who signed the death certificate said the sudden cause of death was something to do with Roy's heart, but Roy was only fifty-five years of age, and fit as a fiddle. I just don't understand it – one moment he was chatting away and the next he was lying dead on the floor. No warning," adds Maren, weeping freely and shaking with grief.

Andrew recounts the similar circumstances surrounding his father's death in Port Glasgow.

Major MacLeod, also a widower, comforts Maren. After retiring from the army, MacLeod had moved to Callander with his late wife, Betty, and purchased two well-established businesses. The owners of the two businesses both decided to retire and move to homes they owned in the Western Isles. MacLeod has standing contracts with the army for the supply of kilts and accessories such as sporrans and kilt belts. One of his customers is Jimmy Reynolds of Bluehill. Major MacLeod and Roy MacGregor had spent many happy weeks fishing for freshwater salmon and trout around the Trossachs area. MacLeod lost contact with his friend Roy when he and his family left Callander and went north to live at Newtonmore.

After the memorial service, the three cousins meet to discuss the fate of young Rory Robertson. They agree that the lad has some good qualities and should be given a chance at an honest form of living. Gregor suggests that Rory stays here at Newtonmore and works with Roddie, helping him to run the tavern in exchange for free room and board. After Rory reaches the age of eighteen, Rory could join the army and billet in the army barracks at Port Glasgow.

"What do you think, Andrew?" asks Gregor.

"Aye, the lad is just in need o' strong direction, and Roddie and the army can take care o' that," replies Andrew.

"He told me he is interested in learning to play the drums," chips in Charlie.

"Well, I will talk to the lad, and if he's willing I will arrange for Roddie to look after him," said Gregor.

Young Rory is relieved at Colonel MacGregor's kind offer

and promises he will stay out of trouble. Roddie for his part likes the lad and agrees to take him on until he turns eighteen, at which time he will pack him off to Andrew in Port Glasgow.

The next day Gregor and his two cousins make their way home. They decide to return home using a shorter route by way of Loch Rannoch and Coshieville, which will save a full day's travel. The weather is still dry and cool. When they reach the town of Aberfoyle, Andrew and Charlie stay with their cousin Gregor for two days to rest. As a mark of respect, the three men visit the grave of their grandfather Rob Roy MacGregor at Balquhidder. Andrew plays 'Rob Roy's Lament' on his Highland bagpipes, beside his grandfather's grave. The grave of Rob Roy is set in a small cemetery behind a church. Aspens and larches stand nearby, now almost leafless. The headstone at the grave is four feet high and is made of grey soft marble.

Andrew stands gazing at the inscription on the headstone. Suddenly he realizes what a fool he has been all those years. It is now so clear to him what must be done – so clear. Written in bold letters on Rob Roy's headstone are the words, 'MacGregor, Despite Them'.

On the journey home, Andrew sits on his horse with a blank look on his face, staring straight ahead as if he is in a dream or trance. He reflects on Heather's comments when they first met: "Andrew, you should be proud of who you are and change yer name back to MacGregor." He remembers his cousin Gregor's words about taking back the clan name and how the MacGregors were descended from the ancient Kings of Scotland. He recounts his lack of willpower and courage to stand up to the Sassenach bullies in the Port Glasgow shipyards who made the Highlanders' lives so miserable with constant abuse and bullying. He recalls the images of the Lowland Scots constantly fist-fighting with soldiers from the Highland regiments while campaigning in Portugal and making their lives miserable. He sees in his mind's eye the brave words of his famous grandfather so boldly and defiantly written on his gravestone and feels ashamed of his lack of action in changing his name back to MacGregor. Griffin feels deep remorse and wishes that he had acted on the advice of his dear wife and cousin all those years ago.

Andrew also recalls the deep sadness he felt inside when the Highland regiments of the Argylls were being cut to pieces during the Battle of Vila Real and the great amount of passion which stirred inside him driving him to come to the rescue of his fellow clansmen. As he rides along a feeling of remorse deepens inside of him and a sense of shame engulfs him. Charlie joins his cousin in their ride south towards the Cardross ferry for the crossing over the River Clyde to Port Glasgow.

"Andrew, y'are very quiet. What are ye thinking about, man?" asks Charlie, who is concerned about his cousin's sudden change of behaviour.

After a long pause Andrew replies in an assertive manner, "I'm thinking it's about time I let people know who I really am!"

Charlie tries to make sense of his cousin's sharp remark, but Andrew rides on ahead.

Soon, Andrew and Charlie find themselves back in Port Glasgow. Their families are delighted to see them, and Andrew and Charlie update everyone on their memorable visit to the Highlands of bonnie Scotland.

Chapter 37

PLANNING A LONG JOURNEY

In the spring of 1813, Major Reynolds calls for a meeting of all of the residents of his piping school at Bluehill. Over 100 people attend. Reynolds explains the generous offer from Gordon Morrison concerning the ownership of the tavern in Oban and the commitment made to Stewart MacGregor about taking the pipe band to Cape Breton, Canada, at the beginning of May. Everyone at the meeting realizes that a replacement for Pipe Major Reynolds will have to be found – 1 September 1806 is the date set for the appointment of a new pipe major. That way, the band can visit Cape Breton in early May and return in time to compete at the Cowal gathering in late August, with Jimmy Reynolds as pipe major.

Reynolds plans to appoint an interim manager to run The Sailor's Hornpipe until after the Cowal gathering in August. On 1 September the new pipe major will take over from Reynolds at Bluehill. It is also agreed that sixteen band members will go to Cape Breton – including Reynolds and his replacement, who is soon to be named. Money has been put aside for the trip. Stewart MacGregor has made arrangements for accommodation of the band members during their stay in the town of Sydney, on the island of Cape Breton, Canada.

Chapter 38

SERIOUS INCIDENT

In April, Griffin finds that the project schedule for the building of the first commercial steamship has slipped, so he gives instructions for the men assigned to this project to work overtime. The tradesmen like overtime because the rate of pay they receive is higher. Dougie Reid and Davie Tosh are not assigned to the steamship project. Reid and Tosh have been assigned to work on the construction of two merchant sailing ships.

"It's no bloody fair," screams Dougie Reid as he downs his tools. "How come we don't get the damn overtime?"

"Aye, y'are damn right," echoes Tosh as he stops work. "It amounts to discrimination."

Soon, the whole day-shift crew of riggers and carpenters stop their work on the construction of the sailing vessels and join their brothers in protest. Sammy Walton, shift foreman, is in the 'materials-laydown' yard checking inventories when an apprentice, wee Ally Liddell, comes running over to him to tell Sammy that all of the day-shift crews assigned to the construction of the two merchant ships have stopped work. Sammy Walton immediately grabs the arms of two security guards and they hastily make their way over to the work area.

"What the hell's going on here?" shouts Walton at the top of his voice.

"It's discrimination, that's what's going on," barks Reid angrily.

"Get back to yer work right away," orders Walton as he brandishes a long, thick pole.

"Fuck you!" replies Reid.

At that moment a fight breaks out between Walton and Reid. Initially Walton has the advantage as he hits Reid on the back and forearms with his pole. However, Reid produces a knife and the fight becomes more dangerous. The two security guards who accompany Walton are attacked and beaten up. The fight between Reid and Walton continues with Reid slashing his long blade at Walton. Griffin, from his office high above the dock area, can see the fighting and quickly makes his way downstairs, where he instructs his staff to round up all of the security guards and get them over quickly to the area of the yard where the fighting is in progress. When Griffin arrives at the scene of the fighting, Walton is lying on the ground bleeding from knife wounds to the body.

"Put the knife down, Reid, right away," demands Griffin.

"Fuck you!" replies Reid.

"This is yer last warning," shouts Griffin.

Reid lurches forward and thrusts the blade of his long knife into Griffin's left shoulder, causing Griffin to fall to the ground. Three security guards, who have just arrived, jump on Reid and wrestle him to the ground. John Wood appears with six other guards, who quickly contain Reid and his followers.

"Send for a doctor right away," screams Wood.

Walton lies motionless on the ground in a pool of blood. Wood tries to revive Walton, but he is dead. Griffin is also lying on the ground, bleeding from his wound. Wood orders four of the security guards to carry Griffin to the main gate. Dr. Sandy Lyle soon arrives and attends to Griffin's wounds. Griffin is taken to the local hospital. Dr. Lyle examines Walton's body and pronounces him dead. Reid is handcuffed and taken by the local constables in an enclosed wagon to jail. All of the tradesmen who stopped work are sent home, and work on the two sailing vessels is suspended.

Griffin has received a deep knife wound to his left shoulder and chest. He has suffered a large loss of blood and is detained in hospital for five days. The blade of the knife entered his body above and to the left of his heart and resulted in a temporary loss of the use of the left side of his body, including his arm and shoulder. Heather and the children are stunned by the incident and the police conduct a full investigation. Sixteen men, including Tosh, are fired. Reid is charged with murder and pleads not guilty, so a trial is set for the first week of June.

A remembrance ceremony for Sammy Walton is held a week later. Over 200 people attend the service. Sammy's wife, Betty, their five children and several of his brothers and sisters are also present. Wood tries to persuade Griffin not to attend the funeral because of his poor condition, but Griffin attends with help from his devoted wife and friends and then returns home.

The whole of the town of Port Glasgow is in shock at the death of Sammy Walton and the attack on Major Griffin.

Work continues on the steamship project at the Meadowside Shipyard. Wood announces to the press that the launching of the first commercial steam-powered boat will be delayed until the middle of June.

Chapter 39

NEW CHIEF OF STAFF

Thomas Campbell, deputy chief of the army, is summoned to London. The Earl of Marshalsea, chief of the army, is very ill and his doctor reports that he will not have long to live. Campbell's brother-in-law, Prince George Augustus Frederick, has been appointed as Prince Regent because of his father's poor health. The Prince Regent is in Europe with the army.

On 15 May 1806, the Earl of Marshalsea dies at his country residence at Sevenoaks in Kent, England. A state funeral is arranged to take place at Westminster Cathedral a week later. General Trimble makes all of the funeral arrangements. Thomas Campbell attends the funeral on behalf of the army. Most of the senior army officers are campaigning in Europe. To show their respects dignitaries from all over the British Isles attend the funeral service.

Thomas Campbell – Old Tom to those who know him well – is appointed as chief of staff for the army, a great honour for the Campbells and for Scotland.

Chapter 40

THE COMET

The launch date of 15 June is a bright, sunny day in Port Glasgow. The boat launch of the first steam-powered commercial vessel is scheduled for 1 p.m. By mid-morning, over 3,000 people have gathered at the Meadowside Shipyard. Local militia line the entrance to the shipyard and additional security guards are brought from Glasgow to ensure that the crowd remains orderly. Dignitaries and newspaper reporters from all over Britain, Europe and Ireland descend on Port Glasgow.

There is a carnival atmosphere. The provost of Port Glasgow declares 15 June a holiday to recognize the importance of the launch of the first seagoing commercial steamboat in the world.

The Argylls' pipes and drums, led today by Major Donald MacDonald, guide the dignitaries to the grandstand, which has been built for this great occasion. Griffin arranges for Major MacDonald to lead the Argylls today because of his other duties as general manager of the shipyard. The dignitaries walking behind The Argylls include Henry Bell and his wife, Sandra; Admiral Percy Chesterton and his wife, Annabelle; Big Willie Meicklejohn, provost of the city of Glasgow; John Lindsay, provost of Port Glasgow; Gordon Morrison, solicitor; John Wood, owner of the Meadowside Shipyards; the Earl of Renfrew and his wife, the Duchess of Renfrew; Major Griffin and his wife, Heather; John Robertson, who built the engine; Davie Napier, from Glasgow, who designed the boiler; and Gordon Templeton, chairman of the Clyde Trustees. The visitors are led to the grandstand overlooking the launching site of the paddle steamer. Admiral Percy Chesterton is given the honour of launching the first commercial steam-powered boat.

"My lords, ladies and gentlemen, today, June the 15th, is a historic moment in the shipbuilding industry because Henry Bell's dream has come true. Today you see the fruits of Bell's vision and endeavours. Bell dreamed of a way to speed up commercial travel by sea. The boat being launched today on the River Clyde will be the first seagoing steam-powered vessel to operate commercially in Europe – or anywhere in the world, for that matter. I name this boat *The Comet*. May God bless her and all who sail in her," states Chesterton.

With that, a large bottle of champagne is smashed against the hull of *The Comet* and the first commercial steam-powered boat is launched to great cheers from the large crowd of onlookers. *The Comet* has been painted maroon and black; the boat is forty feet in length with a ten-foot-six-inch beam. It is fitted with sails and a three-horsepower engine drives four paddle wheels, which are located on the port and starboard sides of the vessel. Soon the paddle steamer is seen puffing its way down the River Clyde towards Greenock and Gourock with six passengers on board. The noisy crowd cheer and wave Scottish Lion Rampant flags.

Wood, Bell and Griffin are interviewed by many home-based and foreign newspaper reporters. All three men interviewed by the press agree the invention of steam-powered engines for commercial travel will mean the beginning of the end for the great sailing ships.

Festivities following the successful launch continue until dusk. Fireworks explode in the evening sky all around Port Glasgow. Celebrations continue afterwards at all of the taverns in Port Glasgow and The Tickled Trout Inn runs out of ale before closing time.

Chapter 41

THE TRIAL

A large crowd has gathered outside the Port Glasgow courthouse on Marshall Street. It is a cool day and a steady wind blows in from the west. The local militia is out in force. About half of the 300 people standing outside the courthouse want Dougie Reid hanged and display banners and placards to clearly show their sentiments. The other half of the crowd is made up of trade-union members, some of whom were fired by John Wood. These tradesmen believe that Reid and the other workers assigned to building the two sailing ships have been unfairly treated.

"I want this crowd well controlled today, men," states Big John McAllister, chief inspector of police for the Port Glasgow area. "If there is any trouble with this crowd I want the troublemakers locked up," orders McAllister, leaving his men in no doubt of his expectations.

Eight additional policemen are brought in from Glasgow to support the twenty resident policemen. A few agitators on both sides get the crowd fired up early and missiles are thrown backwards and forwards.

The trial gets under way at mid-morning, by which time over ten arrests have already been made by local policemen. Trade-union leaders have engaged a Glasgow lawyer, Reilly Franks, from the law firm of McLeish, Reilly and Chalmers to defend Dougie Reid. The Crown Prosecutor's office appoints the law firm of Ogilvie, Urqhart and Donaldson of Edinburgh. Their specialist in criminal law is a brilliant young lawyer, Douglas Ogilvie, who although only thirty-five years old, has

266

successfully prosecuted in no less than seven major criminal cases during the past six years. One case was rendered 'not proven', which was a personal disappointment for the brilliant young lawyer. Ogilvie has been chosen as the lead prosecuting counsel and Gordon Morrison as his assistant for this trial. The trial attracts a considerable amount of press coverage. Newspaper reporters travel from the English cities of London and Manchester, while Scottish reporters travel to Port Glasgow from Aberdeen and Edinburgh to report on the trial.

The Judge for the trial is the Honourable Hamish MacPherson from Edinburgh, who has served for over twenty years with the Bar. MacPherson is a no-nonsense judge and has a reputation for handing down tough sentences. The first day of the trial is to select a jury. This jury selection is incomplete after the end of the first day because the defence lawyer, Reilly Franks, disqualifies many of the jurors on the grounds of prejudice. Franks continues with this approach into the second day of the trial, until the Judge loses his patience and calls a recess at mid-afternoon. In chambers, the Judge meets with the two counsels.

"Gentlemen, it's like this: you have two hours left to agree on yer jury selection; otherwise I will dismiss those jury members already selected and the trial will proceed without the benefit of a jury," states MacPherson forcefully.

Franks protests.

"Protest noted, Mr Franks," replies MacPherson.

By late afternoon that day a jury is in place.

On the morning of the third day, fights break out on the steps of the Port Glasgow courthouse. The local militia is called out to assist an already stretched police force. The hotheads are rounded up and dragged off to jail. The third day's proceedings start off with a plea for a mistrial by the defending counsel, but the Judge quickly dismisses the appeal. Franks' opening comments makes it clear to everyone present that this is going to be a long and drawn-out trial. Defending counsel makes several points to the jury, including reports of unfair labour practices by John Wood Shipbuilders. Ogilvie, the Crown prosecutor, on the other hand, goes to great lengths to discredit Reid's character and speaks about how unbecoming Reid's army record was and the circumstances under which he left the Argylls.

Witnesses appear for the prosecution on the fourth and fifth day of the trial. Jeers and catcalls can be heard from the public gallery when some of the witnesses give incriminating evidence against Reid. Jeannie Reid, Dougie's wife, is in the public gallery and she shouts out obscenities during the trial. The Judge's patience is wearing thin and by the end of the fifth day the Judge orders the courthouse to be cleared of the public and only the reporters and jury members are allowed to remain. This action by Judge MacPherson causes fighting outside of the courthouse to escalate. Several of the police and militia are badly beaten and reinforcements are urgently requested from the local towns of Greenock and Gourock. On the sixth day of the trial, the area around the courthouse is roped off and no one is allowed within 100 feet of the entrance.

Some shipyard employees who are called as witnesses fail to appear. Police reports indicate that these witnesses have mysteriously 'disappeared' or are reluctant to appear. The Judge issues warrants, and the witnesses who can be located are rounded up and brought to the courthouse under heavy guard. The reporters are having a field day covering the trial, and the headlines of all the leading newspapers focus on this event.

Andrew Griffin is one of the witnesses called for cross-examination. Reilly Franks attempts to portray Griffin as a bully. The prosecuting counsel also suggests that through Griffin's decision to approve overtime for the building of *The Comet* he has demonstrated extreme discrimination against shipyard tradesmen working on other important projects. Griffin is grilled for over two hours. Ogilvie objects to Franks' methods of questioning and complains to Judge MacPherson. Eventually Ogilvie is given his chance to question Griffin, and after an hour the reputation of Dougie Reid is well and truly destroyed.

After a break for the Sabbath the trial reconvenes, but Ogilvie fails to appear in court. Gordon Morrison requests a brief adjournment, but Judge MacPherson is in no mood to accommodate such a request and Morrison's motion is denied. Gordon Morrison assumes the role of prosecuting counsel and a search begins to locate Ogilvie. Soon it is discovered that Ogilvie has been attacked by four men on his way to the courthouse and is presently in hospital with a broken leg, fractured arm and concussion.

Security guards are assigned on a twenty-four-hour basis to protect all of the witnesses, the jury and also the prosecuting counsel. Photographs and gory details of the trial continue to dominate the newspapers' daily headlines throughout Britain and Ireland.

When residents of Port Glasgow awake on the tenth day of the trial the chief thought in their minds is how best they can secure a place in the town's courthouse to hear the concluding remarks of Franks and Morrison to the jury. The Judge has issued a directive saying that fifty people would be allowed into the public gallery to listen to the concluding remarks on the proviso that they are searched and agree to remain silent during the proceedings.

Final remarks are made by both Franks and Morrison and the Judge orders the jury to be escorted to a safe house to deliberate on their verdict.

After two days there is still no word that the jury has reached a verdict. On the third day the jury foreman, Andrew Lawrie, indicates that the jury is ready to return with their verdict.

"Has the jury reached a verdict on which you all agree?" asks the Judge.

"Aye, My Lord," replies Lawrie on behalf of his fellow jurymen.

"Do you find the prisoner guilty or not guilty?"

"We, the jury, find Dougie Reid guilty, My Lord, as charged."

The prosecution is delighted. Justice has been done despite extreme intimidation.

In sentencing Reid, Judge MacPherson remarks that in all of his years on the bench he cannot recall a more despicable character than Reid. Reid is sent down and sentenced to be hanged by the neck until dead. Gordon Morrison is commended by his law firm for stepping in when Ogilvie was unable to continue and for doing such a fine job. Ogilvie, for his part, is in hospital recovering from his wounds and provides a detailed description of the four men who attacked him on his way to the courthouse. Within two days the four men are rounded up. One of the four men is Reid's buddy Davie Tosh. The four criminals are charged with grievous bodily harm and sentenced to two years in prison with hard labour.

Chapter 42

AN ENGAGEMENT

During the trial of Dougie Reid, Gordon Morrison stays with the Griffin family at Braemar Gardens. On several occasions Griffin takes Morrison to The Tickled Trout Inn for some of Big Ben's famous ale and a game of cards. Griffin also provides piping lessons to Gordon during his stay and the two men become close friends.

Andrew advises Gordon of his decision to change his name back to MacGregor.

"If you like, Andrew, my law firm can handle your request."

"Thanks, Gordon. I'll take you up on the offer," replies Griffin, feeling relieved that he has at last set actions in motion to adopt his clan name of MacGregor.

"It should take a couple of months to process all o' the legal documents," explains Gordon.

"Have you no young lady friend, Gordon?" enquires Griffin, changing the subject.

"No, Andrew, I have not met anyone yet whom I could seriously care for," replies Morrison awkwardly, as if he did not want to continue discussion on this topic.

Gordon stays on another week after the trial at the urging of the Griffin family on the pretext that Gordon takes piping lessons from Andrew. Griffin has a very different motive for detaining his friend. Helen MacLeod is due to arrive at any moment to take wee Annie Griffin to Argyll for two weeks to teach her Highland dancing. Andrew and Heather are determined that Helen should meet Gordon, so a table is reserved for eight guests at a local restaurant. Andrew's guests include Captain MacDonald and his girlfriend, Lindsay Noble, Ross Noble and the beautiful Fiona, and Helen MacLeod and Gordon Morrison. At dinner Gordon is seated beside Helen MacLeod and can hardly believe his luck at meeting such a beautiful woman. Helen's beauty extends into her personality, her grace and her gentle manner, and Gordon quickly becomes smitten with this young and talented lady. For her part, Helen sees some special qualities in Gordon – he is caring, extremely bright, attentive and a wonderful piper. It is a match made in heaven, and Andrew and Heather do everything possible during dinner to bring these two young people together.

"I am so sorry to hear o' yer great loss, Gordon," says Helen with compassion as she touches Gordon's hand.

"Thank you, Miss MacLeod, for yer kind words. I was very close to my mother. It's been a very unhappy time o' my life," adds Gordon in a stuttering voice.

After dinner the guests make their way over to Braemar Gardens. Gordon has moved his personal belongings into a room above The Tickled Trout Inn to enable Helen to stay with the Griffin family.

"It is very kind of you to give up yer comfortable room for me, Gordon."

"My pleasure, Helen," replies Gordon.

Lindsay Noble plays a few Scottish lilts on the piano and Major MacDonald, who is completely devoted to Lindsay, agrees to sing. The first song chosen is 'Sweet Afton', by Robert Burns. The guests are moved by this song – none more so than Gordon Morrison, whose heart is completely captivated by Helen MacLeod. At the request of Fiona, Major MacDonald sings his very favourite song, 'My Luve is Like a Red, Red Rose', also penned by Robert Burns.

At midnight, all of the guests leave with the exception of Gordon Morrison.

"It's a long and lonely road to Argyll, Helen, for two bonnie lassies to travel unescorted," says Gordon with great concern.

"I came by coach," replies Helen, blushing.

"Would you mind if I escort you and wee Annie back to Argyll just to make sure you both arrive safely?" asks Morrison pleadingly.

Helen is surprised and she does not know how to respond.

"Then it's settled. I will make the arrangements for us to travel together. It will be a great honour," adds Gordon.

The next morning wee Annie and 'Totty', now almost fully grown, board the Argyll coach. Andrew and Heather are delighted with the turn of events and wish them all a safe journey. Gordon arranges to tie his horse to the back of the coach so that he can sit inside the coach beside Helen. By the end of the long journey to Argyll, Gordon has swept Helen off her feet by proposing marriage. Helen feels that this is the right man for her and she accepts Gordon's passionate proposal of marriage.

When the coach arrives in the town of Campbeltown, Argyll, they are greeted by Margaret MacLeod, Helen's sister-in-law. Margaret is startled at Helen's news.

That evening, at dinner, Dr. MacLeod, Helen's brother, welcomes Gordon into the family over a bottle of champagne. Helen displays her beautiful engagement ring, which Gordon purchased earlier that day. It is a half-carat diamond surrounded by bright emeralds, and the diamonds sparkle in the strong sunlight.

Wee Annie and Totty are sent to bed and the adults discuss the wedding arrangements. Following the death of his mother, Gordon has a considerable amount of money in sound investments, so the cost of the wedding, no matter how big, is not an issue. Gordon insists that no expense will be spared to ensure that the wedding will be a happy day for everyone.

With the success of *The Comet*, steam-powered commercial travel is here to stay, and Gordon's mother, before her death, invested heavily in the production of new steam-powered vessels for commercial travel through John Wood, the shipbuilder. Also, Gordon's partnership with Ogilvie, Urqhart and Donaldson of Edinburgh provides him with a handsome salary. Pipe Major Reynolds has offered to pay Gordon fifty per cent of all the profits from The Sailor's Hornpipe for as long as he owns and operates the business.

Helen wants to marry in Campbeltown after the Cowal gathering in August. It is agreed that 16 September will be the wedding day. Gordon has no immediate family. He decides to ask Pipe Major Reynolds to be his best man. Helen has two female cousins who will act as bridesmaids. Dr. MacLeod is to give his sister away as both of their parents died several years earlier. Margaret agrees to make all of the wedding arrangements because Helen is busy giving lessons to her Highland dancers for the Cowal gathering. Gordon provides Margaret with a list of the names of the wedding guests he wants to attend. At the top of the list are Major Griffin and his wife, Heather, and all of their family.

During the next few days Helen spends all of her spare time with her newly found love. It is a heartbreaking moment when Gordon rides north to Bluehill to update Pipe Major Reynolds on his wonderful news.

Major MacDonald and Lindsay are also in the midst of planning their wedding. To everyone's delight, they announce their engagement at the army barracks in the spring of 1812. Staff Sergeant Major Ross Noble makes the announcement on behalf of the happy couple. The wedding is planned for the middle of July in Port Glasgow. That evening the champagne flows freely and many toasts are made to the happy couple. At the request of Major Griffin, Lindsay accompanies her fiancé in singing two Scottish ballads to the delight of all of those in attendance.

Pipe Major Reynolds is very happy to hear Gordon's news of his upcoming marriage to Helen in the autumn. The Scotch flows until the wee hours of the morning and both men do not appear until lunchtime the following day. Reynolds considers Gordon as a son, and is delighted that he has found happiness so soon after his mother's sudden death.

"Aye, I would be honoured to be yer best man, Gordon,"

states Reynolds with great conviction. "She must be some lassie if you proposed on the first date," chuckles Reynolds.

"She is an angel from heaven, Jimmy, and we are deeply in love," replies Gordon with great sincerity.

"Where will you live?" asks Reynolds.

"We'll live in Edinburgh. The law practice is there, so it makes sense, ye ken."

"Well, I wish you all the very best. Yer mother would be so happy for both of you," adds Reynolds with great delight in his voice. Reynolds updates Gordon on his news, including the trip to Canada.

"Sounds really exciting, Jimmy," Gordon says.

"Aye, the MacGregors in Cape Breton are fine folk and we canna let them down," comments Reynolds thoughtfully. "But we'll be back in time for Cowal and yer wedding, do not worry," adds Reynolds confidently.

"Talking about the Cowal gathering, I was planning to enter the individual piping championships. What do you think?" enquires Gordon.

"You know that Major Griffin will be competing and it will be damned difficult to beat him," states Reynolds as he remembers the fine performances over the past ten years.

"Aye, I know. I have taken several lessons from Andrew recently and he has encouraged me to compete at Cowal," says Gordon.

"Aye, Griffin would say that. He's a great champion both on and off the field. Well, nothing ventured nothing gained, laddie," states Jimmy, patting Gordon on the back.

So, with Jimmy's blessings, Gordon convinces himself to go for the Grade 1 piping championship at the Cowal gathering in the autumn.

Chapter 43

VOYAGE TO CANADA

Pipe Major Reynolds and members of the pipe band meet regularly to finalize their travel arrangements and plans for their trip to Canada. When competing at the Cowal Highland gathering, Reynolds uses twenty pipers and drummers. For the trip to Canada it is decided to reduce the size of the band to sixteen members because it is important for the piping and drumming classes at Bluehill to continue while the band is abroad.

"We need to maintain our commitment to the students," states Reynolds to the entire group of band members and instructors resident at Bluehill.

After further discussion it is agreed that eleven pipers will travel to Canada supported by two side drummers, two tenor drummers and a base drummer. A replacement has been found for Pipe Major Reynolds. Reynolds' replacement as pipe major will be Captain Roy Cameron from Inverness, who first came to Bluehill several years ago. Cameron is a first-class piper and good motivator of the men. He served in the army for fifteen years prior to being wounded during the Portuguese Campaign. Shortly after recovering from his wounds at Bluehill he resigned from the army and stayed on at Bluehill as a piping instructor. Captain Cameron has a great sense of humour and is very popular amongst the other band members. His successes amongst the piping students include gold-member winners at the Cowal gathering, and Gordon Morrison is one of his prodigies. Reynolds and Cameron agree that there will be no change in the leadership of the pipe band until after the Cowal gathering in August 1812, and Cameron will travel with the band to Canada to get better acquainted with band members.

There is great excitement amongst the pipe-band members who are chosen to travel to Canada. Many of these pipers and drummers have never travelled outside of Scotland. All sixteen pipers and drummers want to put on a good show at the Cape Breton Highland gathering and do Scotland proud.

"We're leaving Port Glasgow at the beginning o' May," states Reynolds as he steps the band members chosen to go to Canada through the travel plans. "We're to arrive in the port o' Halifax before the month is out, all things being equal," adds the Pipe Major.

"While we are on board the ship to Canada we will have practice sessions," explains Reynolds as he distributes a daily piping and drumming schedule.

"What about dress code while we are travelling on the ship?" asks Tommy Rose.

"You can wear yer trews until we disembark at the port o' Halifax," replies Reynolds.

"Have we got a list o' the pipe tunes for the Cape Breton gathering yet?" enquires Captain Cameron.

"Organizers of the gathering have left it up to us to pick what we want to play. I thought we would agree on this point tonight," suggests Reynolds.

After an hour, the sixteen members of the band agree on a set of six tunes which will be played at the Cape Breton gathering. The set will include two marches, two strathspeys and two reels. Reynolds agrees that he will obtain the music sheets in time for the next meeting of the band members.

"Any other business, lads?" asks Reynolds.

"Aye, I was wondering when the practising would be starting for the Cowal gathering?" asks Tommy Rose.

"Good question, Sergeant Rose. We will get the music from the Cowal organizing committee as soon as we get back from Canada. That should be mid-July. That gives us four weeks to practise for the pipe-band competition at Cowal," explains Reynolds. "If there is no other business the meeting is closed," adds the Pipe Major, who is ready for a drink.

"Is there time for a wee bevy in the mess hall, Pipe Major?" asks Tommy Rose.

"Oh aye," replies Reynolds, rubbing his hands together as he heads quickly towards the bar.

The men are in good spirits and excited about their trip to Canada, and most of the discussions centre around the journey. For many of the men it is their first sea voyage. Over the years, the Boys of Bluehill have maintained a high standard in piping and drumming and as a result the band has continued to attract top-class pipers and drummers. The calibre of piping and drumming this year is as high as in any other year since the band first started playing together.

Andrew and Heather Griffin come to the pier at Port Glasgow to see Pipe Major Reynolds off to Canada. By the time the Griffin family reaches the pier a large crowd has assembled, including Gordon Morrison and his fiancée, Helen MacLeod.

Pipe Major Reynolds is delighted to meet Helen and spends half an hour getting to know her better. Helen likes Reynolds and is impressed by his jovial manner and honest and straightforward talk. Andrew Griffin gives Reynolds a parcel containing a gift for his cousin Stewart MacGregor.

"I'll see that this is safely delivered," promises Reynolds.

Families, sweethearts and friends of the pipe-band members say their goodbyes as the great sailing ship slowly leaves the dockside and navigates its way towards the Tail o' the Bank and out into the open sea.

During the first five days of the voyage to Canada, there is no band practice. Strong winds and bad weather scuttle any thought of the band getting together on deck. Pipers limit their practice sessions to chanters at their bunk beds.

On the sixth day of the voyage, the weather moderates, the

seas grow calm and the winds drop. Pipe Major Reynolds schedules a practice session for all the band members who feel well enough to participate. Many of the passengers join the band on deck to listen to Reynolds put the pipers and drummers through their paces.

By the fifteenth day of the voyage, the Boys of Bluehill are in full swing and the practice sessions become the highlight of the day for many of the travelling passengers going to Canada.

In the evenings, in the main dining room, individual pipers and drummers entertain the passengers. Members of some of the families on board the ship are from villages in the Spey Valley located at the foot of Cairngorm Mountain. These families are the McCullums and Stewarts, who agree to entertain the other passengers by singing Scottish lilts in Gaelic and English.

The captain of the ship is John Munro, son of James Munro who had sailed with the Argylls in 1796 on their South African Campaign against the Dutch. John, like his dad, James, is a competent seaman and has been well schooled by his father in sailing under canvas on long sea voyages in all kinds of weather.

"I appreciate yer boys entertaining us, Reynolds," comments Munro.

"No bother, Captain – it's oor pleasure. Besides, it gives the lads a wee bit more practicing time, ye ken," adds Reynolds.

"You'll find the Cape Breton folk to yer liking, Reynolds," comments Munro. "I married a wee lass from Nova Scotia. We now live in Scotland, in the fair town o' Helensburgh, north west o' Port Glasgow," continues Munro.

During the evening meal another family approaches Captain Munro in the ship's dining room.

"Good evening, Captain. Allow me to introduce myself and my family. We're the Mackenzies from Glenfinnan, on Loch Shiel," explains Alistair Mackenzie, who is a man in his early forties with a fiddle slung over one shoulder.

"Aye, I ken yer village well, Mackenzie. It's on the Road to the Isles," comments Munro.

279

"*Air Lorg Nan Eilean*," comes a quick response in Gaelic from Mackenzie. "Aye, Captain, oor wee village is located on the Road to the Isles," confirms Mackenzie with pride in his voice.

Mackenzie is delighted that Munro knows his village and also understands the Gaelic language.

"Captain, this is my wife, Kayla, my son Kyle and my wee Jessie," explains Mackenzie proudly.

"Very pleased to meet you a'," replies the Captain.

"Would you be givin' us a wee tune on yer fiddle, Mackenzie?" asks Reynolds in an inviting manner.

"I would be pleased, sir, very pleased," replies Mackenzie.

The Mackenzie family has been pushed off their smallholding by landowners whom they have never met and who demand exorbitant tithes. The family is introduced to the rest of the head table, and at the invitation of the Captain they sit down at the table while Alistair gets ready to play his fiddle.

"I'll play a couple o' reels and some jigs," explains Mackenzie to an attentive audience.

Mackenzie tunes his fiddle then opens up with 'Cock of the North', followed by 'Jenny's Bawbee' and 'Caddam Wood'. After five minutes, the audience in the dining room is tapping their feet in time to the wonderful music played so well by Mackenzie. No one in the dining room can sit still. Mackenzie continues with 'Jig of Slurs' and 'Cairney Mount'.

When he finishes his music sets, the diners leap to their feet and clap because they have just witnessed one of Scotland's finest fiddlers in action.

Captain Munro asks for an encore, so Mackenzie obliges. He plays 'Black Dance', 'Scots Polka' and 'Reel of St Anne's'. To finish his performance Mackenzie asks his daughter, wee Jessie, to dance to a fiddle tune.

Wee Jessie is a cute twelve-year-old girl with long blond hair, big blue eyes and a sweet smile. Her mother, Kayla, has been coaching her in Highland dancing for four years and wee Jessie is a natural. She captivates the audience with her version of the 'Sailor's Hornpipe'.

After all of the entertainment is over, Captain Munro thanks everyone. Reynolds and Munro are relaxing at the Captain's table with pipes filled with their favourite thick black tobacco.

"Are you a married man, Reynolds?" enquires Munro.

"No, I never married. Came close, mind you, a couple o' times, ye ken."

Amongst the guests at the Captain's table is Lillie MacFarlane. Lillie is originally from Dumfries in the Border country of Scotland, but she emigrated from Scotland to Canada with her husband, Danny MacFarlane, fifteen years ago and settled in the port of Halifax in Nova Scotia. Danny was a successful merchant and opened four stores in Nova Scotia. Three years ago Danny suddenly died of a heart attack and Lillie is trying to carry on the business. Although Lillie has been left a wealthy woman she does not have the business acumen of her late husband and is having difficulty keeping the business going. Lillie takes pride in her appearance and she dresses tastefully, wearing the latest fashions. Her manners, though simple, are mild and engaging; her heart is perfectly good and benevolent.

"Did you enjoy yer visit to Scotland, Mrs MacFarlane?" asks Captain Munro.

"Well, it could have been better, Captain. I was over visiting with my sister, Margo, for a month. Margo has been sick and she passed away only two weeks after I arrived from Canada," adds Lillie softly with tears in her eyes.

"I'm so sorry to hear that – so sorry," says Captain Munro sympathetically.

Lillie reaches into her purse, removes a handkerchief and wipes the tears from her bright blue eyes. Lillie is in her early forties, with long dark-brown hair which falls on to her slender shoulders. Her sky-blue dress is trimmed with white lace around the neck and sleeves; her shoes are white and she carries a parasol.

"Will you be able to attend the Highland gathering in Sydney in two weeks?" enquires Jimmy Reynolds, who has been sitting observing Lillie.

"Well, I'm no sure, Pipe Major. You see, I have the businesses to run, and the stores will no run themselves, ye ken," replies Lillie firmly. "But I will try and come to Sydney, if I can," she adds in a softer, more gentle tone of voice.

For the remainder of the voyage, Reynolds sees a lot of Lillie MacFarlane, and by the time the ship docks at the port of Halifax, Lillie and Reynolds have become good friends.

Chapter 44

NEW SCOTLAND

The great sailing vessel enters the port of Halifax, Nova Scotia. Captain Munro has arranged with the local port authorities for the Boys of Bluehill to disembark first. The plan is for the band to be met by an army colour party from the army barracks in Halifax, where the Cameron Highlanders are billeted.

It is a fair June sunny day, with a steady breeze blowing in from the west as Reynolds and his band forms up on the pier. A crowd of over 300 people have assembled to welcome home family and friends. Captain Ronny MacKinnon, adjutant at the barracks in Halifax, leads the pipe band down the Wharf Road towards the army barracks in Halifax – a distance of two miles. As the Boys of Bluehill march they play their six-tune set to a crowd of curious onlookers who have gathered along the narrow streets of Halifax. Shopkeepers and merchants, hearing the pipers and drummers, hurry from their stores and join the waiting crowd to catch a glimpse of the famous pipe band from bonnie Scotland.

After marching a mile, some of the onlooking public begin to follow the band. Soon, almost 200 people are following the Boys of Bluehill through the narrow streets of the downtown area of Halifax. As they approach the army barracks in Halifax, Reynolds notices that the local regiment has assembled at the entrance to the barracks. Behind the soldiers stand a crowd of onlookers, who wave flags of St Andrew and the Scottish Lion Rampart banner and cheer the Boys of Bluehill. It is an amazing and unexpected reception.

Lieutenant Colonel Andy Johnstone gives the greeting.

"Welcome to New Scotland," states Lieutenant Colonel Johnstone. "It's a great honour to see you again, Pipe Major. Yer reputation is well known in these parts amongst some of the army pipers you taught so well," states Johnstone enthusiastically.

"I'm truly touched by the reception you folks have put on for us, and, on behalf o' the band, thanks a million," replies Reynolds with great conviction.

Reynolds and Johnstone both served in India and know each other. A big Canadian-type barbecue is organized that evening. Members of the Boys of Bluehill band get to taste their first barbecue, which includes corn on the cob. Johnstone also puts on a ceilidh and Stewart MacGregor and his party of twenty arrives from Cape Breton in the early evening to join in the festivities. Morag, Stewart's granddaughter, who is eighteen years old and a local champion Highland dancer, accompanies her grandfather. Morag has long, dark hair, flashing brown eyes and stunning looks. Two of the pipers who joined the Boys of Bluehill during the past few years, Bill Campbell from Invergordon on the Cromarty Firth and Jimmy Patterson from Gairloch in North-West Scotland, swarm all over Morag and vie for her attention. Bill and Jimmy are sergeants; both are aged twenty-six years old and have played the bagpipes for over ten years.

Chapter 45

CAPE BRETON

After a sightseeing tour around the port of Halifax, the MacGregors and Boys of Bluehill prepare to travel to the island of Cape Breton. A sloop named *Peggy Gordon* is commissioned by Stewart MacGregor to take the party to the fortress of Louisbourg on the east coast of the island of Cape Breton. From there, wagons and carts will transport the band and all of their belongings along the Mara Road to the town of Sydney, where the Highland gathering is being held. The rugged coastline of Cape Breton, the land and the rolling hills are just like the old country, thinks Reynolds. The local Cape Breton folk that the Boys of Bluehill meet are mostly of Scottish descent and many speak in Gaelic and are very friendly folk. As the party travels along the Mara Road to Sydney, Morag MacGregor sings some beautiful Scottish lilts in Gaelic and Bill Campbell and Jimmy Patterson are enchanted.

About a mile from Sydney, the Boys of Bluehill stop and change into their kilts and march the remainder of the way, just as they did in 1796 when they marched from Arrochar to Port Glasgow. As they approach the town of Sydney, a large crowd gathers to greet the Scottish pipe band. Locals wave the St Andrew's flag and cheer their Scottish visitors.

Each member of the band is billeted with a family. Pipe Major Reynolds and Captain Cameron stay at the residence of Stewart MacGregor. The following day the band meet at a local inn called The Moose Head Tavern. Over a hearty lunch arrangements are made for the band members to tour Cape Breton. As luck would have it, Bill Campbell is placed on Morag MacGregor's tour. Jimmy Patterson finds himself with the MacBain family. Ally MacBain is a farmer and has two sons and three daughters. Jimmy soon forgets Morag MacGregor when he meets Islay and Shauna MacBain, twenty-year-old twins, both with long red curly hair, green eyes and stunning looks.

After the tour of the island is complete, the Boys of Bluehill meet daily and practise on the pipes and drums for three hours. The weather is fine, so all of the practicing is done outdoors in the shade of a stand of mature oak trees. Reynolds and Stewart MacGregor agree that, in return for being billeted and fed by the locals, each member of the band will take one student each day for two hours and tutor them in piping and drumming. Most of the students have been taught piping and drumming by ear and many cannot read music. When the Highlanders left their crofts and farms in Scotland to come to Canada, many of them settled in Pictou, Nova Scotia, while others made their way to the island of Cape Breton. Over the years, teachings of the pibroch amongst the Scottish settlers has declined, and by the time Jimmy Reynolds arrived in Nova Scotia only the army-trained pipers stationed at Halifax in Nova Scotia are familiar with the canntaireachd.

During dinner one evening, Reynolds presents Stewart MacGregor with a gift from his cousin Andrew. The gift is a set of brand-new Highland bagpipes, hand-carved with silver-mounted tips. The sheepskin bag is covered with material made from the ancient Clan MacGregor tartan. Stewart is delighted with the gift and asks Reynolds to convey his sincere thanks to his cousin Andrew.

Late in the evenings, Bill Campbell sneaks over to Morag's home and off they go to a local hay barn and make love. Their passion for each other is endless. Campbell cannot get enough of his beautiful Morag, and they make love over and over again. Morag is infatuated by Campbell and can hardly contain herself until nightfall to rendezvous with her newly found lover. This goes on for seven days until one evening Morag's brother discovers the young couple in a nearby barn. Morag's father, Neil, a fisherman, is away at sea. Morag's mother, Flora, died several years ago, so it is left up to Stewart MacGregor, Morag's grandfather, to deal with the young couple.

"What have you to say for yourself, Morag MacGregor?" asks her grandfather sternly.

"I am sorry, Grandfather – I let you down," replies Morag.

"It's a' ma fault, sir," interjects Campbell. "I fell head o'er heels in love the moment I saw Morag," adds Campbell forthrightly.

"And what about you, Morag MacGregor?" asks her grandfather with a look of disappointment on his face.

"Oh, I love Bill, Grandfather, and I want to marry him," replies Morag with great sincerity in her voice.

Stewart can see that both of these young people are in love and he remembers when he first met his wife, Fiona, and how he fell head over heels in love.

"Well, your father will be back in two days for the gathering. We will speak to him then and see what's got to be done," says Stewart in a calm and clear manner.

Neil MacGregor, Morag's father, is speechless when he hears the news. Neil has found it difficult to raise Morag without the help of his deceased wife. Morag has some of her deceased mother's characteristics – she is impulsive, acting without really thinking things through. However after speaking to Morag and Sergeant Bill Campbell he gives them his blessing and agrees to the marriage.

Pipe Major Reynolds is stunned when he hears the news of the young couple's upcoming marriage.

"I cannot take you anywhere, Campbell," states Reynolds. "What are you thinking o' man?" asks Reynolds sternly.

"I love ma Morag, Pipe Major, and I want to marry her," answers Campbell sincerely. "We've talked it o'er and we are going to get married the day after the Highland gathering finishes. We are going to stay here in Cape Breton and make a life o' it," continues Campbell with strong conviction in his voice.

Reynolds cannot respond. He is visibly shaken. Reynolds can see that Campbell has made his bed, and as far as he is concerned he will have to lie on it.

The Cape Breton Highland gathering attracts over 800 people. The spectators come from all over Nova Scotia, New Brunswick, Prince Edward Island and Newfoundland, and from as far afield as the city of Montreal in Quebec. Amongst the visitors are soldiers from the Cameron Highlanders. Many of the Camerons have been taught piping and drumming at Bluehill before leaving for Canada. The Highland gathering is being held over two days. The pace of the events is much more leisurely than at the Cowal gathering and less formal. Campsites are set up and clans post signs outside their tents so that clan members from other parts of Canada can visit. The Boys of Bluehill agree to play four times during the two-day period of the Highland gathering. Aiso, they agree not to enter any of the piping or drumming competitions, because it is recognized that they play at a much higher standard than the locals.

Reynolds and Cameron are invited to judge the events. Reynolds is one of the piping judges and Captain Cameron judges the drumming competitions. Tommy Rose is also appointed as a judge for the Highland dancing, because as a youth he was placed three times in the under-sixteen dancing category at Cowal, winning gold, silver and bronze medals. The Cape Breton gathering is a memorable event. Many exiled Scots who left their smallholdings, farms and cottages after the Battle of Culloden are anxious to find out all of the news from the old country and seek out members of the Boys of Bluehill pipes and drums.

On the morning of the second day of the gathering, Lillie MacFarlane walks into the beer tent looking for her friend Pipe Major Reynolds. Reynolds lights up like a firefly when he sees Lillie. Just the tonic he needs. Lillie wears a beautiful light floral full-length dress with a plunging neckline, which Reynolds does not fail to notice. On her head she wears a large hat and carries a parasol to protect her from the sun.

"I am delighted to see you, my dearie," states Reynolds as he gives Lillie a big hug. "Sit you down. I would like you to meet Stewart MacGregor, who is responsible for all this madness," laughs Reynolds, so happy to see Lillie once more.

"Pleased to make your acquaintance, Mrs MacFarlane," says Stewart, standing up to shake her hand.

"Oh, Lillie will do, Stewart," she replies as she removes the hairpin from her hat.

A young waitress approaches Reynolds' table, and drinks and food are ordered.

"So glad ye could make it, Lillie, so glad," says Reynolds as he reaches for Lillie's hand and gently squeezes it.

Stewart gets the hint that these two folk want to talk in private; so he politely excuses himself, making up a story about checking on the judges for the next event.

"I was no going to come, Jimmy, but if I had not I might never have seen you again," states Lillie with great emotion.

Reynolds recognizes this as a signal. He pulls his chair closer to Lillie, holds her hand tightly and says, "I would have been broken-hearted, ma dearie, if I had never seen you again."

Lillie tells Jimmy that she has spoken to her lawyers about selling the businesses because it has become too much for her. She is unable to cope without the help of someone to manage the day-to-day business activities.

"Sell up and come back to bonnie Scotland, ma dearie," suggests Reynolds with great passion.

Lillie smiles, but does not reply. Instinctively they kiss passionately for a few precious moments and hold hands. Lillie has given Reynolds his answer.

Captain Cameron interrupts this golden moment.

"Eh, excuse me, Pipe Major – we are on in twenty minutes," states Cameron awkwardly.

"OK, Cameron, OK – I will be right there," replies a flushed-faced Jimmy Reynolds.

Later that evening, Lillie and Reynolds make their plans for the future. Reynolds cannot remember what tunes the band has played or how the day has gone. Jimmy Reynolds is in a daze. He pours his heart out to Lillie about Maggie's death and The Sailor's Hornpipe Inn, Gordon Morrison and leaving Bluehill. Lillie listens for over half an hour. The tears roll down Jimmy's face and he becomes very emotional.

"There, there, now don't cry. I know what you have been through. I know," says Lillie with great empathy as she strokes Jimmy's forehead and remembers the difficult time she had after the death of her husband, Danny, three years ago.

The two gently embrace for several minutes, then Reynolds composes himself and walks Lillie back to the local inn where she is staying.

The quality of piping and drumming at the Cape Breton Highland gathering surprises Reynolds. Six local pipe bands compete against one another. All of the bands are from Nova Scotia and Cape Breton Island. Two of the bands – The Sons of Baddeck and the Louisbourg Loyalists – are fine pipe bands. It is difficult to separate them. Finally, the trophy is awarded to the Louisbourg Loyalists because of their better technical merit. Some of the pipers in the Louisbourg band served in the army and their training in piping is the difference between the two bands. In the individual piping competition, Reynolds knows that there are several fine young individual pipers and drummers in Nova Scotia based on the feedback he has received from his own band members, who are instructing many of the competitors.

There is great rivalry amongst the local clans. The Drummonds from Antigonish, Nova Scotia, won the gold medal at the last Cape Breton gathering and are determined to repeat their success this year. Up until the last gathering, the MacGregors won piping trophies, so they are also determined to reassert themselves. However, Reynolds has got wind of a young piper from Glace Bay – Hamish MacGillivray – who might be the man to beat. Hamish MacGillivray is the grandson of MacGillivray of Allendale, who came to Canada from Scotland over forty years ago. Prior to coming to Canada, the MacGillivrays were recognized as producing some of the very best pipers in Scotland. Hamish has inherited some of his grandfather's piping skills and he blows away all of the local competition, much to the dismay of some of the other clans.

After the competition, Reynolds approaches the young man, who is only eighteen years old.

"Aye, I think you could go a long way in piping, laddie. Have ye ever thought o' joining the army as a piper?" asks Reynolds.

"I have given it some thought," replies the young man.

"If you ever visit Scotland, come and see me at The Sailor's Hornpipe, a tavern in the port o' Oban," invites Reynolds as he shakes the young MacGillivray's hand.

The sailing sloop *Peggy Gordon* stands ready at the port of Louisbourg to take the pipe band back to Halifax. There is one more surprise waiting for Pipe Major Reynolds as the wagons are loaded to travel down the Mara Road to board the sloop. Jimmy Patterson and Shauna MacBain advise Reynolds that they are also getting married and plan to live in Sydney. Reynolds soon realizes that he has just lost two of his very best young pipers to Cape Breton and is stunned. Reynolds believes that in Bill Campbell and Jimmy Patterson lies the future of the Boys of Bluehill pipes and drums.

"I wish you all the very best, Patterson," states Reynolds, shaking the young man's hand. "And to you, young Shauna MacBain – I wish you happiness. You have a fine piper in Jimmy Patterson," adds Reynolds, who is visibly shaken with this news.

The band members are subdued as they head down the Mara Road towards the port of Louisbourg. They know that replacing two key pipers at short notice for the Cowal gathering will be a big task and a silence falls over the men as they start on the long journey home.

At Halifax, the band stays overnight at the local army barracks. The ship to Scotland is leaving on the morning tide. Lillie MacFarlane invites Reynolds to her home for dinner. During the visit, Lillie advises Jimmy that as soon as the businesses and her home are sold she will come over to Scotland to join him.

"I canna wait till I see you again, ma dearie. It will be torture waiting for yer message," says Reynolds, embracing his new-found love.

"No matter how long it takes, Jimmy, I will never feel any different than I feel right now," replies Lillie lovingly as she strokes Jimmy's cheek.

All of the MacGregors come to say their goodbyes. The army also turns out in large numbers and Lillie and Jimmy are heartbroken as they kiss and hug each other at the Halifax pier. As the great ship pulls away from its moorings the local army pipes and drums play 'Farewell to Cape Breton', a pipe tune written by Stewart MacGregor's father many years ago.

Chapter 46

SERIOUS PREPARATIONS

The Atlantic crossing from Canada to Scotland is smooth and the great sailing ship makes record time. Reynolds, a skilful motivator with the men, gets the daily practice routine established after a few days at sea. Reynolds and Cameron agree to search for two replacement pipers from amongst the other instructors at Bluehill as soon as they return home.

The ship from Canada docks at Port Glasgow. A large crowd greets the passengers as they disembark from the vessel. Andrew Griffin and Gordon Morrison are amongst those who are on hand to welcome home the band members. Gordon accompanies Jimmy Reynolds and the Pipe band north to Bluehill. Jimmy is anxious to find replacements for Bill Campbell and Jimmy Patterson. Gordon has planned to take advanced piping lessons at Bluehill to prepare for the individual Grade 1 piping competition at this year's Cowal gathering.

Andrew Griffin has three key objectives to achieve during the next four weeks. One is to lead the Argylls to victory in the pipe-band competition. The second objective is to win the gold medal in the Grade 1 individual piping competition, and the third objective is to teach his band a new pipe tune, which Andrew has written during the past year. Andrew names his new pipe tune 'Heroes of Vila Real', and it is written to celebrate the great victory of the Argylls and their Portuguese allies over the combined French and Spanish armies. Andrew has kept the writing of this new pipe tune a secret, even from his wife Heather.

At the first band practice of the Argylls, Andrew discloses his secret to his men.

"Lads, if we win at Cowal I want you to play this new march as we lead the other pipe bands down the long hill and into the town o' Dunoon," explains Andrew.

"Could you play the new tune, Pipe Major, so we can get the hang o' it?" requests Billy MacPherson, one of the up-and-coming stars of the band.

Andrew responds by playing the new victory tune. As Andrew plays the Argylls clap in unison to a very catchy pipe tune. When he finishes playing, all of the men show their support by clapping loudly.

"Great stuff!" "I loved it, Major", "Best pipe tune I have heard in a long time" and "Great wee tune!" are some of the supportive remarks from the band members.

The practice schedule for the Argylls' pipe band is gruelling. The schedule requires practices to be held four times per week. Each rehearsal lasts almost four hours. On top of that, Andrew is practising two nights per week in preparation for the individual piping competition. Heather is unhappy because she never sees her husband during the week. Andrew's work commitments and his piping practices consume all of his time. His shoulder wound and old army wounds are still causing him pain and he visits Dr. Sandy Lyle on several occasions in an effort to ease the pain. Dr. Lyle arranges for Andrew to have massage therapy and also some medication, and this treatment helps him to get through his rigorous piping schedule.

Two days before his wedding, Major Donald MacDonald has the groom's traditional stag party at the The Tickled Trout Inn in Port Glasgow. Big Ben McQuarrie, the owner, closes the tavern to the public so that Donald and all of his friends can have the place to themselves. Heather Griffin arranges a party for Lindsay Noble and all of the invited female guests attending the wedding. Over thirty female guests attend Heather's party.

In excess of 100 guests visit the The Tickled Trout Inn for Major MacDonald's stag party. After a few hours the singing starts and gradually the party gets more boisterous. At 10 p.m. a few of the army cadets start piping and some fights break out amongst the young men who are now intoxicated. An hour later two entertainers arrive, compliments of Big Ben. The entertainment consists of two ladies from Glasgow who perform 'The Dance of the Seven Veils'. Both women are in their late twenties, tall blondes, with full figures and stunning looks. They are professional dancers and entertainers and wear seven silk veils draped over their bodies. When the last of the seven veils is dropped to the floor, some of the younger soldiers try to proposition the female entertainers, but are quickly restrained.

"These entertainers certainly know how to handle themselves," comments Griffin.

"Aye, y'are right," replies Donald, who is feeling no pain.

Later, both entertainers dress in low plunging neckline dresses and large feathered headdresses, and sing a variety of popular music-hall songs. All in attendance participate in the singing. It is 2 a.m. before Big Ben shuts the party down and sends everyone home. Other than some broken chairs and a dozen or so broken glasses, the stag party passes without any major damage to the tavern.

The house party for the visiting female wedding guests is in progress at Heather's home. Some family members and close friends of the bride have come from the island of Islay, where Lindsay Noble was born, and these ladies speak in Gaelic. Unlike the stag party at The Tickled Trout Inn, there are no incidents at this party. Lindsay Noble sings and plays the piano for her guests. A choir from Islay, consisting of four young ladies, entertains the guests with some haunting Gaelic melodies.

The wedding is scheduled to start at 2.30 p.m. on a warm July day. Lindsay has requested a church wedding. Over 150 guests attend the wedding. The minister who conducts the service is

Willie Telfer, a friend of the Noble family. Being a warm and sunny day many of the male guests dress in their clan-tartan kilts, including the groom, Donald MacDonald. The bride wears a full-length white silk dress with a low neckline and a long white veil. Accompanying the bride is her father, Stuart Noble. An army barracks' piper leads the bride and father into the church. Staff Sergeant Ross Noble is the best man. Lindsay's older sister, Morag, is the maid of honour.

The wedding reception is held at Port Glasgow army barracks in the mess hall. Wives of the army officers decorate the mess hall with beautiful lights and flowers. Lindsay is delighted with the whole arrangement. Many toasts are made and after all of the formalities are complete the officers at the barracks arrange entertainment in the form of piping, singing, dancing and a very funny comedian from Glasgow. The newly-weds say their goodbyes and leave on a two week honeymoon to the remote Orkney Isles, located across the Pentland Firth from the Northern Scottish mainland. The wedding party continues well into the wee hours, and it is 3 a.m. before the last song is sung, the last glass of Scotch whisky drunk and the last of the guests make their way home.

When the pipe band arrives at Bluehill Major Reynolds wastes no time in scheduling a meeting with all of the piping instructors. Reynolds is anxious to find replacements for Bill Campbell and Jimmy Patterson, who have chosen to stay in Cape Breton, Canada, and marry local lassies. The meeting is held on the second day after the band arrives at Bluehill.

"Thanks for coming lads, we need to deal with some urgent business. Two o' our pipers, Bill Campbell and Jimmy Patterson, jumped ship in Cape Breton Island, Nova Scotia, and are getting married to two local bonnie lassies. That puts us in a big hole for the Cowal gathering in exactly four weeks. Now, would any o' you fine instructors be willing to join the band and play at the Cowal gathering?" asks Jimmy in his own inviting way.

Three pipers raise their hands. Two of the volunteers have

been around for three years and have very good piping skills and are also fine instructors. They are Johnny McCall and Rory MacNaughton. Johnny is from the village of Brodin on the north-east coast of Aberdeenshire, and Rory hails from the 'kingdom' of Fife. The third volunteer is a newcomer to Bluehill – Niall McIver, from Harris on the Isle of Lewis. Niall speaks in Gaelic and his English is limited to a few words. He has agreed to take English lessons at the local school in Bluehill, but although he is a fine piper Reynolds does not think he is far enough along with his English lessons to join the band at this time.

"Thanks to the three volunteers. I'll meet with you on a one-on-one basis and select two of you for the band," says Jimmy, who looks relieved at the outcome of the meeting.

The next day, Jimmy meets with each of the three men and selects Johnny McCall and Rory MacNaughton. Reynolds knows that he has his work cut out for him to retain the trophy for the best pipe band at the Cowal gathering. He also realizes that he promised Gordon Morrison private piping lessons, so Jimmy has a full slate of commitments between now and the end of August. Reynolds immediately develops a band practice schedule, leaving some openings for Gordon Morrison. As luck would have it, Rory MacNaughton, one of the new band members, receives an urgent message from home that his father, Robert, has died suddenly and that he should return for the funeral.

"What am I going to do?" asks Reynolds as he sits in a slouching position in one of the practice rooms with his fellow pipers. The men have never seen Reynolds so downhearted.

"What about Niall McIver?" suggests Captain Cameron.

"No, he does not understand a word we're talking about," replies a disgruntled pipe major.

At that point Jimmy Reynolds suddenly remembers the two Stewart brothers, Donald and Shaulto, who came to Bluehill in October 1796. A messenger is urgently sent to the Isle of Lewis with a message for the three Stewart brothers.

Two days later Shaulto Stewart appears at Bluehill wearing

297

the Royal Stewart tartan kilt with a set of Highland bagpipes slung over his shoulder.

"Y'are a sight for sore eyes, Shaulto," shouts a relieved pipe major as he embraces his old friend and pats him on the back.

"I could not let you down, Jimmy, after a' the fine piping lessons ye gave me and my two brothers."

Jimmy and Shaulto enjoy a good chat over some Scotch whisky then get down to the business of getting prepared for the Cowal gathering.

In Port Glasgow, Andrew Griffin and his Argylls' pipe band practice four nights a week. During the other three nights, Andrew practices on his own, or coaches young and upcoming pipers. The wound inflicted on Andrew by Dougie Reid is still causing Andrew stiffness and pain in his left shoulder, so he continues to take time off work for massage therapy, which helps to relieve some of the pain. His old war wounds still cause bouts of occasional discomfort.

The Argylls have a fine pipe band this year. Twelve of the twenty pipers and drummers have been with the band for over five years, and it shows in their playing. Amongst the newcomers are two pipers who have won the individual piping championship at Cowal during the past five years. The stage is set for a highly competitive piping-and-drumming competition.

Chapter 47

SIXTEENTH COWAL GATHERING

Old Tom has just attended the final planning meeting for the sixteenth Cowal Highland gathering, which is being held this year on 28 August. A record twenty-eight pipe bands have registered to attend and compete. In addition, Highland-dancing enrolments are at their highest level with over 100 participants. One of the new competitors in the Highland dance competition this year is Princess Augusta's daughter, Marina. In the individual piping competition, there are forty entrants for the under-eighteen category and over sixty pipers for the senior event. The field events also attract record numbers of participants from all over Scotland. The gathering has been well advertised and this is reflected in the high number of participants. With steam-powered commercial boats now operating on the River Clyde, the organizing committee anticipate a record games attendance.

Old Tom opens the gathering mid-morning. The weather is dry and warm and a record crowd of over 3,000 people is in attendance on the first morning.

"My lords, ladies and gentlemen, welcome to the sixteenth Cowal gathering. This year we have attracted the largest number o' competitors ever, and based on the size o' the crowd here today it looks like a record number of attendees," shouts Old Tom at the top of his voice.

There is great cheering from the large crowd, who are in high spirits.

"When I first suggested hosting a Highland gathering back in 1796, I had no idea that it would become an annual event and attract so many folk. On behalf of our organizing committee, I declare the sixteenth Cowal gathering open," shouts Old Tom.

There is great cheering amongst the competitors and attendees alike as Old Tom steps down from the podium. Twenty-four pipe bands make their way on to Cowal Field led by the Boys of Bluehill, last year's Grade 1 champion pipe band. The pipe bands play 'The Gathering of Lochiel' and the crowd cheers their heroes as they make their way around the field. Bands from all over Scotland are present and most of the clan tartans are on display. Soon, all of the other competitors take to the field and complete a circuit, to the delight of the boisterous crowd.

Before noon the competitions get under way. The first set of events is in Highland dancing and Helen MacLeod has brought eight competitors from Argyll. Two of the dancers are defending champions – Kiely and Shauna MacLeod. Kiely and Shauna befriend Princess Augusta's daughter Marina, who is competing at Cowal for the very first time and is extremely nervous. The field events get under way and the most popular event is the tossing of the caber. Most of the competitors in this event are over six feet tall, with bodyweights well over sixteen stones. The men competing in this event are mainly blacksmiths and labourers. Amongst those entered for the tossing of the caber event is the Black Douglas, from Cromarty, who distinguished himself at the Battle of Vila Real in Portugal.

After lunch on the first day, the preliminary rounds of the individual piping championships begin. The under-eighteen competition is in progress and the judges listen to some fine young pipers. After the first round of the under-eighteen competition is complete, the senior pipers take the field. Gordon Morrison plays flawlessly and makes it to the second round. Andrew Griffin competes in the last group, and he also progresses to the second round.

By mid-afternoon, the pipe-band competitions commence. The competitors are placed into various groups. The Boys of

Bluehill are drawn in group number two, while the Argylls are placed in group five. The pipe tunes selected by the judges for the preliminary (first) round are 'John MacKenzie's Farewell to Strathglass', 'Leaving Port Askaig', and 'The Lonach Gathering'.

Fiona Noble and her family cheer on the Argylls and are accompanied by Heather Griffin and her three children. Isla, Andrew's sister, and her husband, Ross MacBride travel from the coastal town of Ayr to visit the Griffin family and to show their support for the Argylls' pipes and drums. The Argylls play well and make it to the second round, which is scheduled for the next morning. The Boys of Bluehill also progress to the next round along with The Isle of Syke Pipes and Drums, who surprise all of the bands in their grouping by finishing first. Other bands to progress into the second round are Shotts and Dykehead, the Sons of Edinburgh, Kilcreggan Pipes and Drums, the Atholl Highlanders and the Gordons. The best two losing bands are the Ballymena Pipes and Drums from Northern Ireland, and the Queen of the South Pipes and Drums from Dumfries, in the Border country of Scotland.

That evening, the Griffin and Noble families meet for dinner. Isla, Andrew's sister, and her husband, Ross MacBride also sit with the Griffin family for the meal. Senior officers of the Argylls appear during the evening and also join the Griffin family.

Major MacDonald and his bride, Lindsay, visit the Griffins and Nobles during the evening. Since Fiona Noble first set eyes on Major MacDonald she has secretly lusted after him. Because Donald has just married Lindsay, Fiona has not made any advances towards him. However, this evening Fiona is inebriated and makes open advances towards Major MacDonald, who is taken by surprise.

Heather notices what is going on and takes the opportunity to follow Fiona into the ladies' powder room.

"What do you think y'are up to, Fiona? Donald is just married and you are a married woman with children," shouts Heather angrily.

"Aye, I know I am married, but I want Donald," replies Fiona, who appears to be talking through too much wine.

Heather grabs hold of Fiona and shakes her.

"Come to yer senses, woman! Do you want to wreck the lives o' a newly married couple, never mind yer own?" shouts Heather.

Fiona bursts out crying and holds on to Heather. "No, I do not want to lose my Ross," cries Fiona.

Both women embrace for a few minutes until Fiona composes herself. Heather tells the guests that Fiona feels unwell and she will take her home. The dinner party continues and Colonel MacGregor appears accompanied by his wife, Mary, and their daughter and her husband, Major Buchanan.

"Yer band played well today, Major Griffin," comments Buchanan.

"Thanks – the band did play very well," agrees Griffin.

"I noticed you were having yer left shoulder rubbed just before you played in the first round of the individual piping competition," remarks Major Buchanan.

"Aye, my shoulder has been bothering me since the knife attack by Dougie Reid," replies Griffin.

"Do you think that you will be able to continue in the individual piping competition, Major?" enquires Buchanan.

"Thanks for asking. I am hoping I can," replies Griffin, who appears to be in some discomfort.

The families retire for the evening and the soldiers linger at the dining table to finish off a few bottles of Scotch whisky, compliments of Major Griffin. Meanwhile, Gordon Morrison and Helen MacLeod have been dining with Pipe Major Reynolds and members of the Boys of Bluehill pipe band.

"You did well today, Gordon," compliments Reynolds as he eats his meal. "Yer tone was just right and you never missed a note," adds a proud pipe major.

"It feels really good. I believe that the extra tutoring you gave me is paying off," replies Morrison, who is happy with Reynolds' comments. "What about yerself? How did the band play today?" enquires Morrison.

"Well, the lads did well. The two new pipers are fitting in, but I think they'll need a wee bit more time to reach the same playing level as Patterson and Campbell. We'll have to go some to beat the Argylls. They have a great tone, and today they sounded like champions in the making," replies Reynolds.

"Enough talk about piping – what about my dancers, lads?" asks Helen, who is determined not be upstaged by the pipers and drummers.

"Aye, we tend to get a wee bit carried away with the piping talk," admits Reynolds.

"Well, my two wee nieces are going to show you men how lassies win gold medals," predicts Helen.

Gordon reaches out and holds Helen's hand and kisses her on the lips. Helen returns his kiss with passion.

"Come on, you two – yer no on yer honeymoon yet," comments Reynolds jokingly.

The next morning starts with the finals of the Highland-dancing competition. In the under-fifteen girls' competition Shauna MacLeod, aged fourteen, has made it to the finals. Shauna is the defending champion in this age group. Joining Shauna is Princess Augusta's daughter, Marina, who has just turned twelve years old two days ago. In the over-fifteen competition Kiely MacLeod, Shauna's older sister, advances to the last eight dancers.

While the Highland dancers compete, the finals of the field events commence. The Black Douglas, from Cromarty, is in the final four of the caber-tossing competition, and he also reaches the final stages of the hammer throwing, which is scheduled for mid-afternoon.

The individual senior piping competition finals get under way. The judges draw lots for the order of piping. Gordon Morrison is drawn fifth of twelve pipers and Andrew Griffin is placed in seventh spot. Also competing is Angus McCall from Tomintoul, whom Griffin has competed against on several occasions. A large crowd gathers for the finals and the weather remains dry. The pipe tunes selected by the judges are 'Edinburgh Volunteers' (march), 'Sandy King's Breeks' (strathspey), and 'Ridhle Mo Nighean Donn' ('Ca' the Ewes' – reel) for the final twelve pipers.

In the Highland-dancing competition for the under-fifteen girls the judges are about to announce the winners. Princess Augusta, the Duke of Argyll and their son James have watched Marina perform flawlessly and are hopeful that she will receive a medal. Helen MacLeod is also anxious as she waits to hear if her niece Shauna is to repeat as gold medalist, a feat not accomplished to date in the competition. The judge, Sandra Magee, a champion dancer in her day and an experienced judge, reads out the result of the under-fifteen Highland-dance competition.

"The bronze medal goes to Marina Campbell from Argyll," declares Judge Magee.

Marina steps forward, bows and receives her first-ever medal to the delight of her family.

"The silver medal is awarded to Shauna MacLeod of Campbeltown," states the judge.

Poor Shauna bravely steps forward and accepts her award with dignity.

"The gold medal is awarded to Sine MacNeil from the island of Barra," proclaims Judge Magee.

The audience gives a big round of applause for the high standard of Highland dancing achieved in the under-fifteen lassies' competition. Princess Augusta hugs and kisses her young daughter.

Helen McLeod, Dr. Sandy and his wife, Margaret, try to bolster Shauna, who is visibly shaken at finishing second.

The over-fifteen female Highland-dancing winners are now announced. "The bronze medal winner is Giorsal Mackinnon from the Isle of Skye," declares Flora MacDonald, the judge from Glencoe.

"The silver medal goes to Jemima McColl from Dunoon," shouts Flora.

A great cheer goes up from the large crowd for the local lassie.

"The champion for this year is Kiely MacLeod from Campbeltown, Argyll," calls out the judge. The cheering is deafening for the crowd realize that they have just witnessed the first repeat winner in the over-fifteen female dance category – a great feat. The McLeod family embraces their repeat champion, and Kiely and Shauna hug each other for a long time. Wee Annie Griffin and her puppy, Totty, also join in hugging her two very best friends.

The winner of the tossing of the caber is the Black Douglas, from Cromarty – a very popular result amongst the large number of soldiers in attendance.

In the men's individual piping competition, the last four pipers are announced. The four finalists are Angus McCall, Gordon Morrison, Donald Lindsay and Andrew Griffin. Heather is very concerned about Andrew because he is complaining about his shoulder wound. Unlike the two bullet wounds Andrew sustained in the Battle of Vila Real, which are only painful occasionally, the knife wound is still causing Andrew a lot of pain in his left shoulder.

The pipe tunes for the four finalists are very challenging. The judges have chosen 'John MacColl's March to Kilbowie', 'Tulloch Gorm' for the strathspey, and 'The Duke of Richmond' for the reel. All four pipers know these pipe tunes fairly well, but one wrong note could mean losing out on the medals. The draw for the order of playing is announced. First Gordon Morrison, followed by Angus McCall, Donald Lindsay and Andrew Griffin. While the four pipers practice, Pipe Major Jimmy Reynolds observes that Andrew Griffin is having difficulty with his left shoulder.

A crowd of over 3,000 people assembles to hear the best four pipers in Scotland. Donald Lindsay has won the gold medal for the under-eighteen competition, but his best effort in the senior piping competition was a third-place finish behind Andrew Griffin.

Morrison leads off and gives a superb performance of individual piping. The crowd shows their appreciation. McCall plays soon after Morrison, and he also gives a very fine performance. Lindsay, who is third, plays well but has a little bit of trouble with the strathspey. Finally, to the cheers of the large crowd Andrew Griffin, defending champion and winner of five individual gold Grade 1 medals in this event, steps out and on to the field and entertains the crowd. The march is played with perfection, as is the strathspey, but in the reel his shoulder begins to bother him and he does not achieve the level of excellence he has demonstrated in the past. The crowd gives him a thunderous applause and he is the sentimental favourite, and hero amongst the soldiers of the Argylls in the audience.

Angus Campbell, the chief piping judge for this event, reads out the results to the hush of the crowd.

"The bronze medal goes to Angus McCall from Tomintoul," shouts Campbell. "The silver medal this year is awarded to Andrew Griffin of Port Glasgow," announces Campbell. "And this year we have a new piping champion – Gordon Morrison from the port o' Oban," proclaims Angus Campbell.

The crowd is stunned at the result, but gives Morrison a big round of applause. Many in the crowd are soldiers from battalions of the Lowland and Highland regiments of the Argylls who will soon be leaving to fight Napoleon Bonaparte in Europe, and feel deflated that their piping hero has lost out on the gold medal.

Helen and Jimmy hug and congratulate Gordon on his great victory. Morrison can hardly believe the result as Angus Campbell awards him the gold medal. Andrew Griffin is amongst the first to congratulate Morrison.

"You did very well today, Gordon. Wear yer medal with pride," Griffin says.

Pipe Major Jimmy Reynolds watches the defeated champion approach Gordon and offers his best wishes. Reynolds thinks to himself what a great competitor and true champion Griffin is, both on and off the field. Reynolds has heard Griffin play 'The Duke of Richmond' reel flawlessly many times in competition and knows that Griffin's damaged shoulder is the reason for him finishing second today.

* * * * *

In the beer tents there is a lot of discussion about the piping competition. The young soldiers who have been tutored by Major Griffin take the judge's result very hard.

After lunch, the field events start to wind down. In the final field event, the throwing of the hammer, the Black Douglas, from Cromarty, completes a gold-medal double by edging out the local favourite and defending champion by only six small inches.

The final event of the Highland gathering, the pipe-band competition, is in progress. Over 4,000 people assemble to watch the best pipe bands compete. The judges announce the order. The Argylls are up first, followed by Kilcreggan Pipes and Drums, the Sons of Edinburgh, the Boys of Bluehill, Shotts and Dykehead, the Isle of Skye Pipes and Drums and finally the Gordons pipes and drums.

As the Argylls wait to be announced, Major Griffin turns to his pipers and drummers and says, "Lads, you have shown me what you can do time and again in practice; now let's see what you can do now that our moment of glory has arrived."

As Major Griffin leads his band on to Cowal Field a great roar is heard from the crowd. The pipers and drummers look magnificent in their Black Watch kilts and their large sporrans. Most of the men sport beards and look imposing to the crowd. When campaigning in Europe, many of the men do not choose to shave early in the morning with cold water in the middle of open fields. As a result, the men grow long beards, which they retain when based at home. The pipe band members wear the large Argyll brooches on their black leather shoulder straps. The brooches, which are made of silver, sparkle in the late afternoon sunlight. Protruding from the top of their stockings are shiny thistle-topped skean dhus. Most of the men in the band are at least six feet tall. The piping and drumming match their appearance. Their performance is near flawless and each of the band members keep in tight formation as Pipe Major Griffin marches up and down wielding his mace in front of the judges' stand. Old Tom, who is observing the Argylls from the stand, experiences a great deep feeling of pride as the pipers and drummers give a performance to remember. All of the endless hours of practice, marching and tutoring have surely paid off.

The Argylls leave the field to a great ovation from a knowledgeable audience. Heather and Isla run up to Andrew and hugs and kisses are the order of the day.

"You were magnificent, Andrew – you and your Argylls were magnificent," cries Heather, who is so relieved that her husband has managed to compete in both events. Isla is crying close to Andrew as a result of the courage shown by her brother, who is clearly in great pain.

The men of Kilcreggan follow the Argylls, and soon the defending champions, the Boys of Bluehill, are called to the field. Pipe Major Jimmy Reynolds is an imposing figure and a legend amongst the piping fraternity in Scotland and abroad. Throwing his mace high above his head, the Boys of Bluehill march proudly on to the field. Pipe Major Reynolds is a magnificent entertainer and instils confidence in his men. Playing their hearts out, the Boys of Bluehill give a fine performance. The two new members of the band play well and Pipe Major Reynolds knows that his pipe band have done their best.

Gordon Morrison and Helen congratulate Pipe Major Reynolds. "You sounded great Jimmy, just great," says Gordon enthusiastically.

"Thanks, Gordon – the boys did play well," replies Jimmy, who is sweating profusely from his exertions.

Shotts and Dykehead play next, and the two Ross brothers, whom Andrew Griffin has trained at the army barracks in Port Glasgow, are members of the band.

There is a lot of interest in the Isle of Skye pipe band this year. Most of the members of the pipe band are army-trained and have been tutored at Bluehill or at the army barracks in Port Glasgow. The band members come from the villages of Broadford and Drumfearn on the Isle of Skye, and most of the men are related to one another. These men have fought with Old Tom in South Africa and in Portugal and are highly motivated. The band members have given a clear example of their excellence in piping and drumming in the preliminary rounds of the competition by finishing first. Their Pipe Major is a Captain MacPherson who has been decorated in the South African Campaign by Old Tom as a result of bravery above and beyond the call of duty. Captain MacPherson was wounded in the European campaigns with the Argylls, and retired from the army two years ago and assembled the pipe band. Several hundred family members have made the long journey down from the Isle of Skye in North-West Scotland and are cheering on their fellow Highlanders. The Isle of Skye Pipes and Drums do not let their family and friends down. They play like true veterans and impress the large crowd.

The shadows are lengthening on this late summer evening as the Gordon Highlanders take to the field. Like the Argylls, the Gordons have a very experienced pipe band. Their drum corps is recognized as the finest in Scotland. The Gordons are led by Pipe Major John Gordon, who is directly descended from Sir John Gordon who was created a baronet of Nova Scotia, Canada, in 1642. Pipe Major Gordon comes from a long line of distinguished pipers. The Gordon Highlanders give a very fine performance and Old Tom sits in the stands in awe, wondering how the judges can separate such very fine piping and drumming.

As the Gordons leave the field the visitors in the audience start singing, "*A Gordon for me, a Gordon for me; if y'are no a Gordon y'are nae use to me.*" The rest of the crowd joins in and the Gordons salute the crowd as they make their way off Cowal Field.

All of the pipe bands now march back on to the field and make their way to the front of the judges' stand. The finest pipe bands ever assembled patiently wait in the evening sun for the judges' decision. Old Tom is requested to present the coveted trophies to the winning bands.

"My lords, ladies and gentlemen, there are no losers here today; everyone who competes here at Cowal Field on this day is a winner in my book. Aye, I have never heard such fine piping and drumming. Congratulations to a' of you," shouts Old Tom at the top of his voice to the cheering and chanting of the large crowd. Supporters of the pipe bands start chanting for their favourite bands, and it is very obvious to all in attendance that this is by far the most competitive Highland gathering to date.

"In third place, taking the bronze medal this year, are the Boys of Bluehill. In second place, for the silver medal, are the Isle of Skye Pipes and Drums. And the champions for 1812 are the Argylls," proclaims Old Tom at the top of his voice.

When the gold-medal winners are announced the crowd erupts in cheering and chanting, and flags and banners are waved high in the air. Hundreds of soldiers and officers from the Lowland and Highland regiments of the Argylls throw their bonnets and glengarries high in the air and there is a great amount of celebrating.

It takes over fifteen minutes before the medals and the Cowal Trophy can be awarded to the winning bands. The spectators surge on to the field and the stewards in attendance are unable to control such a large and boisterous crowd. When order is restored, the trophies are awarded. Jimmy Reynolds is disappointed but in his heart he knows that the Argylls have set a new standard for others to attain.

Heather and the children are unable to get near Andrew to share in this great moment of victory. Andrew is surrounded by hundreds of soldiers and officers offering their congratulations. Eventually, the Argylls are ordered to lead the bands off the field. The tradition over the years is for the winning band to lead all of the other competing bands off Cowal Field and march down the long hill into the local town of Dunoon, a distance of a mile.

It is almost seven o'clock in the evening when the Argylls lead the other pipe bands off Cowal Field and down the long hill towards Dunoon, playing 'Heroes of Vila Real'. Heather carries the Cowal Trophy as she and all of her family members proudly walk behind the Argylls. Ross and Fiona Noble and their children also join the parade. The sun is beginning to dip in the west as the Argylls, playing their tunes of glory, continue down the long slope towards Dunoon. As they approach the entrance to the town Andrew signals the band to play 'Heroes of Vila Real'. There is a large crowd waiting for the champions as they enter the town, amongst them Old Tom and his family. Looking back up the long hill, the large crowd waiting at the entrance to the town of Dunoon can see all of the other pipe bands and their supporters following the Argylls. The line stretches as far as the eye can see and the setting sun catches the clan badges and the silver-mounted tips of the Highland bagpipes. The pipe bands keep in good order as they proudly march down the hill playing their strathspeys, reels and marches. For those who are fortunate enough to be in attendance, it is a memorable sight – one that will always be cherished.

Old Tom and his family congratulate the Argylls for an exceptional performance. The Duke asks Andrew about the new pipe tune.

"It's called 'Heroes o' Vila Real', My Lord, and I wrote it in memory of our great victory," explains Andrew with pride, sweating profusely after the day's efforts.

"I loved it, Andrew – it is a great tune. I would like it to become the signature tune o' the Argylls," shouts Old Tom with great conviction.

"Consider it done, My Lord," replies Griffin, who is thrilled with the Duke's interest and his support for the Argylls' pipes and drums.

Pipe Major Reynolds is the next to congratulate Andrew and the Argylls.

"I swear yer pipers' playing sounded just like one piper, Andrew," says Pipe Major Reynolds with great sincerity.

"You could not pay me a higher compliment, Jimmy," replies Andrew as the men embrace.

"Oh, was that a new piece you played coming out o' Cowal Field, Andrew?" enquires Reynolds.

"I put it together over the last year and named it 'Heroes o' Vila Real'," explains Andrew.

"I love it, Andrew. You have come up with a real winner –

congratulations," says Reynolds as he shakes his friend's hand heartily and pats him on the back.

"Andrew, a messenger arrived while we were at the Cowal gathering," shouts Heather as she prepares the evening meal in the kitchen.

Examining the package, Andrew notices it is from Gordon Morrison's law firm in Edinburgh. Opening the package, Andrew is delighted to read that his request for a name change from Griffin to MacGregor has been processed.

"Mrs MacGregor, is the evening meal ready?" shouts Andrew.

"Andrew, who are you talking to? Do we have visitors?" asks Heather.

"No, no, Heather," says Andrew as he enters the kitchen clutching the covering letter from the law firm. "It's confirmation from the law firm of Ogilvie, Urqhart and Donaldson of Edinburgh advising us of my request to have our name changed to MacGregor."

"Wonderful," says Heather, "I'm glad that you took action after all these years and arranged for the name change."

Chapter 48

ANOTHER SHOCK FOR
HEATHER MACGREGOR

The rain is pouring down in torrents; nevertheless Shore Street
is alive with bustle, especially in the vicinity of The Tickled
Trout Inn. It is Thursday, the day of the well-advertised card
game with no table limits in place. This is not just any card
game; it is a special game with six players renowned for their
skill at winning.

There is a sound of revelry inside The Tickled Trout Inn. A
large crowd of locals has assembled in a room around a card
table as the six contestants vie for a prize in excess of £2,000.
The locals consist of shopkeepers, farmers, shipbuilders and
army officers. The card game has been in progress for over three
hours and none of the players has requested a break. There is
a great deal of tension as the players appear evenly matched.
Andrew MacGregor has been dealt a particularly good hand
by the dealer. As a result Andrew increases the stakes. Three
of the six players withdraw from the game, sensing that the
other contestants have better hands than theirs. In addition to
Andrew, the two remaining players are Captain Thomas Percy
and Gordon Templeton. Captain Percy has travelled up to Port
Glasgow from London and has a reputation for winning high-
stake card games. Gordon Templeton is a rich merchantman
who is known amongst his peers by his soubriquet of the Silver
Fox.

Three thousand pounds are now at stake. Templeton senses
that his two opponents have strong hands – certainly better
than his, he thinks – so he withdraws from the game, leaving

MacGregor and Percy to fight it out. It is nearing midnight when Andrew places £300 on the table to see his opponent's hand. The large crowd of onlookers gasps and silence falls around the room. With a full house, aces full of kings, Andrew is certain that he has a winning hand. Captain Percy places his cigar on an ashtray, but does not immediately make a move to show his cards. Percy stares at Andrew as he slowly turns over each of his cards. When the last card is displayed – the ace of hearts – the silence is broken by a sudden eruption of shouts, gasps and comments from the audience as a royal flush appears for all to witness. Andrew is stunned, and then he feels numbness set in and finds difficulty in reacting to this devastating loss. Meanwhile, Percy casually gathers his winnings, picks up his cigar and begins to leave the card table surrounded by a host of supporters.

"Andrew, it's time for ye to go home; it's past 1 a.m.," says Ben McQuarrie, the owner of The Tickled Trout Inn as he lays a comforting hand on Andrew's shoulder.

Andrew sits slouched at the card table in a daze, stunned and utterly bewildered at the turn of events.

The rain has stopped and the sky is now clear. The moon shines brightly as Andrew walks slowly along a deserted Shore Street towards his home at Braemar Gardens. In the coolness of the early morning air, the realization of his great loss becomes all too clear to him and the shouts of the onlookers at that critical moment echo in his ears. Such a moment as this has never occurred in his life before and he feels a sense of devastation.

Andrew enters his home quietly and walks down the long hallway to a dark living room where the dying embers of a fire and the light from a full moon peeping through the half-drawn velvet curtains greets him. He slouches into a large chair by the fireplace, and his head hangs down in despair. For several minutes Andrew sits in the darkening moonlight of the early morning as clouds scud over the moon. A few minutes later Heather enters the living room wearing her night attire and carrying a lamp.

"Where have you been, Andrew?" asks Heather, sternly holding the lamp closer to her husband.

Looking up at Heather, he catches the anxious look of pain in his wife's eyes as she stoops over him.

"I am so sorry, my dear, so sorry. I have broken my promise to you yet again," replies Andrew with tears forming in his eyes.

"You have not been gambling again?"

"Aye, I have been gambling and, what's worse, I have lost most of our savings."

Heather is stunned at Andrew's statement and sinks down on her knees unable to support herself in the shock of discovery. She has a feeling of revulsion, and bursts into a flood of tears most distressing to witness. A red flush appears in her white cheeks and her sobbing grows louder. As she crouches on her knees she realizes that Andrew has been unwilling to accept any externally imposed discipline and has become a slave to gaming.

Observing his wife's distress as she kneels on the floor, remorse quickly takes a stronger hold over Andrew as he shivers with a feeling of dread.

Moments later, Andrew's son Grieg enters the room and rushes towards his mother, still kneeling on the floor. Heather hugs her son as he helps his distressed mother to her feet and both mother and son slowly leave the room in an embrace.

Early the next morning Andrew is awakened by the sound of a carriage outside his living-room window. He had fallen into a deep sleep on the chair by the fire. Moving towards the window, he draws back the curtains only to witness the carriage pull away. Andrew is unable to view the passengers inside, so he makes his way upstairs to the family bedrooms. All of the bedrooms are empty and there is no sign of the children. Returning downstairs Andrew notices an envelope lying on the hall table close to the door. Andrew tears open the envelope and reads the letter.

Andrew,

Your reckless behaviour and broken promises have caused me much distress. I can no longer trust you. I have to move away.

Your unhappy wife,
Heather

Standing in the hallway, Andrew drops Heather's letter to the floor and bursts into tears. The tears flow freely and he raises his hands into the air and utters a cry of despair. For over ten minutes the tears flow, and as the despair deepens he kneels to the floor consumed with grief and a great sense of loss.

As the carriage makes its way to the south-west along bumpy roads, Heather's thoughts turn to Andrew. She has loved Andrew with impassioned fervour and now she has been rudely awakened by the gradual process of disenchantment. He has broken several promises to her and the family during the past few years, promising many times to stop gambling and spend more time with the children. Certain rumours concerning Andrew's addiction to gaming got whispered about and they unfortunately reached the ear of Heather. She has no reason to believe that they were untrue because she has experienced Andrew's addiction to gaming first hand. Personally, Andrew is loving and indulgent to Heather and the children. No open rupture has taken place until now. Before the world they are as sufficiently cordial with each other as most husbands and wives; but Heather is an unhappy woman, looking upon herself as miserably deceived.

"Heather, what a surprise!" says Isla as the family alight from the coach.

"Sorry to arrive so unexpectedly Isla," Heather replies, hugging her sister-in-law.

The children and the luggage are taken inside the house. Isla takes the children upstairs to their bedrooms and gets them settled. It is almost nine o'clock in the evening and the children are exhausted after the long journey and are all ready for bed.

Isla comes downstairs and searches for Heather. She eventually finds her in a corner of the terrace, shaded from observation by clustering trees. Heather is standing leaning over the rails and gazing on the sloping gardens beneath. Cold and still is her face; cold and still is her unhappy heart, its life blood seeming to have left it. As she hangs over the terrace in the moonlight, her hands clasp together in pain and her forehead presses upon the cold iron of the rails, as if its chill could soothe the throbbing fire within. A cloud of images is in her brain, all bearing the beautiful memories of happier days with Andrew. Silently someone touches her shoulder, and Heather shivers and looks up.

It is Isla.

"Heather!" she whispers, and the tone of her voice is tender, caring and loving. "Heather, are you ill?"

Heather's emotions suddenly overcome her and she begins to sob loudly, her body shaking and trembling, causing Isla to embrace her distraught sister-in-law. Taking her inside the house and seating her beside a brightly burning fire, Isla gives Heather a glass of brandy. The crying continues, and it is all Isla can do to console her distressed sister-in-law. After Heather finishes her brandy Isla takes her upstairs and without any questioning helps her into bed.

The clock in the living room strikes midnight as Ross MacBride, Isla's husband, returns home weary from his long visits to local farms.

"Sorry I am so late, my dear; old man Robertson's newly purchased cow's had a fever."

"Ross, sit down, I have some news," says Isla gently. "We have some unexpected guests; they arrived from Port Glasgow earlier this evening."

"Andrew and Heather?" questions Ross with a surprised look on his face.

"No, it's Heather and the three children."

"Where's Andrew?"

"He did not accompany them on this trip."

Isla then went on to explain the terrible state Heather was in when she arrived and how she thought it best not to question her sister-in-law at this time as she was so distressed.

The next morning is bright and sunny. Isla arranges for the children to come down for breakfast and not to disturb their mother. Soon after breakfast the children rush out to the yard and start feeding the animals. This gives Isla the opportunity to speak with Heather in her room.

"How do you feel, Heather?" asks Isla as she sits down on the bed beside her sister-in-law.

"Much better, thank you, Isla. It was so kind of you not to question me soon after I arrived last night."

"When you feel like talking, my dearie, let me know. I am a good listener."

A deep conflict is going on in Heather's mind as she bathes. Two passions, bad and good, are at work, each striving for mastery. Should I forgive Andrew or should I not? Heather's position is an extremely trying one. In the midst of grief – it may be said *the horror* – she feels the deceit of her husband which is overshadowing her.

Heather sits reading on the terrace under the shade of a large umbrella. The children have gone off pony trekking with one of Isla's hired employees. Heather feels calmer, gentle, pale, her manner subdued even more than usual with the dark distress that is upon her.

As Isla approaches with some refreshments, Heather places her book on the table and Isla pours two cool drinks of lemonade.

"We should not get disturbed, Heather. The children will be gone for a few hours and Ross has been called out by a local farmer," says Isla, drawing a seat closer to Heather.

A few quiet moments pass – time for Heather to gather her thoughts.

"Andrew – Andrew has broken his promise yet again, Isla.

He started gaming again despite all his assurances and has gambled away most of our family savings. He came home early yesterday morning and confessed," said Heather, clutching a handkerchief close to her face.

Isla moves closer to Heather and gently holds her arm. Heather's tears are now dropping fast; she is weak and in shock from Andrew's confession and the loss of the family savings.

Isla comforts her distressed sister-in-law and embraces her. It is clear to Isla that Andrew's addiction to gaming is very serious and that he needs help to slay the gaming dependency which is consuming him.

"Isla, this letter has arrived. It's from yer brother," said Ross MacBride, handing the document to his wife.

The letter is addressed to Isla. Isla grabs the side of her long dress and whisks upstairs and explains to Heather that she has received a letter in the morning mail from Andrew.

"I want you to hear what Andrew has to say, Heather. Would you like me to open the letter and read it to you?"

Heather does not know how to respond, but after a few minutes she agrees.

Isla opens the letter:

Isla,

I am writing to you to advise you that Heather and the children have left me. I have brought disgrace upon the family, and through my wretched behaviour have lost most of our family savings at gaming.

Full of remorse and regret as this moment is, it is only of Heather and the children that I think of rather than myself. I have broken my promises to Heather, not once but on several occasions, and for that I am truly sorry. I caused Heather and the children a great amount of hurt and distress. I have seen our family physician, Dr. Jamieson, and he has referred me to see a specialist. I am leaving for Edinburgh tomorrow for treatment. I will write again. If you hear from Heather, please tell her that I love her and the children.

Your brother,
Andrew

As Isla finishes reading the letter aloud Heather sits hunched up in bed with her hands placed over her eyes.

After a long silence, Heather says, "Tomorrow, Isla, I will take the children home."

"You're very welcome to stay longer, Heather; the children seem to like visiting the farm."

"Thank you, Isla. You are so kind. I want the children to return to school, so we will make arrangements to leave in the morning."

Chapter 49

LEAVING SCOTLAND

Andrew dips a quill into the inkwell and begins to write to his wife, Heather. He barely gets started when he suddenly finds himself shredding the paper and throwing it in a waste-paper basket. For three nights he has tried with all his strength to draft a letter to his wife. After returning from Edinburgh he has rented rooms at The Tickled Trout Inn on Shore Street. During his stay at the tavern he has not ventured outside. Andrew's only visits out of his rooms are downstairs to eat his meals in a quiet corner of the taproom. The only person Andrew notices in the taproom is a ship's captain named MacBride, who also sits by himself on the other side of the room eating his meals. Big Ben McQuarrie, the landlord of the tavern, has personally served Andrew his meals. Andrew's decision to leave Scotland has only been made during the past few days and he does not know how to let his estranged wife know of his plans. While he was in Edinburgh he visited a law firm and instructed them to send £300 to Heather, which represents the remainder of his life savings. In addition, Andrew advised the lawyer to talk to Heather about selling their home at Braemar Gardens and purchasing a smaller, more affordable dwelling for the family.

With the help of Big Ben, Andrew purchases a passage on the *Loch Leven*, which is due to sail to Halifax, Nova Scotia, in a few days' time. It is the most difficult decision of his life. Picking up his quill he again tries to draft a letter to Heather:

My dearest Heather,

I pray that you and the children are well.

I spent some time in Edinburgh and visited a medical specialist, who has given me advice on my gambling addiction. I have been advised that I am indeed addicted to gambling. I have also been told that until I personally acknowledge that I am addicted, I will not be in a position to start the work towards setting myself free of the gambling addiction. I now realize that part of me has been out of control.

The suffering and pain I have caused you and the children has brought me to the realization that I must get away and sort out my life.

I have made arrangements with an Edinburgh law firm for £300 to be made available to you. I also suggest that you sell our house at Braemar Gardens and find a more affordable home for you and the family.

I am leaving for Nova Scotia, Canada, later this week and hope that I can sort out my life and conquer the gambling addiction which has ruined my life and brought so much misery and pain to you and the children.

Please understand that if there is any way to save our marriage, I must pursue this course of action.

Pray for my full recovery.

With all my love to you and the children,
    Andrew

Big Ben agrees to make arrangements for the letter to be delivered to Heather.

Picking up three bags – one filled with clothes, another containing his beloved Highland bagpipes, and the third bag containing food for the voyage – Andrew quietly leaves the tavern and makes his way quickly to the Port Glasgow docks. He had learned from seamen on his voyages to South Africa that fresh fruit is essential on long sea voyages.

As he enters the pothouse by the wharf Andrew is greeted by three adults and a young boy who appears to be about twelve years old. Travelling bags are stacked in a corner of the room. One gentleman, who is tall, thin, has a long pointed nose and is dressed in black, immediately approaches Andrew.

"Reverend John Lindsay at yer service, sir – late o' the parish o' the wee town o' Ayr."

"Pleased to meet you, sir," replies Andrew, taken aback at the Reverend's forthright approach.

Andrew is then introduced to the MacKay family from Portree on the Isle of Skye.

The door of the pothouse opens and in walks Captain MacBride.

"Guid evening to you all. I'm Captain MacBride o' the *Loch Leven*. We sail on the morning tide, so gather up yer belongings and follow me down to the ship."

MacBride is short and sports a thick dark-brown beard which matches his dark brown eyes; his complexion is weather-beaten. His ship, the *Loch Leven*, is a merchantman bound for the port of Halifax, Nova Scotia, Canada.

MacBride leads his passengers up the gangway and on to the ship. Andrew and the Reverend Lindsay are given adjacent cabins on the lower deck.

Early the next morning the sky has cleared and a cool breeze greets Andrew as he makes his way to the upper deck of the ship. The sea appears calm as the Captain gives the order to up-anchor. Within minutes the sails are being set and the great ship slowly starts to leave the dock. A chilling feeling creeps through Andrew with the realization that he is leaving his beloved family and homeland. For a moment he doubts his decision until he feels a hand press gently on his left shoulder. It is the Reverend Lindsay, who takes a position beside Andrew on deck as the helmsman steers the great vessel forward and into mid-channel.

"Is it Halifax or Cape Breton for you, Andrew?"

"Oh, Cape Breton, Reverend."

"Then we are destined for the same place, sir."

Andrew pulls his cloak closer around his body as the breeze freshens from the west. As the ship gathers speed down the River Clyde, passing the town of Gourock, Andrew feels a sense of deep remorse; his heart is heavy with guilt and a feeling of emptiness overcomes him as he shivers. It is really happening? he thinks to himself. He is leaving his family and friends and the country of his birth.

The journey to Nova Scotia is long and tedious. It is a time of deep reflection for Andrew, a time for admitting to himself the recklessness of his addiction to gambling. It is the hurt and shame that he has imposed on his family which cause Andrew the deepest pain.

During the first week of the voyage Andrew stays close to his cabin, practising on his chanter. The Reverend Lindsay, who occupies the adjacent cabin to Andrew, has made several gestures to befriend his neighbour, but Andrew is not ready to develop any new relationships.

At the beginning of the second week Captain MacBride and the Reverend Lindsay are involved in a deep conversation on the poop deck when Andrew appears.

"Good morning to ye, Andrew. How are ye?" enquires Captain MacBride cheerily.

"Keeping well, Captain," replies Andrew as his hand reaches for the rail to steady himself as the ship banks from side to side.

"Aye, we have a bit o' a swell today, gentlemen, so hang on to the rail when yer on deck," suggests the good captain.

"Tell me about yer ship, Captain. Does she ride high or low in the water?" asks Andrew with great curiosity.

"Low, Andrew. We are heavy laden below decks. Cargo bound for Halifax and the port o' Montreal," replies MacBride with great gusto.

"I enjoy yer chanter playing, Andrew; would ye be up to playing the pipes one o' these nights?" asks Reverend Lindsay.

"Thank you. Piping is my great passion – it's in my blood, ye ken," replies Andrew, who feels trapped by the Reverend John Lindsay's request but does not want to further distance himself from his neighbour and the ship's captain. "Maybe I could play a few tunes one night later this week," replies Andrew cautiously.

"Champion!" states Captain MacBride. "Y'are both invited to dine with me on Friday night at 8 p.m. sharp, gentlemen."

The next day Andrew practises on his pipes for fifteen minutes.

During the following days he practises for over an hour each day.

"Take a seat, gentlemen," invites MacBride as Reverend Lindsay and Andrew MacGregor enter the room. Eight places are set for dinner. "Allow me to introduce my fellow officers, gentlemen. On yer right, Andrew, is Midshipman Tommy Burns; seated on yer left is First Lieutenant Rory Macfarlane. On the right o' Reverend Lindsay is Malcy Macpherson, our bosun's mate, and seated to the Reverend's left is my purser, Jamie McDuff. Sitting opposite me is the ship's fine doctor, John Findlater. The wee laddie yonder in the corner is Billy Gunn, cabin boy."

As his name is mentioned a pale-looking young lad, barely fourteen years old, with long dark-brown hair, dressed in a red jacket, frayed waistcoat, white bell-bottom trousers badly stained and black-coloured scruffy shoes, struggles to carry a tray full of drinks to the Captain's table.

"Gentlemen, a toast to our piper and the good reverend."

"The piper and the good reverend!"

During the meal, wee Billy Gunn is kept busy, constantly serving trays loaded with glasses of Jamaican rum, French wine and finally decanters of Portuguese port.

"Now, Andrew MacGregor, it's time to hear some Highland bagpipe music," shouts Captain MacBride above the banter around the room.

Andrew has consumed a lot of alcohol, but before playing he reaches for a glass of water, then pulls himself together, takes a deep breath and starts tuning his Highland bagpipes. Soon the room is filled with the sounds of reels and strathspeys. Clapping breaks out and some of MacBride's merrier officers get up from their chairs and start dancing to the catchy reels so well played by Andrew. Even wee Billy Gunn dances to the lively music.

"More, more, we want more!" are the shouts echoing around the room from the now boisterous and intoxicated dinner guests, who demand Andrew continue playing.

The party continues until Andrew, now completely exhausted, calls a halt and rejoins his guests at the dinner table.

"Great stuff, Andrew, great stuff," shouts an appreciative captain.

The guests return to their quarters around 1 a.m. and the Reverend Lindsay accompanies Andrew back to their cabins on the lower deck.

The next morning the ship is abuzz with news of the 'wild party' in the Captain's quarters.

The Reverend Lindsay, who has risen at his normal time, shaved, and enjoyed his breakfast, is now out strolling on the main deck where he meets Captain MacBride.

"Guid morning to ye, Reverend – fine day!"

"Aye, it is a glorious morning, to be sure."

"Have ye seen the piper this morning?" enquires the Captain.

" No, not a sign – not even a sound coming from his room."

"Aye, I'm no in the least surprised. We kept wee Billy Gunn busy running back and forth all night wi' trays full o' drinks," replies MacBride, laughing.

"Andrew MacGregor is a very fine piper – probably the best in Scotland, I hear," comments the Reverend as he continues his morning stroll around the ship's decks.

It is past midday when Andrew finally stirs. The alcohol and playing the Highland bagpipes to an audience who demanded many encores has taken its toll on him.

It is after 2 p.m. when Andrew finds the strength to venture on deck. First Lieutenant Rory Macfarlane is on watch. Standing beside the Lieutenant is Midshipman Tommy Burns, who is plotting the ship's position.

"Gentlemen, good afternoon to you," says Andrew, who is still feeling groggy after last night's binge.

"Good day to you, sir. Enjoyed yer piping. Great stuff!" said an appreciative Lieutenant Macfarlane.

"Glad ye enjoyed the evening, Lieutenant. As for me, I canna recall much of the goings-on last night after the meal was served," replies Andrew as both of his hands tighten on the ship's rail to steady his stance.

"Mr Burns is also a bit of a piper, Andrew," said the first

officer, looking towards his midshipman, who has just completed plotting the ship's position with his sextant.

Thomas Fraser Burns is the only son of a wealthy Glasgow trader. Burns went to sea when he reached his sixteenth birthday. He is in the process of training to become a commissioned officer, but does find time to practise on the bagpipes.

"How long have you been playing the bagpipes, Mr Burns?" asks Andrew.

"It's been five years now. My father played the pipes and I took lessons from one of the instructors at the piping school at Bluehill."

Andrew's eyes light up at the mention of Bluehill.

"Aye I know about the piping school at Bluehill. It has the reputation of being the best in all of Scotland."

"My father was friends with Pipe Major Jimmy Reynolds and he got me started," replies Burns enthusiastically.

At that moment the Reverend Lindsay appears and invites Andrew for a wee stroll around the deck.

"And how is it with ye, Andrew, this fine day?"

"Wee bit shaky today, Reverend; I hope to find my sea legs before the weather turns."

"There's nothing in this world better than a dose of the Lord's fresh sea air to make a man feel better."

"So what brings you to Cape Breton, Reverend?"

"Well, I have spent the past ten years in Ayrshire, ye ken, preaching the word o' God to farmers, flocksmen, gillies and the like. They're fine honest folk and, as the poet Rabbie Burns said:

"Old Ayr where ne'er a town surpasses,
For honest men and bonnie lasses."

"I have heard so many stories over the years, Andrew, about the Scots who immigrated to Cape Breton and I thought I am forty-seven years old and if I don't go now I may never get another chance. And what's yer reason for going all the way to Canada, Andrew?"

Andrew always knew this question would be asked of him. He had gone over in his mind many times how he would answer, but here was a man of the cloth asking a straightforward question which deserved a truthful answer.

"I see ye know yer Burns poetry, Reverend Lindsay. I am a fan of the works of Burns myself. To answer yer question honestly will take time, Reverend," replies Andrew, still not ready to confide in his new-found friend.

"Take all the time ye need, Andrew. I am a patient man and we still have several weeks' sailing ahead of us."

Andrew is relieved that the preacher did not press him for an immediate answer to his question. The two men continue their walk around the ship, stopping to speak to sailors and other passengers.

As the voyage continues the weather changes, bringing strong winds and heavy rain. All passengers are confined below decks for two days until the storm blows itself out.

On the third day Andrew invites Reverend Lindsay to his room for a drink. The two men enjoy a glass of single malt Scotch whisky and Andrew discloses his addiction to playing cards and gambling. Reverend Lindsay is most attentive to Andrew's account of the events leading up to the separation from his wife, Heather.

"Andrew, are ye a religious man?"

"I believe in the Almighty and I attended the kirk on a regular basis while growing up in Glenstrae in the Highlands when I was a lad, but I have not attended the kirk on a regular basis since getting married. When I was abroad with the army, my wife, Heather, took the children to church frequently," recounts Andrew thoughtfully.

"Andrew, I want to be yer friend. I think I can offer ye some support in the months that lie ahead. Ye only have to ask for help and I promise I will be there for ye," states the good reverend, reaching out and laying his hand gently on Andrew's shoulder.

"Thank you, Reverend. I certainly need a good friend at this point in my life," replies Andrew, embracing his newly found friend.

* * * * *

During the next two weeks Andrew and Tommy Burns become friends. Andrew offers free piping lessons to Burns, but the Midshipman, whose parents are wealthy, insists on paying Andrew for his expert tuition.

The great sailing ship *Loch Leven* finally docks at Halifax on a bright, sunny morning. Captain MacBride and his fine crew are thanked for their excellent service throughout the voyage. The Reverend Lindsay and Andrew make their way to Pier 5, where the mid-sized sloop *Peggy Gordon* is waiting. Twenty passengers board the sloop bound for Cape Breton.

The crossing to Cape Breton is a memorable experience for Andrew and the Reverend Lindsay. The beauty of the land reminds both men of Scotland.

"I can understand now why so many Scots settled this area, Andrew."

"Aye, it's so much like Scotland," replies Andrew as the sloop approaches Louisburg from the east. The fortress of Louisburg is now clearly visible to both visitors as the Captain makes ready to dock.

Arrangements are made to rent a horse and cart, and off go the Reverend Lindsay and Andrew MacGregor down the Mara Road to the town of Sydney, where Andrew's cousin lives. The rugged coastline of Cape Breton, the land and the rolling hills are just like Caledonia, thinks Andrew as the cart bumps its way along.

"Excuse me, sir, how far wid it be to the wee toon o' Sydney," asks the Reverend Lindsay to a knot of local Cape Breton folk who are standing at a crossroad.

"Would ye be visiting some of yer family in Sydney?" replies a grey-haired gentleman wearing tartan trews and a bottle-green bonnet and leaning on a six-foot wooden staff.

"Aye, the MacGregors o' Sydney, ye ken," replies the Reverend politely.

"Now, would that be Rory or Stewart MacGregor?" comes the response.

"Stewart MacGregor," replies Andrew somewhat sternly, becoming impatient with the chatter.

"Aye, Stewart MacGregor and his family live in the cottage opposite the blacksmith's; ye cannot miss it if ye keep on going down the road for an hour or so," replies the local gentleman, while his five companions stare with great curiosity at the two newcomers.

"Well, Andrew, did ye hear the accent o' that gentleman, and did ye notice the Scottish garb? Ye would think ye were back home in bonnie Scotland!"

Andrew smiles and soon realizes that Cape Breton could easily be taken for a part of Scotland.

The door to the white cottage opens and Andrew is greeted by a pretty dark-haired lady, wearing an apron and holding a rolling pin.

"Yes? Can I help you?"

"Would Stewart be home?"

"I'm sorry, he's out on the boat fishing. Can I help?"

"Yes. I am Andrew MacGregor from Port Glasgow, Scotland, and this is the Reverend Lindsay," replies Andrew.

"Oh, I'm so sorry – please come ben," she replies as the door suddenly swings open, and the two visitors enter the cottage.

"Please forgive me, Andrew. I did not recognize you. I remember now we met at a wedding in Scotland. Do please sit yourselves down, gentlemen."

Before Andrew knows what is happening Mary MacGregor whisks up a light meal and a jug of ale appears on the dining table, followed by a plate of hot nourishing oatcakes.

Mary MacGregor is five feet six inches in height, and she has ebony-coloured hair with streaks of grey around the temples. Her eyes are the brightest light blue and her high cheekbones add to her striking facial features.

"Stewart will be so happy to see you, Andrew. He has very fond memories of his trip to Scotland."

The visit continues and Mary arranges for her two guests to have rooms at The Moose Head Tavern, which is located a few minutes' walk from the cottage.

"Please come for dinner at 7 p.m. this evening, gentlemen, and sample some of our fine fresh fish."

When Stewart MacGregor returns with his day's catch of fresh fish he is very excited to hear his wife's news and scurries down the road to The Moose Head Tavern, where he finds his cousin Andrew and his companion sampling the local beer.

"Andrew, so good to see ye," says Stewart as he embraces his cousin.

"Stewart, this is my friend the Reverend John Lindsay, late o' the wee town o' Ayr."

"Pleased to make yer acquaintance, sir," replies Stewart with a strong handshake.

The three men visit for over an hour with drinks appearing regularly on the table. Andrew explains to Stewart about his family situation and Stewart listens intently.

"Andrew, I am so sorry to hear yer news. If there is anything I can do just let me know."

As the visit continues, a young woman with dark ebony-coloured hair and striking beauty appears.

"Father, yer meal is ready. Please come home," says Morag MacGregor youngest daughter of Stewart and Mary MacGregor.

Mary MacGregor is an excellent hostess. Mary treats her guests to a wonderful Cape Breton meal of homemade cock-a-leekie soup, made from chicken, leeks and dried fruit, followed by lobster, potatoes, home-grown vegetables, Dundee cake, shortbread cookies and wholewheat bread.

"I have a visit to make, Andrew, to an old friend in the town o' Baddeck. Will ye be needing the horse and cart today?"

"No – go ahead with yer visit. I have some business with my cousin, Reverend," replies Andrew.

The journey to Baddeck is a pleasure for the Reverend Lindsay.

The people he meets along the way are 'canty, and couthy and kindly the best'.

Baddeck is a small village. The local church is situated in the middle of the village so it is easy to locate. A large sign hung on a white gate boldly displays the name of 'Reverend James Donald Archibald'. As the Reverend Lindsay unlatches the gate a West Highland terrier suddenly appears, barking and snapping at the heels of the intruder.

"Keltie, Keltie – here, girl!" shouts a voice from behind a four-foot privet hedge. The Reverend Archibald then appears holding gardening tools and wearing an apron. "For goodness' sake, is that you, Lindsay? I cannae hardly believe my eyes. Welcome, sir – do come in."

Keltie, the dog, is ushered into another room and the two men talk together in peace and quiet.

"Well, James, I once told ye a long time ago that we would see one another again."

"Yes, I remember the conversation well, all those years ago in Edinburgh when we were training for the ministry. When did you arrive in Cape Breton, John?"

"I arrived in Cape Breton only a few days ago from the port o' Halifax. I travelled over from Scotland in the company of Scotland's greatest piper, Andrew MacGregor. Have ye heard o' him?"

"Of course I have heard o' him. Stewart MacGregor has told the whole of Cape Breton all about his cousin's great piping record in Scotland. So what brings you here, John?"

"After spending twenty years in bonnie Scotland, serving several communities, I thought it was time for a change. I chose Cape Breton because of the thousands o' Scots who immigrated here over the last half-century. So I'm looking for a position with the Church. Do you know of anything that might be suitable for me, James?"

"Well, my flock is a manageable size for me, but if ye were of a mind I could ask you to visit some o' the folk who no longer attend church on Sundays. Also, old man Jock Mackenzie in Ingonish is ready to retire, so I could put your name forward as replacement," said James thoughtfully.

"Splendid, James, splendid."

After light refreshments, the Reverend Lindsay updates James on his friend Andrew MacGregor.

"I have committed myself to help Andrew. He is a lost soul who needs spiritual guidance, and I plan also to spend time with him. Andrew is going to be staying with his cousin Stewart MacGregor for a couple of months until he gets on his feet and can support himself. Who is the minister in Sydney, James?"

"That would be the Reverend Duncan Campbell no less. Duncan has served in the community of Sydney for over twenty years, and during these twenty years Duncan and Stewart have been known to have their differences."

"The never-ending feud between the Campbells and MacGregors, James," comments Reverend Lindsay.

"Aye, the very same. It's going to be a challenge, so maybe you can plan to spend time with Duncan Campbell to try and influence him to help Andrew."

The visit comes to an end and the Reverend Lindsay returns to Sydney happy in the knowledge that his old friend James Archibald will give him a hand up to start a new life in Cape Breton.

"So, Andrew, do you have any plans in mind?" asks Stewart.

"Coming over on the *Loch Leven*, Stewart, I had lots of quiet moments to reflect on my wretched life. I dearly want to find a lasting cure for my addiction to gambling. Also I want to reconcile myself with Heather if at all possible. One other thing, cousin: I kept having this strange and recurring dream night after night during the crossing. I saw myself leading a pipe band on to the field at the Cowal gathering, but the strange part of this dream is that I don't recognize the tartan the pipers are wearing," says Andrew, staring out of his cousin's living-room window.

"Andrew, I truly believe that all of these things can happen, but it will take a great deal of commitment and help. The Reverend Lindsay appears to be committed to helping you."

"It's strange, Stewart – when I first met the Reverend Lindsay I did not care to develop a friendship with him, but now that I have got to know him better I have come to like and respect the man."

"Andrew, I want ye to stay with us until ye get some steady work. Also, Mary and I would like ye to join us tomorrow. We attend church every Sunday."

"Fine by me, Stewart, and many thanks to you and yer good wife for the welcome and all that Cape Breton hospitality."

The Reverend Duncan Campbell preaches with fire and brimstone during his morning service. He is an intimidating individual, over six feet tall. He has grey receding hair, a very loud voice which echoes around the church, and large arms and hands. For a man of the cloth he is an intimidating sight to anyone who has never got to know him; and as for Andrew, seated directly below the pulpit, he certainly scares the living daylights out of him.

"Allow me to introduce my cousin from Scotland, Andrew MacGregor."

"Pleased to meet you, MacGregor. Welcome to Cape Breton."

"Thank you, Reverend Campbell. Glad to be here," replies Andrew, shaking the minister's powerful hand.

The congregation is ushered downstairs, where the local vestry has organized a lunch to welcome Andrew.

"Is this yer doing, Stewart?" asks Andrew, smiling.

"Well, as the Cape Breton folk have all heard about yer piping record in Scotland Andrew, I thought it only right that they meet you in person."

Andrew meets many friendly people that Sunday morning. The older members of the congregation have retained their Scottish accents while the younger folk speak with an accent that sounds North American to Andrew's ears. However, whether the brogue is Scottish or Canadian everyone requests Andrew to play the Highland bagpipes.

"I'm sorry, folks – I did not bring my pipes with me."

No sooner have the words passed through Andrew's lips than all of a sudden his Highland bagpipes appear on a table in front of where he is standing.

"Don't look at me, Andrew MacGregor! I know nothing about this matter," says Stewart sheepishly.

Andrew takes off his jacket and tunes the pipes.

The congregation is hushed as Andrew fills his lungs with a quick, deep breath and he launches into a set of reels, strathspeys and jigs. Members of the congregation soon become involved, clapping in time with the music, and some young females, standing at the back of the room, start dancing to Scottish reels which they know so well.

Clapping and cheering breaks out amongst the congregation, realizing that Scotland's champion piper has given his best performance to a knowledgeable and appreciative audience.

"Andrew, I would like you to meet my close friends the Murrays, from Louisbourg. Allan here owns a small shipbuilding company, 'Murray & Sons', and I was telling him all about yer shipbuilding experience in Port Glasgow on the River Clyde," explains Stewart.

"Very pleased to meet all of you," says Andrew, shaking the hand of Allan, his wife, Kirstie, and two sons, Iain and William.

"Would you be interested in taking a look at my shipyard in Louisbourg?"

"Thank you, Allan. It would be a great pleasure to visit yer shipyard," replies Andrew enthusiastically.

Murray & Sons has thirty workers on its payroll. Andrew spends the morning touring the shipyard and visiting some of the ships being built by them.

"Andrew, we built the brig sloop *Peggy Gordon*, which brought you to Cape Breton. She was our first two-masted brig sloop," says Allan proudly.

"Yes, Allan I really enjoyed the ride. Very smooth journey. According to the captain o' the *Peggy Gordon* we made an average of ten knots," replies Andrew.

"Yes, she can do eleven knots if the conditions are right."

Andrew is shown two new ships under construction. Both are brig sloops with two masts. One sloop is 165 feet long (for the British Navy) and the other is a smaller version, about 100 feet in length, which is on order by a wealthy merchant.

"So, Andrew, what do you think about my shipbuilding company?" asks Allan excitedly.

"I'm very impressed, Allan."

"I was wondering if you would consider working for us, Andrew. You have very good shipbuilding credentials according to your cousin Stewart."

Andrew is flattered by the offer coming so soon after his arrival on Cape Breton.

The two men leave for lunch to talk over the details of the offer.

"Andrew, this is my wife's nephew Colin Grant. He has asked to speak with you," says Stewart as Andrew rises from his seat by the fire."

"Pleasure to meet you, Colin," replies Andrew, enthusiastically shaking the young man's hand.

"I heard you play at church, Andrew, a few weeks ago and I thought you were terrific. I would love to be able to play like you some day," adds Colin excitedly.

Colin Glen Grant is seventeen years old with a crop of blond curly hair. He sports well-developed shoulders from regularly carrying peat almost half a mile to his parents' cottage. Colin has been given piping lessons by his aging father, who was schooled in piping by the Macrimmons of Ingonish.

"How long have you been playing the pipes, young man?" enquires Andrew.

"Well, my father first placed a chanter in my hands when I was nine years old, so that makes it eight years."

"Could you play me a reel?" asks Andrew, seeing the lad is anxious to show what he can do.

"Here, son, try these," says Stewart, handing his nephew a set of bagpipes.

Within a few minutes Colin is entertaining his guests to a

set of reels followed by a strathspey as he taps his foot on the wooden floor to keep on beat.

"Well done, Colin," shouts Andrew, who is impressed by the young man's confidence and talent.

"What do you think, Andrew?" asks Stewart with an anxious tone in his voice.

"I think we have a potential champion in the making, Stewart. The lad has lots of talent and confidence," replies Andrew, patting young Colin on his shoulder.

"Oh, thanks, Andrew – thanks so much," replies Colin as he hands the pipes back to his uncle.

Mary, who has been busy in the kitchen, has been listening to the piping and comes rushing towards her favourite nephew, hugging and kissing him.

"I am so proud of you, Colin. Yer mother will be thrilled to hear this news – so thrilled. All that practising is paying off."

Later that evening Stewart and Andrew talk about young Colin and agree that with some additional tutoring the young man could compete at the Cape Breton games next summer.

"I'll offer to give young Colin some lessons if his father has no objections," states Andrew.

The nights are the worst time for Andrew. Lying in bed, night after night, wide awake, thinking of his family after working at the Murray shipyard. For the past few months the days have passed quickly with his job at the shipyard, teaching young Colin piping and becoming involved with the local church as well as making friends with some of the local parishioners. But when he does get to sleep his dreams are always the same, seeing the children doing their homework after school, and Heather involved in quilt making and sewing. Sometimes Andrew cries out in the night in his sleep and Stewart comes to his cousin's side and comforts him. This sleeping pattern lasts for several months until Stewart suggests to Andrew that he compose a letter to his family. Andrew tries each evening to draft a letter to Heather, but is unable to express the thoughts that are locked away in his heart.

"Andrew have you managed to write home?" asks Mary one evening.

Stewart is out fishing and Andrew is sitting by the fire with a pensive look on his face.

"I have tried several times, Mary, but I just can't seem to choose the right words."

Picking up a quill, Mary draws up a chair and places it beside Andrew.

"Now let's see – why don't I write and you tell me what to say?"

"My lovely Heather, I miss you so much. The people of Cape Breton have been wonderful and helped me settle into my new surroundings. . . . ."

"Thanks, Mary – I can take it from here."

After several moments deep in thought, Andrew writes:

My dear Heather,

I am writing to you from New Scotland. Locals here call it Nova Scotia. The land and people are so much like Scotland. People eat oatmeal, bannocks and lots of fish, play the bagpipes and celebrate Hogmanay just like we do in bonnie Scotland. Some folk I have met also speak Gaelic.

My cousin Stewart MacGregor has been very kind to me, giving me a place to stay and helping me get a job. I am enclosing £25.

Coming across on the ship I met the Reverend Lindsay, who has become a close friend. Lindsay is a compassionate man, has a great amount of patience and has been providing me with spiritual guidance. I have joined the local kirk and also teach piping in my spare time. My job at the Louisbourg shipyard has been rewarding. The owner is a fine boss and is happy with my work at the shipyard.

I miss both you and the children and hope that you are all keeping well. Please tell the children that I love them, and to you I send my undying love.

Andrew

The months pass quickly as Andrew keeps himself busy with his work at the shipyard, teaching piping in the evenings and helping out at the church at weekends. Andrew's nightmares become less frequent with the spiritual help of the Reverend Lindsay, who visits him on a regular basis.

"Andrew, there's a letter for you at The Moose Head Tavern," says Mary as she prepares the evening meal.

Grabbing his coat and boots, Andrew trudges through the snow as fast as he can, thinking that at long last his darling Heather has replied to his letters.

As the barman at the tavern places the letter into his hand, Andrew's manner quickly changes. He studies the writing on the envelope and immediately realizes it is not Heather's fair hand, but that of his sister Isla.

Taking a seat by the fire in the tavern, Andrew slowly opens the letter.

My dear brother,

Hoping that this letter reaches you in good health. I wanted to write to you to let you know how the children are doing. By the time you read this letter it will be Christmas and I can only imagine how lonely it can be in a far-off land away from your loved ones. I see the children on a regular basis. They are all well. Heather sold the home in Braemar Gardens, Port Glasgow, and moved to Edinburgh and settled into a smaller home not far from her parents. Grieg is a big lad now and talks about joining the army. Roy plays the chanter very well and is showing a great interest in the Highland bagpipes. Wee Annie loves animals and I think she may follow in the footsteps of my dear husband and become a veterinary surgeon. The children often talk about you, and Roy goes around telling all of his friends, "My dad is the greatest piper in all of Scotland." Heather has settled into her new life in Edinburgh and sews beautiful garments for the Earl of Midlothian's wife, which brings in extra money. With the money that you send the family does well.

Heather's father has been unwell for the past few months and has taken to his bed. Ross and I keep well. I am not sure how long he can keep working as he gets called out at all hours in dreadful weather, poor man.

Hope that you are well and we send our love.

Your loving sister,

Isla

* * * * *

Andrew returns home and sits quietly by the fire for almost an hour, reading the letter over and over again.

"Andrew, yer meal is ready," says a familiar voice.

"Thanks, Mary – aye, I'll be right there."

It is Andrew's first sleigh ride and he feels exhilarated. Ten of Stewart's family and friends huddle beside one another to keep warm as two large horses pull a sleigh through a newly formed blanket of puffy white snow. It is Christmas Eve and the revellers are making their way to Baddeck for a traditional Christmas Eve gathering of the Clan MacGregor. It is a beautiful still evening as the revellers sing Christmas carols and drink hot toddies from two large bottles, which are being passed from person to person. Cowbells signal the sleigh's progress. It is driven by Stewart MacGregor as it makes its way through a settlement with children skating on a small ice-covered pond.

As the sleigh approaches Baddeck, Stewart can see the flames of a bonfire which forms part of the annual Christmas Eve celebrations. Soon all of the passengers are mixing with family and friends around the bonfire. It is the local custom for an exchange of gifts. Stewart MacGregor, as senior clan member, asks for silence and leads the now forty attendees in a prayer. Andrew is moved with the whole setting. Mary MacGregor, seeing Andrew silently weeping, places her arm around her cousin and wishes him a happy Christmas. After the exchange of gifts everyone makes their way to the village hall as midnight is approaching. Stewart has invited the Reverend Lindsay to lead the gathering in singing Christmas carols. It is 2 a.m. as the sleigh approaches Sydney and the party of ten wish each other a merry Christmas and retire quietly to their homes as snow falls gently over the town.

Chapter 50

SCOTTISH CANADIANS

The last of the winter snow lies in small pockets all along the riverbank as the yawl makes its way towards the open sea. Stewart's sailing boat is like a cutter with an additional short mast at the stern and is painted white and blue. The meadows on either side of the boat signal spring as primroses and hyacinths pop their heads above ground and in the sky herring gulls and other seagulls follow the path of the two-masted vessel in anticipation of a meal of fresh fish.

"What a fine day, Stewart," says Andrew as he takes deep breaths and enjoys the warmth of the early morning sun on his face.

"It is indeed a very fine day, Andrew," replies Stewart as he guides the yawl out of the bay into a calm sea.

Stewart is a skilful fisherman who knows the places where the fish lurk close to the shoreline.

Within a few hours, Stewart has found a shaded deep pool fairly close to the shore where, with the help of Andrew, he and his three companions cast their nets and then carefully place their lobster cages alongside the boat.

As the men wait, Stewart recounts old yarns to his friends of his great moments fishing these waters during the past thirty years.

"The waters around Cape Breton have been good to me, lads. I've witnessed a large variety of medium-sized fish, including cod and skate, but the lobster in this part of the country are the very best you will find anywhere," recounts Stewart proudly.

"If all goes well you'll be feasting on three- or four-pound lobsters tonight."

The day passes and all the men are in good spirits, sharing stories of the sea. By early evening the nets are carefully brought on board, and to Stewart's delight the catch is better than expected. Later, the lobster cages are retrieved from the ocean bed and Andrew marvels at the size of the lobsters Stewart so proudly displays. The day's catch is placed in creels and neatly stacked. Soon they up-anchor and hoist the sails, and with the assistance of a fair westerly breeze the yawl is homeward bound.

It is after dusk when the boat is moored and the men gather their creels and make their way home to Sydney.

"You have done so well, gentlemen," says Mary MacGregor as the evening meal is prepared.

The men settle down in the living room sipping locally brewed beer. One of the guests, Billy Paterson, a Scottish Canadian from Dundee, is anxious to get to know Scotland's former champion piper.

"Andrew, I was wondering if you have any openings in your busy piping schedule. I have two brothers and we are all army-trained pipers. We have heard what a fine piper you are, so we would like lessons to improve our playing," explains Billy.

"Don't listen to him, Andrew. Billy and his bothers just want to beat the Campbells at the next Highland gathering," shouts Stewart, who is nearby filling the men's beer glasses.

"Billy, I have two fine students right now, but what I would really like to do is form a local pipe band," replies Andrew.

"Great idea, Andrew," shouts Stewart. "You should have no problem recruiting ten or even twelve pipers and drummers."

"Well, to tell ye the truth, I was hoping for sixteen pipers and drummers," replies Andrew as he sips his beer.

"I guess you have to think big these days," retorts Stewart laughingly.

"I was thinking o' placing notices around Sydney, Baddeck, Ingonish and Louisbourg, lads. What do ye all think o' that?"

"Great idea, Andrew!" and "Fine idea!" are the responses.

The following day Andrew engages the help of a local printer, Andy Farquharson, originally from Old Aberdeen, and arranges for a few dozen posters to be printed. The local printer is tickled pink with the idea and offers to have the posters distributed around Cape Breton at no extra cost.

Five days later, as Andrew is returning home from the shipyard, he notices a large crowd assembled outside Stewart's home. As he approaches the house several people notice Andrew and come running towards him. Others soon follow. Surrounded by people from all over Cape Breton, Andrew is overwhelmed with the interest his poster has stirred amongst local communities. Soon Andrew is rescued by Mary and Stewart MacGregor.

"Gentlemen, please, please, can I have your attention?" shouts Stewart.

It takes several minutes for the crowd of people surrounding Andrew to be silent.

"Thank you, thank you, gentlemen. Can I suggest we all go down to the town hall so we can conduct an orderly meeting?" requests Stewart, sounding very flustered.

The crowd swells to over eighty people as they make their way towards the town hall. Curious bystanders also start to join the throng.

"Thanks, Stewart. I had no idea the response would be anything like this," said a very relieved Andrew MacGregor.

It takes Stewart several attempts to convince the town-hall custodian, Jimmy Telfer, to allow Andrew and his new recruits to use the facility. Telfer has been recruited by the townsfolk to be custodian of the building, which was originally erected with the assistance of the local folk ten years ago. Telfer, who came over to Canada from Scotland twenty years ago, has become known as the 'wee general' because of his authoritarian style in deciding who can and cannot make use of the building. Eventually, after much persuading by Stewart, Telfer allows the large crowd to use the main meeting room for two hours.

Looking around the audience seated in front of him, Andrew

notices that there is a wide range of ages in the room. Some of the men come dressed in their army uniforms, while the older gentlemen are kilted and carry bagpipes under their arms. Others appear to be teenagers. Also Andrew observes two females with a set of Highland bagpipes held in their arms.

"Good evening, ladies and gentlemen. Thank you for responding to my poster. I had no idea there was such an interest in the surrounding communities to form a pipe band," states Andrew as more and more people appear at the back of the room. "I would like to set up a schedule for this weekend. For those of you who are available this weekend, I would like you to write down yer name for Saturday or Sunday. Mary MacGregor has paper, ink and quills at the back o' the room. Please write down yer name and come back on Saturday or Sunday and be prepared to play three tunes for me on the pipes. You can choose yer own tunes," adds Andrew. "For those of you who have training as side, tenor or bass drummers, please also write down your names and when you are available."

Before Andrew can finish speaking, people sitting in the front rows of the meeting room suddenly jump to their feet and scurry to the back of the room. It takes over an hour for everyone to write down their names, and people push, jostle and become irritable.

"Can you believe what's happening here tonight, Stewart? It's amazing," comments Andrew as he leans against a pillar, wiping his brow.

"Listen, Andrew, the folk who sign up for the weekend are from all different clans and communities around the island. Most of them are decent pipers and drummers. I know many of these people. Piping and drumming is a big part of their lives. The problem you will have, dear cousin, is choosing the best twenty pipers and drummers. Remember to pick a piper from each clan or there will be hell to pay!" states Stewart, looking sternly at Andrew.

Looking down the list of names, Andrew notices the names of two females, Catrina and Shauna Rose.

* * * * *

Mary MacGregor sweet-talks Jimmy Telfer into allowing Andrew to use the town hall for the weekend. Telfer has admired Mary MacGregor from afar for years and Mary is aware of this admiration and uses it to her advantage.

All of the MacGregor family assist Andrew in controlling the number of pipers and drummers entering the town hall during the weekend. The first person on Saturday morning to play his pipes is an army officer from Louisbourg, Fergus McWilliams. McWilliams introduces himself in a broad Scottish accent and opens his bag and produces a beautiful set of silver-mounted Highland bagpipes. Within two minutes McWilliams tunes his pipes then confidently launches into a set of three pipe tunes. Andrew is impressed with the confidence, poise and technique of McWilliams.

It is almost 8 p.m. on Saturday night as the last person for the day enters the hall. Iain Cunningham has played side and tenor drums for over ten years.

"So which part o' the island are you from, Iain?"

"St Ann's. Ma father settled in St Ann's when we came to Canada frae Glasga'. We moved tae Ingonish and I met a bonnie wee lassie and got wed," explains Cunningham.

"Well, ye have no lost yer Glasgow accent after all these years!"

"No, ma dad and I are proud o' oor Scottish heritage and wid'na have it any other way."

Iain plays for twenty minutes on the side and tenor drums and Andrew realizes that here is someone whom he could rely on to lead the drum corps.

"Who taught ye how to play, Iain?"

"Ma dad taught me. He played wi' the Gordons in Scotland, and they are renowned for their drum corps. Big Bill Gordon from Old Aberdeen was ma dad's instructor and he was a first-class teacher, ye ken, Andrew."

Sunday is an entirely different day. Members of the Campbells and MacGregors get into a fight outside the entrance to the town hall after the church service is over. Stewart McGregor and his brothers intervene and pull the adversaries apart.

"He started it – he's to blame," shouts out young Duncan Campbell as he is held tightly by Stewart MacGregor.

"It's a lie, Uncle Stewart. He called me names and said that we MacGregors were only good for shovelling shit," screams Roy MacGregor.

"I don't care who's to blame. It's bad enough that you're fighting, but on the Sabbath it's a disgrace. Both of you are going home, and neither one of you will get a chance to play the pipes today," shouts Stewart, who is furious with the conduct of his nephew and the Reverend Duncan Campbell's son.

"You can't stop me from playing in the pipe band. My father will get me a spot in the pipe band, you'll see," shouts a defiant Duncan Campbell Junior as he struggles to break free from a tight hold.

Arguments also break out in the afternoon and again Stewart and his brothers have to intervene. Young lads from Pleasant Bay are the culprits.

In the evening two female pipers enter the room wearing Clan Rose tartan kilts and carrying Highland bagpipes.

"Ladies, pleased to meet you," says Andrew, surprised at having two females apply to join his pipes and drums band.

"I am Catrina Rose and this is my twin sister, Shauna."

"Tell me, ladies: how long have you played the pipes?" asks Andrew.

"Seven years, Andrew. Our father, John Rose, learned to play in the army and he taught us. We started learning to play the chanter when we were nine. That was ten years ago," replies Catrina confidently.

"Well, can you play a few tunes for me now?" requests Andrew.

The twins chat for a minute, then together they start to play a reel, followed by a jig, then a strathspey. They both start well and finish well and achieve a nice tone playing together. Andrew is surprised and asks the twins to play another reel.

The twins chat and then play a reel flawlessly.

"Well done, ladies. I am so impressed," says Andrew.

"Well, I'm glad this day's events are over," comments Stewart as he passes a bowl of potatoes to Andrew during the evening meal.

"Aye, I agree, Stewart," replies Andrew, looking more the worse for wear.

"You see, Andrew, the hatred between the MacGregors and Campbells still exists even in this part of the world," states Stewart in a disappointed manner.

"I am sorry to hear that. I would have thought that after leaving Scotland and travelling to the New World both sides would have buried the hatchet," replies Andrew, who has been told of the fighting earlier in the day.

"Anyway, have you any thoughts on whom you may pick for the pipe band?"

"Aye, I have a list o' fourteen pipers and four drummers. Take a look at this list and let me know what you think, Stewart."

"Good stuff, Andrew! You have chosen folk from many different clans," he replies, sensing that when the islanders hear who is picked to play the fighting will stop. What is this, Andrew – two female pipers?"

"Yes, Stewart, the Rose twins from Halifax. They have relatives nearby and are willing to relocate."

"But how are their piping skills, Andrew?"

"They are good pipers, and with some more coaching they could be very good, Stewart."

Chapter 51

CAPE BRETON PIPES AND DRUMS

During the past two years Andrew has worked hard training the local pipers and drummers to play as a band. It has been an extremely difficult task and Andrew's patience has been tested to the limit. Fortunately under the guidance of Iain Cunningham the drum corps has flourished. Four side drummers, two tenor drummers and a base drummer now form a drum corps which Andrew believes can excel in competition.

"Don't feel discouraged, Andrew – the pipers are trying their best," comments Stewart MacGregor as Andrew sits at the dinner table looking very discouraged.

"Aye, I know, Stewart, but there are a couple o' the pipers who just do not have the ability to meet the grade despite countless hours of practice."

"Well, Andrew, you'll just have to replace them!"

"The problem is, Stewart, that they are both Campbells."

"Oh, dear me. Yes – that's a big problem," states Stewart rising up from the table and reaching for a bottle of single malt Scotch whisky.

The two men talk over a drink of Scotch for a couple of hours, and Mary MacGregor leaves her husband and Andrew and scarpers off to bed, sensing that this discussion is developing into an all-night affair.

The following day Andrew and Stewart journey to Fort Louisbourg and meet with Captain Robbie Bruce McWilliams, a friend of Stewart.

"Great to see you, Stewart. How is the family?"

"Very well, Robbie. Thanks for asking."

"Robbie, this is my cousin, Andrew, from bonnie Scotland."

"Welcome to Fort Louisbourg Andrew," says Robbie as the men shake hands.

Stewart explains the situation regarding Andrew's efforts during the past two years to try to form a top-class Cape Breton pipe band.

"It's a very tough assignment, Andrew, with the ongoing feuding between the local clans. I sympathize with you. Have you tried recruiting some of our ex-army members? Many of these men are army-trained and continue to play the pipes in civilian life."

"Yes, we have two of your ex-army pipers, Jamie Robertson and Johnny Graham, both fine pipers," replies Andrew.

"Yes, I know both men very well. They are, as you say, Andrew, fine pipers indeed," states Robbie enthusiastically.

"Now, if I had two more like them and one was a Campbell we would have a competitive pipe band, Robbie."

"Leave it with me, gentlemen, and I will do some digging."

A week later Stewart receives a message from his friend Captain McWilliams.

"Andrew, it looks like McWilliams has struck gold," shouts Stewart at the top of his voice.

"Three ex-army pipers, and two of the pipers are Campbells!" says Andrew excitedly as he reads Captain McWilliams' letter.

Stewart and Andrew waste no time contacting the three ex-army pipers and arrange meetings with them. One of the three pipers, Malcolm Campbell, has recently returned to Cape Breton after working in the port of Montreal. The other two recommended pipers, Billy MacLeod and Rory Campbell, reside in Halifax.

"My first visit to Halifax, Stewart," said Andrew as both men check into a local boarding house.

"It's a fine town, Andrew, and I am glad we are staying the three nights so you can tour around and see all the sights."

On the following day Andrew and Stewart meet Billy MacLeod in a local pub called The King's Arms, a red-brick building located on Prince Street close to the harbour.

MacLeod is thirty years old. He has sandy-coloured hair and sports a large moustache.

"I served with the army here in Nova Scotia for ten good years. I learned to play the Highland bagpipes when I was nine years old in Aberdeen, Scotland, before my family made the move to Halifax," says MacLeod as he sips a jug of locally brewed ale.

"Andrew here is one of Scotland's very best pipers and we are so glad he is trying to raise Cape Breton's piping standards," said Stewart with great excitement in his voice.

"I have heard your name mentioned, Andrew, several times in the barracks at Halifax," comments MacLeod.

"I hope the barrack comments were good ones," replies Andrew, laughing.

The conversation lasts for an hour and Andrew likes MacLeod's easy-going manner and thinks that he would be a good addition to the Cape Breton Pipes and Drums. During the discussion, Andrew mentions his plan to take the pipe band over to Scotland to compete at the Cowal gathering, which excites MacLeod.

After lunch the three men amble over to a park and MacLeod plays a set of three pipe tunes which Andrew knows well. As MacLeod plays, local folk gather around to listen to the piper with some onlookers clapping their hands in time with the stirring music. It soon becomes clear to Andrew that MacLeod is a fine piper, so he asks him to play a few more tunes.

It is agreed that MacLeod will talk with his wife, Katie MacLeod, to see if she would be willing to relocate to Cape Breton to be close to the band members.

The following morning Andrew and Stewart meet with Rory Campbell. Rory is about five feet two inches in height, has a loud abrasive voice and is a chain-smoker. Rory has two boys at home who are attending school. Since leaving the army Rory has not played much on his Highland bagpipes. He indicates that he did play laments at some funerals and also piped at a few weddings. When asked to play a set of three tunes his playing did not resonate well with Andrew. Rory's timing was off and he missed several notes playing a reel.

"So you have not played with any pipe bands since retiring from the army, Rory?"

"No, Andrew, I went back to working on the fishing boats and did not play with any of the local pipers," replies Rory.

Andrew and Stewart thank Rory for taking the time to meet and indicate that they will contact him in the future if the need arises.

The next day Andrew and Stewart go touring around the town of Halifax. The weather is mild and Stewart introduces Andrew to several of his friends, who recount the history of Halifax to Andrew. Of particular interest to Andrew, as a former worker in shipyards in Scotland, is the construction of a permanent naval yard and the building of HMC *Halifax* in 1768. This was the first naval warship of this class to be built in Halifax.

Back in Cape Breton Andrew and Stewart locate Malcolm Campbell. Campbell held the rank of sergeant major with the army when he retired and went to Montreal, where he served as a foreman in the port of Montreal. He is almost six feet tall with dark curly hair and appears fit and healthy.

"Pleased to meet you, gentlemen," says Malcolm as he places his bagpipes on a nearby table.

Stewart introduces Andrew to Malcolm.

"Yes, I have heard a lot about you, Andrew, from folk I worked with in Montreal – ex-army pipers who played at the Cowal gathering in Scotland," recounts Malcolm.

"It's amazing how small a world we live in," replies Andrew.

During the next hour Andrew explains his plans to Campbell for the band to compete at the Cowal gathering in Scotland and the need for experienced pipers to raise the pipe band's standard.

"Sounds like the very thing I would love to do. Playing at Cowal would be a dream come true for me," says Campbell with great conviction in his voice.

Shortly afterwards Campbell tunes his pipes and plays a reel, a jig and a strathspey. Andrew likes the tone of the pipes and the smooth change in tempo when moving from a reel to a jig.

"Well done, Malcolm!" exclaims Andrew, patting him on the back.

It is agreed that Malcolm will join the Cape Breton Pipes and Drums.

Chapter 52

TRIP TO MONTREAL

It is Andrew's fifth year in Cape Breton. For the past year his Cape Breton Pipes and Drums has competed successfully at local competitions in Cape Breton and throughout Nova Scotia. The quality of the piping has increased dramatically with the additions of Malcolm Campbell and Billy MacLeod.

"Are you ready to lead the pipe band on to Cowal Field, Andrew?" enquires Stewart.

"No, Stewart, the band is not ready yet, but with more practice they can become more competitive."

"For God's sake, man, how many more nights of practice will it take?"

"A lot more."

Grunts and groans are heard around the town hall when Andrew tells the members of the pipe band that he is increasing the practice sessions from four times per week to five times. Some of the younger pipers complain.

"It's like this, ladies and gentlemen: you are the best pipe band in Nova Scotia, but at the Cowal gathering you would not win a place in the top four bands in Grade 2 competition based on where you are right now. I'll make you a deal," continues Andrew: "if you agree to compete in Montreal in two months' time and win the gold medal I will take you to Cowal Field next year."

There is great excitement amongst pipe band members and

everyone agrees to the extended practice times.

The Cape Breton Pipes and Drums stand at the ready. The band is next to be called upon to enter the field of competition here in Montreal. Four pipe bands have already played and the judges are about to signal Pipe Major Andrew MacGregor on to the field. It is a sunny day and a large crowd of onlookers have assembled to watch pipe bands compete. The Cape Breton Pipes and Drums consists of twelve pipers, four side drummers, two tenor drummers, a bass drummer and a pipe major. Each of the pipe band members wears their own clan tartan.

"Forward march!" is the Pipe Major's call as the band moves forward in good order on to the field, stopping in front of the centre stand, where three judges wait. The band keeps in tight formation and launches into a three-piece set of music selected by the judges. Stewart and Mary MacGregor and some of the parents of the pipers and drummers have accompanied the band to Montreal and show their appreciation with loud cheering and clapping when the band completes their playing.

"The band sounds good, Andrew," shouts Stewart as he congratulates all of the pipers and drummers leaving the field.

"Thanks a million, Stewart. I hope the judges agree with your assessment," comments Andrew.

One other local band now takes the field to compete.

About an hour later, all of the competing bands march on to the field to await the judges' verdict. The results are announced in reverse order, and all of the members of the Cape Breton Pipes and Drums hold their breaths, hoping for a first so they can travel to Scotland next year to compete at Cowal Field.

"Here are the results of the Pipe Band competition: Longueuil South Shore Pipe Band placed third; in second place, Montreal Boys Pipes and Drums; winning band, Cape Breton Pipes and Drums."

The result is such sweet music to Andrew's ears, and the

other members of the Cape Breton band jump for joy, throwing their bonnets into the air.

"Now, Andrew, you need to devote all your leisure time to getting the band ready for the big trip to Scotland next summer," says Stewart, patting Andrew on the back.

Chapter 53

CAPE BRETON TARTAN

The town hall is packed to welcome back the heroes from Montreal. The pipe band enters the town hall in single file, playing the three pipe tunes they used to win the gold medal in Montreal. Stewart MacGregor follows the band into the town hall carrying the newly won trophy from Montreal. There is great excitement amongst all the people present.

"Ladies and gentlemen, I know you are all very proud of what the band achieved in Montreal, and so you should be," states Stewart MacGregor, holding the newly won trophy above his head for all to see. "Now we must help our pipe band get ready for the big trip to Scotland next summer. We will need to raise money for the trip and for the accommodation. Are you willing to help us?"

"Yes, yes," is the loud reply from all of the excited local folk packed together in the main hall.

"You'll get no help, Andrew, from the Reverend Campbell. Since you banned his son from playing in the band for fighting, he has been bad-mouthing you all over Cape Breton," says Stewart.

"Well, I am sure there are good honest folk in the community who will ignore his comments and support the pipe band," replies Andrew.

In the autumn a committee is formed of ten members whose mandate is to identify fundraising activities and seek out donations from local business and some of the richer folk living on the island.

It soon becomes apparent to Andrew that the bad mouthing from the Reverend Campbell is being ignored by almost all the population living on the island. Donations come pouring in and lots of activities are held to raise money for the trip to Scotland.

As a member of the fundraising committee, Andrew is asked what else the band requires, other than transportation, food and lodgings for their trip to Scotland.

"We will need funds to replace some old Highland bagpipes. Also, I am asking the committee to consider coming up with a Cape Breton tartan so all band members' kilts will be the same tartan," explains Andrew.

There is silence following this request.

"But, Andrew, we do not have a Cape Breton tartan," points out a committee member.

"Aye, I realize that, but I recommend that you form a subcommittee and they come back with a recommendation for a Cape Breton tartan," replies Andrew.

"Getting agreement on a Cape Breton tartan will not be an easy task, Andrew," comments the chairperson of the committee.

"Well, if that's how it is I suggest ye'd better get started right away," replies Andrew in an assertive manner.

"Oh, and another thing to note is that if we get the kilts with the Cape Breton tartan, the band members will also need new Harris tweed jackets, shirts, bonnets, belts, sporrans, socks, flashes and shoes," adds Andrew as he makes his way to the door of the meeting room.

The fundraising committee meets every week. After some major fundraising activities across the island, enough money has been raised to pay for all known expenses, including new kilts, jackets and accessories for all of the band members. The subcommittee assigned to choosing a Cape Breton tartan is struggling to come up with a tartan that every committee member can agree upon. It's mid-March so Andrew MacGregor requests that he be allowed to attend the next scheduled meeting of the subcommittee charged with recommending a Cape Breton tartan.

"Ladies and gentlemen, time is running out for a decision on a Cape Breton tartan for the pipe band," explains Andrew.

"Well, Andrew, it's no for the want of trying," states the chairperson in a manner that suggests a high level of frustration.

"Can I suggest a few things, Mr Chairperson?" requests Andrew.

"Please go ahead" is the quick response.

"Well, can I go around the table and ask each one of you what colours you would prefer for the kilts?"

"Aye, yes, go ahead," is the response.

"I would like green and some yellow," says the chairperson.

Other preferences were some blue to represent the sky and sea; some green for fields; and some yellow.

"Ok folks, I hear green, some yellow and some blue."

All members nodded agreement.

"So why don't you pass this information on to some local weavers and dyers and ask them to come up with samples of cloth woven with green, yellow and blue?" asks Andrew.

Agreement is reached and a follow-up meeting is scheduled for two weeks' time to review the samples of cloth woven by the weavers.

The practice sessions for the pipe band are proving successful and all members attend every scheduled meeting of the band. Listening to the pipers play, Andrew likes the tone of their pipes. Getting the right pressure in the airbag of the pipes is critical to eliminate over- and under-blowing. There is just one adjustment to be made by the drummers. The drummers are getting ahead of the beat of the music.

"Iain, yer drum corps is terrific. Their performance in Montreal certainly helped us win the gold medal. To help us play our very best in Scotland I would like the drummers to make a timing adjustment. I notice at practice sessions that when playing reels the drummers tend to get ahead o' the beat, so if you can make that adjustment we should be in great shape for Scotland," explains Andrew.

"I'll talk tae the lads and we'll make the adjustment, Andrew," replies Iain Cunningham in a confident manner.

Chapter 54

BATTLE OF THE BANDS

There is great excitement at the dockside at the port of Halifax on this beautiful July morning. The Cape Breton Pipes and Drums wearing their Cape Breton tartan kilts are in the process of boarding a ship to Scotland to compete at the Cowal gathering. Over 200 Cape Bretoners have accompanied the band to Halifax to see them off at the pier. Many of the family members are also travelling to Scotland with the band, including Stewart and Mary MacGregor and the Reverend Lindsay.

For Andrew MacGregor it's a moment he has dreamt about for the past five years. Thanks to his sister Isla, all of the arrangements for the visit of the band to Scotland to compete are in place. Although Andrew has not heard from his estranged wife, Heather, Isla has kept him updated over the past five years with the family affairs.

As the great ship slowly leaves the pier shouts of good wishes can be heard from the shore. Cape Breton passengers wave to the well-wishers on shore. It is an emotional and daunting scene for the members of the pipe band to travel all the way across the Atlantic Ocean to bonnie Scotland to represent their beloved Cape Breton.

After three days at sea members of the pipe band find their sea legs, so Andrew organizes practice sessions on deck as the weather is fair. Andrew has taught the band members the ten most popular pipe tunes previously used by the Argylls' pipes and drums when they competed at the Cowal Highland gathering.

"Lads and lassies, today I would like to teach you a new pipe tune which I wrote when I lived in Scotland. It's a catchy wee tune which I think you will all like."

Andrew then launches into 'Heroes of Vila Real'. As he plays the band members clap in time with the music. When Andrew finishes playing, the band and family members standing nearby all applaud, showing their appreciation for the stirring music.

During the following two weeks the band members master the playing of 'Heroes of Vila Real', and during their free time the Rose twins can be heard singing the notes of the tune on board the ship.

On the last day of July, the ship docks at Port Glasgow from Halifax. The crossing has been smooth with just two days of choppy seas.

The plan is for the pipe band and family members to stay in Ayrshire at The Ploughman Inn, which is about three miles from where Andrew's sister Isla resides. Since Andrew's last visit to The Ploughman Inn, several years earlier, the new owner, Lefty Brown, a retired prizefighter, has expanded the size of the inn and built several additional rooms for overnight visitors. Isla has reserved all of the rooms at The Ploughman Inn for the stay of the band members and their families. Andrew agrees to stay at the inn and visit his sister Isla between band practice sessions.

"It's so good to see you, Andrew, after all these years," says Isla as she hugs her brother, who has returned to his native Scotland.

"Good to see you too, Isla."

"Looks like you're becoming distinguished, Andrew, with all that grey hair and beard," comments Isla.

Isla's dogs surround Andrew as he tries to negotiate a path into the house.

"Sit down, Andrew. Would you like some tea?"

"Thanks, Isla."

"I hope the accommodation at The Ploughman Inn is suitable for you and the band members and their families, Andrew."

"It's just fine, Isla. The new owner, Lefty Brown, has gone out of his way to accommodate us and make us feel welcome. He attends our band practices every day and told me last night over a few drinks that he thinks the Canadians have a good shot at a Grade 2 medal. He also told me that we were the only competing band with two female pipers."

"So glad everything's working out, dear brother. And how have you been keeping?" continues Isla.

"Very well, Isla. Thanks for asking. The Reverend Lindsay, whom I met travelling to Nova Scotia five years ago, has been a great help to me fighting and killing the gambling demon which was consuming me, Isla. He taught me so much. To be properly cured I first of all had to admit that I had an addiction to gaming; then, with the good reverend's constant help and encouragement, I fought to slay the demon. I am pleased to tell you, Isla, that I have never played cards or gambled since I first landed in Cape Breton."

"Wonderful news, Andrew; I'm so glad you have overcome your addiction, so glad," says Isla, hugging her brother.

There are many tears shed by brother and sister, and hugs last for several minutes.

"I owe a great debt of gratitude to the Reverend Lindsay for rescuing me from a reckless lifestyle. Lindsay taught me about my conscious desires and my unconscious desires. Becoming the best piper in Scotland was, of course, a conscious desire, but, unknown to me, my unconscious desire was to be a successful gambler. It was only after Lindsay explained this to me that I began to understand the decision I had to make to cure myself of the deep-rooted dragon that has been lurking inside me all of these years. It took all of my willpower to make the decision to slay the gambling dragon once and for all time. And so each day I faced the dragon and fought it until one day I awoke and it was finally gone."

The tears run freely from Isla's bloodshot eyes as she listens to her brother's account of the struggle to kill the addiction that had consumed him and brought so much pain and suffering to his family.

"The Reverend Lindsay has been a godsend to you, Andrew. I would very much like to meet this man."

"Have you heard from Heather and the children, Isla?"

"Aye, I have," replies Isla, wiping away the tears from her cheeks. The family still lives in Edinburgh and they're all keeping well," replies Isla as she holds her brother's hand.

"What about the children? They must have grown some since last I saw them, Isla?"

"Oh yes, Grieg's a big lad now. He is very clever and is attending university in Edinburgh, Andrew."

"And Roy? Did he take up the bagpipes?" asks Andrew in an anxious tone.

"Aye, he did. In fact he's playing at Cowal with the East Lothian Boys Pipes and Drums."

"Grade 2, Isla?"

"Yes, it would be Grade 2, Andrew."

"Then Cape Breton will be competing against my son."

"Yes, Andrew, I believe so," replies Isla, observing the anxious look on her brother's face.

"And wee Annie? How is she doing?"

"Oh, Andrew, she is such a joy! Like me, she just loves animals. I think when Annie is older she will look after the health of animals, just like my dear husband did."

"Isla, I need yer help to get Heather back. More than anything else in this world, I want to be reunited with my Heather. Can you help me?" pleads Andrew.

"I want that too, Andrew, but it's been five years since ye went to Canada."

"Look, Isla, there must be a way – please, Isla. Heather respects and loves you."

"OK, Andrew, I'll see what I can do in the short time we have to make this happen," agrees Isla.

Andrew hugs his dear sister.

The day before the start of the Cowal gathering, Andrew puts the Cape Breton band through their paces.

"Now, lads and lassies, from the moment you line up at Cowal

Field you will be under the judges' eyes. What I demand is that you keep the formation we have practised for the past three months. Heads up and follow my lead when marching on to the field. This is the first time the Scots have seen you or heard you play, so we want to make a first-class impression. Remember there are no wrong notes. We play like we do in practice: good tone, even blowing into the bags, no over- or under-blowing, drums keeping pace with the beat. Now, if it rains, I want you to cover your pipes until we get the nod to enter the field. Any questions?" continues Andrew.

Fergus McWilliams steps forward.

"Andrew, on behalf of all of the pipers and drummers, we would like to thank you for your tutoring and encouragement. You have taught us so much and instilled that winning attitude in us during these past few months. We are all committed to doing our very best for you and for Cape Breton in this major piping and drumming competition," states McWilliams with great conviction.

All of the band members then clap their hands and give loud cheers for their pipe major Andrew MacGregor.

Large crowds have assembled at Cowal Field as the Cape Breton Pipes and Drums make their way to the south-west side of the field, where the Grade 2 competition is scheduled to start in an hour. The competing bands are already warming up as Andrew directs his band to their practice area. It is a cloudy start to the day with a light wind out of the west.

"OK, lads, take ten minutes to practise."

As the band members practise Andrew goes around adjusting pipes and asking some members to change the reeds in their pipes. The drumming corps sounds good to Andrew.

"Andrew, my dear friend, how are ye?"

Turning around Andrew sees none other than Jimmy Reynolds barrelling towards him.

"Jimmy Reynolds, so good to see ye, man," shouts Andrew as both men embrace one another.

"My God, Andrew, whit's wi' this grey beard?"

"Aye, I thought I would try and look a wee bit more distinguished for the homecoming, Jimmy," replies Andrew jokingly.

"So how did ye find the Cape Breton folk, Andrew?"

"Well, I discovered that Scottish families who emigrated to Canada slowly became more Scottish than the Scots themselves, Jimmy, for one simple reason: when you are far away from home you tend to cling to your identity – that is what defines you," explains Andrew with great conviction.

Cape Breton band members observe this reunion of old comrades with great curiosity. It's the first time they have seen such a joyous side of Andrew MacGregor.

Andrew introduces Jimmy Reynolds to all of Cape Breton band members. Jimmy has put on a lot of weight during the past five years.

"Too much beer, Jimmy," jokes Andrew, patting Jimmy's midriff.

"Well, five years running the bar at The Sailor's Hornpipe Inn in Oban," shouts Jimmy, patting his tummy with both hands and leaning back. "I see you have two female pipers, Andrew. That's a first for the Cowal gathering."

"Yes, Jimmy, twin girls, and damn good pipers to boot."

"Andrew, yer boy Roy is playing over there in the trees with the East Lothian boys' band. That's him with the blond curly hair," says Jimmy, pointing towards young Roy.

As Andrew gazes towards his son Roy, the clouds above part and the first rays of the sun break out all over Cowal Field. Andrew anxiously looks around for any sign of Heather and Grieg and wee Annie, but only members of the East Lothian boys' band are in view.

"Gather around. We are drawn to play in fifth place for the first of two rounds. To get to the second round we need to finish in the first three. Are ye ready to give it yer very best shot?" shouts Andrew.

"Yes, yes!" is the immediate response from the pipers and drummers of Cape Breton.

Cape Breton Pipes and Drums, all wearing their Cape Breton tartan kilts, assemble on the starting line waiting for the command to move forward into the playing area. Four fine bands have already played their sets of tunes, and now Andrew waits for the judges' signal to move his Cape Breton Pipes and Drums into the playing arena in front of the stands.

"One, two, three, forward!" shouts Andrew, and the band moves ahead playing 'John MacColl's March to Kilbowie Cottage'. The band keep their tight formation then form a circle. The judges for this competition are experienced pipers and drummers, having played with the Boys of Bluehill pipes and drums and with the Argylls. The Cape Breton band smoothly leads into a strathspey and finishes off well with a reel. Andrew and his band leave the field to warm applause.

The final band to compete in the Grade 2 events is the East Lothian Boys Pipes and Drums. Andrew finds a good vantage point to view his son Roy's band. As the pipers and drummers come into view, it appears to Andrew that his son Roy is the youngest member of the pipe band. Also, the Pipe Major looks like Ross Noble, a good friend of Andrew's from his days with the Argyll and Sutherland Highlanders. The East Lothian boys' tartan kilts are of Clan Bruce. Their kilts are predominately red with smatterings of yellow and green.

As Andrew observes his son's pipe band he is joined by Fergus McWilliams.

"Hi, Andrew. The East Lothian lads sound very good to me. What do you think of their playing?"

"Fine wee band, Fergus. Nice tone."

The bands for the Grade 2 competition stand anxiously waiting for the judges' results for the first round.

"Ladies and gentlemen, here are the placings for the first round o' the Grade 2 pipe band competition: placed first, East Lothian Boys Pipes and Drums; second, Macgillivray Western Isles Pipes and Drums; and third, Cape Breton Pipe Band."

You would think they have just won the Grade 1 World Pipe Band Competition as all of the members of the band jump for joy, tossing their bonnets into the air.

"Great effort, lads!" shouts an exhilarated pipe major as he joins his pipers and drummers in celebrating getting to the second round of the Grade 2 competition.

"You are now guaranteed some sort of medal, lads," shouts Andrew.

"Congratulations, Ross, you have a fine pipe band," says Andrew, shaking the hand of his old friend.

"Thanks, Andrew – great to see you, man!" replies Ross, patting Andrew on the back.

"Dad, Dad," calls out young Roy as he embraces his father.

"Oh, son, it's so good to see you again."

Father and son embrace for several minutes and Ross leaves them to enjoy this moment.

"Son, are Grieg and wee Annie and yer ma here today?" asks Andrew anxiously.

"Yes, Dad, Grieg and my mother and wee Annie are here, but I don't think my mother wants to speak to you, Dad," replies Roy, looking down at the ground.

Over lunch, Andrew goes over some adjustments he wants to make for the second round in the Grade 2 competition.

"You played well to get to the second round of the competition. You beat three other very good bands. Now, this afternoon's challenge will be tougher, to finish ahead of the East Lothian and Macgillivray pipe bands, but I believe you can do it. You should also believe that you can do it!"

Andrew spends the next twenty minutes going over the adjustments he wants to make in piping and drumming.

"Now, remember, if it rains today cover yer pipes until we are called to the start line to play."

Andrew goes looking for his son Grieg, wee Annie and his wife, Heather.

"Congratulations, Andrew – yer band played well to finish third, very well," says Reverend Lindsay as he finishes his meal.

"Thanks, Reverend. I am very proud of the band getting to the second round of the competition," replies an elated pipe major. "Will ye join me, Reverend? I am on the lookout for my son Grieg, wee Annie and my wife, Heather."

"Certainly, Andrew."

Both men walk around Cowal Field. Andrew meets many of his former friends, but there is no sign of Heather or his son Grieg or wee Annie.

"Andrew, Andrew, wait up!" calls out a voice behind him.

"I'm sorry I missed the first round of yer playing. We lost a wheel from the carriage on our way to the gathering which delayed our arrival," says Isla apologetically.

"Isla, I'm so glad you made it. This is the Reverend Lindsay," says Andrew looking around for his family.

"Oh, so pleased to meet you, Reverend. I've heard so much about you during the past five years," replies Isla, shaking the Reverend's hand heartily.

"Delighted to make yer acquaintance, Isla."

"Isla, I met young Roy a few hours ago. His band was placed first going into the second round. We finished third."

"So happy you and Roy met each other. Roy has followed in your footsteps, Andrew, and is becoming a fine piper," replies Isla.

"Are Heather and Grieg here today, Isla?"

"Yes, Andrew. Heather and Grieg and wee Annie are visiting with Roy at the moment. You will meet one another after the second round of the piping competition."

Andrew and the Reverend Lindsay return to the Cape Breton band.

"OK, everyone, gather round. We have been drawn to play in second position. The Macgillivrays go first, then us followed by East Lothian. Now, pipers, remember, do not over-blow or under-blow; drummers, keep pace with the beat. You know the three tunes we have been asked to play. We have practised these pipe tunes over and over again. I want a nice tone, a flawless start and a good finish. Keep in tight formation, and remember if it rains cover the pipes until we are ready to play. Best o' luck!"

The sun disappears behind the clouds as the Macgillivray pipe band takes the field in their hunting tartan to a rousing reception. The wind picks up from the west and there is a threat of showers. The band plays well and gets a well-deserved round of applause from the large crowd in attendance.

Cape Breton Pipes and Drums stands ready in their new Cape Breton tartan kilts, Harris tweed jackets, beige socks, green flashes and black bonnets and shoes. Many of the onlookers are curious about this band from abroad, because it is led by one of the greatest pipers Scotland has produced over the years and this is the only band with female pipers competing this year. A buzz of excitement can be heard around the stands as Pipe Major Andrew MacGregor leads his Canadian pipe band into the arena. The Canadians keep a tight formation then form a circle while they play a rousing march. The transition into a strathspey is smooth and the band's tone sounds good to Stewart MacGregor, who is roaring the band on to victory. The wind freshens from the west, but still the rain holds off. Finally the band plays a reel and they complete their performance. As they march from the arena the large crowd applaud the Canadians from Cape Breton.

Just as the East Lothian Boys Pipes and Drums take the field there is a sudden shower. The wind drives the rain down on to the band members and the spectators and the heavy shower lasts for several minutes. The judges wait to see if the shower will pass. After five minutes the rain eases and showers become intermittent, so the judges call on Pipe Major Ross Noble to take the field. The East Lothian band did not cover up their pipes during the rain squalls so the tone of the pipes does not appear to be as crisp or sharp as in the preliminary round, thinks Andrew MacGregor, who has played many times in similar conditions here in Scotland. The rain stops as the band marches proudly from the arena to a big ovation and chanting from the supporters of the band from Scotland's east coast.

The tradition is that all six bands that compete assemble on the field in front of the stands to hear the judges' verdict. As the six band members wait for the results, the younger lads in the Canadian band appear very nervous.

"I thought my heart was going to burst out of my chest," states Jimmy Patterson, a promising young Canadian piper.

"My stomach has turned over many times, I am so nervous" is another comment from Keith MacDonald from Pleasant Bay, Cape Breton.

"Steady – stay calm. It will not be long now before we get the result," states Pipe Major Andrew MacGregor.

After the passing of another ten agonising minutes, a state of restlessness begins to take hold amongst all of the members of the six competing Grade 2 bands.

"Ladies and gentlemen, the judges have now come to a decision on the Grade 2 pipe band competition. In first place, Cape Breton Pipes and Drums; second place, East Lothian Boys Pipes and Drums; third place, Macgillivray Western Isles Pipes and Drums."

At first the spectators appear surprised at the judges' announcement, but supporters of the Canadians who travelled all the way across the Atlantic ocean to Scotland are joyous – no one more so than Stewart and Mary MacGregor.

Members of the Cape Breton band start jumping up and down for joy when they realize they have won the gold medal. Andrew MacGregor is thrilled that the band played their very best and got the judges' nod for first place.

To his credit, Pipe Major Ross Noble approaches Andrew and congratulates him for an amazing achievement.

"Andrew, ye have achieved something very special here today in bringing a brand-new band to first place in a major competition," comments Ross Noble.

Young Roy MacGregor is devastated at the loss and is being comforted by Heather as Andrew approaches his family.

"Congratulations, Andrew, on a great victory for Cape

Breton," comments Isla, who is standing beside her sister-in-law.

"Thanks, Isla. The Canadians were magnificent – never missed a note," replies Andrew. "Hello, Heather. How are you?" asks Andrew tenderly.

"I'm well, thank you," replies Heather.

"Grieg, how are ye doing, son?"

"Well, Father, I am studying law in Edinburgh," replies Grieg.

"Grieg is top of his class, Andrew," states Isla with passion.

"Congratulations son. I wish you a successful career in your chosen profession," says Andrew, patting his son on the shoulder.

Andrew tries to console young Roy, who is still visibly shaken by the result. Kneeling down on the ground, Andrew speaks to his distressed son.

"Yer band played very well, son. I think that heavy rain shower just before you started playing may have dampened some of the reeds, making the tone sound not quite as sharp as during the first round this morning. Don't be discouraged – your band will win many trophies. You'll see," says Andrew in a comforting manner, embracing his young son.

At that moment the Reverend Lindsay appears, congratulating Andrew on the amazing victory. Andrew introduces the Reverend Lindsay to Heather.

"Very pleased to make yer acquaintance, Heather," says Lindsay.

"Andrew, the family is travelling back to my home in Ayrshire this afternoon. Tomorrow we are having a family dinner. You and the Reverend Lindsay are most welcome to come," says Isla in an inviting manner.

"Thanks, Isla – we would be delighted to come for dinner," replies Andrew, feeling so glad that he may have a chance to talk to his wife, Heather, in private.

The tradition at the Cowal gathering is for the winning bands in Grade 1 and Grade 2 competitions should lead all of the other competing bands from the field and march down the long road into the town of Dunoon. After the Grade 1 bands march from the field, the Cape Breton Pipes and Drums lead the other five competing bands from Cowal Field and down the long road into the town.

It is after 6 p.m. as the Canadians march towards the town of Dunoon. The clouds have gone and the sun is low in the sky away to the west. Pipe Major MacGregor signals the Cape Breton band to play 'Heroes of Vila Real'. As the band marches, onlookers clap and cheer the Canadians. Stewart MacGregor marches behind the Cape Breton Pipes and Drums proudly carrying the winning Grade 2 trophy for all to see.

Chapter 55

MACGREGOR AND PROUD OF IT

Andrew MacGregor and the Reverend Lindsay arrive at Isla's home at 4 p.m. Wee Annie, Andrew's youngest child, and her brother Roy run to greet their father.

"Daddy, Daddy, look what I have. It's a wee white rabbit which I have named Timmy. He's so cute. Look, Daddy!"

Andrew hugs his daughter, who has long, curly dark hair and big dark eyes like her mother.

"Ross, this is the Reverend Lindsay," says Andrew as they enter the living room.

"Aye, my wife, Isla, met you at Cowal and speaks very highly o' you, Reverend," comments Ross MacBride.

"Thanks, Ross. You have a very kind wife."

Andrew sits beside Heather, and Isla serves some drinks. The guests include Stewart and Mary MacGregor.

"You have done a wonderful job, Heather, with the children. Grieg excelling at university, Roy becoming a member of a good pipe band and wee Annie continuing with her deep love of animals," said Andrew, trying to strike up a conversation with his estranged wife.

"It's been a challenge, I can tell you. Moving to a home closer to my family has helped me cope better with the children."

Heather has retained her grace and beauty over the past five years. Other than her ebony hair showing some signs of greying, she looks the same to Andrew as when he last saw her.

At dinner Isla places the Reverend Lindsay and Andrew on

either side of Heather. Isla asks the Reverend Lindsay to say grace, then the meal is served.

"How do ye like Canada, Reverend?" asks Heather.

"Oh, it's a bonnie place, Heather, especially Cape Breton. Looks just like Scotland."

"Aye, I can confirm that," comments Andrew. "Also, many of the locals can speak Gaelic and the food is just like we eat here in Scotland," adds Andrew.

"Of course Nova Scotia has the best lobsters in the world," shouts Stewart MacGregor. "Is that not the case, Andrew?"

"Aye, the lobsters are delicious and plentiful," replies Andrew.

The atmosphere during the meal is positive, and Isla works on hatching a plan to get Heather and Andrew together.

After the meal is finished and the children tucked in bed, Isla invites Heather, Andrew and the Reverend Lindsay for a walk around the property. The weather is fine and Heather grabs a shawl and the party sets out for a walking tour. Ross MacBride entertains Stewart and Mary MacGregor. Isla walks beside the Reverend while Andrew and Heather follow behind.

"I was wondering if you and the children would like to visit Canada. It's a wonderful country."

"I don't know, Andrew."

"Heather, with the help o' the Reverend Lindsay I have broken my addiction to gambling. Since I last saw you I have never gambled, played cards or even been near a card table. It took lots o' willpower, but that part o' my life is now behind me," states Andrew with a great amount of conviction.

"You hurt me and the family, Andrew, very deeply. How can I ever trust you again?"

"Heather, please take some time to talk to the Reverend Lindsay. He is the one that cured me o' my addiction to gambling. He is a fine man and a Good Samaritan. I owe him so much."

At this point Heather and Andrew join Isla and the Reverend and continue their walk. It's gone 10 p.m. when all of the guests reassemble by the fire in Isla's living room.

"The land here is very good for growing vegetables," remarks the Reverend. "My former parish was about ten miles to the north-west o' here."

"Stewart, when will the pipe band return to Canada?" asks Isla.

"Well, we are scheduled to travel home in one week. The families who accompanied the pipe band want to visit their families here in Scotland before returning home."

One week, thinks Andrew: one week to try and reunite with Heather.

After the guests depart, Isla and Heather have some tea by the fire.

"Didn't Andrew look well sporting that grey beard, Heather?" remarks Isla, anxious to direct the conversation towards her brother.

"Yes, the beard was an unexpected surprise," responds Heather as she stares into the brightly burning fire.

"Andrew and I had a wee talk, Heather, about his life in Canada during the past five years and how he has desperately missed you and the children. With the help o' the good Reverend Lindsay he has cured himself of the gambling addiction."

Hearing no response, Isla continues trying to get a reaction from Heather.

"Andrew's here for one more week and he would love to spend some time with you and the children. Can I suggest we plan a day's outing with the children?" asks Isla, placing a hand on Heather's shoulder. "That would allow the children to get to know their father again."

At first Heather does not respond. She sits, leaning forward, staring into the flames of the brightly burning fire. Then turning to her sister-in-law Heather says, "Very well, Isla – you can plan a day's outing for the family."

Early the next morning Isla makes her way hurriedly to The Ploughman Inn. Isla finds Andrew at breakfast with Stewart and Mary MacGregor.

"Guid morning, Isla," says Andrew, somewhat surprised to

see his sister so early in the morning.

"Is something wrong?" asks Stewart, bracing himself for bad news.

"No, no, gentlemen," replies Isla as she hurriedly removes her cloak and hat and sits down at the breakfast table. "Oh dear, I'm breathless," says Isla as she reaches for a glass of water. "There now, I feel much better."

"You also had me worried there, sister. I thought for a moment it was bad news," comments Andrew.

"On the contrary, gentlemen: I have spoken to Heather and she agrees that I can organize a family outing for one day this week, and ye are all invited," explains Isla excitedly.

Andrew is the first to respond: "That's wonderful, my dear sister."

Andrew reaches out and joins hands with Isla. A discussion follows about where to go. Andrew remembers the family's first holiday in May 1802.

"Can I suggest something?" says Andrew with excitement in his voice.

"Please do, dear brother."

"Well, in May 1802 we visited Isla and Ross at Applecross Farm and spent a wonderful day beside the beautiful River Doon, about ten miles from the farm. Do you remember, Isla?"

"Yes, I remember it well, dear brother," replies Isla. "It's a favourite spot o' my husband, Ross. Leave the arrangements to me," says Isla as she rises from the table.

With the help of her brother, she places her cloak around her shoulders, grabs her hat and disappears like a puff of smoke.

It's a bright start to the day. Ross MacBride, with the help of two farmhands has been loading the hay wagon for a trip to his favourite spot by the beautiful River Doon. Heather's children are excited as they board the large hay wagon pulled by two great Clydesdale horses.

"First stop is at The Ploughman's Inn to pick up the Reverend Lindsay, Andrew, Stewart and Mary MacGregor," shouts Isla to her husband.

"What a beautiful spot," comments Stewart MacGregor as he helps unload the hay wagon.

"I'm so glad you like it, Stewart. It's my favourite spot in all of Ayrshire," remarks Ross as he stands with his hands on his hips taking in the magnificent view.

Soon the children are swimming in the River Doon and playing with Isla's dogs.

Heather speaks to the Reverend Lindsay while Andrew helps Isla and Ross prepare the lunch.

"How did you and Andrew meet, Reverend Lindsay?"

"It was five years ago on board the ship to Canada. Andrew's cabin was next to mine, ye ken, and we were both bound for Cape Breton, which is where Stewart and Mary MacGregor reside," replies Lindsay.

"I hear ye spent a lot of time with Andrew in Cape Breton, helping with his gambling addiction."

"Aye, we spent many a long night together fighting the gambling dragon," recounted Lindsay thoughtfully.

"Do ye believe Andrew is no longer addicted to gambling?"

"If ye had asked me that question three years ago I would have said that he was on his way to a cure. During past two years, Andrew, through his actions and strong character, has proven to me beyond any doubt that his wretched past addiction to gambling is truly gone. Yer husband has shown great willpower, and I, and many others, admire him for the strong actions he has taken to cure himself."

After lunch Ross and Andrew organize games for the children. Isla spends time with her sister-in-law and tries to encourage her towards reconciliation with Andrew.

On the way home from the day's outing, Isla starts singing, and before long everyone joins in. It's a happy time for all.

Lefty Brown, owner of The Ploughman Inn offers to organize a ceilidh at the inn before the Canadians depart for Canada.

"Thanks, Lefty – that's a good idea. We can celebrate the pipe band's great victory at the Cowal gathering," said Stewart MacGregor.

Andrew is delighted with this news and pays a visit to his sister Isla.

"So what do you think, Isla, o' holding a ceilidh at the inn?"

"Wonderful idea, Andrew. There's only one problem: Heather and the children are planning to return to Edinburgh tomorrow. Leave it with me, Andrew, and I will try to persuade Heather and the children to stay one more day."

Heather's children do not need much persuading. They jump at the idea of attending a ceilidh. Heather on the other hand needs all of her sister-in-law's powers of persuasion to agree to stay one more day. Isla's winning manner triumphs as Heather agrees to attend the ceilidh and return home the following day.

Isla, Stewart MacGregor and Lefty Brown, agree to organize the ceilidh. Sixty guests have agreed to attend, so Lefty closes the inn for the day. Hurried changes are made to accommodate seating for everyone and also make an area free for the dancing after the meal.

By 5 p.m. on the day of the ceilidh all of the guests have assembled in the inn. The Cape Breton Pipes and Drums are outside waiting for Lefty's signal to pipe in the haggis. Pipers enter the building playing 'Heroes of Vila Real' and guests clap in time to the beat of the music. Stewart MacGregor carries in the haggis and places it on the head table.

The meal surpasses everyone's expectations. The bill of fare includes cock-a-leekie soup, smoked salmon, kippered herrings, haggis, Scotch eggs (boiled eggs covered in sausage meat, rolled in breadcrumbs, then fried), clootie dumplings and custard, Dundee cake and shortbread cookies.

After the meal the room is rearranged for the Scottish traditional dancing. The Cape Breton Pipes and Drums provides the music and Isla arranges the dances.

"Ladies and gentlemen, boys and girls, the first dance is 'Strip the Willow'," announces Isla.

Within a few minutes partners are chosen and the dance floor becomes crowded. Andrew approaches Heather and asks her to join him for 'Strip the Willow'. At first Heather hesitates, then agrees, and both Heather and Andrew squeeze past friends and find themselves at the head of the line of dancers. The music begins and Andrew and Heather lead off this long dance and everyone has a great amount of fun.

Later, wee Annie MacGregor entertains the guests with the sword dance, which requires great skill and dexterity. Heather is so proud of her daughter's dancing skills.

Isla then continues with announcing the dances.

Later Stewart, Ross and Andrew are invited by Lefty Brown to the bar for a celebratory drink. Suddenly, without any warning, Andrew crashes to the floor beside the bar. Stewart is the first to respond.

"Quick, Lefty – get a doctor as fast as you can," shouts Stewart.

Lefty immediately sends a servant on horseback to fetch a local doctor. Stewart tries to revive his cousin, but Andrew does not respond. A big commotion starts with people rushing towards the bar to see what has happened. Ross and Stewart remove Andrew from the bar area and with the help of two servants carry Andrew upstairs to Stewart's room. Isla, seeing what has happened, rounds up Heather's children. Isla takes the children outside. Heather comes to see what is happening and is told by Lefty that Andrew is ill and has been taken upstairs. Lefty and his staff do their best to bring about calm. The pipe band stops playing and leaves the building.

Dr. Moncrieff arrives later and examines Andrew. Turning slowly towards Heather, Dr. Moncrieff pronounces Andrew dead. Heather is stunned and is in shock. Mary MacGregor comforts her and takes her slowly to her room.

Arrangements are made for Andrew's body to be taken to a hospital for further examination.

Back at Applecross Farm the children have been put to bed and told that their dad is sick. A weeping Heather is consoled by Isla and Ross. Heather is now in deep shock.

The next morning Dr. Moncrieff visits Heather and prescribes medication. On the advice of the doctor, Heather remains in bed.

Dr. Moncrieff meets with Ross, Isla and Stewart MacGregor.

"I am so sorry for your loss. I examined Andrew's body earlier this morning and, based on the suddenness of what happened, I can only conclude that Andrew died of a massive and sudden heart attack."

Isla, with tears in her eyes, is the first to speak.

"Our father died exactly the same way, Doctor, in Port Glasgow. One moment he was standing near us talking to our mother in the kitchen of our house and the next moment Father collapsed on to the floor. We tried to revive him, but he was gone," recounts Isla with tears now flowing down her cheeks.

"I'll wait for your instructions regarding the funeral arrangements, Ross," says Moncrieff as he leaves the room.

There is a long silence in the room. The silence is broken by Heather as she enters the living room in a dressing gown.

Isla walks towards her distressed sister-in-law and both hug each other for several minutes.

"Ross, we will need to attend to the funeral arrangements and meet with the pipe band and guests over at the inn," says Stewart solemnly.

"The pipe band and the families will be travelling to Port Glasgow to board the ship back to Canada in two days," adds Stewart.

"Aye, I understand, Stewart. We will have to make arrangements," replies Ross solemnly.

There is silence as Ross MacBride stands up to address the Cape Breton pipe-band members and their families, who are all assembled at the inn.

"Andrew's death was so very sudden and unexpected. The family are in deep shock as a result o' this tragic event. The death certificate says 'sudden and unexpected fatal heart attack' as the cause o' death. I know ye all will miss your dear friend Andrew MacGregor. He was Scotland's greatest piper and will be sorely missed. As for the Cape Breton Pipes and Drums, I am sure Andrew would want you to keep the band together and build on yer success at Montreal and here at Cowal. Stewart and Mary MacGregor are staying on to help me plan the funeral and memorial service. I thank them for that. I wish ye a' a safe journey home and hope to see you all again at future Cowal gatherings."

News of the sudden death of Andrew MacGregor is sent to the MacGregor clan chief, Gregor MacGregor; the piping school at Bluehill; the Argyll's army barracks in Port Glasgow, and Meadowbank Shipyard; and announcements appear in the *Port Glasgow Chronicle*, the *City of Glasgow Evening Standard*, and the *City of Edinburgh Herald*, providing information about the funeral arrangements and memorial service.

Gregor MacGregor, the clan chief, recommends to Heather that, following the memorial service in Port Glasgow, Andrew's body be buried beside his grandfather's grave at Balquhidder. Heather agrees to Gregor's recommendation.

By early morning on the day of the memorial service large numbers of people have arrived at Port Glasgow to attend the memorial service, which is scheduled to start at 2 p.m. Carriages from the north and south continue to arrive during the morning. By 1.30 p.m. the local army barracks is packed full of Andrew's relatives and friends, including clan members, shipyard workers and soldiers from the Argylls. The Reverend Lindsay has been invited to lead the memorial service.

Just before the service starts, a large coach with gold trim and pulled by six magnificent white stallions appears at the entrance to the barracks, followed by an escort of twenty mounted soldiers. Gregor MacGregor recognizes the crest of the Duke of Argyll on the side of the coach as it comes to rest beside the barracks' entrance. Thomas Campbell, the Duke of Argyll, exits the carriage followed by his beautiful wife, Princess Augusta. Gregor greets the royal couple and escorts them to their seats in the army barracks.

The Reverend Lindsay opens the memorial service with a prayer. Some of Andrew's favourite songs, penned by the poet Robert Burns, are sung at the request of Heather MacGregor. Several tributes are made. The first tribute is made by former Pipe Major Jimmy Reynolds.

"Aye, I can only say that the sudden death o' my dear friend and fellow officer Major Andrew MacGregor is a great loss not only to his beloved family, but to all o' Scotland. Not since the Macrimmons o' the Isle o' Skye have we been treated to such excellence in pipin'. Andrew's great piping legacy will continue through all of the hundreds of army pipers he has taught so well over the years. It will be a great challenge for any young-up-and-comers to beat Andrew's piping record at the Cowal gathering. Andrew's march 'Heroes o' Vila Real' will continue to be played on battlefields all over the world by the 98th. Aye, his legacy will continue long after we are all gone."

The Duke of Argyll offers his deepest condolences to Andrew's family and praises him for his great courage in battle and for what he achieved with the Argylls.

Andrew's cousin, Gregor MacGregor, the clan chief, gives his blessing to Andrew's family and salutes his memory for the great contribution he made over the years to Scotland for keeping the piping tradition alive amongst the Scottish clans.

Other tributes are made by Henry Bell, the inventor of the first steam-powered engine for commercial travel; John Wood, shipbuilder; and Gordon Morrison, barrister with Ogilvie, Urqhart and Donaldson of Edinburgh.

As the coffin is taken by eight soldiers of the Argylls to a waiting hearse, members of the Argylls' pipe band play a lament outside the army barracks. A huge crowd lines the streets of Port Glasgow as the hearse, escorted by a detachment of mounted soldiers, makes it way north to Balquhidder, to Andrew's final resting place.

The next morning Heather and the children make their way to Balquhidder followed by Andrew's sister's family, close friends and a detachment of mounted soldiers of the 98th.

On reaching Aberfoyle, the entourage turns to the north-east, passing the towns of Callander and Strathyre and onward to the village of Balquhidder, situated on the north shore of Loch Voil. The grave of Andrew's grandfather Rob Roy MacGregor is located in front of the east-facing gable of the old church of Balquhidder and is marked by a carved grave slab. The family, friends and soldiers assemble at the graveyard. The clan chief, Gregor MacGregor, has arranged for a burial plot close to Rob Roy's gravestone. The Reverend Lindsay conducts the graveyard service and Gregor MacGregor gives a brief eulogy. Former Pipe Major Jimmy Reynolds plays a lament and the coffin is slowly lowered into the grave. A company of the 98th, composed of Sassenachs and Teuchters, fires a three-round-rifle volley as a salute to Major Andrew MacGregor. A headstone is placed on the grave.

The inscription reads, 'MacGregor and Proud of It'.

EPILOGUE

Genetic Defects and Your Family History

Although it would not have been recognized in the nineteenth century, the early deaths of male members of the Clan MacGregor are characteristic of a genetic defect known as Brugada syndrome, a little-known but very real genetic mutation primarily associated with males and discovered by Belgian doctors in the mid 1990s.

Brugada syndrome strikes without warning, resulting in a heart attack and possible death. From my research, it appears that I was the only male member of my extended family to have survived a heart attack as a result of a genetic mutation. I did not identify any female deaths associated with the syndrome in my family group.

One of my purposes in writing this novel is to raise the awareness level amongst the public at large of the syndrome. Sometimes families lose young and healthy loved ones in life as a result of heart attacks. In many cases, the reason for the sudden and unexpected heart attacks is not known. It is important to understand the medical history of your family, including the cause of death, especially if the deaths come about as a result of a sudden heart attack at an early age to an otherwise healthy individual.

For people like me who have survived a sudden heart attack caused by having Brugada syndrome life can be very normal. I continue to be active in soccer, golf, cycling, walking and Scottish country dancing, although I have discovered my limits and realize that I cannot go at the same pace as before the heart attack.

Medical technology advances during the past few years have made it possible for people to be tested from home rather than at hospital. For people who have a small implantable cardioverter defibrillator (or ICD) installed above the heart, tests can be done remotely from home using the Medtronic Carelink service. The results of tests of the heart using this technology take a few minutes of the patient's time and can be done when the patient is asleep at home. The test results provide the medical staff at the hospital with information related to the functioning of the patient's heart.